THE FALL DUOLOGY

ECHO OF DEATH

BOOK ONE

JOYCE GEE

Ebook ISBN: 9781763650695

Paperback ISBN: 9781764474009

Hardcover ISBN: 9781764474016

A NOTE ON LANGUAGE

This is just to let you know that I'm from Australia.

The English I use is Australian English, which is not the same as American English. In Australia, we like S, not Z. The letter U appears in words where it does not in American. Smelt is the past tense for smell. There are certain words that we use on a regular basis which make Americans blush. I'm sorry. Not really. It's all English in the end.

So, I love you readers from America, but please remember that my spelling is not incorrect, it's simply a different version of English to what you use.

Trigger Warning

Please only read this if you have triggers, otherwise you may spoil yourself. This book is about fighting to save the people who matter when it seems the enemy cannot be defeated.

To start, I will tell you what isn't in the book. There is no on page rape, no cheating, no incest, no minors, no pregnancy, and no substance abuse.

This is **NOT** a romance. Let me make it clear that this is first and foremost, an epic fantasy. While there will be an ending with some semblance of a HEA in the second book, romance is not the driver of The Fall duology. However, there are depictions of sex. There is violence.

Please always put your mental health first.

This one is for Anita.

You asked for this background story, and I delivered.

It is also for all those who would do anything to save the ones they love.
For the ones who carry the weight of the world and feel like they need to
have all the answers.

To Kyle,

Yes, you can read this one.

I guess.

If you must...

It's fine.

One

Eirian

Her nose twitched at the scent of pear blossom and mint saturating the air, and she shoved her hands into the folds of shimmering black fabric. With hundreds of eyes on her, the last thing Eirian could do was pinch her nose to fight off a sneeze. She dreaded the lengthy ceremonies, but as the High Priestess of Endara, they were unavoidable. At least her position granted her the power to nominate who would lead them, leaving her free to ruminate on more important issues facing the city.

There was something about the monotone of the priest leading the ceremony that made Eirian wonder why she could not hear snoring from the pews below. Her balcony overlooked the sanctuary, situating her above the bulk of worshippers. It put her on display, something she had needed to get used to after her powers manifested. As the first Altira born after the death of the previous High Priest, there had never been a day when Eirian could forget who she was. In her veins ran the power of the god her family was bound to. She was the heir to Death, and it was her job to oversee the spiritual wellbeing of Endara while guiding those who dedicated their lives to serving Death.

Her nose twitched again, the desperate urge to sneeze prompting Eirian to scrunch up her face to fight it off. She knew from experience that if she sneezed, the sound would echo through the temple and draw the attention of the congregation. Gaze drifting to the young man standing to her left, she signalled for him to come closer. His eyes widened in surprise, and he bent over to bring himself level with her. Drifting forward, the layers of black fabric adorning him fluttered over her arm. Realising his clothes had touched the High Priestess, the cleric mumbled his apologies and scrambled to flatten the robe.

"Stop your fussing," Eirian said, keeping her voice low. "Make a note to have the incense switched out to something less irritating. Have whoever changed it placed on kitchen duty for a month. I don't appreciate feeling a constant need to sneeze."

"I'm dreadfully sorry, Your Eminence."

It was an effort not to roll her eyes, and her lips thinned. "I said, stop fussing. You are a cleric serving in the Temple of Death, so behave like it."

He shrunk back, head bowed. "Yes, Your Eminence."

Lifting her gaze to the ceiling, she examined the intricate latticework of marble crafted centuries before by master stonemasons. Veins of black laced through the cold white, a perfect material for the temple dedicated to death. There were days when Eirian wished she were as cold as the marble caging her. If her daughter had a say in it, Delyth would certainly argue her mother was colder than stone. She knew the girl was not among the worshippers, despite having received the command to attend when they sat down for dinner the previous night. Wherever she was, Eirian suspected Delyth was not thinking about the duty she owed Endara as one of the Altira family, and she envied that freedom.

In the sanctuary below, the priest led the congregation through their prayers. A buzz of energy filled the temple, and Eirian cocked her head to breathe in the anticipation. It fed her magic, coaxing the darkness from where it sat coiled inside her. With the ceremonies nearly over, she needed to prepare for the hardest part of the month. Petitioners came to her in the temple gardens to plead their case. Guilt stabbed through Eirian as she offered the same silent prayer to the gods. This was the part of her duties she hated the most. Having to pick from those desperate to die. They were suffering, and in their pain, they wanted their deaths to have meaning.

Existence was a delicate balance. It was the first thing they taught all children, and it was drilled into mages from the moment their power manifested. Life was a precious blessing from the gods, and to waste it was a sin. As his High Priestess, it was Eirian's task to ensure people knew how offensive it was to Death if they did not appreciate the gifts given to them. And it was her job to deliver his blessing to those who had reached a natural end to their time among the living. Those who suffered from illnesses the healers could not fix, or whose minds no longer wished to go on. They presented their situations to a council of priests for the chance of an audience with the Altira. After that, it fell on her shoulders to choose worthy sacrifices.

The priest below shifted to face her balcony, and raised a hand as he said, "Blessed are the chosen of the gods. May your life be worthy of being collected by our Lord Death."

Rising from her seat, Eirian stepped forward to bow to the crowd below. She held the position for five steady taps of her foot before straightening. When she stepped away from the rail and out of sight, she listened to the burst of sound echoing through the temple. A group of priests and clerics waited at the back of the platform, where the curtains protected her from the view of anyone traversing the pathways between sections. Other balconies played host to important officials from the twin cities and other nations, as well as prominent members of society. Attending the public ceremonies was a requirement of power, and no one dared raise Eirian's ire by failing to present themselves without good reason. Certainly not if they wanted to gain a private audience with her at a different time.

"Has anyone seen my daughter?" she hissed, icy blue eyes dancing from one person to the next. "I want Delyth found and brought to me as soon as possible."

With all the noise that had broken out, Eirian finally surrendered to her need to sneeze. The young cleric she had spoken to squeaked in terror and rushed from the balcony to follow through with her instructions. Sneezing a second time, the High Priestess held up a hand to signal for the others to keep their distance. It was a temporary relief, and her eyes stung, telling her she needed to leave before it got any worse. One of her attendants was a healer, and the mage huffed, shaking his head as he murmured something in the ear of a cleric. He plucked a kerchief from a pocket, extending it to her with a stern look.

"Cover your nose and take shallow breaths until we're outside. I've sent for medicine to help clear your airways of irritation. When did this start?"

"It's the new incense," she muttered, accepting the square of white fabric. "Thank you, Rince. How many petitioners do you have for me today?"

"Two dozen made it through the assessment, but one died overnight. A woman with advanced cancer, brought in from a seaside village to the north. Her heart failed."

"Gebael bless her spirit and see her at peace. Give my condolences and prayers to her family, and ensure they have enough supplies before their journey home. We shall give her the same farewell as the chosen and add her name to the wall of remembrance."

A priest made a noise of protest that died in his throat when Eirian glanced his way. "Your Eminence, are you sure? She did not give her life energy to the city."

Squaring her shoulders, Eirian towered over the man and raised an eyebrow. "Are you sure you wish to question me? I'm aware of how she died, and instead of spending her last days surrounded by her kin and community, she journeyed here to offer herself to the temple. She deserves to be honoured for her sacrifice, as I suspect she would have been among those I chose today, had she lived a few days longer."

"It honours her family, and her community," another priest said. "We are servants of our people, and we must always give them the respect they deserve. Small blessings matter."

Smoothing her hands over the silky fabric of her formal robes, Eirian moved toward the corridor. The people standing between her and the rest of the temple parted like water, falling into place at her back. As the healer in charge of presenting the petitioners, Rince took the prime position to her left, while her aide settled on the right. Joshua was ten years her senior, but he had served Eirian faithfully since the day he entered the temple and swore his life to Gebael, the god of death.

"Lord Madoc sends his apologies for not attending this morning. He was called away to deal with a collapsed building in the new district. Apparently, a child came into her powers and caused the foundations of a housing complex to cave inwards. Thankfully, it was empty."

In the twenty-three years she had been married to Madoc, Eirian had never heard Joshua say his name with anything but disdain. "My husband wasn't around for breakfast, so I assumed something important had called him away. A pity about the building."

People moved out of the way when they saw her approaching. A few bold politicians called her name, hoping to steal Eirian's attention away from her task. It never worked, and she had commanded her attendants to take names years ago, ensuring those who interrupted her time were not granted an audience. On any other day, her time was fair game. Ceremony days belonged to her role as the Altira mage. She was the only human capable of drawing the life energy from willing sacrifices and feeding it to the city crops to ensure they grew healthy and plentiful to feed the citizens of Endara and Ensaycal.

Eirian knew what the others with her ability were called. They were husk makers, the Ravens of Death, and attendants to Death's Executioner. Only a few dozen remained alive, the rest slaughtered by Annawyn, the god of thoughts and emotions. She had never met them, though in her younger days, she would have given anything to learn from those more experienced in the deadly power coursing through her veins. Dullaghan frequently visited Endara, and Eirian enjoyed having tea with the headless riders who served Gebael as she did. The insights she gained from their conversations were invaluable, and they provided news about things happening throughout Tir. It was a dullaghan who had warned her of the wars breaking out across the lands, and the tightening grip of Annawyn's madness on the First People.

Only a select few in Endara and Ensaycal were aware of the information she had gathered. None of them wished to send their people into a panic over the possibility they would soon be at war. The gods of war and death had blessed their cities, and it was not uncommon for their deities to be seen walking the streets as though they were ordinary people. Eirian was aware of what Gebael liked to do, and she kept his secret close to her heart. If Death wished to stalk the shadows to deliver punishment to those who sinned, then no one had the right to question him.

Wrestling her thoughts away from Gebael's cold eyes and even icier touch, she scowled when Joshua nudged her arm. "What is it? Did I miss something?"

"No, you didn't. I know your expressions well. You've never been able to hide it from me when your mind wanders. If Delyth arrives while you're with the petitioners, what would you like me to do with her?"

"She can spend the day in the kitchens."

Joshua arched a brow in amusement. "Really? You'd subject the kitchen staff to her?"

"Madoc spoils her, and I'm tired of my daughter thinking she is above attending the ceremonies. Just because I allowed her to dedicate herself to academics does not mean she is excused from her duties as an Altira. She needs to be reminded I can rescind my permission and insist she take her place among the clergy."

"Delyth shows promise. Perhaps you should have her apprentice with a council member. It would channel her studies in a manner suitable for an Altira."

Grunting, Eirian hid her relief at the sight of the large doors that led into the tranquil gardens. They were a work of art, so fine the sunlight gave them an ethereal glow. Whoever had created them had possessed a skill that few could match, making delicate filigree from stone that would make a silversmith weep. It was a thing of beauty to welcome those in pain to a place where they could find peace. Beyond the doors was a carefully maintained garden with the most vibrant of blooms, and tall trees under which petitioners could sit and wait to learn their fate. Winding streams of water cut through the space, filled with darting fish and drifting lilies.

"You make a good point. We'll discuss it in a few days once we're done with the ceremonies. She needs a focus for her future. I won't tolerate her fluttering around like a Zarthein."

Rince chuckled, shifting the focus to him. "My radiant High Priestess. The day Delyth flutters around like a Zarthein is the day you leave us."

"I worry about her," she muttered, shoulders dropping as a priest carefully drew the doors open. "She's nearly twenty, and I don't know what to think."

Placing a hand on her shoulder, Joshua shared a look with Rince. "You're an exemplary mother."

"Don't be ridiculous! My daughter complains to Madoc at least three times a week that I'm a terrible mother and she wishes he were her only parent. Perhaps she has a point."

Clearing his throat, Rince nodded at an approaching healer. Glancing at the young woman in her sage green robes, Eirian hoped she had brought something to ease the irritation in her nose. Bowing low, the healer held out a box to Rince without daring to look at the High Priestess. He lifted the lid to examine the contents, humming thoughtfully while fussing over what was in it. With a snap, the box was closed, and he took it from her, murmuring his thanks before waving for Eirian to enter the gardens. She huffed, rolling her eyes to look at Joshua, only to find him smiling faintly.

"The petitioners await your judgement, Your Eminence," the priest at the door said.

"Go get started, and I'll bring you some tea to help with the inflammation." Rince flapped a hand, urging her to continue on her way. "If she has trouble breathing, fetch me immediately, Joshua. I doubt it'll happen, but just in case, monitor her."

His hand slipped from her shoulder to her lower back as Joshua encouraged her to move. "You have my word, Rince. It is my job."

Fresh air filled her lungs, but it did not feel as wonderful as usual, and Eirian sneezed. "Just do whatever you need to do, Rince. I feel dreadful, and it's a busy day."

Two
Delyth

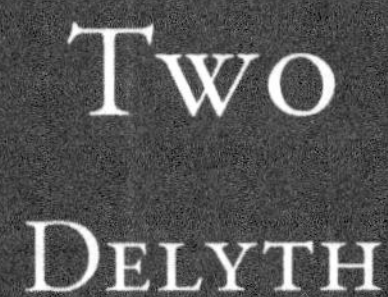

Water lapped at her feet, the cool an enticing contrast to the warmth of the day. In the distance, the peal of bells informed the group that the morning ceremony at the temple had ended. The deep ring was a reminder of what she had done, and the trouble waiting for her when she returned home. Deciding to ignore the warning echoing across the city, Delyth tossed her head back and closed her eyes, enjoying the bite of the sun on her skin. Her arms protested the position they were trapped in. At the back of her mind, a voice that sounded too much like her mother suggested she should take more care to avoid the pain unless she wanted to regret it.

"We should go for a swim," one of her friends said.

Someone laughed, and drops of water left cool spots on Delyth's face as they replied, "If Del starts swimming now, she might escape the wrath of the Altira. If she's lucky."

"My mother will be too busy with the selection today to punish me for my non-attendance," she muttered, cracking open an eye to stare at the woman beside her. "Besides, I'm not the only one who is absent."

A sly grin tugged at the corners of Amelia's lips, and the elf twisted around to tug a stray lock that had escaped the tie restraining Delyth's wild brown hair. "My aunt doesn't care where I am today."

"Gods, I wish I were a Zarthein and not an Altira."

"Don't say that," Amelia purred, leaning closer. "I wouldn't be allowed to kiss you."

One of their other friends scooped up water and threw it at them. "Except you're not allowed to kiss her! Everyone knows only the reigning heirs may fraternise romantically."

Delyth sat up to stretch her arms and groaned at the pinch in her shoulders. "Because we follow all the rules, especially stupid ones. It's not like I can get Amy pregnant."

Amelia grinned, nuzzling her neck. "Thank the gods."

"Talk about forbidden," someone grumbled.

"We know, Laryn. The bloodlines of the gods must be kept apart to prevent the potential muddling of heirs. No one wants an Altira mage with the gifts of war, or the other way around. It's why they scattered the other bloodlines across Tir," Delyth said before sighing. "Fuck, I sound like my mother. I thought I asked you to slap me when I did that, Amy?"

"Oh, you did, Del. Patton was there. Weren't you, Pat?" Amelia pulled away to point at a sullen elf lying face down on the jetty with his arms dangling over the side.

"I know nothing," he grumbled. "Except it's hot, and we should go swimming."

Swiping the back of her hand over her brow, Laryn agreed. "I vote we swim. If we put it off, a priest is bound to find Del, and then our fun will be over."

Watching her friends shed their outer layers of clothing, Delyth rubbed the hem of her shirt between two fingers. The surrounding water glittered, ripples turning the reflection of the sun into thousands of shining drops of light. It was mid-morning, so the tide had long since gone out, but the sea currents tugged at the waters of the Bay of Blades, forcing them to lap gently against the floating jetty. Further back, the wall keeping the outskirts of the Fishers District from collapsing into the depths hummed with energy as it drew from the force constantly drumming against it. Whoever had designed the wards on it had been clever enough to use the infinite source of power supplied by the current to feed the protections.

Amelia poked her cheek, grinning when the action received a huff. The elf had shed everything but her shirt, opting to keep it on. They had learnt from experience that being lectured by a stone-faced priest of Death's temple while naked and in public was an unpleasant situation. A somewhat embarrassing one as well. What worried Delyth the most was being found by someone higher in the hierarchy. Over the years they had been lucky no one recognised Amelia and reported it back to Eirian, who would tell the leader of Ensaycal. Teleri Zarthein was as terrifying as her human counterpart in Endara.

Openly admiring the well-built, muscled body of her lover, Delyth wished she cut as impressive a figure. When it had become abundantly clear her inclinations were academic, her mother had allowed her to withdraw from combat training. Most Altiras either joined the temple or became prominent members of the army, where they fought side by side with the Zartheins. The joint forces of Ensaycal and Endara were the greatest collection of human and elven warriors in Tir. She prayed to Gebael daily, hoping her inclinations would not condemn her to a life spent upholding the ways of his temple. As the daughter of his heir, Delyth knew things about the god of death that others did not, including his love of books and crafting. Her mother always wore the jewellery he had made for her.

"You've got that look, Del," Amelia murmured, holding out a hand to help her up.

"I can't help it. I started out thinking about how beautiful you are, and then I remembered my mother could decide any day that it's time for me to join the temple."

Grasping Amelia's hand, Delyth let the warrior haul her upright. They stood close together, fingers entwined, as the warrior pressed a kiss to her nose. Splashes sounded from nearby, reminding them that their friends were diving into the cool waters of the bay. Lips curling into a smirk, Amelia released her hand and set to work on the buttons of her overshirt while Delyth unbuckled the braided belt holding her trousers in place. She had kicked off her sandals earlier to dip her feet into the water. The linen tumbled to the ground with nothing keeping it secure, and the elf shoved the shirt from her shoulders. Stepping free, Delyth let the garment join the others on the timber slats of the jetty and tugged the thin fabric of her undershirt from her skin.

A breeze fluttered the hem, causing the tiny hairs on her body to rise. Catching her shiver, Amelia chuckled and slid her arms around her waist to pull them together. Leaning into the embrace, Delyth rested her head on her lover's shoulder, breathing in the faint scent of salt, and the special mixture she used to clean her leather armour. At only thirty years old, elven standards considered Amelia too young and untrained to use anything heavier than leather and mail. It did not matter that she was a Zarthein, or that she was as physically capable as someone fifty years her senior; they expected her to adhere to the same rules as the rest. Leaning back, Delyth scrunched up her nose and stuck her tongue out before shoving Amelia just enough to send her staggering backwards and off the jetty.

Spluttering as she resurfaced, the elf glared and swiped her sodden hair from her face. "That was mean."

Flashing a grin, Delyth dived in and enjoyed the icy water surrounding her. It stole the warmth from her skin, plastering her shirt to her body. Treading water once she surfaced, the young mage watched her friends splashing each other and laughing. Arms wrapped around her from behind, Amelia's tongue chasing the droplets on her neck.

"Delicious," she murmured, and her teeth grazed Delyth's skin.

"Sometimes I worry about your love of salty things."

"I'm a Zarthein. They raise us on a diet of the tears of our defeated opponents."

Arching back when teeth latched onto her earlobe, Delyth groaned. "It's not fair you get tears to drink when us Altiras get nothing but haughty righteousness."

"You know how much I adore your haughtiness, Del. I enjoy making it beg."

Her hand wandered down from Delyth's hip to stroke between her legs. Eyeing Amelia sideways, the mage knew the flush of her cheeks was from more than exertion and hoped their friends would not realise what they were doing. The elf had a fondness for exhibitionism that sent a thrill down Delyth's spine. They did nothing obvious, preferring the danger of possibility. With the water being too deep for them to stop kicking, Amelia could do nothing more than tease. Across the bay, the towers of Ensaycal seemed bigger than normal, casting shadows over the rest of the city. Compared to Endara, the dominion of war was a sprawling beast curled around a temple dedicated to battle.

She remembered the last time she had visited the arena and wriggled her arse against Amelia. "I'd say the begging is fairly equal."

Amelia laughed and sunk a finger into Delyth's cunt while her thumb circled her clit. "Oh, dear heart, it's never equal. I only let you think it is, so you don't get bored."

Whatever she had planned to say faded from thought when a second finger joined the first. Biting her bottom lip, Delyth slid an arm between them to seek Amelia's entrance. It was a twist, and rarely effective, but she knew from experience it was enough of an encouragement to lead to better things when they got the opportunity. The thumb on her clit pressed harder, and a moan tumbled from her mouth before she could stop it. Amelia's breathy chuckle spread warmth on her cheek.

"Blood and bone, I love how responsive you are, Del."

"Are the two of you going to swim or just float there?" Laryn drifted closer, kicking her legs slowly.

Squeezing her legs tight to trap Amelia's hand, Delyth arched a brow at their friend. "We're enjoying watching you idiots try to drown each other. Some of us have been up since before dawn."

"Sure you are."

Resting her chin on Delyth's shoulder, the warrior grinned, and kept stroking her lover. "You can join us if you want, Laryn. We're just talking about the many differences between our families."

Eyes narrowing, the other woman cocked her head and made a point of directing her gaze to the water in front of Delyth. "I'm sure you're having a great conversation, but it would be nice if you could keep your hands off each other and spend time with your friends."

Guilt clouded Delyth's mind, and she wriggled out of Amelia's grasp. "You're right; we're neglecting you. Come on, Amy, let's help Laryn drown Calleth. Patton as well. If we can catch him."

She heard a huff from Amelia, and the tone of it told Delyth the warrior was unimpressed. The two men were treading water further out, hands waving toward a merchant galley flying the colours of a distant daoine nation. Sometimes they talked about bartering their skills for passage on one of the many trading ships that came to the Bay of Blades so they could explore the world. It was an idea Delyth liked to contemplate when her mother was being particularly frustrating. Laryn, Calleth, and Patton possessed a freedom she and Amelia longed for. They could leave if they wanted, but if she or her lover did the same, they would be hunted down and returned to face the consequences of their choices.

Signalling to Amelia, Delyth angled herself toward Calleth. His red curls gleamed in the sunlight, and she envied the speed at which they dried out. The delicately curved tips of his ears stuck out at an angle that had made him the target of bullies when they were younger. Laryn and Amelia had always come to his defence, and it was an unspoken understanding among the group that he would do anything for them.

He worshipped the ground Laryn walked on, and she happily kept him close.

They moved slowly to ensure their approach was silent, even when the flow of the current was pushing them back towards the jetty. As soon as they were close enough, Laryn dipped below the surface to grab Calleth's legs while Delyth prepared to launch herself at his body. She could tell from the narrowing of Amelia's eyes that the warrior was planning to attack Patton, even though he was the strongest swimmer. Her chance came the moment the red-haired elf began struggling to break free of Laryn's grasp. With a kick of her legs, Delyth launched herself at him, arms wrapping around his shoulders. From the corner of her eye, she watched Patton streaking through the water like a fish while Amelia chased him.

A flicker of magic came from the man beneath her, the only warning the two women got before he sent them flying with a ward that knocked them backwards. The impact left Delyth dazed, and she gave thanks to the ancestors she had mostly been in the water instead of above it. She had seen what happened when a defensive ward forced someone against the surface of a body of water. Recovering from it quicker than she would have elsewhere, the mage looked around for Laryn, only to find her and Calleth missing.

His head broke the surface, and the panicked look on his face sent chills down her spine. "Where's Laryn? I can't find her. Del, where is she? Oh, gods, what have I done?"

The sound of his shouting brought Amelia and Patton swimming back while Delyth reached for her magic. She was an Altira. It was easy for her to spread her power through an area to sense the energies of anything living. Locating the familiar touch of Laryn's magic, she pointed in the right direction before taking a deep breath and diving. Following the thread of power she had wrapped around her friend, Delyth felt the burning of her lungs as they protested the situation. It was only when her hand closed around the other woman that she felt the fear fade. Patton was there as well, and together they dragged Laryn upwards, breaking through the surface to suck in deep gulps of air.

"You fucking idiot!" Amelia had Calleth by the arm. "You could have killed them!"

Spluttering, Laryn clung to Patton and Delyth. "It was our fault for scaring him."

"Scared or not, there's no reason to use a knock back in water."

Calleth stared at his friends. "I'm sorry! I should know better than to react like that."

Shrugging off their hold, Laryn swam over to pull him into a kiss. "I'm not hurt, just a little breathless and keen to get out of the water now. The ward sent me a bit too deep."

They all understood what she did not say out loud. If Patton and Delyth had not reached her, she might not have made it to the surface before passing out. She had already been underwater when it happened. Watching the fair-haired elf slip an arm around Calleth to swim to the jetty, Delyth did not stop them. What fun they had been having had ended. Joining her lover, she leaned in to kiss Amelia's cheek reassuringly. There was a flicker of fear in the warrior's eyes when she stared at her, a hand coming out of the water to brush sodden strands of brown hair away from her face. Neither of them spoke, preferring to take a moment to appreciate the fact they were alive and well when things might have gone differently.

"I love you," Amelia murmured. "If you had been hurt..."

"Hush, Amy. I'm fine. Come on, let's join our friends. Don't be mean to Cal. He didn't mean to hurt us, and the guilt he must be feeling is punishment enough."

THREE
TELERI

THE LAST OF THE soldiers settled into position, their boots thumping heavily on the cobblestones of the courtyard. Sweeping her gaze over them, Teleri nodded slowly, her mouth twisted in contemplation. Each month she selected thirty to form the honour guard who accompanied the fifteen petitioners chosen by Eirian for the sacrifice. It was a highly sought-after position. Something she had never quite understood. She supposed most saw it as an opportunity to support those who willingly offered their lives to serve the community.

"Are you happy with this selection, Mother?" Her eldest son touched her arm, and Teleri sighed. "I know you find this process tedious, and I would take over for you if I could…"

Rubbing a thumb against the polished cerapter horn hilt of her sword, she gave him a thankful smile. "I know, Yestin, and I appreciate your eagerness to ease my burden."

"But you're the Zarthein mage, and the burden is yours to bear."

"How did I raise such a wise young man?"

Yestin chuckled, lifting his dark gaze to the sky. "I'm fairly sure Grandma did most of the work."

Covering her heart with her hand, Teleri pretended to be hurt by his comment. The sting had once been painful, but she had long since come to terms with missing most of Yestin's early years because of a military campaign. It had taken time for their relationship to grow, and it had helped that her mother had taught him everything she knew about the role of War's heir. Nothing had called her away from raising her other children, something Teleri was thankful for. Her family was important, and if there was one thing the separation from her firstborn had taught her, it was that family mattered more than duty to a path dictated by the ill-luck of birth, and the blood of a god.

"I'm glad you will never know the pain of leaving your family, my dearest boy," she said, and reached out to ruffle his raven-black hair. "And I hope you never know the burden of raising the next heir."

Bumping his mother with his shoulder, Yestin smiled faintly. "Knowing my luck, I'll be the grandfather telling my grandchild why I understand their feelings."

"Luckily, the power goes to the first person in the bloodline born after the death of the heir. All I can do is hope for you and your children to be spared. I know it sounds terrible to wish this on others, but I wish the burden belonged to some other family instead of ours. It's too much."

"Have you ever talked to Eirian about how you feel? Or the Altira before her."

Snorting, Teleri slung an arm over his shoulders and squeezed. "Eirian Altira believes there is nothing greater than serving her god. In more ways than simply as his High Priestess, and especially on her knees."

"Mother!"

Her smile was one of amusement. Once he was old enough to understand the complexities of being a god's heir, she had sat him down and explained the bond between her and the man who had been the Altira mage at the time. After his death, Teleri had kept her distance from Eirian, forbidden from witnessing her growing up. Beyond formal occasions, they avoided their counterparts until they came of age, and it was torture. Certain gods were bound, each a part of a whole, and their heirs felt the bond as well. Teleri hated her inability to resist the pull to Eirian and the previous Altiras. Part of her hated that Death's heirs were human, and it was likely she would face at least two more Altira mages before the fading finally claimed her life. She dreaded it.

"You're a married man, Yestin. You know exactly what I'm referring to."

Groaning, he slapped a hand to his face. "Yes, but you're my mother. It's embarrassing to talk about such things with my mother. Though I suppose I'm thankful it's not about Father."

"Who do you think I should select?" Nodding at the lines of soldiers, Teleri redirected their focus to why they were there. "As my child, it may be your duty to guide the next heir. It's about time I trained you. If you wish. Otherwise, I'll ask Caelia if she would do it."

His eyes widened in surprise, and she felt a sliver of doubt. It was a heavy request, one that placed the prospect of her death in his mind in a way that no parent wanted their child to deal with. But she had celebrated her two hundredth birthday, and if she was fortunate, Teleri hoped to spend another hundred and fifty years with her family. Asking Yestin to learn from her was a purely selfish request. There were years to go before she needed to teach anyone, but she wanted to spend more time with the son she often felt distant from.

"You honour me with the offer. Caelia is better suited, but I'd like to. Perhaps we could both learn, and spend the time together as a family," he replied, leaning in to kiss her cheek.

Pursing her lips, Teleri pretended to consider his suggestion. "We could do that."

"I'm not fooled, Mother."

"And I'm sure I don't know what you're talking about. Now, pick thirty soldiers from the ranks. Remember, their duty for the next few days is to accompany those selected to feed their life energy into the cities to ensure our local food supplies continue to flourish. Not just those people, but their families who have come to witness the sacrifice they're making, and to remember the beauty of life."

He arched a brow, and the gleam in his eyes suggested he was indulging her. "So, we want people who have a reverence for the ritual. Those who would cry with the crowd if they weren't on duty."

"Those who will leave offerings to the ancestors when the ceremonies are over."

Despite being a Zarthein and the son of the current heir, Yestin spent much of his time training side by side with the soldiers lined up in front of them. They were his comrades, and they all answered to the High General. Studying the familiar lines of his face, Teleri wished she shared the same relationship with the members of the army as he did. There were so many Zarthein among the ranks that he had never been treated any differently. She knew Yestin was highly regarded as a warrior, and it filled her with pride. For all her failings as a mother, her children were capable, serving their people with integrity and respect.

"Show me the list. We're too high for me to pick out everyone clearly," Yestin said, holding out a hand for the book resting on the rail in front of Teleri. "I'll have a better chance with the names."

Half-smiling, Teleri plucked the thick book from its perch and handed it to him. It carried a weight that was more than physical. She had record-ed every list of names for every ceremony. There was sentiment in it, but it was mostly out of respect. No one knew the truth, and Teleri never planned to tell anyone she did it to remember the soldiers she had lost in battle and to ensure their families received the recognition they deserved. The honour she believed belonged to them for all their sacrifices. Eirian had caught her leaving offerings but never pushed to know why. For all the complicated emotions she felt for the High Priestess, Teleri was relieved every time her Endaran counterpart knelt by her side in silence to light the candles.

There was a reverence on Yestin's face as he stroked the book that suggested he had his own theories about why she kept her list of names. It brought a sad smile to Teleri's lips, her heart clenching when he shot her a thankful smile. He took care in opening it, leafing through the pages to find the most recent entry. She had penned it the night before, offering a prayer to the gods as she copied each name from a list provided by her advisers.

On some level, she found peace in her little ritual when she sat alone at her desk, surrounded by dancing shadows and the silence of the night. Only the scratch of her quill against paper, and the smell of lemongrass infused candles cut through her solitude. Drawing the memory to the front of her mind, Teleri gazed out at the soldiers awaiting their orders. Their excitement was palpable, the thrum of their magic filling the air with a heady thickness.

"Right, here, these people are my recommendation," Yestin said.

"You tell me who, and I'll call out the names so the rest can get on with their day."

Beaming at his mother, he told her the first name. The tension broke in the courtyard, congratulatory cheers accompanying each selection. For once, the pride Teleri felt was more for her son than for the fine warriors being chosen to accompany the sacrifices. At the edge of her awareness, she sensed one of her advisers waiting with an air of anxiety surrounding him. It was an irritating scratch that detracted from her enjoyment of the event. Yestin kept glancing back at the man, the concern furrowing his brows telling her he was as sensitive to the cloud of emotion. By the time they reached the last name, Teleri was more than ready to find out what was wrong. They waited for the soldiers who had not been selected to depart while those who had gathered around the officers for their orders.

"Would you like me to return this to your desk, Mother?"

Eyeing the book clasped tightly to his chest, Teleri shook her head. "No. You can hear what Wyatt has to say. Whatever it is, it's troubling him, and it might be best if you're here."

Straightening when they approached, the shorter man ran a shaky hand through his hair, leaving it even messier. "High General, Yestin. I didn't want to interrupt the selection, but it's important."

"Yes, I can tell. What's wrong, Wyatt?"

"I received a report from Kirrama. The city has fallen."

Dread turned her cold, and Teleri rubbed her mouth while she considered the implications of a city as large as Kirrama falling. At her side, Yestin was muttering curses between demanding to know why they had not been informed the distant city was at war. She could not remember any reports concerning conflict in that region, so it bothered her to find out that something had happened without her knowledge. If they had been aware, they would have sent legions to assist their ally. Worse, it was not the first city it had happened to, and now she needed to speak to Eirian.

"Was there any information about who attacked?" She lifted her gaze to the arched doorway above them, studying the swirl of the lattice carvings. "Or was it like the others?"

Jerking around to blink at her in confusion, Yestin said, "What do you mean?"

"Kirrama isn't the first city to fall in recent months. We've kept the information quiet to avoid panic."

Wyatt's mouth twisted, making his displeasure clear. "And I argued against doing so. These cities are being betrayed from within, their gates cast open for an enemy we can't identify. We need help."

"I know! Which is why I'm going straight to Eirian. She can get a message to Bellenden, and you can be sure that her sister will be here as swiftly as Igraine can fly. The dragon riders can scout out the enemy. And I believe we need their help, or we'll be chasing our tails."

While his anger had turned his magic into a furious swirl, Yestin kept his visage blank. It was a testament to his training, but Teleri hoped he would relax his control once they were in private. It was better for him to express his fury before he returned to his home. If there was one thing she understood well, it was that taking home excess rage did not benefit a family. Not in any manner. Sometimes she recalled all the occasions when she had taken her anger home and the terrified stares of her children.

"With your permission, High General, I will command the keepers to prepare the tower for the dragons. We will need to inform the local farmers. At least we can ensure they're compensated for any additional livestock required to feed our guests while they are here," Yestin said, refusing to meet his mother's gaze. "Is there anything else you need me for?"

"No, that's all. Thank you for taking the initiative."

He snapped a fist to his chest, his slight bow appearing stiff and uncomfortable with one arm keeping her book tucked to his side. Watching him go, Teleri pursed her lips while Wyatt shuffled. The impatient huff escaping his control had her shifting her focus to him, and the man arched a brow in expectation. She suspected he was waiting for her to scold him for arguing with her in front of Yestin. Sweat trickled down her spine from the heat of her armour. It was a familiar sensation; one she could focus on while dragging out the silence between them to make Wyatt grow nervous.

"High General, we need—"

"Do not tell me what we need, Wyatt. I've barely begun training my son to one day guide the next High General, and what you did undermined his trust in me. Do you know how fragile our relationship is?"

There was a glimmer of shame in his gaze, but the twist of his mouth suggested he felt no remorse for his actions. "No, I'm testing it. If Yestin cannot see why you kept it secret, then he has no place among the future leadership of Ensaycal. When you die, it will be his responsibility to make these decisions."

A muscle twitched in her cheek, and Teleri longed to strip out of her heavy layers to replace them with a light robe. "I need a horse and an escort. Send a pigeon to the temple to inform the High Priestess."

"Would you like me to give her the details?"

"No," she replied, shaking her head slightly. "I'm unsure of who Eirian has informed among the clergy. We'd better keep the information from spreading as a rumour. I'll tell her myself."

"I'll see to your horse and escort."

"Thank you. While you do, I'm going to fetch a bottle of elderberry wine."

His brows shot up, almost disappearing beneath his fringe. "Why?"

Snorting, Teleri smirked. "Because Eirian likes elderberry wine, and I know from experience she'll do anything for me after a few glasses. She can't resist. Which is exactly what I need, since the relationship between her and her sister is unconventional."

Four

Briallen

Icy wind rushed past, leaving her thankful for the thick layers of her riding leathers. Wards sat close to her skin, trapping the warmth within the armour to ensure she could still move the moment they landed. There was no view as beautiful as the glittering blanket of stars that stretched beyond all imagination when viewed from the back of a dragon in flight. Except perhaps, the setting sun against an angry mass of clouds heralding an approaching storm. When she had been younger, Briallen had begged her father to take her on the back of his bonded to fly among the brilliant colours of a sunrise, and no disappointment stung quite like what she had felt to discover the clouds only appeared that way from a certain angle.

"I hope you never lose your wide-eyed wonder, little Bri."

A layer of wool covering her face hid her smile. *"You've known me since my mother brought me to my father in Bellenden, Igraine. Have I ever changed? It's been fifty years."*

The dragon's chuckle resonated through her mind, and Briallen relaxed her hold on the pommel of her saddle. Stretching, she rolled her shoulders and peered across the darkness to seek the shadows of her companions. Knowing Tristan and his dragon, Ysgarlad, were with her on this mission provided more relief than she would admit out loud. Only Igraine knew how much it mattered to her, and the dragon would never betray her innermost thoughts to anyone. Her bonded was the clutch sister to her father's, and Igraine had always been there for her even before she began her training. There had never been any question about who would become her bonded.

A dark shape swooped past, and Tristan's laughter carried on the wind. Despite being younger than Igraine, Ysgarlad was a bigger dragon, and in the right light, her scales looked as though someone had painted them with blood. When the two dragons stood next to each other, they were a study in opposites. One appeared built for battle, her broad chest and massive size terrifying in red, while the other was born of cold misty mornings, and known for her speed. But Briallen knew the truth. Igraine was one of the most vicious dragons in Bellenden. Ysgarlad was a soldier, and she took her orders from the more experienced dragon. Which was how Tristan had come to live among the dragon riders of Bellenden as a child. They had rescued him after Igraine had roasted his mother.

Sensing where her thoughts had gone, Igraine snarled, *"Goblins are terrible."*

"And yet you and Ysgarlad brought home a goblin child."

"He's a boy. They're not as bad. Just wait; one day he'll build you a nest."

Feeling her cheeks burn beneath the thick wool of her mask, Briallen did not respond. She knew what Igraine was suggesting, and she was well aware of the confusion Tristan stirred in her heart. Without warning, the dragon tucked her wings in tightly and began diving towards the ground. Scrambling to grab the pommel, she held on while wrapping herself in wards to ensure she did not lose her hold. It was magic all potential riders had to master long before they were allowed to climb onto a dragon's back. If they could not protect themselves in flight and fight, then they would never be allowed to bond, even if one of the mighty creatures was interested in claiming them. One day, Briallen hoped she would master the ability to change shapes like her father's people, and she prayed to the gods her animal form would have wings. She liked to imagine how it would feel to fly beside Igraine.

Before they hit the ground, the dragon spread her massive wings, catching the air to slow their descent. Whooping in delight, Briallen leaned sideways to peer down at the town sprawled across the land. Lights flickered in windows, smoke drifted from chimneys, and the few people who were walking the streets turned their attention skywards. She knew what they saw. Two terrifying shadows blotting out the stars as they circled the town in their search for a suitable landing place. In daylight, they brought out feelings of awe, but in the dark of night, they were the dangerous monsters from stories about ancient battles. Dragons changed the outcome of war, and no one wanted to deny hospitality to them or their riders out of fear poor impressions would lead to the destruction of their homes.

Ysgarlad had already set down in an open field outside the town. From the way they kept it clear of crops and livestock, Briallen suspected it was the community gathering place used for festivals and other large events. Igraine's landing jolted her, stealing the air from her lungs as it always did. Unbuckling the bindings securing her in the saddle, she stretched before climbing down. Hot breath greeted her once she was stable, the dragon scrutinising her. Rubbing a spot above her nostrils that Briallen knew she favoured, she poured love over the bond to assure the beast she was fine. Igraine liked to fuss over her as though she were her hatchling, and since her mother had never bothered to show the same affections, Briallen let the dragon do as she wished.

"Stop dawdling, Bri," Tristan said, approaching her while Ysgarlad nudged Igraine's neck. "We're supposed to be meeting the informant from Oisin's court, and we don't want to miss our chance."

"He's right, little Bri. You cannot be late, or the spy will leave."

Giving Igraine a sideways look, she nodded at her friend. "You owe me an ale."

"Oh, fuck off! You owe me."

Hooking a finger around the lower half of her mask, Briallen yanked it down to expose her mouth. Doing the same, Tristan was quicker to shove the upper half into the gap between the top of their head and the hood clinging to them. She knew that once they were in the light, he would take the time to tease her about the redness of the skin around her eyes, where the mask did not protect them from the chill. Most riders wore special goggles over their eyes, but neither of them had taken that step yet. It was a common joke in their community that young riders liked the sting, while those with experience knew protecting their vision was more important. Considering most riders were mortal, Briallen understood the concern. Few were true immortals like Tristan, and though she was unlikely to die of old age, she could be injured and killed.

Briallen slung an arm around his shoulders and pointedly snapped her teeth at Tristan. "Now, remember, this is a human town. Keep your claws retracted and try not to let them see inside your mouth."

"I'm older than you, Bri," he grumbled.

"And yet only a month ago you caused a panic in that elven city we visited."

"It's not my fault how people react when they find out I'm a goblin."

She kept her arm around him as they walked toward the town. Listening to the snorts and scuffs of the two dragons settling down to wait, Briallen understood the resentment in Tristan's voice. Her mother had been human, and her father was a duine who was thousands of years old. As a half-blood, she dealt with the scorn as much as he did. It had brought them together, forging their friendship. Tristan had found her being bullied by older daoine youths for being half human and threatened to eat them all. At fifteen years old, rejected by her mother and kept from being a sister to her younger sibling, Briallen had happily clung to him, much to the dismay of her father and his older children. But they had stuck together through everything, and Igraine and Ysgarlad protected them as best they could.

No walls surrounded the town, but barely armed people patrolled the streets to keep the peace. Their eyes widened at the sight of the two riders in their distinct leathers, and Briallen wondered if they had ever seen anyone wearing as many weapons as the two of them were. As a goblin, Tristan was deadly without the need of any blades, but he preferred to keep his claws in. So long as he kept his mouth shut, people would assume he was human, but no one could mistake her for being anything other than a duine when her riding gear did not cover her head to toe. Even half-bloods possessed the telling moon glow that was unique to the daoine. Keeping their distance, the guards followed them to a tavern near the centre of the town, and the tense smile Briallen gave them had hands darting to their short swords.

"Not the least friendly greeting we've gotten," Tristan muttered, shaking her arm off.

"You can't blame people for being nervous when dragons land outside their homes."

"Why do you think this woman wanted us to meet here?"

Bounding up the stairs onto the verandah of the tavern, Briallen shrugged and headed inside. The walls had muffled the noise, but it hit her as soon as she passed through the doorway. People stared at the riders, so she stared back with a grin. Tristan elbowed her, his lips pressed shut. He would avoid talking to hide the sharp points of his teeth that gave away his goblin heritage. Shoving her hood back, she rearranged the top half of her woollen mask to sit over her hair, keeping any stray bits from sticking up. In the corner of her vision, she watched her companion do the same. Everyone knew what they were, but there was no need to appear even more intimidating. Unwilling to wait for the tension to ease, Briallen made her way to the counter, leaning on it with what she hoped was a friendly smile.

"Two ales, please!"

Tristan was a silent presence at her side, his gaze sweeping the room for the woman they were supposed to meet. All they knew was that she was a duine and had travelled a long way from the daoine kingdom of Talaroo with information. Studying his face, Briallen saw when he located their target, his sensitive nose twitching. It was a useful aspect of being a goblin that had helped them out many times on missions. He could smell the other duine in the tavern, even if he could not see her. Scowling at them, the barkeep delivered a pair of mugs, and she withdrew a silver coin from a pocket, sliding it across the counter. When he saw it, his eyes widened, and he hesitated to pick it up.

Ignoring the exchange, Tristan whispered, "She's in the far corner. Let's go."

Collecting the mugs, Briallen followed him across the packed room to a corner tucked in beside a staircase leading up to what she suspected were rooms for other uses. Muffled sounds came from above, and Tristan's flinch confirmed her thoughts. The woman at the table did not look up from her book as they sat, and through the layers of the robe she wore, Briallen saw the glow of her skin. Giving Tristan his drink, she studied the narrow eyes of the duine and watched the twitching of her cheeks that betrayed her agitation. Whatever the information was that she had to give them, it had to be more important than they realised, otherwise her father would not have sent them on this mission.

"No one could ever mistake what the two of you are," she said, and Briallen wanted to sigh in delight over the sweetness of her voice. "Fucking riders think they're amazing."

Her delight faded, and the rider huffed. "You try bonding with a dragon."

"I can already fly; I don't need a dragon."

Tucking away the information about her animal form, Briallen took a sip of the ale. "I'm Briallen Altira. He's Tristan. You have information for Lord General Valerian."

Curiosity lit the deep brown eyes of the other woman. "You're his half-blood daughter."

"Aye."

"Your sister is the Altira mage, the heir to Death. My job is to deal in information. I've been undercover in Oisin's court for more years than I want to remember, and what I have for the Lord General is important. Are you aware of the attacks on cities all over Tir?"

Briallen stared at her drink, watching the flickering lights shift the colours. "I am."

"Annawyn is behind it. Oisin and other loyalists received instructions to attack anyone who won't bow to the mad god. She is using her mind mages to twist people to betray those who stand against her from within. Her influence is spreading across the world, driving mortals and immortals alike to insanity."

Beside her, Tristan went still, reminding her of a predator preparing to strike. She supposed that in a tavern filled with humans, he was. In the back of her mind, Igraine's presence was a constant comfort, and the press of the dragon's awareness confirmed she was paying attention to the meeting. What was happening throughout Tir was a concern, and as long-lived as dragons were, they were as mortal as humans, elves, and daoine. War had claimed the lives of many of them, and Briallen had overheard her father arguing for the formation of a secret place to take clutches of eggs and young hatchlings where they would be safe from those who would bring harm to the dragons. Those who had sworn themselves to the god Annawyn, donning the mantle of Unseelie.

"Wait, doesn't Talaroo share a border with Diwan?" Tristan muttered, eyes never leaving the woman opposite them. "Queen Malena is a Raven."

"Indeed. Where do you think Oisin plans to attack first? Their youngest daughter is a husk maker like her mother."

"As the daughter of a Raven, can the princess be bonded to a danann pairing?" Igraine demanded.

Sipping her ale, she wished it were one of the wines her father preferred to drink. "Has Queen Malena taken her daughter to the Vale? Most husk makers are Ravens."

"Except for the Altira," the woman replied, lips twitching in amusement.

Unappreciative of the comment about her younger sister, Briallen schooled her features to remain blank. As a child, she had never understood why Eirian had been kept from her, and why their mother had delivered her to her father at three years old. No matter how many lectures she had endured about the importance of the heirs, and the role played by the Altira mage, Briallen had longed to belong to the human family she had been born into. Even now, despite their ages, she tried to endear herself to her sister every time she visited the twin cities. At least her niece adored her, and Igraine was always happy to sneak Delyth into the skies without Eirian's permission.

"As far as I know, Queen Malena attempted to give Princess Silaine to Neriwyn, but he rejected the girl even though she is a husk maker. This is information they kept secret. Oisin has plans for the princess. I'm telling you because it's important. Husk makers can turn the tide of a war just as easily as a dragon. If the mad god controls daoine born with the ability, then she could destroy entire mortal armies with a handful of people."

"She's right, Briallen."

Glancing at Tristan, Briallen saw the tip of a fang digging into his lip. The information worried him, and she understood why. Husk makers were terrifying in a battle, something they had witnessed not long after Igraine had bonded with her. Eirian had been called into battle by Death, and they had been among the riders assigned to protect her. Watching hundreds of soldiers turn to dust and bones had left her with nightmares for months. Sometimes they returned, and Briallen knew she would be plagued by them again.

"We can bring you to Bellenden if you wish to convey everything to the Lord General," she told the woman. "Or arrange for you to meet him outside of the city in a secret location."

Head cocked, the other woman chuckled. "It has been a long time since I saw Valerian. The last time our paths crossed, I seduced him and stole vital documents from the study to the left of his bedroom."

Tristan gawked at her while Briallen gasped. "That was you?"

"Ah, you've heard the story?"

"Yes. My father uses it as a cautionary tale."

"Well then, I'll take you up on your offer. However, I find it challenging to fly at night. Will one of your dragons allow me to ride on its back with you?"

Chewing her bottom lip, Briallen studied the elegant curve of the woman's features and wondered what they would be like twisted in pleasure. "I'm sure we can sort something out. You've ridden before?"

Growling, Igraine flooded her mind with suspicion. "*You're not to sleep with her.*"

"I certainly have. Once daylight arrives, I'll fly myself. And yes, I would prefer to ride with you, little Altira, just in case the goblin decides he's hungry."

Five

Eirian

Exhaustion had seeped into her bones, settling with no intention of leaving. Between the ceremonies, the sacrifices, and the news Teleri had delivered about another city falling, she had barely stopped long enough to rest. Dispatched to Bellenden, messenger pigeons carried a request for a visit from her older sister. They had kept the reason private in case the bird was intercepted on its way to the mountain city that housed the dragons and their riders in their part of the world. Anyone who did not know them would simply view the letter as an invitation from one sister to the other to visit her family. Briallen would know better, but Eirian suspected she would hope otherwise.

With everything going on, she had yet to find the time or the energy to be angry with Delyth for absconding from the ceremonies. Part of her was glad her daughter was acting out. If more cities fell, Eirian knew the war would find them, and it would spare no one. Better for her only child to steal some happy moments with her friends. Standing in front of a mirror to study the lines marking her face, Eirian wished someone had let her have the same chance. Guilt rippled through her like a wave, offering faded memories of Briallen begging to be allowed to be her family. Their mother had never encouraged their relationship, and not for the first time, Eirian wondered how different things could have been.

The truth in her reflection was kinder than her thoughts. Blue eyes stared back from a face that did not look like it belonged to a woman barely over forty years old, who had shouldered nothing but duty all her life. It was a gift from Gebael that left Eirian resentful. Death liked his heirs to remain beautiful for as long as possible despite being human. Looking away from the mirror, she regarded her chambers with regret. They were hers alone, and she contemplated slipping down the hall to the quarters she shared with her husband to see if he was home. She knew he would not be there, but anything was better than facing the silence alone. Too many thoughts chased through her head like rowdy children.

Shedding her clothes with the slow care of a woman putting off a task, Eirian did her best to keep her mind from drifting to the god she served. Teleri had suggested she summon Gebael to find out what information he would willingly offer, but she did not know if she was in the right state to deal with his demands. And Death was always demanding. Even as she dreaded him, desire slithered through her exhaustion, whispering reminders of how talented the god was with his mouth and hands. There had been too many times over the years when the only way Eirian found peace was at his mercy. It was a craving that had become ingrained in her when she had turned twenty, and Gebael had shown himself.

No one would disturb her until dawn. It was clear the events had worn her down, and turning back to her reflection, Eirian focused on the dark shadows beneath her eyes. The last time she had slept was after Teleri had plied her with elderberry wine as a bribe to convince her to send the letters to Briallen. Over the years it had become the High General's preferred way of getting Eirian to do what she wanted without a fight, and she let her. Sometimes it was easier to surrender to the desires of another, especially when they were one of the few people she trusted without question. Teleri was the only person who understood the weight of responsibility forced upon her by the misfortune of birth.

Moving to a set of drawers, Eirian pulled one open to pluck a bundle of black fabric from it. If she were going to summon her god, then she needed to dress for it. Gebael liked it when he arrived and found her adorned in the sheer black silk robe he had gifted her. Better if she were on her knees. She could almost guarantee his good mood by presenting herself in the right manner. To get the god of death to answer her questions, Eirian needed to ensure he felt like indulging her, even if she felt too tired for it. Delaying until after she had slept would only add to her stress, and the anticipation of needing to speak to him would keep her from resting. It always did. The sooner it was done, the sooner she would have answers.

Dragging a brush through her dark brown hair, Eirian clipped it back with a delicate silver contraption the god had made for her. He had taken her through the gateway stones to the eternal valley of winter, Ellinjaa, and one of her favourite memories of the trip was of seeing his workshop. As beautiful as the frozen valley and its tower of black stone were, they did not compare to the pure happiness that had turned Death's icy blue gaze into a warm summer sky. After showing her around, Gebael had fucked her on one of his workbenches, and Eirian had known she would never deny him anything he wanted.

Satisfied with her efforts, she rearranged the position of the robe, so it clung to her curves before returning to the mirror. Using her foot to drag a cushion from beneath the carved timber frame, Eirian positioned it before sinking to her knees. His fondness for making her watch what he did to her was one thing she refused to question. She knew enough about the hedonistic ways of the gods before the Sundering to understand Death enjoyed a show. They all did. It was why the ceremonies had become what they were: an elaborate performance intended to soothe the vicious temper of a god who could kill them without hesitation.

Her eyes fluttered shut, and the bone-deep weariness reached for her mind, hoping she would finally rest. Doing her best to stave off sleep, Eirian focused her thoughts and magic on Gebael. There were two easy ways to summon the god she was bound to. If she were injured badly enough, he would come to check on her. The other way, the one she used the most, called on her to stretch her mind over the chains between them to draw Death's attention. Sometimes it was almost too easy, but Eirian dared not question it. She knew he drifted across Tir doing whatever he pleased to spite the god of life, and getting in the middle of a dispute between the gods was ill-advised.

An icy chill settled over her skin, familiar in its agony, and the desire it brought with it. Clenching her thighs together, Eirian counted to five before she opened her eyes to drink in the sight of the man behind her. When she took in the amused curl of his lips, the anxious fist clutching her heart relaxed, and she sighed in relief. In the flickering light of the lanterns hanging around her chamber, Gebael drew all the shadows to him. They crept over the walls and floor, dripping from the ceiling to greet him with the enthusiasm of a loyal hound, pulling her magic along with them. His cold blue eyes were dark, and Eirian held his gaze in the mirror, making a point to draw her bottom lip between her teeth.

"Darling, this is unexpected," he murmured, placing a hand on her head. "But not undesired. Spread your knees more, and hands behind your back. I haven't visited you in too long, and I'm sorry for it."

It was easy to slip into a state where she thought of nothing but pleasing him. He was her god, and his power flowed through her veins to give her life a purpose. Everything Eirian had become she owed to him, and adoration replaced resentment with each beat of her heart in his presence. A knowing smirk appeared as she shifted to spread her knees, and the translucent black fabric slipped to the side. Rolling her shoulders to lift her breasts up, she clasped her hands behind her back. In the mirror, her reflection taunted Eirian with the idea that she remained a highly desirable woman despite her age. As though Gebael sensed the negative thoughts clawing through her mind, his hand trailed down from the top of her head to her throat, and he bent over to kiss her cheek.

"Your beauty grows with every passing year, Eirian."

The touch of his lips left an icy spot on her skin that fed the desire pooling between her legs. "I've missed you, my Lord Gebael. These last few months without you near..."

Something flickered across his expression that she could not name. A look she knew too well swiftly replaced it. Gebael's hold on her throat tightened as his other hand grabbed a handful of her hair to yank her head back. His kiss was hard, the ice of his power stealing her breath with more finality than the restriction on her neck. As soon as dark spots began to dance in her vision, Eirian felt him let go, and she did her best not to collapse in a heap at his feet. The hunger in his stare was one she had endured before, but even though she had enjoyed it in the past, the exhaustion remained buried in her bones, reminding her she had a job to do. With lips parted in horror, Eirian broke her pose to cover her face.

"Eirian?"

Shaking her head, she drew a shaky breath between her teeth. "I'm sorry, my lord, please forgive me. The last few days have been exhausting, and I thought I was doing the right thing."

"You never need to apologise to me for being tired."

"You're not disappointed with me?"

Gebael chuckled, stroking her hair gently. "I would be remiss if I were. No one serves me as devoutly as you, my darling High Priestess. Besides, I'm aware of what troubles you."

Lowering her hands to her lap, Eirian stared at him in the mirror. It startled her to see remorse on his face; the emotion seemed out of place on the god of death. Ashamed of her assumption, she reminded herself of the first thing about the balance they taught all children. Death drew purpose from life, and wasting it was an insult to the gods. The man behind her tolerated wars out of necessity, but he had told her many times he did not enjoy them. Gebael preferred to allow people to live out their days in meaningful pursuit of the things that made their hearts and minds soar while doing their best not to bring harm to others. In truth,

Eirian had never understood how he could wish that for people while doing the terrible things she knew he did.

"It's Lady Annawyn, isn't it?" she murmured, dropping her gaze to the edge of the cushion beneath her knees. "You warned me one day her anger with you and the other gods would bring war here."

"Yes, it is. Her madness is spreading across Tir, and there is nothing I can do to stop it."

"My city is going to fall."

"Eirian..."

Exhaling heavily, she lifted her chin and regarded the mirror. "There must be something that can be done. Surely Lady Shianeni will not allow her wife to destroy all her mortal creations in a temper."

They stared at each other, neither willing to flinch. A hint of pride cut a path through his remorse, and Gebael inclined his head. Her heart hammered fearfully against her ribs, aware of how easily the man touching her could stop it. There was a reason Eirian refused to keep any potted plants in her quarters to liven the place up. When he was not being careful of his power, living things suffered, and she did not need the reminder that he could end her existence as easily as blinking.

"You're right, there is probably something that could be done if only I set aside my pride to work with my estranged wife. I know what's coming, and I cannot see the other side of it. Not yet."

Twisting around, Eirian grabbed the fabric of his trousers and peered at him pleadingly. "I'm not so foolish as to think I mean anything to you in the grand scheme of things, but I'm begging you to do something. We will fight this war, but I don't need you to tell me we will lose."

His eyes were a bottomless lake of crystal blue, threatening to drown her. "Hope can be found when all else has been lost. I suspect any chance we have of bringing an end to Annawyn's madness will require us bowing to Shianeni's whims. Her games started it."

"I will pay whatever price is asked of me."

"Therein lies the problem. She knows how precious my heir is. She will take you."

"Better to let Lady Shianeni have me than to let Lady Annawyn destroy Tir."

He closed his eyes, lips pressed in a firm line. If she had not known better, Eirian would have thought he was struggling with his emotions. There was a stillness to him that gave the impression of being carved from ice. As his heir, she knew what it meant. Gebael was sorting through the visions given by his power. When he had first come to her, Eirian had asked how she would die. The explanation he gave her, along with three possibilities for her death, remained locked in her memories. People were blessed with the freedom of choice, and it was the paths they took that led to their end, but along the way, there were always forks that could take them on a different road. Decisions made by those around them played a part. Nothing was certain until it happened.

"Have I ever told you why I cling to my heirs so tightly, Eirian?"

She rested against his legs, letting him toy with her hair. "I never tire of hearing it."

"You keep me grounded. I cannot forget what I am as long as I have my precious Altira reminding me," he said, studying her reflection in the mirror. "My beautiful, fragile, High Priestess. The one person who understands I'm a monster but worships me anyway."

"I am yours, my Lord Death."

A sad smile appeared at her comment. "I will meet with Shianeni and Neriwyn. Annawyn needs to be stopped, even if it means I must give you to the one person who has the power to keep you alive forever to punish me. I hope you can forgive me for what she'll do to you."

Eirian's heart fluttered at the thought that her god would grieve her. "Thank you."

Six

Delyth

Light filtered through stained glass windows, casting ominously coloured shadows throughout the chamber. She hated the effect it had on her eyes at certain times of the day, but Delyth knew why they used a particular pigmentation in the libraries. Immovable structures stretched from one side to the other, with archways interspersed at random intervals to allow people to flow between them. There was no way of fully grasping how much knowledge each library housed, and Delyth wished she could spend her lifetime trying.

"Lady Altira," the librarian said, bowing slightly. "I found the manuscript you were after."

Beaming with delight, she eyed the heavy tome on the tray held by the grey-clad woman. "Oh, excellent, thank you. I'm done with this one, so I won't exceed my limit."

"May I ask what you're looking for?"

Wary of sharing her plans, Delyth glanced at the papers spread across the table she was using. Sketches of weapons and the proposed wards she was considering stood out accusingly, and she scrambled for the simplest excuse. No one need know her plans were for a birthday gift for Amelia. If the rumour spread that she was interested in a respectable soldier who did not belong to the Zarthein lineage, then her mother might be pleased with her for a change. Not that Eirian had bothered to spare a glance in her direction in recent days. Delyth did not know what was going on, and all she cared about was that it kept the High Priestess out of her hair so she could do what she wanted without hassle.

"I'm planning to have a gift commissioned for a friend's birthday," she replied, giving her best impression of a flustered girl caught writing the name of her infatuation. "It's a surprise, and since they have other weapons, I wanted to put some different wards on it."

The librarian smiled indulgently and tutted, "Ah yes, I see. What about a return ward? That way, their gift will always get back to them."

"But that's a compulsion ward, and short-lived."

"Only when used on a living creature. When worked into an object, it compels anyone who possesses it to return it to the owner. It's commonly used by jewellers to ensure special pieces are difficult to steal. Though the skill and power of the caster influence its strength."

Clearing a spot on the table, Delyth signalled for the librarian to place her tray down so she could exchange the new book for the one she no longer required. While she did, the young mage mulled over the suggestion, wondering if it would be a useful ward for Amelia to have on a weapon. Drumming her fingers on her chin, she suspected the practicality depended on the style of fighting preferred by the warrior receiving the gift. If she had a pair of throwing knives crafted, it would suit Amelia's stealthy nature, and compared to something bigger, like swords, a small blade was more likely to be misplaced in a fight. Delyth sat up straighter, grinning at the possibilities.

"I would love to see the designs of some return wards. Thank you for the suggestion."

"No need to thank me. Watching the wheels turn in your mind while you considered the possibilities was an absolute delight. You do your father proud, Lady Altira. He'd be overjoyed with your creativity."

Eyes darting towards the main entrance, Delyth watched a pair of clerics enter. "Fortunately for me, pleasing my father is easy to do. My mother, on the other hand."

"Yes, I imagine it's difficult having Eirian Altira as a parent," the librarian grumbled, mouth twisting. "At least you have Lord Madoc Vasser. He is a truly good man."

Delyth cocked her head, narrowing her gaze at the older woman. The disdain in her voice when she spoke of Eirian had been unmistakable, and the mage wondered what her mother had done to earn it. She knew why she felt conflicted emotions towards the High Priestess, and as far as she was concerned, that was her undeniable right as her daughter. Most people in the twin cities seemed to worship the ground Eirian Altira and Teleri Zarthein walked on. They were the heirs of two of the most powerful gods who ruled over their world. If anyone deserved the reverence they were treated with, it was them.

"Indeed, he is. Thank you. Those references?"

Straightening, the librarian frowned when the two clerics Delyth had noticed halted a short distance away. She wanted to ignore them; to pretend they did not exist, and her mother had not sent them to fetch her. Deliberately turning her focus to her work, the young mage listened as the other woman hurried off while pretending to shuffle through some notes. The clerics remained where they were, standing at the edge of her vision in silence. If they were waiting to be acknowledged, Delyth intended to make them suffer until they gave up on the proper procedure the temple taught.

"Lady Altira," the shorter cleric finally said.

"Go away."

They whispered to each other, and Delyth was thankful she could not hear what they were saying. Hand gestures suggested an argument before the taller one spun on his heels to hurry from the library. Scoffing, she made the mistake of glancing up from her work to examine the man in his black robes, with his arms crossed and a disapproving scowl directed at her. Amused by his expression, Delyth smirked.

"Yes, go fetch my mother. You clerics are very fetching. Perhaps one day they'll promote you to priest, and you'll get to fetch people who want to be fetched."

"The High Priestess has commanded your attendance at a meeting."

Pulling a face, Delyth returned to her work. "She can command away. I don't care. I'm not one of her precious clergy members who must dance to her tune."

She felt his gaze following her every action. It made her skin crawl, distracting her from her research, and leaving her very aware of the fact he was close enough to catch a glimpse of her sketches. Gathering the sheets of paper, Delyth carefully stacked them in a pile with an innocuous picture of a swirling vine design she had devised earlier. Tracing the lines with her fingertips, she recalled the painting she had seen that inspired her. Whoever had done it had given the plant tiny, delicate purple flowers amongst spear-like leaves that reminded her of Amelia. When she spoke to the bladesmith who had agreed to take her commission, Delyth hoped he would etch the design into the knives.

Hearing the footsteps of the librarian returning, she shot a glare at the cleric and continued to tidy her work. "I'm sorry to inconvenience you, but could you please reserve these books for me?"

"I understand," the librarian replied, eyeing the cleric with distaste. "When do you expect to return?"

"Honestly, I have no idea. Hopefully tomorrow, but it'll depend on whatever Her Eminence wants of her lowly daughter. The sooner I turn twenty, the better."

Aghast at her comment, the cleric gasped. The two women ignored him, neither willing to invite a lecture on the importance of the Altira mage. Helping Delyth with the books she had been using, the librarian discreetly slipped a folded piece of paper onto the stack of notes. Curious, the mage did not reach for it, preferring to place another sheet on top to avoid drawing attention. Whatever was written on it, the older woman did not want the cleric to notice. Delyth hoped it was simply a list of wards that were not commonly found on weapons, but which would make for a useful addition. As much as she resented her mother, she refused to participate in any talk of rebelling against the government of the twin cities. No matter what, she was still an Altira, and nothing Delyth could do would change her bloodline.

Gathering her work, she nodded to the librarian. "Thank you for your help."

"It was my pleasure."

Rising from her seat with her papers clasped to her chest, Delyth stalked past the cleric, who attempted to protest her departure. The sound of the librarian laughing reached her ears before she was out of range, and it brought a smile to her lips. By leaving, she had forced the cleric to decide between losing her in the city or letting the High Priestess arrive to find her daughter gone. It was a delightful conundrum to push on him, but it was also one that would earn further lectures from her mother once they finally faced each other. Outside the main chamber of the library, coloured light from more stained-glass windows bathed the long corridor. Unlike the ones illuminating the books, these were exquisitely crafted scenes of historical events that held a certain significance to the twin cities.

"There you are, daughter," Eirian said, startling Delyth out of her observations.

Not bothering to hold back her groan, she glared at the cluster of people surrounding the High Priestess. "Your Eminence. To what do I owe this pleasure? What have I done this time?"

"I don't appreciate your disrespect in public, Delyth. We need to talk."

Clearing his throat, Joshua directed a pointed look at her that had the young mage biting down on her response. The priest constantly tried to facilitate a positive relationship between her and her mother, which always surprised Delyth. It was obvious to her that he was in love with

Eirian, even if it went unsaid. But the seriousness in his gaze seemed different from his usual stern expression. Reluctant to give her mother the time of day, she rolled her shoulders, shuffling her feet as she sneered at the cleric who had caught up with her. His face was red, and he waved at her while struggling to catch his breath.

Rolling her eyes, Delyth nodded at him. "I think he needs to spend more time training."

"Delyth," Joshua said, his voice lacking the scolding tone her mother's would have held.

"Fine. But make it quick. I'm busy."

Eirian sighed, and the tired defeat in her gaze had Delyth recoiling. "This conversation needs to be held in daylight. Will you give me that, or are you too busy?"

Icy dread entwined her spine, and she nodded silently. Following her mother, Delyth contemplated what the problem might be. She doubted Eirian was there to inform her she was disregarding everything her daughter wanted to force her to join the temple. There was something terrible going on. Amelia's last letter to her had said Ensaycal was preparing the dragon tower, and her family was behaving strangely about it. Having grown up in the middle of politics, Delyth was not so foolish as to miss the signs of a problem unfolding.

"There's a small garden out here," she said quietly, waving at a narrow door set deep into the wall. "I enjoy having lunch there when I need the fresh air after hours of study."

One priest pushed his way through to inspect the courtyard garden and to ensure it was empty before allowing Eirian to drift through. When she had been younger, Delyth had wished she possessed the strange elegance that seemed to come naturally to her mother. Always swathed in long robes, the High Priestess flowed like a calm stream. As she got older, it had become obvious it was part of the mask her mother wore to give herself an air of divinity as heir to Death. Joining Eirian in the garden after Joshua waved her through, the click of the door closing startled Delyth and left the two of them alone in the quiet space, surrounded by creeping vines and sweet flowers.

"I know we don't have the best relationship, Delyth, and we disagree a lot." Eirian drifted to a stone bench, collapsing on it with a heavy sigh. "But you're nearly an adult, and it's time I treated you like one. Teleri and I recently received news that Kirrama has fallen."

It felt like she had been kicked in the gut, and Delyth staggered to the second bench, dropping her bundle of paper on the way. Sheets fluttered to the ground, covering the mossy cobblestones. Neither spared them a glance. Rubbing her face, Eirian waited for her daughter to say something.

"But Kirrama was a merchant city..."

"There have been others. We kept the news secret, thinking we were doing the right thing. Except it kept happening, and now with Kirrama being so close to us. Darling girl, it's the mad god. She has finally made her move, and we mortals are her target."

"Did you know they were under attack?"

Shaking her head, Eirian let the mask fall, and Delyth was shocked by how exhausted she appeared. "No, we didn't. Considering Annawyn is the god of the mind, we believe she is twisting people within the target cities, and they are betraying their people from within, allowing her Unseelie forces to attack without warning. I fear she is already spreading her darkness within our cities."

Delyth wanted to run away, to find Amelia and their friends and get on a ship to escape. She was an Altira, and her education had left nothing out when it came to the gods and the First Peoples. They had no way to defend themselves against those who had declared their loyalty to Annawyn and formed the Unseelie faction. Even dragons could not kill those immortal races, though their fire did enough to slow them. As a husk maker, Eirian could slow them as well, but she was only one, and the mad god had destroyed almost all the rest. Covering her mouth, Delyth blinked away the tears forming.

"What can we do?"

"Gebael has agreed to speak to the other gods, and I offered to pay whatever price they asked. She is a god. There's nothing we can do without their help. All we can do is prepare. I've sent for Briallen, so hopefully she will arrive soon enough."

What joy she felt at seeing her aunt was lost in a sea of horror. "Can we evacuate?"

"And go where?"

"I don't know. Tir is a large place. Surely there is somewhere safe."

"From a god?"

She gave up trying to fight her tears, feeling the damp trail they left on her cheeks. "But the people, Ma. What about our people? Is Annawyn just going to kill everyone?"

"The rage of a god is a terrible thing."

Leaping up from her seat, Delyth darted across the small space to throw herself into Eirian's embrace. Clinging to the black robes with their familiar scent, she sobbed. The arms wrapped around her squeezed tight, but she felt the slight shudder of her mother's body as they cried together.

"Whatever the gods ask us to do, I'll help you, Ma. You don't have to do it alone."

Clenching her eyes shut, Eirian kissed the top of Delyth's head. "Oh, my darling girl. I want you to know that I love you, and I am proud of you. You will always be my precious child, and I wish I had been a better mother."

"I love you too, Ma."

Seven

Teleri

Dark stone sucked in the heat from the day, leaving the cavernous chambers within chilled. Boots clicked against the flooring, accompanied by the occasional muttered curse when someone did not pick up their feet enough when crossing one of the ventilation grids. Teleri found many of the older buildings in the cities wondrous, but none so much as the tower that hosted the dragons when they visited. It was an architectural marvel crafted from stone, with a melting point high enough to resist the occasional bout of fire that might escape the iron control of the mighty beasts. They had put care into ensuring the tower was as cool as possible, with massive openings and ventilation shafts running through every wall to allow air to circulate. Magic thrummed, layers upon layers of wards spun to hold everything together no matter what struck it.

"Because we don't know how many to expect, we've purchased three dozen cattle for the yards, and paid a reserve fee for more as needed. Do you think we should get more?"

Teleri scowled at the woman before returning to her inspection of the dragon roost. "Are the handlers bulking out the feed for those cattle? I hope you didn't demand prime breeding stock. If our fears are unfounded, they'll need those animals."

She stammered, shooting a look at the man hovering beside her. "We followed procedure."

The slow rise of an eyebrow had the aides scrambling back to the door, huddling together to discuss what had been done. Craning her head back, Teleri wished she had been around when the tower had been built. Far above them, a domed ceiling provided ample room for a dragon to stretch its wings. In her many conversations with the riders, she had learnt sizes were so varied from dragon to dragon that it was difficult to pick an average. All of those who came to the twin cities tended to be considered medium. She had been told that the larger ones found the tower too small for their needs. Recalling the enormity of the ones who visited, Teleri struggled to grasp what a large one was like.

"I don't think all the riders will remain here for long once we meet with them. The High Priestess said she sent letters inviting her sister to visit, but kept the reasons out of it. Briallen knows Eirian would not invite her without something else going on," Teleri said, kneeling to trail fingers over scratches on the stone floor. "But the question is whether her father, the Lord General, will believe her. In all likelihood, he'll send no more than five."

One of her nieces had accompanied her to the inspection, and the girl stared out at the distant glittering waters of the Bay of Blades. "Aunty Teleri, have you ever met the Lord General of Bellenden?"

"I have."

"Is his dragon as nice as Igraine?"

"And how do you know Igraine is nice, Amelia?" She kept her tone gentle, hoping to avoid embarrassing the girl by revealing she was aware of her relationship with Eirian's daughter.

Shoulders drooping, the young warrior glanced away. "The last time Lady Briallen visited, a group of us dared each other to approach the dragons while they were sunbathing on a beach."

Chuckling, Teleri believed the story. Mostly because it was something she would have done as a child if they had allowed her freedom. Studying the girl, she wondered what Eirian would say if she knew her daughter was carrying on behind her back with a Zarthein despite the relationship being forbidden. Part of her wanted to draw Amelia aside for a lecture, but she failed to see what harm would come of it. They were two young women who were about to learn how terrible the world was.

"I'm glad none of you were hurt."

"Igraine let us touch her. So did a big red one. The others just huffed smoke, and pretended we weren't there." Amelia straightened, an eager smile appearing. "Do you think Rider Tristan will accompany Lady Briallen this time? He found us at the beach and showed us how to use handfuls of wet sand to scrub the dragon's scales the way they like it."

Mouth twisting, Teleri did not voice her opinion on the dragon riders allowing a goblin to join their ranks. As much as she liked Tristan, she knew the stories. Even before the Sundering of the gods, the goblins had delighted in preying on mortals. Now they were wholly sworn to serve Annawyn. What she had heard about Queen Calista terrified her. If the Unseelie forces came to the twin cities, Teleri knew they would have no way to defend themselves. Everyone would die horribly.

"Be careful around him."

"Why? Because he's a goblin?"

"Yes. Rider Tristan is bound to a dragon, but his kind serve Lady Annawyn."

Crossing her arms, Amelia ignored the scolding looks directed her way by the others accompanying them, and approached her aunt. "But he's in love with Lady Briallen, and would never betray us."

Teleri spread her fingers, laying two of them into the gouges left by a dragon claw. "Is he now? And how did you come to have such information, Amelia? Did he tell you that?"

"Well, no, he didn't."

"Then who did?"

Aware she had trapped the girl in a corner with no way out except to reveal her relationship with Eirian's daughter, Teleri chuckled softly. Dropping to a knee next to her, Amelia pressed her hand to a different grove, her eyes wide with awe. Hair as black as her own was drawn back in a tight braid with a blue ribbon wrapped around the end. The colour reminded the general of Eirian's eyes, and she suspected it had been picked for exactly that reason. Like the Zartheins, the Altiras all had much of the same look to them. Something about being tied to a god left the bloodlines carrying certain traits of theirs. She counted herself fortunate to have never met War, but from what Eirian had shared of Gebael's descriptions of him, Neriwyn possessed the same raven hair and dark eyes that all Zartheins did.

"I know," she whispered to Amelia. "And I understand. You need not fear that I'll force it to end."

Biting her lip, her niece frowned. "How do you know?"

"I know everything that goes on in my family. But considering the circumstances, I don't see an issue. Sometimes, finding love and happiness is more important... especially now."

"Del is everything to me."

Shifting her weight slightly, Teleri covered Amelia's hand gently. "I'll talk to her mother. Sometimes the rules are silly. It's not like the two of you can mix the bloodlines."

Amelia searched her aunt's gaze, her suspicion obvious. "Aunty Teleri, is there something wrong? Everyone is so tense."

She was not given a chance to respond when the rest of their group issued surprised greetings to the freshly arrived priests. Closing her eyes, Teleri waited to find out if they had been sent to ensure things were prepared, or if they were accompanying their High Priestess. A cold power brushed against hers, too familiar and enticing to be anyone other than Eirian. No matter how many Altira mages she dealt with, the desperate longing to be close to them left the same deep ache in her heart.

"Keep quiet, and observe," she murmured, receiving a sharp nod in response.

The tap of Eirian's boots on the stone drew her focus. Each step was measured; her performative serenity never faltered. Teleri turned slightly so she could watch the High Priestess drift closer with an expression of disinterest. At her side, Amelia stiffened, nose flaring as her eyes settled on someone who had accompanied the Endaran leader. Suspecting it was Delyth, she cleared her throat, arching a brow, and her niece shrunk down, dropping her gaze to the claw marks on the floor.

"Teleri." Eirian's hand landed on her shoulder, and it took an effort not to nuzzle it. "How go things?"

"We're as ready for dragons as we can be without knowing how many or when they will arrive."

Humming thoughtfully, the High Priestess squeezed her shoulder before moving past her towards the ledge jutting away from the main part of the tower. Each level had one connected to the roosting caverns to allow the dragons to come and go as they pleased. It was another aspect of the building that Teleri admired. There had been no need to build a second dragon tower, but she prayed to the god of crafting the mages responsible for such things were still capable. All the schematics were preserved and kept in the archives in duplicate. Every architectural plan used in the twin cities was.

Leaping to her feet, Teleri followed her to the edge. "Have you heard anything?"

"Not yet. Briallen gets overly excited when I write, so I expect she won't stop long enough to respond before flying here. Dragons are faster than pigeons."

"And the other matter?"

"He hasn't returned. I need to beg a favour of you, darling Teleri." Eirian turned a fearful gaze in her direction, eyes darting to where Delyth stood near Amelia. "She wants to help. I can't let her."

Lips parting, Teleri could not speak. Her thoughts went to the arguments that had raged within her mind over what to do with her family if war with Annawyn's forces came to their cities. Not bothering to hide her anguish, she looked at the two young women who were trying their best not to steal secretive glances at each other that anyone observing would notice. They deserved to live.

"You told her everything?"

"I did. Have you?"

"Only those over a hundred. The children need not worry yet. Not until we know what we're doing."

Fingers touched hers for a moment before Eirian clasped her hands in front of her. "I've made too many mistakes in my life, and most of them involve my daughter. With what is coming, I owe it to her to treat her like an adult, and pay her the respect of being truthful."

Recalling Yestin's anger over her decision to keep the truth from him about the cities that had fallen, Teleri wondered if she was continuing to make a mistake. She glanced back at Amelia and Delyth in time to catch them staring at each other longingly. Eirian sighed, drawing her attention back to the High Priestess. There was a deep sadness in her blue eyes that confirmed she was aware of the two girls.

"Should we send them away?" Teleri murmured. "Briallen could take them to Bellenden."

"Dragons are not immortal, and the riders serve the gods as peacekeepers. I fear Annawyn may set her sights on Bellenden and the other dragon cities. In all honesty, I've realised I fear for Briallen's safety just as much as Delyth's."

"As you should. She is your sister."

Eirian chuckled, the sound striking the other woman as bitter. "And what a terrible little sister I have been. This war with Annawyn will be the death of me."

"Perhaps she won't risk angering Gebael and Neriwyn more by attacking their heirs?"

"Wishful thinking will get us nowhere. Best to assume she's destroying cities close by as a method to drag out our torment. She wants a battle between the gods, and we're the bait."

Rage rippled through her magic, curling around her comfortingly. It was easy to wrap herself in her bloodlust, to let her mind seek reassurance in memories of battles won, but Teleri knew this was one they would lose. There was no hope to be had, no matter what she told herself. From the defeated slump of Eirian's shoulders, and the sorrow in her eyes, it was clear she had surrendered to the truth. All they were doing was waiting to find out how they would fight their way to the world beyond the Veil. Maybe the god of death would return to his High Priestess with something better than an apology.

"We should start preparing to inform the people. They have a right to know so they can make their plans," she said, pushing her rage down to avoid being distracted from her job.

"Let's wait until Gebael returns. Once we know whether the gods are abandoning us completely, we make our plans. I know it's better not to hope, and to assume the worst, but it's wrong to deny there might be a chance. Whatever the cost, we should be prepared to pay it."

Inclining her head to where Amelia and Delyth had crept close enough to subtly brush their fingertips together, Teleri asked, "What if the cost is them? Will you give our children to the gods to stop their war?"

Tears welled in Eirian's eyes as she stared at the bay. The view from the dragon tower was easily the most magnificent in the region, and it was a place Teleri knew her human counterpart liked to visit, even when there was no need to. Stretching away from the line of sloping cliffs, Ensaycal and Endara were like the wings of a bird, ruffled by the wind. There was no uniformity in the height of the buildings, or in the colour, but at a distance, it did not matter. Gleaming deep blue, the Bay of Blades was the body between the two cities, just as ruffled by the wind, and as likely to bite the wings as it was anything else. Sometimes she wondered if their ancestors had chosen the region to settle because it was a battle to survive, and it was only through the strength of their magic and resolve that they flourished.

"I want to say no, Teleri, but what if it means saving the rest of Tir? Are we in a position to refuse?"

"What is a handful of lives when millions are at risk?"

"Exactly. But what if they leave us to die? What will Annawyn do when she has killed every human, elf, and daoine, and there's no one left but the First People?"

It was a terrible prospect to imagine. The wars would continue until their world was nothing but ash and unending rivers of blood. Teleri did not know if the gods could change the First People to make them mortal, and it felt like blasphemy to request Eirian to ask Gebael if it was possible. The gods had created mortals because they realised immortality was boring, so she wanted to believe they would have changed things if it were possible. But imagining the gods were incapable of altering their creations opened her to questioning other things, including why they bothered with having heirs. Too many questions left Teleri feeling like their entire existence was nothing more than a game.

Eirian's soft hands clasped hers as she said, "Promise me, if they ask for a life, you will let me accept the burden. You've got more years to give, and I need you to protect Delyth. She has so much potential if only she embraced it."

Grief lanced through her, and Teleri nodded sadly. "I can promise you that."

Eight

Briallen

A dragon's roar echoed through her room, drawing Briallen to the open balcony doors. Watching the mighty creature swoop down from the sky, it did not surprise her to see another giving chase. They swirled around each other, dancing splashes of red and grey against a clear blue sky. There was no mistaking Igraine and Ysgarlad; their broad wings never touched each other or any of the buildings they darted through. Other dragons cast wide shadows from above as they enjoyed the day. Unless needed, they came and went as they pleased, leaving their riders to deal with their lives. Though most rarely went far, preferring to keep close to the people they were bonded with.

Ysgarlad came close to her balcony, and Briallen grinned at the speed of the two dragons sweeping past. Her attention was pulled to the shadows inside the door when she felt the presence of another. Looking over her shoulder, she watched Tristan step free of the murky darkness, his lips curled in a smugness that was well deserved. It was his favourite trick, and neither of them ever tired of it. Part of Briallen wished she could learn to shadow walk like a goblin, but all she could hope for was learning to shapeshift once her powers matured. As a half-duine, there were still years of waiting until then.

"You done packing?" Tristan straightened his coat, and she watched his hands stroke over the brown leather. "Please tell me you're done, Bri. For once, just be organised on time."

Giving him a wide-eyed look, she avoided glancing at her bed where her pack waited to be filled. There was no need to because Tristan's smirk faded into a frustrated twist. Stomping over, he grabbed her arm and dragged Briallen back into her bedroom. Hiding a grin, she listened to him mutter about the absurdity of her inability to complete simple tasks when they needed to be done. The prick of his claws slipping free of his control was a reminder that her ridiculous behaviour annoyed the goblin. She did not do it on purpose, but Briallen avoided discussing how she felt about the unending internal struggle completing tasks was. Even with her best friend.

"Honestly, Bri! All you must do is pack some clothes appropriate for dinner with your sister. Every time we go somewhere, you do this. One of these days I should leave you to sort it out yourself with no help from me. Then we'll see how you go."

Briallen pouted at him, wishing she could articulate how much she appreciated his help. "I was going to pack, but then Igraine and Ysgarlad put on their performance."

"Oh, so you're telling me you would have been packed on time?" His eyes narrowed.

"Don't you have any faith in me?"

"None whatsoever. You're good at a lot of things, Bri, but keeping yourself organised is not one of them. Now, do you think the High Priestess will expect us to attend anything formal?"

Pulling a face, Briallen did not know how to answer the question. Her sister rarely invited her to anything public. Tristan frowned, glancing between her and the mostly empty bag before sighing heavily. Plonking down on the bed, he patted the spot next to him.

"Tell me what's wrong."

She shook her head, stumbling over to her wardrobe to yank the door open. "There's nothing wrong."

"And I'm the king of Lonsellis."

"Well, it's very nice to meet you, Your Majesty. I'd bow, but I'm busy."

Tristan bit back a laugh, and she winked at him while rummaging through the clothes hanging from a rail. Most of it was casual wear for when she had free time and no expectations of needing to ride anywhere. Snagging her fingers on a silk coat, Briallen pulled it from the hanger to pack. It was dark grey, reminding her of rain-laden clouds, with bright blue embroidery of flowering vines decorating it. Tossing it at the watching goblin, she continued to examine her choices. She did not know why it was so hard to pick a few things out when the chances were that she would spend most of her time in the typical rider's gear. Thinking back to Eirian's letter, Briallen doubted she needed much.

"You've met my sister, Tris, and I know you have strong opinions about her," she said, pulling out a simple green linen dress. "Did her letter seem unusual at all?"

"She normally has instructions as to why she wants your presence in Endara. I told you it was strange that she asked you to visit because she's missed you."

"I know you think I'm too forgiving."

"We're well past too forgiving," he grumbled, folding the clothes to shove into her pack.

Retrieving another elegant silk coat, this time in a rich blue that made her eyes stand out, Briallen decided it was enough. "Eirian is my sister. We're family."

"Sharing blood does not make you family. I'm your family, the Lord General is your family, Igraine, and Ysgarlad are your family. Eirian Altira is simply the other daughter of your mother. A mother who abandoned you to your father."

"I'm sure if she hadn't been one of those chosen to be the mother of the next Altira—"

He laughed at her, shaking his head in disbelief. "Listen to yourself, Briallen."

"What do you mean by that?"

"When will you stop making excuses for them?"

Snarling, she stomped over to stand in front of him. His emerald eyes met her glare without blinking, framed by curls as dark as the night. Without touching, Briallen knew they felt like the softest silk between her fingers. Anger fading, she rubbed her eyes and wondered how to admit he was right. He was always right. Tristan was the only person who never hesitated to give her the truth, even when it was painful. Even Igraine tried to gentle the harsh realities of their world.

"I'm going to outlive her. She's ten years younger than I am, but just looking at us, you would never know. For the rest of my life, I'm going to look like this, and in thirty or so years, Eirian will be gone."

Sympathy filled his gaze, and Tristan cupped her cheek. "You do yourself a disservice by pretending she's a good sister. Yes, you'll outlive her, but is it worth the knots you tie yourself in?"

"Maybe."

"And maybe if she hadn't been born the Altira, things would be different."

Leaning her face into his palm, Briallen gave him a sad smile. "I try so hard because I don't want to be the family disappointment, or the burdensome sister, or the accident."

"Fuck, Bri, you're none of those things, and if anyone tries to say you are, I'll..."

"You'll what, Tris?"

Shaking his head, Tristan withdrew his hand. "Tell Igraine what they said."

Lips thinning, she did not push him for the truth. In the back of her mind, Briallen sensed Igraine's amusement, and it left her wondering what Ysgarlad was saying to Tristan. If her dragon knew, she was keeping it to herself. There were times when she wished her bonded would tell her everything, and others when the silence was preferred. Knowing

Igraine's opinion about the goblin, it was likely that no comment was the safer option.

"You need more clothes," he said, plucking the blue coat from her grasp. "Unless you plan to go shopping while we're there. Do you want to buy some new clothes, Bri?"

"I might. Delyth enjoys taking me to the markets and showing me all her current favourite places to go."

Fiddling with the bag, Tristan did not respond. She dismissed his silence, returning to her wardrobe to grab a few changes of clothes for use under her riding leathers. Tossing them at him, Briallen scurried around the room to gather any random item she thought she might need, only darting to the bed to dump them next to her pack when her hands got too full. If there was anything unnecessary amongst the collection, Tristan would set it aside for her to put away when she remembered they existed. Every few weeks, someone took the time to sort through her chambers, returning things to their places so Briallen could restart her piles of misplaced, and generally forgotten belongings all over the rooms.

"Are you sure this is enough clothes?"

She scratched her head, staring at the neatly packed bag in confusion. "I think so. Is it?"

"How many times have I told you I can't think for you?" he replied with a huff.

"Ah well, I don't remember. Tell me again for good measure, and I promise to forget it before we leave. No, you're right; it's enough. If I've missed anything important, it's not like we won't be in a city."

"You'd forget your head if it weren't attached to your body."

"Well, it's a good thing I'm not a dullaghan then!"

A knock sounded at the door. Even though it was in the other room, the repetitive thump was loud enough to make Briallen flinch. She did not need Tristan's nose to tell her who it was because the pattern was the same as it had been since her childhood. Lord General Valerian was a lesson in consistency.

"Can you finish packing for me? I should speak to my father."

Tristan blinked, lips curling up on one side to flash his pointed teeth. "When don't I finish packing for you? If I didn't, you'd end up leaving everything important behind."

Pressing a hand to her chest, she smiled thankfully. "And see, this is why we make such a wonderful team. You're the organised one, and I'm the one who's always happy to take on the dangerous tasks."

"Go speak to the Lord General before he breaks open the door."

Hurrying through to the other chamber, Briallen knocked into the corner of a table with her hip. Biting back her yelp, she pulled the door open with a forced smile. The first thing her father did was arch an eyebrow, his lips twitching with thinly veiled amusement. As stern as he could be, many accused Valerian of spoiling her, and she knew she was lucky to have a parent who loved her.

"I fear you'll never learn not to walk into things, but I'm thankful the healers no longer question me about your never-ending bruises," Valerian said, stepping past her into the room. "Greetings, Tristan!"

"Good afternoon, Lord General," the goblin called back.

Remaining at the door, Briallen observed the way her father swept his gaze over the mess of her sitting room with his usual dismay. He said nothing, but she knew he was the one who had arranged for someone to tidy things up. Shame burnt her cheeks, leaving her wishing she were better at keeping things organised. It was not something she did on purpose, but no matter how hard she tried, Briallen never managed to maintain the new habits.

"What can I do for you, Father?" She released the door, letting it slide back into place with a click.

Valerian shifted, tilting his head to glance her way. "I'm concerned about the letter."

"From Eirian?"

"Yes. As your Lord General, I've kept information from you because you're a low-ranked rider; however, as your father, I fear the consequences of continuing to do so. Considering the mission you were sent on most recently, you may well suspect. Or rather, Tristan does."

Scowling at the underlying suggestion that she was unobservant, Briallen huffed. "War."

"Indeed. The Unseelie have been attacking unprepared locations across Tir, but only after the mad god has twisted key targets within the population. I believe the Altira is aware and hopes to use you to communicate with me. If she fears for the safety of Endara and Ensaycal, she may wish to ask for our help but suspects it's not safe to send the request by bird."

"*I fear your father is right,*" Igraine whispered at the edge of her mind.

Briallen stared at where Tristan had come to stand in the doorway to her bedroom. "Seems a bit extreme to send a letter to request a visit from her sister just to use her as a fancy messenger pigeon."

"Bri," Tristan said, shaking his head.

The Lord General chuckled, giving the younger man an indulgent smile. "She'll never change. Normally I would agree with you, Briallen, but this time I must admit the Altira is showing a great deal of wisdom in taking this course of action. Messenger pigeons go missing or are intercepted. A dragon and its rider? Far harder to do the same to them. It's the right move to make in this war."

"But we're not at war?" Briallen felt the prickle of nervous confusion down her spine.

Warmth flooded across her bond from Igraine to offer her a shred of comfort. Eyes closed, she took a deep breath and mentally leaned into it, letting the dragon fill her with strength. A hand stroked her hair, Valerian's soft murmurs barely forming words. She did not need them to be coherent, just reassurances.

"If we fight the Unseelie, we'll lose." Briallen opened her eyes to gaze at her father.

"Yes, my little love, we will. Dragon fire will slow them. It will cause pain, but they're immortal and we're not. If war comes, we'll fight, but we'll die trying to protect the innocent."

Shuffling his feet, Tristan replied, "As is our duty to the balance. The strong protect the weak."

"I'm sending Calea and Zern with you as my representatives. They're selecting three other pairs as an escort. Should the Altira need to send me a message, two pairs will return to Bellenden, leaving you with the rest. We're preparing to coordinate forces as needed to defend against the Unseelie. All we can do is buy as much time as possible. Hopefully, the two heirs have their gods."

Lurching forward, Briallen wrapped her arms around her father, hugging him tight. "I wish the gods would stop her. Why do we have to pay the price when the gods are mad at each other? It hardly seems fair. Eirian has always told me Lord Gebael is a just god."

"He is Death, Briallen. There is no greater justice." Valerian rested his chin on her head and met Tristan's gaze across the room. "You will protect my daughter, Tristan."

"Always, my Lord General. I will never let you down."

She grunted, scowling at him while clinging to her father. "I don't need protecting."

Kissing her hair, he chuckled. "It's my duty to worry, my little love. Call it a father's prerogative to be concerned about his headstrong, and occasionally reckless daughter."

Nine
Eirian

The first time she had stood in one of the cavernous rooms to watch a dragon land, Eirian had learnt there were things in life that seemed better than the role life had given her. She had been around six years old, and it had been one of the Lord General's older children bringing Briallen for a visit. Envy had soured her attitude towards her only sister, turning her into a miserable child who lashed out in temper every time Briallen told her about some exciting adventure she had gone on with her best friend and the dragons. When she thought back on that visit, Eirian wondered if she might have had a closer relationship with her sister if she had not wished their positions were the other way around. But then she realised the consequences if Briallen had been born the Altira mage instead of her.

Death's heir needed to be human. To grow old and die. There was a beauty to life and death that those who lived forever could not fully appreciate. Even though the daoine were mortal, their unending years robbed them of seeing the world in the same light as a human or elf. If anything, Eirian wondered why Gebael had allowed Briallen to be born. Any children she had would carry the Altira bloodline further out of the carefully controlled human lines, putting them at risk of having one of Death's heirs born to live thousands of lifetimes. The fear for her sister it stirred always surprised Eirian.

"Any sign of them?" Teleri appeared at her side, a hand on the hilt of her sword.

"They were sighted recently, but no one has approached the tower yet. It's worrying. What if they've spotted something we're unaware of?"

Patting her arm, the elf smiled patiently. "Why, Eirian, are you worried about your sister for a change? I'm sure everything is fine, and the dragons are simply surveying the land."

"Of course I'm worried!"

Slapping a hand over her mouth in surprise, Eirian stared at Teleri. She had always kept her concerns to herself, preferring to keep any fondness she harboured for her sister a secret. When people possessed the power she did, others went out of their way to find weaknesses. It was part of the reason she had resigned herself to having only one child. Far easier to protect one, especially when they were as capable as Delyth had proven to be. Maintaining distance from Briallen ensured no one was overly inclined to use the dragon rider against her. But the sorrow and understanding in Teleri's gaze reassured her. Eirian knew the truth would remain between them without question.

"The Lord General is thousands of years old; the gods created him. Whatever is going on, you can be sure he's already aware of it," Teleri said gently. "If I were him, I'd have told Briallen everything. I wouldn't send her into a situation unprepared."

Eirian pictured the statuesque duine in command of the army of dragon riders based in Bellenden. As a child, he had terrified her. Every time they met, it felt like he could see straight through her and found her lacking. In recent years, Valerian filled her with more unease than fear. While she aged, the ancient man remained trapped in eternal youth. Soon enough, Delyth would appear older than her aunt. Thinking about them reminded Eirian she needed to have another discussion with her daughter about it.

"He'll have sent a senior officer to accompany Briallen. The Lord General is protective of her."

Teleri chuckled, a hand sweeping outward to gesture at the massive chamber built to house a dragon. "So protective that he allowed a dragon to choose her as its rider."

"Well, let's be honest, few people would confront a dragon. I suppose I'd happily let one choose Delyth if I knew it would ensure her safety in the coming war. Except the riders will be on the front line."

"Sometimes the best way to protect our children is to give them the tools they need to protect themselves. All we can do is build their confidence, provide everything required to grow, and encourage learning as much as possible. The rest is up to them. But we do them no favours by sheltering them."

A roar sounded through the air, like a distant rumble of thunder. Several more joined it, acting as a warning to those in the tower awaiting their arrival. Hurrying across the chamber toward the door, Eirian's lips twitched when Teleri placed a hand on her back, guiding her to a safe position. Wind buffeted them as one of the mighty creatures landed heavily on the extended platform designed specifically for that purpose. Wings flapped while it settled, and the High Priestess kept her face sheltered until it stopped. With the dragon came warmth and a whiff of smoke.

"They never cease to be amazing," Teleri said.

Lowering her arm, Eirian took in the sight of the dappled grey dragon. The disapproving gleam in its eyes confirmed its identity before Briallen had bothered to shout her greetings. Whatever the dragon thought about her, the High Priestess was glad she could not hear its thoughts. Igraine had snapped her teeth at her on more than a few occasions, and it was a warning Eirian did not take lightly. Laughter accompanied the half-duine rider leaping from her saddle to scramble down her dragon's extended front leg.

"Eirian!"

Stepping free of Teleri, she approached her older sister with as blank an expression as she could manage. "Rider Briallen, welcome back. I'm pleased to see you."

Igraine's head whipped around, catching her rider as the woman seemed to trip on nothing. Pressing her lips together, Eirian resisted the urge to make her usual snide comment about her sister's clumsiness. If they were to face a war together, she needed to make an effort to be kinder. She did not want to die with ill feelings between her and her family. There was a moment of confusion when Igraine blinked one enormous eye at her before withdrawing her head to allow Briallen to finish walking over to Eirian. Deciding she had nothing to lose, the High Priestess greeted the other woman with open arms, pulling her into a stiff hug.

"What's wrong, Eirian?" she murmured, returning the embrace hesitantly.

"Not here. That's a conversation to be had in comfortable chairs with wine," Eirian replied, pulling out of the hug to bow to the dragon. "It's wonderful to see you, Igraine. You are as magnificent as ever, and a blessing to our fair cities. I hope you find the cattle we have supplied to be delicious."

There were roars echoing from the other chambers, and she suspected the other riders would soon appear in the hallway beyond. Watching Briallen cock her head, it was obvious she was listening to something being said by either Igraine or another duine who had accompanied her. Gebael had spoken into her mind, and Eirian was thankful she did not possess the ability as a normal part of her powers.

"High General Teleri, good to see you! Though if you're here to welcome me, then my father was right." Briallen nodded at the elf, fingers closing around the straps of her pack to adjust the weight.

She did not understand why a pang of jealousy struck her when Teleri welcomed Briallen with a hug. While she had scorned her sister, Eirian knew the elf had spent a lot of time with her. Part of her supposed they had more in common. It was rare for Briallen to confide in her about what she had seen and done as a dragon rider. Something Eirian realised she regretted, because she wondered how often they could have provided comfort to each other when their duties weighed too heavily on their shoulders.

"And it is always wonderful to see you, Briallen. Is your sullen companion here?" Teleri gave her a knowing smile, glancing at the door. "I'm looking forward to sparring with him."

"He's determined to beat you this time."

"I wish him luck, but he's still a boy. Sadly, by the time he's fully grown into his abilities, I'll be long dead. Such is the cost of mortality. I regret I'll never know your animal form."

Eirian clenched a fist, frowning as she realised she had not thought about her sister one day being able to shift into an animal. "Are you planning to stay in the tower, Briallen? Or would you like to stay with me? I know Delyth is excited to see you, even if it's not for the best reasons."

The sorrow on Briallen's face told her everything she needed to know. "I'd like to stay with you. Do you mind if Tristan does too? Father made him promise to look after me."

Her mind churned with the possibilities. Most people viewed the goblin with distrust, but Eirian appreciated what he was capable of. He would be a valuable asset in discovering if Annawyn had already dug her twisted claws into the cities. As a goblin, Tristan could slip from shadow to shadow unnoticed, listening in on private conversations while the participants thought they were alone. The unwavering loyalty he displayed towards Briallen gave Eirian an advantage. If he thought it would protect his friend, he would help her with almost anything she asked of him.

"Of course. Tristan is always welcome to stay. I suspected you'd ask, so I had two chambers prepared, side by side, with balconies facing the tower. We wouldn't want your dragons to fret." Eirian offered Igraine a warm smile, but the dragon huffed smoke at her.

Staring at her dragon, Briallen nodded. "Igraine thanks you for your consideration of her and Ysgarlad. While she would rather I stayed here, she understands why I don't want to."

Bowing deeply, Eirian hoped the dragon knew she was being truthful as she said, "Please don't worry about Briallen. She will be perfectly safe with me. I swear on my life."

Igraine arched her neck, spreading her wings wide. A large, golden eye held Eirian trapped in place, and there was suspicion in its depths she knew was wholly deserved. She hoped she could come back later without her sister and Teleri to witness her telling the dragon all her regrets. Though Igraine had never spoken to her, Eirian wanted to tell her everything she kept hidden in her heart so she could tell Briallen if the worst happened before she could do it herself. It was better than writing a letter to entrust to someone else in the hope it would reach the rider when the time came.

"She said that if anything happens to me, she'll eat you for dinner."

Unable to resist laughing, Eirian nodded in agreement and turned to her sister to hold out her arm. "Come, let's find the rest of your party and make sure everyone is settled."

She did not miss the surprise in Briallen's eyes as she slipped an arm through hers. Nor did she fail to see the warmth in Teleri's as the elf gestured for them to go out the door in front of her. When they reached the hallway outside, they found Tristan waiting for them, his green eyes glittering in the dim light. Those responsible for designing the tower had placed chambers for the riders opposite each dragon roost, ensuring they were never far apart. He was leaning against the door to the room Briallen would have used if she had chosen to remain in the tower, but the dismayed twist of his mouth told Eirian the goblin was aware of her decision. Glancing him over, she wondered when he would admit the truth to her sister. It had been obvious for years that he was head over heels in love with Briallen.

"We should wait for Commander Calea before going anywhere," Tristan said, eyes never leaving Eirian. "High Priestess, High General. It's good to see you both."

Extending her arm to clasp his in greeting, Teleri grinned. "I heard you're eager for an arse-kicking."

"I'll beat you this time, High General."

"Perhaps I'll join you for training." The words left Eirian's lips before she could stop them.

The excited smile appearing on Briallen's face warmed her heart. It was unexpected, but Eirian was glad of it. She could try to be a better sister, and it was not too late for them. They would be stronger for it when they faced the war Annawyn was sending their way.

"I'd love to spar with you, Eirian," Briallen murmured, and her smile did not fade.

"You'll need to be gentle with me. I don't train as much as I did when I was younger."

Footsteps silenced their conversation and shifted their focus to the approaching group of people. There were four individuals adorned in the typical brown leathers of the riders, and it surprised Eirian to see one had the wide leathery wings of a peropuan. They were a peaceful people dedicated to mastering the healing arts. To discover a dragon had selected one as its rider struck the High Priestess as very unusual. Each of them was heavily armed, and only one was vaguely familiar. A tall woman with even wider wings than the peropuan led the way, each deep rose-pink feather immaculate despite her having been on the back of a dragon in flight not long before.

Briallen and Tristan stiffened, while Teleri stepped forward to greet the danann. "Commander Calea, it's an honour to welcome you to the twin cities. I hope your journey was fair."

Memories flashed through Eirian's mind of the woman hissing threats to her as a child whenever she had been spiteful towards Briallen. Her smile was forced, but she patted her sister's arm and moved a few steps closer to the group of riders and their escorts. Teleri had selected the warriors as an honour guard to assist the visitors from Bellenden.

"Welcome back, Commander Calea. It fills me with relief to see you here at this time of uncertainty. Lord General Valerian has paid us a great honour by sending you."

Nose twitching, the danann warrior stretched her wings slightly, and she replied, "Indeed. We have much to talk about, High Priestess Eirian, and High General Teleri. However, that can wait until after we've all settled in and had something to eat. I'm sure you wish to catch up with your sister."

"Indeed." Eirian inclined her head. "Briallen and Tristan are going to stay in my home so I can spend more time with her. You're welcome to take up guest quarters in the temple if you wish."

"No, but thank you for the offer. We'll remain here. Rider Briallen has her orders from the Lord General, as does Rider Tristan. Everything else can wait until tomorrow."

Eirian looked at her sister, taking in the solemn expression she wore. "You're right. Everything else can wait until tomorrow. Today is for reuniting with family."

Ten

Delyth

She had watched the dragons circling the Bay of Blades at sunset, their roars almost as loud as the thunder of a storm rolling in from the ocean. Two of the mighty creatures had swooped low through Endara, almost touching buildings with the tips of their wings, and Delyth had recognised them the moment she set eyes on the dappled grey and red scales. Igraine and Ysgarlad represented freedom, so she was eagerly counting down the hours before she could quietly beg her aunt to take her to join the clouds. Only the dinner gong had been enough to pull her from her balcony to find out if Briallen was staying in her home instead of the dragon tower situated between the two cities. Her mother had promised to invite her to stay.

It had felt like torture to remain in her quarters instead of impatiently prowling the hallways until Eirian returned. Whenever Briallen visited, they gave her chambers on the other side of the building overlooking the distant tower. With so many rooms between them, Delyth did not know if the rider had accompanied her mother. Or if Tristan was also present. Her heart fluttered at the thought of the goblin as she hurried towards the smaller dining chamber used for family affairs. As much as she loved Amelia, Delyth liked to dream of being courted by the beautiful man who followed her aunt everywhere. He had been her first infatuation, and the obsession refused to fade as she got older.

The door to the dining chamber had been left propped open, and she slowed her pace to creep along the wall. Wrapping a sound-dampening ward around herself, Delyth flattened against the cool stone beside the opening. Ears pricking at the sound of her mother and aunt's voices, she did her best to soften her breathing so that no other sound interfered with what she was listening to. Part of her felt guilty for eavesdropping on a conversation between Eirian and Briallen, but she knew they were more likely to speak openly between themselves without her presence. Despite all her mother's assurances that she would not be excluded from serious discussions, Delyth suspected they would soften the information given to her.

"How dare you make such an offer without talking to anyone, Eirian!"

Her mother's grunt of annoyance was unmistakable. "What else was I supposed to do, Briallen? I needed to ensure the gods knew someone was willing to pay the cost of salvation."

"Do you expect me to sit idly by while you sacrifice yourself?"

"I expect you to do whatever it takes to protect Delyth. She is what matters most, and you know it. You've always been closer to her than to me, and I know it's my fault, so please, sister, save her."

Eyes widening, Delyth realised her mother intended to have her taken away if war came to their home. Covering her mouth with trembling fingers, she debated letting the two women know she had overheard their words, but she did not want to interrupt their moment. Part of her was thrilled Eirian was willing to admit she had made a mistake by not building a closer relationship with Briallen, but a darker part of her mind argued the only reason it was happening was because the High Priestess knew there was no hope. They were the admissions of a person who knew the end was coming on swift wings.

"You know I would do anything to protect Del," Briallen snarled. "And you."

"My beautiful, strong, and courageous sister. I'll carry the guilt of my failures beyond the Veil, and they are heavy indeed. Do not add more weight to them by throwing yourself onto the pyre with me."

There was a long silence from the dining room that had Delyth wondering what was going on. Chewing on a knuckle, she watched the deepening shadows fill the hallway. They seemed to roll across the stone, creeping closer to where she stood until they pooled on the other side of the doorway. Biting down hard on it to silence her surprised yelp, she blinked furiously when Tristan appeared, leaning against the wall. He held a finger in front of his mouth to caution her to remain silent, an eyebrow arched in amusement. Delyth wished her heart would stop pounding against her ribs so loudly, and did her best not to let the goblin see how flustered his presence made her.

"You're forgetting one thing, Eirian. I am a dragon rider, and it is my duty to defend the weak. If war comes to your home, I'll be one of the first to join the battle. It will be Igraine's fire leaving a trail of broken bodies on the front line. We will do everything we can to slow the Unseelie down."

Tristan's mouth twisted into an angry snarl, but no sound escaped his lips. Shadows crawled up his legs, and Delyth dragged all her knowledge of goblins to the forefront of her thoughts. Their command of darkness was unique to them, as was their ability to walk from shadow to shadow in a manner similar to the veil walking used by others like the dullaghan, danann and pixies. It made them useful spies, and she wondered how many conversations he had observed.

"Let the other riders fight and die!" Eirian shouted, and the sound of glass breaking made Delyth twitch. "I just want you to save my daughter... and her beloved. Take Delyth and Amelia and fly."

"Wait, you know about Amelia?"

It felt like her heart was going to beat its way out of her chest, but the stern look Tristan gave her kept Delyth pinned in place. Amelia had informed her Teleri knew about them, but she had not expected to learn her mother was also aware. She did not know how to deal with the truth because for so long, she had convinced herself the rules forbidding relationships between Altiras and Zartheins would mean Eirian would punish her for being involved with Amelia if she found out.

"Of course I do. They're young, and their feelings may change, but until then, I don't see any harm in letting them be in love. It's not like they can mix the bloodlines. I want Delyth to be happy."

"Because you never got to be young and carefree?"

"Those are not things any heir to a god is allowed to be. I'm glad my daughter is just another Altira."

"Me too. I wish you could have grown up knowing freedom."

Shaking his head, Tristan stepped away from the wall and held out his hand to her. His shadows urged her to move, so Delyth nervously slipped her fingers into his, allowing the goblin to guide her into the dining chamber. He wore a disarming smile that hid the points of his teeth, and if it were not for the wisps of darkness chasing his feet, she could have been fooled into believing he was as human as she was.

"See, I told you they'd be here already," he said cheerfully, winking at her.

Her gaze drank in the sorrow on her mother's face as the High Priestess stared at her. Shattered glass decorated the floor next to Briallen, but the dragon rider did not seem bothered by it. Looking between them, Delyth realised how similar they were in appearance, their blue eyes almost identical. It was a reminder of how infrequently she had seen them so close she could observe their similarities. Meeting Briallen's gaze, she found a hint of knowing that suggested her aunt was aware of her lurking presence outside the door. Giving Tristan a suspicious glance, she plucked her hand from his grasp.

"I'm so happy to see you, Aunty Bri!" Flouncing over to the older woman, Delyth threw her arms around her. "How is Igraine? I can't wait to say hello to her. Are you staying here?"

Arms tightened around her, and Briallen kissed the side of her head. "How are your studies going, sweetling? Learnt anything exciting since your last letter? I meant to look up some wards for your project, but I completely forgot."

"I did find some interesting combinations for it. Not that it matters while we have more important matters to deal with," she replied, pulling back to turn to her mother. "Where's Pa?"

Eirian's mouth twisted in disappointment, and she did not need her to say anything to know the truth. Busy with city business, Madoc would be absent from dinner. As much as she often resented her mother, Delyth appreciated her efforts to always be present.

She spoke before Eirian attempted to excuse his absence. "Probably better he's not here. The sky could turn green, and he wouldn't notice until someone wrote it on a plan."

No one mentioned the shattered glass on the floor, but Delyth saw her mother flinch each time her gaze drifted towards the shards. The slip in her temper was unusual for the High Priestess, and a sure sign that she was under strain with everything going on. For once, she felt like she had an opportunity to be a rock for Eirian. All her life, her mother had been a pillar of stone for people to lean on, so Delyth intended to seize her chance to return the favour. If her mother needed someone to shoulder some small portion of the weight of her duty, then she would be there. Starting with guiding them to the table to enjoy a delicious hot meal together while pretending there was no war heading their way.

Delyth gestured at the table, eyeing the open bottle of raspberry wine. "Let's sit. The servants will be along with dinner soon enough, and I'm so hungry it's ridiculous!"

It was obvious her mother and aunt were thankful for the suggestion, and she watched closely as Eirian took her place at the head of the table. Selecting the seat to her right, Briallen stuck her tongue out at Tristan when he rushed to pull her chair out for her. Envy stabbed a knife in Delyth's heart when she caught the goblin gazing down at his fellow dragon rider with adoration. Leaning on the back of the seat opposite

Briallen, she smiled at her mother before glancing at the doorway in contemplation.

"Do I need to run to the kitchens?"

Reaching for the open bottle of wine, Eirian shook her head. "No, I asked for the gong to be rung early. They'll be along shortly. Though don't ask me what they've cooked."

While Tristan and Delyth sat, Briallen held a wineglass out to her sister. "We visited a small town a few months back while on patrol, and let me tell you about this thing called bacon."

"We have bacon," Eirian muttered. "It's cured pig meat."

"Not like this. The town is on the edge of a cooler mountain region, where they have snow for a good half of the year. Anyway, they have something called maple trees, which they harvest the sap from."

Giving them an apologetic look, Tristan pinched the bridge of his nose. "I'm sorry, she's been obsessed with this information since we spent a few days there exploring."

"I have not been obsessed!"

Biting back a laugh, Delyth watched Briallen smack Tristan's arm. "So, what do maple trees and sap have to do with bacon? I'd like to know. Also, where was this?"

Eyes narrowing at her friend, the dragon rider huffed and turned back to her niece. "Well, they harvest the sap and turn it into syrup. It's delicious. I wanted to bring a bottle, but I used it all. These people put it on all sorts of things, including bacon. Honest to the gods in their eternal valleys, maple bacon is the most amazingly delicious food ever created."

"Flavoured bacon?"

"It's sweet, and sticky, and salty, and I wish I had some to share with you."

There was amusement in Eirian's eyes as she sipped wine and studied her sister. "I'll have you know we have flavoured bacon. Sure, it's not done with tree sap, but I've been told there are butchers who carefully smoke meats with different woods to infuse them with certain flavours."

"Is anyone else planning to join us?" Tristan inclined his head at the door.

"Not unless Madoc finishes work. I decided I wanted tonight to be just the family. Tomorrow will be a long day spent debating in council."

Silence descended on the table at Eirian's reminder of what was to come. Chewing her lip, Delyth wondered if it would be the Endaran council only, or if they planned to have the joint councils working in unity from the onset. Defence of the twin cities was a matter for both, and no one would attack one without involving the other. An image of the Bay of Blades bathed in the colours of sunset flashed through her mind, and Delyth froze in horror, eyes wide as she stared at the others.

"Wait, have the ocean-dwelling First People joined the Unseelie?"

Scowling, the High Priestess drained her glass, and a few stray drops looked like blood on her chin. "Yes, I believe so. Not all, but as far as I'm aware, the kelpies and sirens have. Merfolk might have too. At least the bunyips are unwilling to leave their swampy homes."

Her shoulders slumped, tendrils of fear worming their way into her. Delyth wanted to cling to the possibility they could hold off the Unseelie long enough for the gods to deal with their treacherous member, but attacks from the water would divide their focus. Not only that, but she could not see how the dragons could help. Their fire would not deter water-dwelling enemies who could lure defenceless mortals to their death simply by singing. Everything she had studied about the First People rushed through her thoughts, a confusing whirl of information that left Delyth feeling like someone was sticking needles into her scalp. Eirian's hand found hers, squeezing tightly to remind her she was not alone.

"Can we close the sea gates?"

Eirian shook her head. "Not without undeniable evidence. Until then, the gates remain open for trade. At least they are warded to keep the sea folk out. Though there have been reports of ships going missing. It's not something the dragons can investigate. As mighty as they are, they are not inexhaustible. Perhaps the danann or pixies will."

Tristan allowed a single claw to emerge on his finger, and he tapped a glass with it. "Not likely. They're immortal, but they also need to rest. Not to mention the struggle to fly with wet wings."

"He's right," Briallen said, a faraway look in her eyes. "One good storm would plunge them to the depths where any Unseelie water dwellers would take them captive and delight in watching them drown for eternity. At least Lord Charnel remains aligned with the other gods."

"Are you suggesting we entreat the god of water to help us?" Delyth mulled over the possibility.

"I don't see why not. Isn't that what the gods are for?"

Lips thinning, the High Priestess hummed. "I'll ask Lord Gebael about it when I see him next. But please, I didn't want dinner to be clouded by these issues. Tell me, Briallen, have you made any progress in being able to shape-change? I know Delyth has questions."

She wanted to be thankful to her mother for shifting the conversation, but staring at the three older people seated at the table, she knew it was all empty. They could not shake the sorrow shadowing their eyes, or the moments when their minds provided some fresh thought that filled them with horror. Everything else they discussed was decoration to hide the truth. Letting her gaze linger on the doorway, Delyth could not smile when the servants finally arrived with their meal. Each plate of food was beautifully arranged, and she wondered if they would still put in the effort once they knew what was coming. It seemed so pointless to sit at tables, sipping wine and eating elaborate meals while the mad god whispered in the minds of those who would destroy them all.

Eleven

Teleri

"Thank you for coming early, Rider Tristan," Teleri said as the goblin emerged from the shadows. "I know this is a lot to ask, but I could use your skills today."

He cocked his head, staring at the massive round table occupying the centre of the chamber. Each district of the cities was represented, elegant name cards serving as reminders of who had been elected for that period. It was not just the city officials who held seats at the table; there were places for the guild leaders, the banks, the temple, and the army. At opposite points, two chairs sat slightly higher than the others, their timber so beautifully carved it felt wrong to use them. Tristan did not need her to explain that those chairs were for the two heirs, and Teleri wondered what he thought as he drank it all in.

"I'm happy to be of service, High General. What do you need me to do?"

Following his gaze as it swept around the room, she pursed her lips. "I need you to be my ears in the shadows. You're skilled enough to ensure no one knows you're there?"

Tristan's lips twitched. "I'm 103 years old, High General, and nought but a child to my kind. But I can manage to fool a room of humans and elves into not noticing my presence."

"No need to be modest, Tristan. Lord General Valerian would've ensured you had training in those abilities from the moment you could wield the power. I know I would have. There are so few goblins who aren't Unseelie, and that makes you invaluable to our side."

"Which many people like to remind me of. I'm a high-born goblin raised away from the Spire, and my leader has done his best to teach me, even though no one else in Bellenden has my powers."

She suspected he led a very lonely existence among the dragon riders, even with the devotion he showed Briallen. There were times when she felt isolated, but Teleri knew she had others around her with much the same magic. They were not War's heir, but there were plenty, especially among the Zartheins, who could confidently spar with her. Lifting her gaze to the extensive map of Tir painted on the ceiling, she located the Spire.

"Do you ever regret not being among your kind?"

The flash of his pointed teeth brought her gaze back to him, and Teleri observed the wicked claws extending from his fingertips. "No. I'm curious, High General, what do you know of goblin culture?"

"I know it's matriarchal, and males aren't treated the best."

"When Ysgarlad found me, I had tried to run away, and my mother had hunted me down. You can't imagine what it's like to be told from the moment you're born that all you'll be good for is licking the boots of your betters. That if you don't want to be one of the wretched grunts or sold to a pleasure house, you need to make sure the women want you around. Our job as men is to look pretty, to please, to make shiny things to decorate the homes we tend to. We own nothing, and we have no freedom. So no, I don't regret having a dragon light my mother on fire to save me."

Her throat felt like it had seized, and Teleri tried to swallow to dislodge the blockage. He was right. She could not imagine what it was like for the goblins, and it made her heart ache with sorrow for all those trapped in the Spire. Looking at the table, she thought of the ever-changing mix of people, wondering if they realised how fortunate they were. Things were not perfect in their cities, but at least there was relative equality. They had programs to ensure the less fortunate were cared for. Healing temples where anyone could seek help, and public food halls to feed anyone in need. All of it was the tireless work of Death's temple. For people to live a life worthy of the gods, they needed to survive.

"I wish there was something we could do to help," she said, stroking the back of a chair. "Though perhaps that's a sentiment born from privilege. Many goblins, men included, wouldn't welcome change."

"You're worried about this meeting," Tristan replied.

Laughing at his astuteness, she nodded. "I am. Hence my request for your help."

"I'm afraid I cannot tell if someone is under the mad god's influence. All I can do is observe and hear things others won't. If you feel there is someone you'd like me to keep an additional watch on, write it on a slip of paper. While I'm here, I'll do my best to help."

Teleri arched a brow, wondering why she had not thought of his suggestion. It was a promising idea, and one she needed to tell Eirian about. Between them, they were familiar with every person who would soon arrive for the joint council meeting. There was no one else they could trust to decide who to keep a closer eye on. If she were the mad god, she knew she would target people placed in higher authority to twist first. Corruption nearly always began at the top, filtering down to those with less power to manipulate the situation. It was why the cities were ruled by councils that underwent public elections every three years, and no council member could serve consecutive terms.

"What would they do to you if they captured you?"

Meeting his jewel-like gaze, it startled Teleri to see fear as he said, "I'd rather not find out."

She did not press further, her magic creeping outwards to meet Eirian's icy power. Shifting her focus to the smaller entrance the two of them used, Teleri watched Tristan fade into the shadows before the High

Priestess swept through the door. Several high-ranking priests accompanied her, their black robes decorated with the symbols of their position. Of them, the only one she had any tolerance for was Joshua, and the priest gave Teleri a tense smile that confirmed she was not alone in her concerns.

"Oh good, you're already here, High General," Eirian said, waving in her direction as she hurried around the table to her chair. "Everyone else is in the building."

Frowning at the group following their leader, Teleri felt a pang of confusion at discovering Briallen was not among them. "Where's your sister? I thought she would be with you."

"No, she's off with Delyth. Something about shopping. Commander Calea will attend this meeting as the representative of the dragon riders. That's a point. Please fetch a few chairs suitable for our winged guests. I'm unsure if the peropuan will be present."

Head lifting, Joshua gave Eirian a startled look. "Did you say peropuan?"

"Indeed. I was amazed when I saw them at the tower yesterday. Does anyone else find it odd that a dragon would pick someone with wings of their own to be their rider?"

Chewing the inside of her cheek, Teleri did not admit she agreed with Eirian. "At least they won't die if they fall off. Gives them quite an advantage."

"That is true." Settling on her chair, Eirian held out a hand to Joshua for the folder he carried. "Thank you."

Eyes narrowing, Teleri recognised the object Eirian placed in front of her. Whenever she had documents she wanted kept from the eyes of the other council members, she carried them in the stiffened leather folder, bound shut with a warded black ribbon. Anyone who dared open it would receive a nasty shock, ensuring the High Priestess knew who had dared invade her privacy. A faint smile tugged at Eirian's lips, and she nodded to Teleri's chair opposite her, fingers drumming against the table.

"The Lord General sent me a letter."

"Briallen gave it to you last night?"

"It was quite the read," she said, giving the folder a hard push to slide it across the table.

Teleri caught it before it fell off the edge, settling into her seat before opening it. There was an undeniable beauty to Valerian's writing, each letter perfectly formed as it swirled over the page. Remnants of his wax seal clung to the top and bottom of the pages, the bright purple harsh against the creamy colour of the paper. She did not need to read beyond the first page to feel the cold slither of fear making its way down her spine. His words left her certain that their cities were doomed to fall at the hands of Annawyn's Unseelie army, aided by those residents turned by her manipulations.

"We're fucked. Has Lord Gebael returned?" Teleri snapped the folder shut.

From the look on Eirian's face, she knew the god of death had not visited again. An anxious voice wriggled free of her forced sense of calm to suggest the High Priestess should summon her master, but Teleri shoved it back behind the wall she had built in her mind. It was easier to leave the other woman to deal with a god, and to make deals to scrape some semblance of survival from the mess their creators had made of Tir. If she had truly wanted to speak to a god, she knew she could summon her own. Lord Neriwyn was not present in her life, and Teleri preferred it that way. But should the situation demand it of her, she would set aside her distaste for the gods to call upon the man who had done nothing to prevent the Sundering and subsequent millennia of war.

The doors burst open, a pair of guards using their bodies to keep them in place while council members ambled in with their assistants. Dropping her gaze to the folder beneath her hand, Teleri lifted it again to meet Eirian's stare. They remained locked in place for a moment before the younger woman nodded slightly. Giving it a shove, the High General sent it sliding across the timber while everyone else was busy finding their spots. People milled around, passing documents and other things to those seated at the table. High above them, slatted windows cast beams of light that seemed to increase the shadows. Glancing at the nearest dark pool, Teleri wondered where Tristan was lurking. It always took longer than she liked for the council to organise themselves, leaving her impatient.

Before she had a chance to demand order, Eirian rose and clapped her hands three times. Surprise rippled through the room, focus settling on the High Priestess. Teleri listened to the scuff of feet as those standing shuffled away from the table to take their places behind the line drawn around it. No one expected the council members to dismiss their staff, and it was important for assistants to remain close so they could do their jobs. Sweeping her icy gaze around the table, Eirian barely lingered on Teleri, but the elf felt an affectionate caress of power against her magic. She wished they had been given more time to prepare a plan, but whatever her human counterpart intended, she knew she needed to support it unconditionally in public. It was the only way they could wrangle the joint council into believing there was a threat coming for them.

"My dearest members of the joint council, I apologise for this highly irregular summoning," Eirian said, her voice carrying a hint of her magic and the weight of her position. "However, the High General and I have not undertaken this action lightly. We summon you here today to inform you of a most unfortunate development, and to set into motion what is needed to ensure our survival."

The doors had not shut, drawing Teleri's gaze to the dragon riders who had arrived with Briallen and Tristan. Calea's wings were spread wide, almost filling the doorway with their size, and obscuring the others accompanying her. She was not the only one to look in their direction. The council members burst into conversation as they questioned why a high-ranking commander of the dragon rider army was attending. Admiring the steady precision of Calea's steps, Teleri observed how she lifted her wings, folding them back to reveal the peropuan to her left, and a duine to her right. Eirian's assistants had prepared a space for the commander halfway between the heirs, at the spot for guest attendees. A slight smile of appreciation appeared on Calea's face when she observed the stools provided for her and her fellow winged rider, but it faded swiftly.

"Commander Calea, welcome to the joint council of Ensaycal and Endara," Teleri said, raising a hand in greeting while the danann inclined her head politely. "We are thankful to Lord General Valerian."

She rested a hand on the table, eyes moving from one person to the next with a piercing gaze born from millennia of watching conflicts unfold. "Council members, I'm not here simply to visit your beautiful cities, though the waters of the Bay of Blades are a welcome sight. Sadly, I am the bearer of misfortune, for the mad god is finally making her move, and the Unseelie march to war."

"What does that have to do with us?" A council member demanded, and Teleri eyed the man thoughtfully. "Surely the dragon riders aren't here to ask for our army."

"No, I'm here to prepare you for the likely destruction of your cities. Do not be fooled. You cannot fight the Unseelie and survive. Many cities have already fallen. Even Kinara."

Shock froze Teleri in place, horror filling her. She had never had the privilege of visiting the mighty city of knowledge, where creativity reigned over conflict, and the small part of her that had dreamed of it withered with the truth that she never would. Meeting Eirian's mournful gaze, the elf suspected she had been as unaware of Kinara's destruction as the rest of them. If the god of thought could turn on a place of learning and art, they had no chance of avoiding her attention. Their home would burn.

Covering her mouth with a trembling hand, a council member seated two places over from her stared at Teleri and asked, "Why would they destroy Kinara? It is a city of peace."

Next to Calea, the peropuan drummed his fingers on the table. "Not just Kinara. My homeland has come under attack. The Unseelie have destroyed the houses of healing, where everyone was welcome. No one is safe."

"No one is safe unless they bend the knee." Rising, a woman pointed at Eirian. "If we offered the Altira and Zarthein families to Lady Annawyn, pledging our loyalty to her instead of Lord Neriwyn and Lord Gebael, perhaps our cities would be spared the destruction."

Picking up a pencil, Teleri wrote her first name down for Tristan. She suspected the goblin was already close to the councilwoman, familiarising himself with her scent to make it easier to track her down. The room filled with sound as people descended into arguments, and there were too many voices lending their support to handing over the members of the two godly bloodlines that guarded their cities. From the shadow that had appeared on Eirian's face, Teleri knew it was what the mad god wanted. Destroying the bloodlines ensured the gods remained trapped in their current forms, unable to pass over their power when existence became too much to deal with. No heirs meant no rebirth.

Teleri sensed it was time to act and slammed a fist against the table to demand attention before her power crept outwards, urging calm. "That is enough. Sit down, all of you. We will not bow to a mad god bent on destroying all mortals to punish the other gods. Now, Commander Calea, what does Lord General Valerian suggest we do?"

Twelve

Briallen

With their arms linked, they walked down the street to meet Amelia, Laryn, Calleth, and Patton. Under the shade of the path keeping pedestrians out of the way of faster-moving transport, Briallen decided it was easy to pretend there was nothing wrong with the world. She could ignore the prickling sensation trailing down her spine, urging her to be on alert. Delyth behaved as though she were unaffected, and the dragon rider suspected it was the case. Doing her best not to peer at every shadow, and glare suspiciously at every person they passed, Briallen prayed it was simply her nerves getting through to her. With the looming threat of war, jumping at nothing was reasonable behaviour when there might be servants of a mad god waiting to attack them.

"If you don't stop fretting, you'll spoil Delyth's day," Igraine grumbled at the back of her mind, reminding Briallen the dragon was enduring her every emotion.

Eyes narrowing at a man leaning against a doorway, she wished she could control her thoughts better. *"I can't help it. The mad god could be watching us right now, and there's nothing I can do."*

"You can enjoy the time with your niece. Considering we don't know what will happen, there's no time like the present to have some fun. Happiness matters."

Delyth squealed, hopping madly as she pointed to the four elves heading in their direction. "I see them! You know they're going to want to go to the dragon tower."

Smiling faintly, Briallen felt the delight of her bonded. If the group wanted to go to the tower to see the dragons, she would take them. She always did. Igraine loved indulging them, especially Delyth, and Ysgarlad happily endured whatever the grey dragon wanted. When she remembered what they had done to rescue Tristan from the terrible fate of growing up in the Spire, Briallen understood their willingness. All dragons doted on children to a certain point, even if a person was not considered an adult in their culture. To Igraine, they were all children until she decided otherwise, and she would protect them with everything she had.

Letting her niece launch herself at Amelia, Briallen smiled at the other three. Their friendship with Delyth had blossomed in recent years, but she remembered a time when the four elves had seen the human girl as nothing more than an annoyance. It was something she recognised from her own youth when her father commanded her much older half-siblings to spend time with her. At least they were only ten years older than Delyth, unlike the hundreds of years between her and her daoine family. But there were also only ten years between her and Eirian, and sometimes that gap was unbridgeable. Not without an excellent reason for things to change, as she had learnt the day before.

"It's good to see you all," Briallen said to the three waiting to the side while the lovers embraced. "How has training been treating you? Worked out your specialities yet?"

Calleth dropped a hand to a short sword at his hip. "I remain a soldier, and always will, Rider Briallen."

Scoffing, Laryn smacked the back of his head and grinned. "He lies. They keep talking about running away on a ship to travel the world, living by the edge of their blades."

"Right, because you won't come along with us," Patton replied, rolling his eyes.

The faint smile he wore told Briallen the two men enjoyed her teasing. It had her heart aching with envy, and Igraine's chuckle at the back of her mind confirmed she would be on the receiving end of another lecture once the outing was done. Brushing the observation aside, she winked at the trio and nodded at Delyth and Amelia pointedly. They stood with their arms around each other, lips barely a finger's width apart as they whispered sweet words to assure themselves of their love.

"Yes, they're always like this when they're not worried about being caught." Laryn pulled a disgusted face, and the two men laughed, elbowing each other. "It's annoying."

Making a rude gesture, Amelia sneered at her. "Blood and bone, you're annoying."

"Am not."

"Are too!"

"Children are such a delight."

Pinching the bridge of her nose at Igraine's comment, Briallen muttered, "Is this normal for them?"

Patton gave her a blank look that confirmed it was. Laughter filled her mind, and for once, she wished she could block Igraine from observing everything through her eyes when she wanted to. It was frustrating, and outside of a handful of situations, Briallen struggled to convince the dragon to give her privacy. Aware they risked drawing unwelcome attention, Delyth and Amelia separated, but the rider decided the smile her niece wore was as bright as the sunlight beating down on them.

"So, where are we going first?" Delyth bounced on her toes, her eyes suggesting she could go all day. "I was thinking about lunch at that cafe we found."

It was impossible not to smile indulgently at her niece before a prickle at the back of her neck had Briallen shifting to observe the street. Oxen pulled a pair of wagons laden with nondescript crates and painted with the same family emblem. They were moving slowly enough to have caused a disruption to the flow of traffic, and she settled her gaze on the wildly gesturing driver of a coach stuck behind them. Drawn by a pair of patient horses, the vehicle bore the emblem of the couriers' guild, and Briallen decided it was no surprise the driver was fed up. Couriers took their jobs seriously, and as someone who had used their services many times, she appreciated his dedication.

"What do you sense?"

Mouth twisting, Briallen moved on from watching the road to studying the individuals on horseback, carefully picking their way past. *"I don't know. It's probably paranoia."*

Igraine huffed, and she imagined an indignant puff of smoke. *"Your power is growing, child. Don't dismiss the gut feelings you get. Little Delyth is the only child of the High Priestess, and that makes her a prominent target for the mad god's followers. Be on guard."*

She hated the thought of anyone hurting her niece for a reward. Realising the group had continued to discuss their options, Briallen returned her focus to them. Meeting Amelia's gaze, she nodded once, moving a hand to the pair of sai secured at the back of her belt, their hilts in easy reach. The elf drew her bottom lip through her teeth, a glimmer of rage crossing her eyes. Flicking her gaze to Delyth, the dragon rider watched the rage become understanding. If there was one thing Briallen knew she could count on, it was the younger woman doing anything to protect her beloved.

"Where's Rider Tristan?" Patton asked suddenly, turning the group's focus to her.

Shrugging, she waved a hand in the direction she thought the joint council building was. "He's attending the meeting today. Unlike me, he has useful skills to offer."

"Don't be like that, Aunty Bri!" Delyth crossed her arms, eyes narrowing. "I hate it when you talk about yourself like you have nothing to offer. You're not setting a good example for us children."

"Sorry, I don't mean it like that. It's just hard when your power still hasn't fully manifested, and most people in your life don't think you should be allowed to be bonded to a dragon yet, let alone go on missions. They only let Tristan go because he's a goblin and has useful abilities."

Pulling a face, Calleth muttered, "We get it. Our powers are mostly manifested, but we're only thirty, so as far as everyone else is concerned, we may as well be fifteen. Del is the only one here who's technically an adult now."

They took a moment to feel the solidarity of their positions while Delyth scratched the side of her head. It was clear how much it bothered her, and the worry in her gaze when she looked at Amelia had Igraine sighing at the back of Briallen's mind. Dismissing it as a conversation for later, she slung an arm around Patton's shoulders and waved at the street.

"So, where to? I'm looking forward to a day of relaxing with my favourite niece and her friends."

Delyth arched a brow, an amused smile making her lips twitch. "I should hope I'm your favourite, considering your other ones are older than you. Unless something has changed?"

"No, you're still the youngest."

"Well then, I'm hungry, so I vote we head to the food market and see what vendors are there. Last week there was a cheese stall, and I swear they had the best selection of goat cheeses I've ever tasted. Bet they would go well with that maple bacon you mentioned."

Placing a hand over his stomach, Calleth said, "Forget the cheese. I need meat."

"Curry," Laryn replied. "She's always there, and her extra-spicy curries are amazing."

Laughing, Briallen agreed to eat first. "You had me at cheese, but I'll need some meat. Did you know that being bonded to a dragon means you get the worst cravings for meat? Because no one warned me about it before Igraine initiated the bond."

"No way!" Patton laughed. "Maybe Calleth is secretly a dragon rider."

Making their way along the street, Laryn led the group while Amelia kept close to Delyth. Happy to remain at the back of the group with Patton, Briallen watched the shadows and the passing people with a suspicion she hated. It felt wrong to fear that any person they crossed paths with might be one of Annawyn's servants. An overprotective sense she knew was partially Igraine's fault screamed they should not be wandering the streets of Endara, but it was a voice she refused to give in to. To stop living, to cower in fear while the mad god burned the world around them, was worse than dying. So long as they fought back in whatever way they could, Briallen believed they could win. She had to believe or go mad with despair.

Laryn turned down an alley between buildings, unlit lanterns hanging from hooks signalling it was a popular path. When they reached the other end, Briallen took a deep breath, inhaling the scents drifting from further away. Distant music suggested they were approaching the food market, and memories of previous visits promised an enjoyable time. There was always entertainment to be had, with street performers plying their skills to earn handfuls of coins from their passing audience. Swaths of coloured fabric decorated the narrower street, and instead of wagons drawn by beasts of burden, people carried their cargo, or dragged hand-drawn carts along behind them. She knew the food market was a permanent thing, and long ago, it had been written into law that no livestock was permitted.

Hopeful vendors shouted for the attention of people passing by. Drawn to a stall with silver charms on display, Briallen stopped to admire the delicate work. Milling around her, the others took turns to examine what was on offer. Hearing a delighted gasp, she watched Delyth pluck a charm shaped like a stack of books from the table and reach for the purse tucked into her belt. Amelia grabbed her wrist, shoving a hand with a few coins at the seller, her expression filled with eagerness. Returning her attention to the wares, Briallen saw a simple crescent moon with a sun trapped between the points and felt a pull to it. She did not know why, but it made her think of Tristan. When she paid, the seller flashed a thankful smile.

Ice slid down her spine, and Briallen stiffened. The others had moved away, but Patton remained with her, watching the people wandering the street. Staring at the vendor they had just bought from, she frowned when fear flashed across his face. He met her gaze, shaking his head before turning away to hide at the back of his stall. Feeling the weight of Igraine's attention settling into her mind, Briallen moved her focus to the street. Delyth and Laryn were examining a stall three spots along where brightly coloured fabrics hung from rods, while Calleth and Amelia waited patiently. No one had approached them, but she saw a trio of men lurking on the far side of the street. It was easy to dismiss them as nothing more than creeps, so she kept looking.

"*There,*" Igraine said, her growl making Briallen flinch.

It was a lone woman standing in front of a stall, seemingly examining an arrangement of hats. Elbowing Patton, she made a slight gesture in the direction of her target, and he shifted his position to watch covertly. They carefully moved to catch up with their companions, and the moment they joined them, Amelia frowned suspiciously. Out of the corner of her eye, Briallen observed the woman keeping pace from the other side of the street. She was slightly behind, so they remained in front without it being obvious she was trailing them.

"I'm sure it's nothing," she murmured to Patton. "But we should be alert."

"How quickly would Igraine get here if needed?"

Amelia followed his glance, her focus settling on the unknown woman. "I've seen her before."

"Where?" Briallen signalled for them to keep walking towards the food market.

"She was hanging around the training yards yesterday. I thought she was just there to feast her eyes on some half-naked men with their swords out, but maybe not."

"*We thought she was following Delyth, but perhaps she's watching Amelia. It makes sense; the mad god will seek the destruction of both families. They're equally at risk.*" Briallen sensed Igraine preparing to leave the dragon tower. "*My wings need stretching.*"

"*Has Ysgarlad told you what Tristan is up to?*"

"*The High General has our goblin spying on the joint council while the meeting is in session. He's going to be busy. I want you to stay with the young Zarthein and her friends.*"

Delyth peered at her, a hint of amusement cutting through her worry. "I can tell you're talking to Igraine. You get this weird, distant look that makes it seem as though you're not here."

"Sorry. She's going to stretch her wings, so she's nearer if we need her. We should keep going and pretend we haven't noticed our shadow. I doubt that woman is the only one. Besides, some of us are hungry, and we might need the fuel." Licking her lips, Briallen tried to muster some enthusiasm for the sake of her niece. "Someone promised me cheese."

Linking her arm through Amelia's, Delyth's expression became delighted, and her aunt wondered how often she forced herself to act as though nothing was bothering her. It troubled her to think it was a frequent occurrence because of Eirian. The important thing was to ensure that anyone following them did not realise the group was aware they were being tracked. Any sign of suspicion would send their shadows into the wind, and Briallen longed to get her hands on one. She needed to know if they served Annawyn or if they were following them for some other reason. Eirian had not mentioned having people from the temple tracking her daughter, and with the current situation, she knew her sister would have told her to avoid causing undue concern if they were noticed.

"Does your mother have you followed?" She kept her tone cheerful despite the low volume.

"Yes, but they're easy to spot. Any priests or clerics are usually her servants. If you spot a crafter, you can be sure they'll report back to my father that they saw me. Politics is all about earning favour from those with the power, so you too can one day possess power."

Briallen glanced at the woman she now felt certain was following them. "She's no cleric."

Rolling her shoulder, Amelia grunted. "No, she's not. What are you thinking?"

"How much do you know?"

"My aunt told me everything. She didn't want to, but after she found out Delyth knew, she decided she had to. Do you think you-know-who has corrupted her?"

It was almost as though the young warrior feared drawing the attention of the god by saying her name, and Briallen wondered if it was possible. "I really hope not, but yes."

"All we can do is stay alert," Patton said, smiling at a soldier who passed them. "And smile. Please."

Thirteen

Eirian

Trapped within the bottle, the colour of the wine was too dark to appear as anything other than ink. Using her teeth to yank the cork out, Eirian did not bother with a glass, swigging from the bottle directly. The tart flavour of blackcurrants hit her tongue, but she was not interested in savouring it. Leaning back in her chair, she took another mouthful, eyeing the growing stack of documents on her desk. Her assistants dealt with the bulk of her work, ensuring only the most important things reached her, but with everything going on, those items were piling up. Mouth lingering on the bottle, a trickle of wine trailing from the corner of her lips, Eirian decided they probably did not matter anymore.

It was hard to see the value in dealing with paperwork and other city matters when she knew about the approaching destruction of her home. The letter from Valerian had only reminded her of what really mattered. Family. Her sister, daughter, husband, and even the cousins she only interacted with when necessity demanded it. There was still time to repair the broken bonds, and to seek forgiveness for her neglect. If Lord Gebael demanded her life in return for saving her people, she wanted to give it with her conscience clear. Part of her hoped the god she served would respect her efforts. Tipping back the bottle, she swallowed more, not caring if she woke up the next day with a pounding headache.

A knock at the door had her turning to blink at Briallen. Her sister was slumping, hands shoved in the pockets of a short green jacket decorated with brightly embroidered birds in flight. It looked like the sort of thing

Delyth would pick out, and she could not help smiling at it. Signalling for the rider to enter, Eirian wondered if her daughter would appreciate it if she asked her to select clothes for her. Before taking a seat on the other side of the desk, Briallen plucked the bottle of wine from her grasp, eyes sweeping the area for a glass. When she failed to locate one, she shrugged and took a swig, pulling a face when the dark liquid hit her tongue. Passing it back, she dropped onto the chair with a grunt.

"Fuck today, and the beast it rode in on."

Eirian arched a brow, not surprised by her sister's words, and she wholly agreed with them. "I'll tell you about my day if you tell me about yours. Though I was hoping yours would be uneventful."

"So was I," she replied, staring at a painting on the wall unhappily. "Do you recognise this person?"

Frowning when Briallen pulled a book from her pocket, Eirian watched her flip it open to a page with the corner folded down. Holding it up for her to examine, the rider ground her jaw, gaze flicking back to the painting on the wall. Studying the intricate sketch of an unfamiliar woman, the High Priestess questioned her initial assumption. There was a tug of recognition at the back of her mind, the faint sort that suggested she may have encountered the person in passing, interacting briefly enough to stir memory.

"I want to say no, but at the same time, I'm not certain. Why?"

Briallen grunted, snapping the book shut and dropping it on the desk. "Because she followed us all day. We didn't think she was one of yours. Delyth was quite certain you normally assign clerics. I didn't think you'd have bothered today since I was with her."

"True, I didn't. Do you think I'm a terrible mother for having my daughter followed when she's wandering the city? I never thought it was wrong since I was trying to protect her."

"You wouldn't be the first parent in a powerful position to do so. My father certainly did, and he still commands Tristan to watch over me.

Love is shown in so many ways. Are you a terrible mother for it? I don't think so because you don't control her freedom."

Humming thoughtfully, Eirian reached for the book with the drawing. Flicking the cover open, she gasped at the beautiful sketch of a dragon she knew to be Igraine. The next page was of a different dragon, followed by a smiling picture of Tristan. Lingering on it, she glanced at Briallen when her sister grabbed the bottle of wine, tossing her head back to take a bigger swig than her last one. She wanted to try her hand at being an irritating younger sister and prod until the other woman was agitated enough to admit her feelings for the goblin. It seemed ridiculous to keep denying it when war was coming.

"This is the work of someone who cares deeply for her subject," she murmured, tracing the line of Tristan's face.

"Well, yes." Using the side of her hand to rub her eye, Briallen waved at the book with the bottle of wine. "He is my only friend who isn't a dragon. We've been through a lot."

She turned the page, finding a picture of the Lord General with less detail than the one of Tristan. "I had no idea you could draw, Briallen. I'm sorry, I should've been a better sister."

"It's strange to admit, but I started drawing as a child because I found it helped me remember things I otherwise forgot. I'd draw the face of a person, look at it, and recall instructions they gave me. Or a picture of an object would prompt me to remember whatever I needed to about it."

"Do you ever wonder why you forget things so easily?"

"Sometimes, and then my attention is caught by one of the thousands of thoughts in my head. It's rather noisy in there all the time except when I'm on Igraine's back, drawing, training, and fighting. Those tasks take up all of what's up here," Briallen said, gesturing at her head with a half-smile.

Leaning back in her chair, Eirian tried to imagine what it would be like to have a thousand thoughts competing for attention. She knew other people who endured the same chaotic brain as her sister. It was not uncommon, and the healers did their best to identify it in children so that they, and their families, could be provided with all the support they needed. Many of them became the greatest mages the city knew. Her husband was one. Madoc had learnt as a child how to turn his busy mind into something so skilled it created buildings wonderful enough to rival those made by the original builders of Endara and Ensaycal. He believed progress lacked art and worked hard to bond the two aspects together in ways she could not comprehend.

"I'm never sure if I'm glad Delyth didn't inherit a mind like yours and her father's." Eirian continued to flip through the pages, noting how often Tristan appeared. "Though she's a brilliant girl either way. Perhaps it's for the best she doesn't have the advantage because she'd be terrifying."

Briallen cocked her head to the side, confusion twisting her expression. "Advantage?"

"Yes, advantage. Healers do their best to identify children with minds like yours. A long time ago, it was discovered that when given the right support, most had the potential to do brilliant things. We don't like to leave people behind here."

"A wonderful sentiment, but when was the last time you walked the streets of your city?"

Eirian opened her mouth to reply, but the words died in her throat when Madoc stumbled through the doorway, a bottle of something clasped in each hand. He hesitated when he saw Briallen, but his gaze moved to the open wine, and the obvious lack of glasses. No one spoke as he placed his additions on the desk and picked up the bottle of black-currant to take a swig as he sat on the other chair. Pursing her lips, Eirian studied her husband, concerned over his dishevelled state and the dark spots on his face. She had a sinking feeling the marks were dried blood.

"Have you heard?" he mumbled, waving the bottle at her.

Not knowing what he was referring to filled Eirian with dread. "No, I haven't, Madoc. Please tell us."

"Someone slaughtered one of my teams. I found them when I attended the site for an inspection after we were done with the council meeting."

Gasping, Briallen covered her mouth, and Eirian clenched her jaw. She desperately wanted to argue that it could not have happened. Not in her city. While they had issues with crime, and Madoc's teams of crafters had discovered more than a few murder victims, the slaughter of multiple people in one place was unheard of. Between Briallen and Delyth being followed, and Madoc's news, the High Priestess knew the truth. The mad god was putting her plan for Endara and Ensaycal into action.

"How bad was it?"

Madoc met her gaze and took another swig. "I'd rather face a battlefield than see it again."

For her husband to describe it that way scared Eirian. He was a gentle man dedicated to the art of building. It was a reason she had fallen in love with him when they first met. Theirs had not been a romance approved of by her mother and the others responsible for her upbringing, but in the end, their opinions had not mattered. Madoc was her peace, and though their relationship was strained at points, Eirian had never stopped loving him.

"Briallen said she was followed today while out with Delyth."

"I didn't have anyone assigned. Didn't think it was necessary." Madoc gave Briallen a grim smile, inclining his head slightly. "Thank you for protecting my daughter."

She nodded as she reached for one of the bottles he had brought with him. "I will always protect Delyth. We're family, Madoc, and I'll do whatever I must to keep her safe."

Returning her attention to the little book of sketches, Eirian realised it was open on one of her. "This is the mad god beginning her efforts to destroy us. Those under her sway will strike at whatever they can to throw the government into disarray. Anyone with Altira or Zarthein blood is at risk."

"Briallen can put Delyth on the back of her dragon and leave." Wine sloshed from the bottle with the force with which he waved it around. "I don't care about anything else, just her."

There was a distant look in Briallen's eyes that Eirian suspected was a sign she was communicating with Igraine. Knowing what she did of her sister, it was likely that they were discussing the feasibility of doing what Madoc demanded. She watched sorrow appear before her sister took a mouthful of wine, the bottle dangling from loose fingers threatening to fall. All Eirian could think was that she was glad there were no rugs in her home office to be ruined by broken bottles of wine.

It was obvious Madoc had worked out what Briallen was going to say, but the flash of anger twisted his features. "Why? If you'll do anything to keep her safe, why won't you take her and go?"

"Igraine said Bellenden is in danger. She was under orders not to tell me unless necessary. Apparently, demanding we take Delyth was a good reason. My father is planning to do what he can to save our people, but he doesn't know who he can trust. Calea knows."

Grabbing the untouched bottle from her desk, Eirian set the book of sketches down and hoped her sister would forget it. She did not know why, but she wanted to keep it. Another part of her wanted to ask Briallen to do larger pictures of her family she could put in her office. It seemed so trivial when destruction was coming for her home.

"Valerian has the gift of foresight," she said, revealing information her mother had given her before she died. "It's not overly powerful, fortunately for him, but he gets visions of the future occasionally."

"You think he's seen the fall of the dragon riders?" Madoc shook his head in horror.

"I do. His letter told me that the destruction of Endara and Ensaycal is inevitable. That you asked Igraine to take Delyth back to Bellenden means you don't know what he wrote."

Briallen shrugged, closing her eyes as she slumped back and lifted her legs to prop them on the desk. "No, I didn't. The letter was for you, and I'm not the sort to read correspondence intended for another."

The folder containing Valerian's letter sat next to the stack of paperwork, and Eirian picked it up to pass to her sister. While the rider showed no inclination to take it, Madoc did not hesitate to pluck it from her grasp. Staring at a splotch of dried blood, she realised they were smears from his fingers that he had missed when he scrubbed his hands clean. He took his time reading the letter, but Eirian could not stop thinking about how devastated he must have felt when he found his slain mages.

"We can't tell the general population about this," Madoc said, voice cracking.

"And yet, we must. They should know the danger they're in. If people want to flee to find somewhere safe, then we owe it to them to provide that chance."

Cracking open her eyes to observe her sister, Briallen sighed. "Our enemy is a god. Considering what she did to cause the Sundering, where on Tir is safe?"

He closed the folder, tossing it onto the desk. "She's right. If being in an Eternal Valley did not protect Death's Ravens and their danann mates, where on Tir could someone hide from the god of the mind?"

"If we can capture one of her servants, perhaps the mind mages can detect something," Briallen murmured, jolting upright to glance between them. "Maybe we can find those under her influence."

"That's a good idea. It's more than we have." Eirian licked her lips, contemplating whom she trusted among the mind mages of the temple to accomplish such a task. "I'll get Rince and Joshua to compile a list."

Draining the bottle she originally opened, Madoc gave a broken sob. "It's not fair! Why must we pay for things that had nothing to do with us? The gods should deal with their own problems."

"You're right, my love. We shouldn't pay for their fucking mess."

"Can you summon Lord Gebael?"

The temptation was strong. Eirian was feeling the strain of waiting for him to return with answers, but she knew he would not look kindly upon her impatience. Managing Gebael's temper was a delicate dance. One she had learnt the hard way when she was younger. There was nothing to be gained by risking his ire when they needed him to negotiate with the other gods to stop Annawyn.

"No, he said he would return when he had something. I might anger him if I try, and we cannot risk losing his support. Lord Gebael doesn't want us destroyed, but he is a god."

Madoc slammed a fist into the desk, startling Briallen. "So what, we just wait?"

"Getting angry will not help us." The dragon rider put a hand on his shoulder.

She expected him to shake Briallen off, but instead he slumped back in defeat. "I know, but I'm so angry with the gods. We never asked to be game pieces in their fight with each other."

Eirian blinked away tears, knowing her sister and husband would notice them. "We will fight, and whatever it takes, we will do it. Delyth and the other children of Endara and Ensaycal will survive."

A flicker of magic caused Briallen's skin to glow brighter than her sister was used to seeing. "My father will send more dragons and their riders to help us with whatever plan we come up with."

"I just hope this fight doesn't cost all our lives."

Fourteen

Delyth

It was strange to have an armed escort surrounding her, but Delyth could not help feeling thankful for it. After breakfast, her father had shared what had happened, carefully picking each word to be gentle in his delivery. Not that it mattered how Madoc said it because there was no way to make the news of a group of crafter mages being murdered sound anything less than what it was: a complete tragedy. Her parents had invited her to join them at a joint council meeting, but Delyth had not wanted to listen to a bunch of politicians discuss the darkness coming for them. Instead, Briallen suggested they tend to Igraine and Ysgarlad.

She would be the first to admit that when she looked around the familiar streets of Endara, she no longer felt safe. The illusion of peace that had ruled her youth was shattered. There was no doubt in Delyth's mind that had she been alone the day before, the woman stalking her would have tried to kill her. From the continuous concerned glances, it was clear her aunt could tell the news had shaken her. Only a fool would be unmoved, and Delyth refused to be labelled as such. Lifting her gaze to the sky, she wondered how quickly things in the twin cities would unravel. With one slaughter, it might be possible to keep information under wraps, but if there were more, then people finding out would be the least of their problems. There would be panic.

"Igraine is looking forward to seeing you," Briallen said, false cheer making the pitch of her voice rise. "She said if you do a good job polishing her scales, you can go flying."

Before finding out about the attack, Delyth would have been overjoyed to take to the skies on Igraine's back. "Thank her for me. It'll be nice to soar with the birds."

"You know, when I finally shift, I hope my animal form has wings."

"Because then you don't have to worry about dying if you fall off?"

Her laughter was bittersweet. "No, so I can fly with Igraine."

Watching a dragon circling high above the city, Delyth did not need to ask to know the mighty grey beast was tracking them. She tried to imagine how amazing it would feel to fly side by side under the power of her own wings. It was a pleasant distraction from the cold weight of fear that had settled into her stomach.

"Delyth, you're allowed to be scared. I don't know if your parents told you that, so I thought I should say something. Fear is perfectly reasonable in this situation."

Casting a nervous look at the nearest soldier, she rolled a shoulder. "I know. Blood and bone, I know that logically, I am right to be scared. But, Aunty Bri, I don't want to be. My mother is the High Priestess of Death, the Altira, and people will look to us for strength."

Briallen stared at the sky, her eyes tracking the dragon. "It is the duty of the strong to protect the weak. Sometimes the best thing we can do is to be honest with those we're serving. The Unseelie are immortal, and we are very much not. Anyone who isn't frightened is a fucking idiot."

The soldier grunted, tucking a wispy clump of hair behind his ear. "It's true."

"What is important is how you put those feelings to use. Letting your fear hold you down is the quickest way to fail the people who matter. It's only by accepting the truth of your emotions that you can turn them into a positive force with which you can help others."

"Were you scared when Igraine chose you to be her rider?" Delyth hoped she knew what the answer was, but a part of her did not want to hear it if it meant seeing her aunt as anything other than the indomitable dragon rider she had always believed her to be.

"Absolutely!" Briallen replied, a half-smile accompanying the knowing gleam in her eyes. "And I still am every time I get on her. If something went wrong and I fell, the chances of survival are slim. Igraine would do her best to catch me, but I'd still be badly hurt."

It made sense; Delyth knew it did. The joke she had made about why her aunt hoped for a winged animal form had seemed funny, but it was too close to the truth. A large number of daoine who were dragon riders had wings when they were shifted, almost as though it was a preference of the dragons themselves. She supposed it made sense. From what she understood, the bond breaking was a painful thing some did not survive. Much like the power bond between two mages.

"I hope you get wings."

"So do I. I wouldn't mind being a lorikeet. They make me laugh."

She giggled at the thought of Briallen shifting into the form of a lorikeet. "What kind?"

"Oh, a rainbow, of course! All those bright colours."

The levity of the subject helped pull her from the previous conversation. Hearing the distant roars of dragons, Delyth searched the sky for them. At her side, Briallen muttered under her breath, but she caught the name of the bay. Pace quickening, the young woman felt a fresh eagerness to reach the tower, though she wished they could take horses there. It would have been quicker, but most horses had not undergone the training needed to keep them from panicking around dragons. They had ridden from the temple grounds to the outskirts of Endara, but the walk to the tower was a long one.

"If I could shapeshift, I'd like to be a big cat. I've seen pictures of them in books, and I think the ones with the orange and black stripes are gorgeous. They're called tigers."

Humming thoughtfully, Briallen nodded slowly. "I've seen something like that in the Aluca Mountains. They're called snow leopards, and they're gorgeous. I haven't met a duine who can shift into a large cat, but my father once told me King Vartan Malfaer is a black leopard."

"What is the most unusual animal form taken by a duine you've met?" Delyth watched a line of wagons ambling along the road and wondered where they were coming from.

"Well, recently Tristan and I were sent to meet a spy who had been in the kingdom of Talaroo. She could shift into a cerapter. It was amazing. Granted, I've encountered natural ones, and I wouldn't willingly get so close to a living one. I asked if she's as vicious as the real thing."

"And was she?"

Briallen's nervous chuckle was all the answer she needed. The unmarked wagons drew level with them, the driver of the lead one nodding respectfully as their group stepped off the road to ensure there was enough space. Dirt crumbled beneath her boots, but Delyth was more interested in what the covered cargo might be. Part of her mind pointed out that the canvas was not as well secured as one would expect, and there was a distinct lack of netting to hold it in place. None of the soldiers seemed bothered, but Briallen was staring at the line as it moved past. Her magic possessed a familiar coldness that reminded Delyth of her mother, and it troubled her almost as much as the wagons did.

A dragon circled lower, red scales gleaming like freshly spilled blood in the sunlight. Ysgarlad drifted above them, close enough for Delyth to see the vicious claws on each of her feet. The horses pulling the wagons startled, drivers shouting along the line as they wrestled with the animals for control. Inhaling sharply, Briallen's hand headed for the hilt of a blade, and her niece pressed closer in concern. Watching the nearest wagon, she thought she saw the flash of hands grabbing the edge of the canvas to hold it in place while the unhappy horses picked up their pace. They kept walking, remaining off the side of the road until the last wagon had gone by, leaving them coughing in the cloud of dust. Though they were now behind them, Delyth noticed Ysgarlad remained close enough for everyone to admire her.

"Something isn't right," Briallen said, earning an amused look from a soldier. "I've asked Igraine to pass a message to the others since Calea is with the joint council."

Glancing down, Delyth noticed a dead plant at her aunt's feet that reminded her of when Eirian used her powers. "What makes you think that? And are you feeling well?"

"I'm fine. As for what makes me think there's something wrong with that wagon train? Honestly, I'm not sure, but all my instincts are screaming danger. Don't tell me you sensed nothing because I saw the suspicion in your eyes when you were watching them."

The dragon tower was within sight, and Delyth was pleased to see Igraine's mighty form waiting for them where the road forked towards the bay. "The canvas seemed wrong, but what do I know?"

"You're a brilliant girl, and I trust your observations."

Hearing those words from someone she admired as much as she did her aunt left Delyth buzzing with joy. That her magic had never presented with a strong inclination to a discipline had always left her questioning what she was capable of. She knew plenty of others like her, each a powerful mage dedicated to academics. If it were not for belonging to the Altira family, Delyth would have taken a position at a university where she could focus on her interest in complex wards. Magic danced between her fingertips, stirred by the desire to show Igraine and Briallen how her skills had advanced.

Poking her arm, Briallen grinned. "Igraine said you've grown."

Staring at the dragon as she stood and ambled towards them, Delyth gasped when Ysgarlad landed on the other side of the road. "Tell her she is even more beautiful than last time. Also, ask her to tell Ysgarlad she is as resplendent as the sun. I am humbled by the magnificence of her presence."

The soldiers looked at her like she had grown a second head, but Briallen laughed, while the red dragon settled back on her hind legs, wings spread, and neck arched. If Delyth could make a guess at the expression on Igraine's face, she would have sworn the grey dragon was giving Ysgarlad her best disapproving look. Her large eyes narrowed in on her rider, the gold flickering with a hint of fire. It seemed likely there were threats being exchanged, but Briallen's mirth did not fade.

"Did they notice anything about those wagons?" She ignored the mutters from the soldiers.

Lowering her head, and stretching it closer to the group, Ysgarlad blew smoke over them, and Briallen said, "Igraine said they smelt strongly of rotten onions and potatoes."

"Which explains why they were covered. Both crops need to be kept out of direct sunlight once harvested." Delyth frowned, recalling the wagons, but her suspicion remained. "Something still doesn't feel right. Did anyone else notice those smells?"

A soldier shrugged, running a hand through her short hair. "Can't say I did. Which is strange, since those vegetables smell bloody awful when rotten. We should've gotten a whiff if the wagons were carrying loads of them because there's never just one or two bad ones."

"Yeah, but a dragon's sense of smell is a lot better than ours!" Another one waved at the two dragons. "So, it stands to reason they would pick it up when we couldn't. Besides, why would anyone fake it?"

The two dragons stared at where Endara sat on the sloping cliff, a gleaming city of stone and magic overlooking a perfectly calm bay. Whatever Igraine was saying had Briallen paling, and Delyth could not help marvelling at the way her skin took on a strange glow, like someone was trying to trap moonlight. It was a reminder that despite having a human mother, her aunt was a duine. When Igraine snapped her mouth shut, gaze dropping to Briallen's feet, Delyth followed her focus. Seeing a slowly creeping circle of withered plants sent a chill down her spine, and she reached for the older woman's arm to shake her. Stopping with her hand two fingers' width away, her brain screamed at her not to touch her aunt.

"Aunty Bri, look at me," she whispered.

Eyes flashing to her, Briallen frowned. "What's wrong?"

"Look down."

Peering at the ground, the dragon rider appeared befuddled. She glanced at Igraine, head cocked as her confusion deepened. The circle had stopped spreading, but the exchange had drawn the attention of the soldiers. Listening to their murmurs, Delyth went through the possibilities in her mind. Everyone knew the only human with husk maker powers was the Altira mage, but it was not an unheard-of ability among the daoine. Death's Ravens were the original husk makers, and the power occurred among born daoine. Every ounce of logic she could muster told Delyth it made perfect sense that as her aunt manifested her powers, she would be a husk maker.

"That wasn't me," Briallen mumbled, shaking her head and meeting Delyth's gaze. "I'm not... no."

"It makes sense."

"Igraine said the same thing. I can't be developing those powers. Do you know how people view husk makers? It's not always considered a good thing to be, and I don't know of any who are dragon riders."

Confident that her aunt was not going to accidentally suck the life out of her, Delyth put a hand on her arm. "Well, it's a good thing you're the sister of the Altira mage. Ma will help you figure it out."

Fear flitted through her eyes before being replaced with determination. "We have more important things to worry about right now. I have an awful suspicion those wagons were hiding something."

"You think they were using rotten vegetables to hide the scent of what they were really carrying?" asked the soldier, who had voiced her own doubts about what Igraine reported.

"It doesn't have to be enough for us to notice, just enough to throw off a dragon. All the Unseelie need to do is get a few goblins or mara into the city to cause damage."

Ysgarlad flapped her wings, leaving the ground with a swirl of magic. Watching her gain height, Delyth was not surprised when other dragons swept from the tower, heading towards Ensaycal. Roars ripped through the sky like thunder. She did not know if a rider accompanied the ones heading to War's city, but she prayed the dragons practised patience instead of their burn first, ask questions later nature. Briallen grabbed her arm, pulling her close.

"Stay with the soldiers. The tower will be safe, and I'll be back as soon as I'm sure there's nothing wrong. You're not a warrior, Delyth, so please do as I ask."

Clenching her jaw, she wanted to argue that she had useful skills, but the fear in her aunt's gaze made the words freeze in her throat. Nodding in agreement, Delyth did not move when her arm was released. Igraine strode forward, lowering herself to make it easier for Briallen to clamber up her front leg and onto her back. Soldiers closed in around her, watching in awe as the mighty dragon launched into the air with a tiny figure clinging to her scales without a saddle. Dust swirled around them, prompting Delyth to weave threads of her magic into a shield to protect them from it.

"Right, you heard Rider Briallen." Delyth looked at the nearest soldier, mouth set in a grim line. "We're to head to the tower and remain there until she returns. If there's something going on with those wagons, the dragons will deal with the issue and alert the joint council to the danger."

Fifteen
Teleri

Teleri had once thought that watching the members of the joint council argue in circles over the most trivial of matters would never cease to amuse her. With the fate of the twin cities in question, she quickly found the sound of their voices was wearing her down. She wanted to scream at them to be silent, that every moment spent arguing in this chamber was time wasted when they could have been searching for solutions. They needed to inform the general population, so families were free to decide what they wanted to do. Many would pack their bags and flee, seeking safety in small communities and hidden spots that felt like no one else would find. What mattered was making the announcement so they could do what they believed to be the right thing.

Meeting Eirian's gaze across the table, Teleri saw her frustration reflected back at her. It felt like a thousand thoughts passed between them, a silent agreement that they could not allow the arguments to continue. Their duty was to Endara and Ensaycal. Each person seated around the table had sworn an oath to serve the citizens of the cities. Her magic coiled around her like an angry serpent ready to strike. It longed for a fight, and teaching the council members a lesson seemed like the easiest way to deal with the need. For too long she had allowed them to forget how powerful she was, instead letting Eirian endure the fear that being the heir to a god induced among the wise.

Sudden movement to the side drew her attention. Wings spread wide, Calea shot from her seat, while the other two riders accompanying her did the same. Their actions brought silence to the chamber, focus settling on them instead of whatever petty matter had stirred the arguments. The danann warrior appeared calm, but Teleri noticed one of her wings was lower, the feathers along the top bristled like an agitated bird. It was strangely reassuring that despite her millennia of experience, Calea had little tells that betrayed her fear. She did not need the rider to say a word to know the dragons had communicated bad news. What mattered most was that it was not a battle before they were ready.

"High General, we need to speak," Calea said, gaze locked on Teleri.

Her words caused the council members to break into fresh arguments, their voices a rising cacophony that had the peropuan recoiling. From what she knew about the reclusive race, they were sensitive to sound, and the distress in his expression had Teleri signalling to her assistants to clear the way to the smaller set of doors. Eirian swept around the table, Joshua trotting at her heels like an ever-faithful hound. Catching Calea's gaze, she nodded towards the doors, receiving a sharp nod in return. The three riders moved swiftly through the room, but Teleri remained in place, holding a hand up in a plea for silence.

When they ignored her, the High General let her magic flood the chamber, forcing the council members to sit in silence. Their eyes glazed over, expressions becoming slack as she used a side of her power they were less familiar with. Instead of a lust for battle, a desire for peace infected them. It was something Teleri preferred not to do, but if she was going to find out what was wrong, it was better to leave the argumentative ones trapped in a state of euphoria. At least that way, they were not being a thorn in her side. Slipping from the table, she strode across to the waiting door, flashing a smug look at the soldiers waiting for her. They snorted in amusement, eyes darting to the dazed joint council.

"Why is it so suspiciously quiet in there?" Eirian did not look at her when she joined them in the small corridor. "Did you put them to sleep? It's been a while since you last felt forced to do that."

"I wanted to before the disruption. Commander, what happened?"

Calea exchanged a glance with the peropuan, their wings held at a similar height. "Rider Briallen and Lady Delyth encountered a wagon train on their way to the tower. Igraine and Ysgarlad grew suspicious and investigated. As did the others. Zern headed to Ensaycal, where they spotted a second wagon train displaying the same attributes that roused suspicion in the first place."

"You want to join them," Teleri replied, mouth twisting as she considered the news.

"Our dragons are on their way here. Would you like to join us?"

The shadows grew thick, and Tristan stepped free. "I'll head off now. I can shadow walk to the gates. No one will see me, and I'll keep an eye on things from the ground."

"Go. Try to keep Briallen out of trouble," the peropuan said.

No one blinked when he faded back into the shadows, but it felt like the corridor grew lighter once they cleared away. Eirian's arms were crossed, and she stared at a door. At her side, Joshua fussed, the older priest clearly unsettled by the situation. There was no doubt in Teleri's mind that she wanted to accompany Calea to see the wagons, especially if it meant a short flight on the back of a dragon. She knew it was wrong to be excited, but the thrill of flying made her heart sing.

"I'll go with you, Commander."

The danann warrior smirked, but it faded when Eirian cleared her throat and said, "I will as well. If there is something wrong, I might be of more use than you, Teleri."

"Husk makers are always useful when the First People are involved. Not that I'm suggesting there's any involved when we don't even know yet if there is something wrong... but I trust those two dragons." Calea's wings drooped, curling around her slightly. "Even though she's young, Rider Briallen is smart."

Eirian lifted her chin, eyes narrowing in annoyance. "Of course she is. My sister is an Altira."

It surprised Teleri to hear her defend Briallen so quickly. "Let's not delay. Eirian, I'd like you to ride with Commander Calea. We cannot risk anything happening to you."

"Nor can we risk you, Teleri," she snapped.

The peropuan rider flashed a grin at the High Priestess. "I will protect High General Teleri. She will not fall from Laszlo's back while I am with her. He understands how important she is."

"Fine. This way."

She could not resist finding the irritated twist of Eirian's lips amusing, or the way she spun on her heel to storm down the corridor. Wriggling her brows at the riders while Joshua trailed after the High Priestess, Teleri saw nothing but concern in their gazes. Indicating for them to go first, she watched Calea lead the way with the duine second, and the peropuan third. Her soldiers waited for orders, their hands on the hilts of their short swords. Lingering, the High General debated what to tell them. If she commanded them to head to the gates, they would arrive after her, and might not be necessary. But if she did not, they would be needed.

"Send a bird to Ensaycal, alert them to the danger. Hopefully, they'll realise something is wrong because of the dragons, but best not to assume. I want more soldiers sent to the dragon tower. Lady Delyth is there, and we can't risk her safety. Inform the council there is a potential threat and then keep them here until I send confirmation it is safe to leave. If they argue, I'm giving you permission to lock the doors. Station guards at all entrances to the building to watch for danger."

"Do you think there will be?" a soldier asked.

Pursing her lips, Teleri hoped there was not. "Better to be prepared. All the leaders of both cities are in that chamber. If I were in command of the Unseelie, I would send a stealth attack to wipe them out."

A whistle from the far end of the corridor prompted her to hurry away, leaving the soldiers to deal with her orders. As she went, Teleri debated recalling her power from the council chambers, but left it. They would come out of the daze eventually, feeling like they were caught in a dream with no comprehension of how long it had been. Until that happened, they would be easy for her soldiers to deal with. With their training, they would know to wait, not that rousing them was something anyone could do without her help. Flashing a smile at the peropuan, Teleri slipped through the door to join the rest of the group. It was a private route through the joint council building, one reserved for the heirs.

"Everything sorted?"

Glancing at the rider, a pang of guilt struck Teleri as she said, "I'm sorry, I don't remember your name. If I'm going to ride on your dragon, and put my life in your hands, it feels incredibly rude not to ask. Not sure what your duine companion is called either."

"Don't feel bad, Calea never bothered to introduce us," he replied, chuckling as he tucked his wings in, so he did not bump her. "My name is Hadrian. The duine is Jacinta, and her dragon is Anund. We left Val at the tower, but they are investigating your city with Idrun."

Ahead of them, the broad wings of the danann warrior blocked Teleri's view of Eirian. The rose-pink feathers were flat, no longer showing signs of agitation. Aware she had never felt a flicker of bloodlust escape Calea's control, doubt struck her. It was easy to fear War's precious winged warriors when that was all they were, but there was a magical side of them that was far worse. If the commander was a blood mage, Teleri suspected she had been sent for a reason.

"Tell me, Hadrian, is your commander part of a pairing?"

He arched a brow, a slight smirk lifting one side of his mouth. "No. She's never met her warrior, and you'll never hear her say she regrets it. In all the years I've known her, Calea has remained the same."

The wording he used confirmed her suspicion. "She's a blood mage?"

"Aye. Will be very useful having one of those around if we need to question the enemy."

"How did you end up being a rider?"

"My people try their best to remain neutral. We're healers by nature and believe all people have a right to medicine. That doesn't mean the Unseelie leave us alone. I'm not Laszlo's first rider, and it was my efforts to heal his previous bonded that had him choose me. It was strange," Hadrian said, giving her a look that Teleri could only describe as haunted. "They were there to defend my village, and the elf who was his rider took an attack meant for me. You can't imagine how intimidating it is to try to heal a woman who has been gutted by a goblin while her dragon is chewing on the attacker in front of you. I failed, but the fact that I exhausted myself to do so endeared me to Laszlo."

Blinking at him, Teleri did not know what to say. He was right; she could not imagine the situation he had found himself in, but she admired Hadrian's strength. Peropuans were immortal, but that did not stop the Unseelie from taking them captive. It was rare for any of them to be born with a connection to War, leaving them without the bloodlust that made a warrior. For him to have accepted a dragon's bond and picked up a weapon to defend the weak meant defying the nature of his people.

"Don't take this the wrong way, Rider Hadrian, but I think you might be one of the people I admire most in this world. You possess a courage the rest of us can only dream of."

"Thank you... I think."

A roar vibrated through the walls, prompting Teleri to take note of where they were. The scrape of a door opening drew her focus to the rest of the group ahead of them. Sunlight flooded the hallway, almost too bright as it reflected off the stone rooftop of the building. When they stepped through, she gazed at the massive form of a dragon waiting for them. Eirian stood to the side, whisper-arguing with Joshua while Calea spoke to Jacinta. Giving a quick salute, the duine darted over to the dragon and scrambled up his extended front leg. Above them, two more dragons circled, waiting for their chance to land.

"Laszlo said he is honoured to carry you, High General." Hadrian remained at her side; his leathery wings folded in tight. "However, he is concerned this roof is not intended to take the weight of a dragon, and suggests I carry you to him as he passes by the edge."

Approaching, Calea nodded to her. "Zern suggests the same. Do you trust us not to drop you? Those of us with wings have done this before, so you'll be perfectly safe."

She had no issue with it, and as long as they got there quickly, she did not care how she ended up on the back of a dragon. "Let's go. I'm ready if you are, Rider Hadrian."

"As am I, Commander," Eirian said, joining them as Joshua walked back to the door.

Her wings spread, the breeze ruffling her feathers, and Calea held her arms out. "Zern will glide past, letting us land on his back. Apologies for the impact, he can only go so slow."

Watching the danann scoop her human counterpart into her arms, Teleri shifted her focus to the dragon swooping towards them. He banked, wings slowing his descent before he reached the rooftops of taller buildings nearby. Calea did not seem bothered by Eirian's weight, taking a few running steps and launching them into the air as her bonded glided past, the tip of a wing brushing over the stone. For a moment, her heart plummeted, but then she saw them settle onto his back, Eirian secured in front of the commander. At her side, Hadrian chuckled, his eyes tracking Zern's ascent into the sky.

"Our turn. Luckily, Laszlo is smaller, so he's confident he can go slower."

It was impossible to stop her yelp when the peropuan scooped her up, breaking into a run with his wings spread wide. Eyes wide, Teleri watched the floor disappear from beneath her feet, giving her a view of the distant ground before a dragon's wing cut into her vision. He did not let go of her until they were at the saddle, and the impact of two flying creatures colliding stole the breath from her lungs. Instinct took over, sending Teleri straight for the reinforced leather straps securing the saddle to the dragon, her hands digging into them. Hadrian helped her into the saddle, settling behind her with his wings protecting her from the wind until he was certain she would not fall.

Teleri wanted to scream with delight, unable to tear her gaze from the view. Laszlo's wings lifted them high above the city, chasing after Anund and Zern. An arm was wrapped around her waist, a tight presence refusing to let go in case she fell, while Hadrian's other hand joined hers in clinging to the leather strap. There was a strange intimacy to the position that had her wondering how different it would have been if they were not pressed for time and racing to check out a potential threat. His face was beside hers, and from the corner of her eye, Teleri watched the flutter of his long lashes.

"Hold on tight, we're going down," he murmured in her ear.

The flash of a red dragon racing past caught her attention. Ysgarlad was unmistakable, but there was no sign of Igraine close by. Heart pounding, Teleri hoped Briallen was safe. She had smelt no smoke, and she doubted the dragons would risk setting the cities aflame. Not unless they had no other choice. There were few places where the massive creatures could land, so Laszlo circled as close as he dared while Hadrian wrapped his arms around her tightly. Without questioning his actions, she held on as the peropuan leapt from the dragon's back, carrying them to the ground where the others waited.

She did not need long to gather her wits, and the sight of Briallen standing on the back of an empty wagon with rotten onions at her feet sent an icy chill down Teleri's spine. "The Unseelie have come."

Sixteen

Briallen

"They were empty when I got here," she told them, kicking an onion. "I waited too long to come after them. Igraine believes they picked up the pace once they were past us."

Crouching in front of the wagon, Jacinta sniffed the timber before lowering her nose to the ground. "I've got the scent, but it's contaminated by the rotten produce. Give me a moment to strip and transform, and I'll be able to get a better read in my hound form. Hadrian should join Val in Ensaycal."

Briallen jumped down, careful not to land on the onions. Sweeping her gaze over Teleri and Eirian, she wanted to grin at the windswept appearance of her sister. It had amazed her to see Calea land with the prim High Priestess in her grasp, but the awe on her face had been a welcome reminder of things she took for granted. Above the city, their dragons circled, searching with their superior eyesight for any sign of a threat. Holding out her hands, she let Jacinta pile weapons and armour on them while she made quick work of stripping. As soon as the older woman was naked, magic twisted around her as she transformed.

"*Tell them I will hunt now,*" Jacinta said, her voice a brush against Briallen's mind.

"She's going now." Scrunching her nose, Briallen watched the massive hound leap up onto the wagon to get a better sample of the scents she needed to follow. "I'd offer to follow her, but my hands are full."

Wings spread, Hadrian shrugged, and waved at the sky. "I can help, or I can join Val."

The hound bared her teeth at him, launching from the wagon to chase after the trail she had caught. Eyes narrowing, Calea pointed at the dragons, and the peropuan nodded. He did not linger; his powerful wings carrying him into the sky to meet his bonded. Catching a flash of red, Briallen watched Ysgarlad follow Laszlo, her scales dark at a distance unless the sun caught them at the right angle. Tristan's absence bothered her, but she was sure he had a good reason for it.

"I'll follow Jacinta. You stay with the High General and High Priestess." Calea gestured at them, and Briallen nodded. "You'll be able to relay information to them. Did you see anything useful?"

"No, I'm sorry, Commander. They looked like they should, mostly. Delyth and I had a bad feeling about them, but not all the soldiers escorting us agreed. Maybe we'd have dismissed it if Igraine hadn't mentioned the smell of rotten potatoes and onions the rest of us didn't pick up."

There was a flash of fear on Eirian's face. "Where is Delyth?"

"I told her and the soldiers to go to the dragon tower and remain there until we were sure it was safe."

Calea nodded in approval, her wings spreading as her magic pulled threads of the Veil into her grasp. "I'm going to catch up with Jacinta. Please wait for your soldiers, High General. Briallen will guide you."

Watching her fade from sight, the three women did not speak. The weight of Jacinta's belongings made her arms ache, so Briallen walked around the nearest wagon to the driver's seat. Without horses, it sat at an awkward angle, but she did not care. It was clear of rotten food, making it the only spot she could dump the weapons and armour. Examining the harnesses from the animals that had pulled it, she felt her sister and the elf at her side. Guilt flickered through her, and she looked at Eirian, contemplating whether she should mention what had happened with her magic. She knew she should, but there were more important matters to deal with, and Briallen did not want anyone distracted.

"I should have seen it. They weren't true horses," she muttered, rubbing her face. "There are fucking kelpies running around in the cities, and they were right in front of me."

Eirian sighed, putting a hand on her shoulder to give it a reassuring squeeze. "You weren't expecting it. I don't blame you for not noticing. The rest of us wouldn't have either. They chose rotten food for a reason."

"*She's right,*" Igraine murmured.

Giving her sister a tense smile, Briallen kicked a collar, listening to the jingle of straps. "If it makes you feel better, Igraine agrees. It doesn't help me, even though I know it's true. I feel responsible if anything happens because they were right in front of me, and I knew something was wrong. Every instinct in my body was screaming to stop them, but I didn't."

"Don't beat yourself up, Briallen. If you'd done something, they'd have killed you, Delyth, and the soldiers. Your inaction protected her," Teleri replied from the other side of the wagon, where she was leaning in to examine the area around the driver's seat.

Those words did nothing to calm the guilt plaguing her, but Briallen appreciated the assurance her failure had a positive result. Images of Delyth being torn to pieces and eaten by a kelpie drifted through her mind, making her shudder. Teleri was right. If she had tried to stop the wagon to quell her suspicions, they would have attacked, killing the group. Igraine and Ysgarlad would have swooped in, summoning the other dragons and their riders, but probably not in time to save them. The last thing Briallen wanted to be responsible for was the death of her beloved niece. Her safety mattered more than anything, and she would sooner throw herself into the fire than bring harm to Delyth.

The sound of soldiers drew their attention away from the wagon. Heavily armed people swarmed into the street, scattering the crowd. Thoughts clicked into place, and Briallen spun around to gesture wildly at Teleri. Arching her brow in amused confusion, the elf spread her hands. At the back of her mind, Igraine muttered something about using her words, reminding her that others did not always follow the same line of thinking that she did. Forcing herself to stop and take a deep breath, the rider pointed at a cluster of intrigued onlookers under the shade of a building. Teleri stared at them, brow furrowed before she nodded slowly and jumped up onto the wagon to address the soldiers.

"We have Unseelie loose in the cities. I want two-thirds of you to spread out and search buildings. The rest can speak to witnesses. We need to find out how many people were in these wagons. Since there are no horses present, we suspect kelpies drew them. Work in trios, and guard your backs," Teleri shouted, her voice carrying over the soldiers. "The dragons are watching. If you find anything, signal and they'll relay the information. Do not engage anyone you think might be Unseelie. You will die, and that would be a damn shame."

Soldiers sorted themselves into groups of three, most rushing in different directions. Turning her gaze to the sky, Briallen watched Zern and Anund circling over separate sections of the city, and knew Igraine would relay Teleri's words. It was one of those times when she was thankful her bonded observed through her ears and eyes. Since Jacinta had not reached out with her mind voice, she assumed the duine hound had found nothing yet. Or she was being cautious. Other shape-changing races could also mind speak, as could those with wings. The only way to keep a conversation private was to touch the other participants. At least no one could listen to them talking to their dragons.

"Do you want to go with them?" Eirian asked, but Briallen was unsure if she was talking to her.

Teleri beat her in responding. "No. Better for me to stay here. There will be more soldiers arriving, and this is a central point for issuing orders. Have you heard anything, Briallen?"

"Nothing," she replied, shaking her head.

"Thought so, but I needed to ask. When Calea received the news, she sent Tristan ahead to search. Have you seen him? They can't hurt him, can they? He's a goblin."

Ice slivered down her spine at the thought of Tristan being hurt by Unseelie attackers. "Ysgarlad would know if he got into trouble, and Igraine would tell me. He's fine."

"But did you see him?"

"No, I did not. Not since this morning when he left to do what you asked of him."

Huffing, Eirian scowled at her elven counterpart. "I can't believe you asked him to spy on council members. That's crossing a line, Teleri. If they found out, I dread the reaction."

"I don't care what their reactions would be, Eirian. The mad god is coming for our people, and if having a goblin on our side who can spy on those in power means finding her servants, I'll use him." Teleri spread her arms, lifting her chin in challenge.

She was unwilling to get involved in their argument, and wanting to keep out of the way, Briallen drifted towards the nearest building to escape the warmth of the sun. Sweat clung to her skin, turning her armour into a stifling layer she longed to shed. Listening to Eirian and Teleri debate the ethics of tasking Tristan with spying on members of the joint council, she felt an almost immediate relief in the coolness of the shadows. Scratches on the wall caught her attention, drawing her further from the wagon where her sister stood. Briallen rubbed them, feeling the peeling paint disturbed by claws scraping over the timber panels. They were familiar, turning her thoughts to Tristan.

"Goblins," she muttered, turning a fearful eye to the shadows she stood in. "*Warn Ysgarlad.*"

"*He already knows and is on his way to you. Be careful, my little Bri.*"

There was comfort in the brush of Igraine's mind against hers. Aware she needed to alert Teleri to what she had discovered, Briallen withdrew her hand, intending to call for the elf. As she turned, a shift in the shadows caught her eye, magic prickling with warning. A dragon roared, fury filling it as claws dug into her arm. The goblin did not move fast enough to stop her scream, but a tentative voice at the back of her mind told the rider that if the Unseelie had wanted her dead, she would be. Teleri and Eirian rushed towards her, but the goblin clicked her tongue, pulling Briallen back against her chest.

"Let my sister go!" Eirian snarled, magic twisting around her in warning.

A tongue trailed over her neck, eagerly lapping up the trickle of blood from where claws pierced her skin. "Let go of this tasty little treat? I don't think so. Now, Altira, why don't you let go of your magic."

Teleri had a hand on the cerapter horn hilt at her hip, but there was no familiar thrum of bloodlust in the air. Anger filled Briallen, dark whispers circling her mind suggesting she could deal with the threat on her own. All she needed to do was trust the magic raging through her body, demanding to be let go. Shadows thickened around them, Tristan stepping free to snarl at the strange goblin, his fearful green eyes locked on her. In the sky above, Igraine and Ysgarlad waited, desperate to help but unable to do anything without setting the city on fire and killing thousands of innocents.

"Let her go." Tristan's claws appeared; his teeth bared. "If you hurt her..."

"You'll what, boy? Kill me?" Her nose pressed into Briallen's hair. "I smell you all over her. Put your claws away. Try anything, and I'll rip her throat out."

With a hand over her mouth, and claws digging into her jaw, there was nothing she could say. Holding his gaze, Briallen pleaded with him to step back. It did not matter how much he wanted to kill the goblin woman for hurting her, nor did it matter what Eirian and Teleri wanted to do. The moment they tried something, she would die, and Briallen really did not want that to happen.

Ever the sensible one, Teleri released her hold on her sword. "What do you want?"

"Your blood on my tongue, and that of the Altira. My illustrious queen has offered quite the reward to whoever kills you. I'm most fortunate to have stumbled upon this opportunity."

Closing her eyes, Briallen knew she could not stand there, bleeding, and ignoring the whispers of her magic while the woman holding her threatened the lives of two people she cared about. Trusting her instincts, she snapped her eyes open and relaxed her hold over her power. It felt like ice slithering across her skin, creeping to where the goblin held her. The moment it latched on, it became a flood of warm energy filling her, a shriek making her ears ring. Flakes of dust coated her, and Briallen whimpered as the claws tore her skin, but the power was there, mending it with the life it sucked from the goblin. Breaking free, she stumbled back against the wall, staring in horror at the hollowed-out figure.

"Briallen, look at me," Eirian said, eyes wide with shock. "Let go of your magic."

She shook her head. "I can't."

"You can, and you will. She's a goblin; you cannot kill her, and the longer you hold on, the more at risk you are of losing control. We can capture her if you stop what you're doing."

Lips trembling, Briallen focused on drawing the magic back into her. It protested, longing to taste more. At the back of her mind, she heard Igraine, but it was as though a cloud muffled the sound. The goblin had crumpled to the ground, a withered husk of flaking skin wrapped around brittle bones. She would heal in time, a long and agonising process that gave Briallen some delight. When the last tendrils of her magic returned to her, Tristan leapt at the woman, claws tearing through her shell.

Eirian rushed over, fingers brushing where the claws had damaged her face. "How? When? Why didn't you tell me? Do you understand the danger of this power, Briallen?"

"Am I a husk maker?" she whispered, hands trembling as she grabbed her sister.

"It appears so. You didn't know?"

"When the wagons passed us, Delyth pointed out I'd drawn the life out of the ground. I had noticed no changes before then and wouldn't have if she hadn't said something."

Igraine's form filled the sky above them. "*The signs have been there, but I wasn't sure.*"

Pulling her into a hug, Eirian sighed. "We need to keep this quiet. I fear what Lord Death might do."

Tristan was suddenly there, yanking her from her sister's grasp and into his arms while shadows crawled over them. "I'm sorry, Bri. I failed you."

"Don't be silly, Tris." Pressing her face to his neck, Briallen listened to Teleri directing the soldiers drawn over by her scream. "I let my guard down. We're just lucky she wanted something."

"I don't know what I would have done if you'd been killed."

Clearing her throat, Eirian reminded them she was there. "Rider Tristan, can you accompany the soldiers to the temple cells? I know it'll be a long time before the prisoner is capable of anything, but I'd rather have someone with your abilities overseeing things."

Feeling his muscles tense, Briallen kissed his cheek. "I'll be fine, Tris."

"Come with me, Bri," he said, ignoring the arch of Eirian's brow.

"I can't. Calea ordered me to remain with Eirian and Teleri."

Her gaze caught sight of the soldiers struggling to drag the withered body onto the canvas from a wagon. Bile filled her mouth, and Briallen turned away, retching. Hands stroked her back, Eirian's soft murmur a reminder that her younger sister understood the enormity of her actions.

"Everything will be fine. I can teach you how to control it. We are Altiras, and this is ours." Eirian helped her straighten; blue eyes filled with sympathy. "You did what was needed. I am proud of you."

Blinking back tears, Briallen nodded. "I'm a dragon rider, and an Altira. My job is to protect the defenceless, and I'll do whatever is required to ensure the people are safe."

"It doesn't get easier."

"Then I shall have to get harder," she replied, forcing herself to watch Tristan assist the soldiers.

Seventeen

Eirian

Her sister was a husk maker. The thought kept repeating through her mind even as they coordinated a city-wide search for the Unseelie. Eirian wanted nothing more than to go home, hide in her office with at least two bottles of wine, and forget the horror she had seen in Briallen's eyes. She dreaded what would happen when Gebael found out the half-duine Altira he had allowed to exist was a husk maker. It should not have mattered when all others with the power were daoine. Most people were aware he had created the power for his Ravens, giving them an advantage over the immortal First People to buy time for the Executioner to kill them. A dragon bound Altira with the husk maker power, and the long life of the daoine felt like a threat to the balance.

Every time Briallen shifted closer to her, the blue eyes so like her own were wide with a desperate need for reassurance. Despite being ten years older, her sister seemed younger, leaving Eirian wondering if the power was manifesting too early for a duine. That thought joined the dozens of others battling for attention whenever her focus slipped. She was thankful Teleri was there to take command of the situation, because for once in her life, the High Priestess felt completely useless. And every time she met the gaze of her elven counterpart, she saw nothing but concern and understanding. Those dark eyes filled Eirian with guilt over her inability to do something useful, even though she knew she would be called upon to use her power if they found the Unseelie.

"Do you think this is the start of the war, or simply an opportunistic attack?" she asked once Teleri sent a fresh group of soldiers off to search. "It seems strangely timed."

Briallen craned her neck to locate her dragon. "We just got here."

"Exactly. It's hardly a secret we're sisters, or that your father is the Lord General of Bellenden. If Commander Calea sends a rider back, he'll send more dragons to defend us."

Whipping her head around to stare at them, Teleri's nose flared in a way Eirian knew meant she was unhappy with a thought that had crossed her mind. "That's their plan. This isn't just about us. Valerian is doing his best to help cities within his region of care, spreading the dragons thin. He will pull forces to send them here to protect the bloodlines of War and Death, leaving other cities vulnerable."

"Igraine agrees with you," Briallen murmured, wrapping her hands around her braid.

"Have you heard anything?"

"Jacinta is struggling to find a scent that doesn't vanish. Commander Calea believes her inability to do so means the wagons only contained goblins. The kelpies pulling the wagons would have headed straight to the bay because they cannot pass as humans. She recommends you increase patrols along the waterfront and warn people not to approach strange horses lurking on the shore."

Eirian thought about how often her clerics reported Delyth had joined her friends to go swimming in the bay. Thousands did every day. It was a normal practice to enjoy the cool waters, and children were taught to swim at an early age. There were wards at the entrance to the Bay of Blades to keep the sea folk from entering, but those did not prevent them from using the city to gain access to the water. Chewing her bottom lip, Eirian stared into the distance, her mind churning over all the information she had about how far from the sea a kelpie could go before the magic binding them to it forced them to return. That knowledge might help them work out where the wagons had come from. They had to have stuck close to the coastline.

Frustration tore through her when she could not remember, and she scowled at Briallen and Teleri. "How far from the water can a kelpie go? Or any of the sea folk?"

"Kelpies can roam farther than the others, except sirens, but they have wings. Merfolk and selkies won't go far from the water; as for puca, they can follow any creek or river. Bunyips don't leave their swamps, and they're mostly Seelie. What are you thinking?" Briallen blinked at her, and Eirian was glad to see her determination. "Wait, you're thinking about where they started."

"The Spire is across the ocean from us."

Teleri grunted, nodding slowly as she studied the watching crowd of ever-changing people. "But there would already be goblins here. Other cities have fallen already."

"But those cities weren't ours. Those cities weren't Bellenden. They've sent more goblins over, and I'll wager the ones here are fresh off the ship, and hungry for blood. It makes sense with wagons being pulled by kelpies. When we follow their trail, we'll find they came along the coast," Eirian replied, and her fingers found a loose thread on her robe.

Rubbing it between her fingertips, she wondered how many more goblins were already in the city. Or mara and strigoi, who could also pass as humans. It made sense to slip them into the cities, and if it had not been for Briallen and Delyth, they would not have known. There had never been a reason to search incoming wagons, only to record their arrival so the relevant guild could deal with them.

"What if these aren't the first?"

Briallen and Teleri froze, staring at her with growing horror. A cluster of clerics and priests waited in the shade of a building, assisting with preparing statements to deliver across the cities, as well as taking any information provided by helpful citizens. Signalling to them, Eirian moved away from her companions, intending to meet the three priests who responded to her summons. When the two women followed, she did her best to hide her irritation. She wanted a few moments away from the churning energy of their magic to clear her mind so she could work out what she needed to do.

"We need the records examined," she said to the priests once they finished bowing. "I believe these aren't the first Unseelie to arrive in our cities. There will be more abandoned wagons. To avoid rousing suspicion, they'll be spaced out. While you're at it, have a look at the reports of missing people, as well as death reports. The enemy is here, and they won't be starving while they wait."

The priests exchanged horrified looks, and Eirian ground her teeth. She wanted them to rush off to follow her instructions, but it was clear the enormity of her words was sinking in. Not just them, but anyone else within hearing, including Teleri, Briallen and a handful of soldiers. For a pair of cities built around the worship of their patron gods, neither Endara nor Ensaycal was prepared for what would happen when the god they did not kneel to came to destroy them. Their homes would fall. There was no more time for debate, or for a collective decision from the joint council. It was time for her and Teleri to decide as the heirs to their gods, and to bear the weight of it together.

"Eirian, if you're right..." Teleri rubbed the back of her hand over her mouth. "We're already too late. The time we thought we had to prepare, and to warn our people was a lie."

"Fuck the council. It's time for us to do our jobs."

Head bowed, Briallen's hands were clasped in front of her, and the distant look on her face told Eirian she was busy talking to Igraine. Or Jacinta. She could not tell the difference, and it did not matter. Whatever parts of the conversation that held any relevance would be shared when it was done. That was something she could trust her sister to do. Igraine roared above them, a plume of fire lighting up the sky as the dragon expressed her rage over the situation. It had always baffled Eirian why such mighty creatures bothered to care about the lives of people like them, but now she was thankful for their help.

"Commander Calea wants to send Val and Idrun back to Bellenden to inform my father of your decision as soon as you make it. If you plan to evacuate the cities, it is our duty to assist," Briallen said, expression blank except for a slight twitch in her cheek. "Jacinta has given up on tracking the scents. They're returning here to discuss what you plan to do, so we can respond accordingly."

Realising she no longer felt safe in her city was a punch in the gut. One Eirian knew she would never recover from. As much as she did not want to summon Gebael, she could not keep waiting for him to return from wherever he had gone to meet with the other gods. Sweeping her gaze over the skyline, Eirian located the distant temple rising above everything else. Energy thrummed through the city, her power reaching for it to remind the High Priestess of who and what she was. It drew Teleri's attention, the elf frowning at her.

"What are you thinking, Eirian?"

"I have to summon him."

Briallen stiffened, and she wrapped her arms around her stomach. "Will he kill me?"

"I'm hoping he'll leave you be while there is a battle to be fought. Surely he knows how badly we could use a second husk maker. There's only so much I can do."

"You can't mean to throw Briallen into battle. She's barely coming into her power!" Teleri shot forward, grabbing a handful of her robe to jerk Eirian closer. "I won't let you."

Baring her teeth, the High Priestess ignored the desire to snarl. "Would you rather let them tear your family to shreds? Because Briallen, the dragons, and I are the only effective weapons we have."

"She's right, Teleri. The First People cannot be killed by anything except the swords, Oblivion and Eclipse. All we can do is damage their bodies badly enough to buy time to run. I might not be magically mature, but I can do something that's better than nothing. Besides, I'm a dragon rider, and I know the risks," Briallen replied, shoulders slumped and a tired resignation in her eyes that had not been there earlier.

They stared at each other in understanding. Two sisters with an ocean of missed opportunities between them united with one purpose. It should not have filled her heart with warmth, but Eirian looked forward to standing side by side with Briallen to show the Unseelie why they should fear the Altira family. They would make Gebael proud of his bloodline, and when it was over, he would grant them peace beyond the Veil. At least in the war to come, Eirian could rest knowing the chances of having her spirit bound to her bones like countless Altira mages before her were slim. She would not be trapped for eternity, waiting to be summoned by those who shared her blood.

"I'm aware of your duty, Rider Briallen. My concern is that you're untrained. As a husk maker, you could do more harm than good as you are now. It's too dangerous to everyone else."

The bitter laugh that fell from Briallen's lips surprised Eirian. "Bold of you to assume I'd be in a position to hurt innocents if I was being forced to use my untrained powers."

"Are you planning to jump from Igraine to land among the Unseelie?"

"If I have to."

Recoiling, Eirian gasped. "That would be suicide."

It felt like the temperature dropped, and she looked around fearfully. Instinct screamed at her that Death was walking among them, watching, and listening to everything they said. When she returned her gaze to her sister, Eirian saw ice in the rider's eyes. Nothing would deter her from doing what was needed, and the High Priestess respected it because she was the same. Teleri could voice as many protests as she desired, but her blood would soak the ground beside theirs.

"The strong protect the weak," Eirian murmured.

Her sister gave a sharp nod. "Such is our duty to the balance."

Igraine's roar was a reminder that the dragon was always watching through Briallen's eyes. She saw and heard everything her rider did. It was hard to imagine what such a bond felt like. Eirian could still feel the chill in the air. Awareness made her skin prickle, but she did not know where Gebael might be lurking. There was a chance that everything she felt was nothing more than a mix of wishful thinking and paranoia. Because if he were there, he would know what Briallen was and might punish his High Priestess when she failed to mention her half-duine sister was a husk maker.

"So, are we going to tell our cities that war with the mad god has come for them?" Teleri finally asked, breaking the silence that had fallen on the group. "Do we tell them to run?"

Slipping into her role was easy and comforting. "I don't see what choice we have. Some might survive if they can find places to hide in small numbers. Considering how many of the Unseelie enjoy eating humans and elves, I can't see the mad god letting everyone be killed. Or at least, the Blood Queen won't deny her people."

Briallen grunted, and Eirian would have sworn she heard amusement in it. "They don't need to. Don't forget they existed for millennia before the gods got bored with only immortal playthings and created mortals. Or do your history lessons conveniently leave off that part?"

"Or maybe we were trying to find a light in the situation?"

"It's better to face the dark with honesty in your heart than false hopes that fade when they run out."

Pinching the bridge of her nose, Teleri sighed. "We have to give our people something to believe in, or they'll succumb to the darkness of the mad god and let the Unseelie feast."

Anger at the gods for their failure to deal with their problems filled Eirian. Lifting her chin, she glared at the shadows, hoping that if Gebael was watching, he felt the rage coursing through her. She wanted to make their creators fear the wrath of their creations. They might have been born from the boredom of immortality, but they had minds of their own, and a strength spun from the fragility of mortal life. If they worked together, throwing everything they had into it, Eirian knew they could bring down the gods.

"We're going to evacuate the cities and bring this war to them," she said, ice dripping from her voice as the dark whispers of her magic laughed in the back of her mind.

Teleri arched a brow, her dark eyes filled with suspicion. "Dare I ask what your plan is?"

"This war is not our fault. All we have done is exist. So, let's deliver it to the ones who started it. If we march to their home, the Unseelie will follow. Let's see how the god of life likes it when it's her precious heir facing a brutal and bloody death at the claws of a goblin."

"You can't be serious!"

"I'm fucking serious. This is it, Teleri. This is the line in the sand that we must cross. What else can we do? If we stay and fight, we will die. Everyone here will die. At least some will survive if we run."

With a twist of her mouth, Briallen stared at Igraine's circling form. "She says to do it."

"Is this really what you think we should do?" The High General shook her head. "Because you're right about there being nothing else we can do except stay and die."

For the first time since news of Kirrama falling reached her, Eirian felt like she was in control of the situation. "Yes, it is. Now, we need to prepare. It's time to ring the bells."

Eighteen

Delyth

The longer they sat in the tower waiting for news, the worse she felt. It was torture not knowing what was going on. From her vantage point on the landing platform of an unused roost, Delyth watched the dragons circling Endara, and prayed everything was fine. She knew it was not, but that did not prevent her from hoping otherwise. Briallen would have returned if everything had been as it should be. Left alone by the soldiers, who preferred to wait at the bottom of the tower, she could not help but consider the possibilities.

Endara and Ensaycal were under attack from the Unseelie. There was no other logical possibility. The wagons had been sneaking people aligned with the mad god into her city, and they would never have known if not for her and Briallen. It left her wondering how many more had rumbled into the cities, a cargo of Unseelie hidden within. Turning her thoughts to the attack on her father's team of crafters, Delyth knew in her gut goblins had slaughtered them. While they had been arguing over what to do when the Unseelie army arrived, they had forgotten to consider the possibility that it was already there, hidden in the shadows.

"Del?"

Amelia's voice broke through her spiralling thoughts, pulling her gaze from the distant city. Twisting around, she stared at the elf, relief rushing through her to summon tears. Startled by the distress on Delyth's face, the warrior rushed across the roost, crashing to her knees to wrap her arms around her. They clung to each other, listening to the distant roar of a dragon. Burying her face in Amelia's neck, she breathed in the comforting scent of leather and eucalyptus. It was easy to pretend their world was not crumbling beneath them when they were together.

"Have you heard anything?" she whispered, unsure if she wanted to know.

"There are Unseelie in the cities. I know it was you and Briallen who realised something was wrong. What you did for our people by trusting your instincts... Del, you might have saved us all."

"I'm glad you think so. Only a couple of the soldiers believed us."

She growled, and the sound seemed so absurd that Delyth had to giggle. The arms holding her tightened as Amelia nipped her ear, which only made her laugh more. Squirming to break free, the young mage shook her head, waving at the door. It did not matter that there was no one there. She suspected their friends were wandering the corridors of the tower, waiting for them. There was no way Amelia had come from Ensaycal to join her without Laryn, Calleth, and Patton. Not that she would complain about their presence. Friends always made stressful situations better.

"I'm sorry." Delyth shrugged sheepishly. "I didn't mean to laugh."

Snorting, Amelia arched a brow. "I won't deny my feelings were hurt."

"Don't be silly, they weren't."

"You laughed because you're tense. How long have you been here without a clue of what was going on? I'd be crawling out of my skin."

The truth of the statement made her sigh. "Well, yes. It's been a while. Though maybe less time than I think. Do you know anything else?"

"Not really. I was in the training yards when the birds arrived with messages from Aunty Teleri. As soon as I heard you were here, I fetched the others, and we argued our way out of Ensaycal. Unfortunately, it took longer than I would have liked, and we still had to walk. The rule banning horses remains. Though I suppose it makes sense. People would know something was wrong if they spotted horses being run to the dragon tower when everyone knows it's not allowed for safety."

Fear seeped through her at the prospect of walking back to Endara. In the tower, Delyth felt safe. She could not put her finger on why, other than her doubt that any Unseelie would be stupid enough to risk being caught in a dragon roost. They would not die, but they would wish they could once a dragon got a hold of them.

Her thoughts flashed back to what Briallen had done. "Amy, I think my aunt might be a husk maker."

Eyes widening, Amelia gasped, a hand shooting up to cover her mouth. "What?"

"When the wagon train passed us, and we suspected something was wrong, there was a dead patch at her feet. I recognised it because I've seen it happen to my mother." Dismay twisted her mouth, and Delyth drew her knees up to her chest. "It makes sense, right? She's a duine, and an Altira. Other than our family, the husk maker power is only found among the daoine because that's who Lord Gebael gave it to."

"It makes sense. But isn't she a bit young to show signs of that power?"

"Maybe. I don't know if being half human would change that."

It was easy to spot the wheels turning in Amelia's mind, and Delyth knew it was a sign of what was to come. They could not kill their enemy. All they could do was slow the Unseelie down while praying to the gods for help. Powers like that of a husk maker would work better than anything else they had, and Briallen would be used as a weapon. So would her mother, which turned her blood cold. She hated the thought of her mother standing on the front line, wielding her destructive powers for as long as she could stand so the rest of them could flee. Biting the inside of her cheek, Delyth wanted to scream at the unfairness of the situation.

"I'm going to lose my mother and aunt in this fight," she mumbled, rubbing her cheeks in a desperate attempt to banish her tears. "They'll be the ones to fall while we hide."

"Del…"

"Will you fight? Am I to face a bleak future without my family or without you? What about Laryn? Calleth? Patton? Are all of you going to abandon me to sacrifice your lives so that I might live? Because I'm as useful in a battle as a rag in a flood. Not that you're much better when the enemy is immortal."

Amelia sighed, shaking her head. "I don't know."

"The enemy is already here. People are dying."

"As long as we breathe, there is always hope."

She did not fight the desire to scream, and her lover recoiled in surprise. Magic swirled at her fingertips, bringing resentment with it. Delyth wished she could turn it into something useful. With the future they faced, she saw no use for her skills when what they really needed was warriors to hold back the enemy long enough for everyone else to escape. Her pretty tricks and intricate wards served no purpose except to drive her away from the ones she loved. Even her mother could fight.

"They're going to come for us, Amy. We'll be hunted across Tir until the death of every Altira and Zarthein satisfies the mad god. She wants to make the other gods suffer. What are we supposed to do?" Delyth did not know whether she wanted an answer.

"We make it as hard as possible. There's bound to be something we can do."

"Like what?"

Head hanging, Amelia did not meet her eyes. "I don't know. We're too young and inexperienced for this, Del. What are we supposed to think of that people like Commander Calea have not?"

"Sometimes youth brings a fresh perspective."

"Maybe. But the Unseelie are ancient. It's not like we can cut their heads off."

Delyth wondered if her mother would summon Death once she was finally free to retreat to her chambers. She had spied on them once, and the memory of his cold eyes often tormented her dreams. For a long time, she had feared he would punish her for spying, but he never had, and she never spoke to Eirian about it. There were some things better left unmentioned. But those memories stirred at the back of her mind, leaving her heart hammering against her ribs at the thought of what the High Priestess would be forced to do and offer to their god in return for the survival of everyone else.

"Can your aunt summon War?"

Choking in surprise, Amelia stretched her legs out and stared at the city. "I don't know, but I imagine so. You said your mother summons Death, so I don't see why Aunty Teleri can't summon War."

"Do you think she has, and she already knows how this fight will go?"

"Well... I mean... I don't know. There are a lot of things kept secret, and what relationship my aunt has with our god is one of those."

Behind them, the door scraped open, and she heard the arguing whispers of their friends. "Do we stay here, or should we head back? I don't know if there's been any news."

Patton was the first one to join them, his hands shoved into the pockets of his coat. "There's food downstairs in the hall if you're hungry. Or not. Are you?"

It felt strange to consider food when her stomach had become a knot of anxiety after watching Briallen climb onto Igraine's back. She had not eaten since breakfast, and it felt so long ago Delyth knew she needed something. The thought of it brought on a wave of nausea.

"I'm too worried to be hungry, but we can go down there and sit with whoever else is waiting," she replied, giving her friend a grateful look. "What do you say, Amy?"

Her dark eyes were filled with something unreadable. "Could we go for a walk?"

"We can ask the soldiers."

"A walk will do us good. Besides, who knows when we'll be able to enjoy one again?"

Extending his hands to them, Patton braced while Delyth hauled herself up. Her joints protested the movement, reminding her how long she had been sitting there. A walk was exactly what she needed to clear her mind of the shadows crowding her thoughts. Once Amelia was on her feet, the man slung an arm over their shoulders, guiding them to the door where Laryn and Calleth waited.

"They want to go for a walk, so let's annoy some soldiers," he said, grinning.

No one argued with the plan, and Delyth ambled along in silence while she listened to them attempting to distract her. It seemed wrong to worry about training schedules, and who was sneaking into whose chambers behind the backs of their commanding officers. Not even Laryn's decision to learn how to fight with sai because she liked Briallen's pair stirred her from her silence. The weight of her thoughts left Delyth with just enough energy to smile faintly and nod in agreement when needed. Every flickering shadow made her nervous, and the watchful gazes of the soldiers they encountered added to her questions. She wanted to shake each of them, demanding to know what they had heard, or if they had received fresh orders.

When they arrived on the bottom floor of the tower, they found a crowd of soldiers standing in the first chamber. There was an uncomfortable energy surrounding them, and far too many hands on weapons for Delyth to be at ease. As soon as they spotted the group on the stairs, the hum of conversation fell silent. Pushing to the front of the group, she hoped her position as daughter of the High Priestess would encourage them to reveal what was going on. Instead, the warriors stepped back, giving them space to move away from the stairs. Halls led to various chambers, including the dining hall and kitchens that were only staffed when dragon riders were in residence. More soldiers stood in them, watching the larger room as though they feared something would send everyone running.

"Has something happened?" she demanded, her voice sharp in the strange silence.

A soldier cleared his throat, glancing at his fellows. "Yes, Lady Delyth. They found a goblin in Endara. It attacked the High Priestess, the High General and Rider Briallen."

Gasping, she grabbed Amelia when the elf shot to her side. "Are they hurt?"

"No, milady, they're fine. Rider Briallen dealt with the goblin."

"Did you hear, Del?" Amelia said, pressing her face to the side of Delyth's head. "They're unharmed. I bet the goblin is in chains and on its way to the temple cells."

Her thoughts churned like the bay during a storm. "How did she deal with it?"

Murmurs rippled across the crowd of soldiers, and the knot of anxiety in Delyth's stomach became an inferno of fear. Her suspicions had been right. Briallen was a husk maker. It was the only way her aunt could have dealt with a goblin attack and survived. Had they said Eirian was responsible, she would not have questioned the explanation. But they had not, and now she needed confirmation.

"I was there," a woman pushed her way through the soldiers to stand in front of Delyth. "And I was sent to warn everyone here about the goblins and the kelpies. Rider Briallen is a husk maker. I saw her in the goblin's grasp, and she sucked the life from the Unseelie bitch."

Amelia huffed with delight. "You were right, Del."

"Thank you. Now, what did you say about kelpies? The bay is warded against water folk entering from the sea. How could—oh." Her dread became a thorny vine wrapped around her spine.

The soldier nodded, eyes wide. "There were no horses found with the wagons, and no reports of any running loose. We're working on the assumption that there are kelpies in the bay."

Patton whistled in disbelief. "Fuck me. Kelpies. Guess we won't be going for a walk."

It had been one thing to suspect the Unseelie had infiltrated her home, but having it confirmed carved out a hollow place in her heart. Closing her eyes, Delyth searched for the strength to stay upright, while Amelia's hold on her tightened. She felt her friends press closer and listened to the soldiers talking. When she opened her eyes again, every shadow became a threat where goblins might lurk. The irrational part of her mind wanted to be somewhere bright, an open space under the sun where no darkness could lay deadly fingers on them. Those ideas were torn to shreds by the voice of logic reminding her nightfall would come, and the goblins in the twin cities would have the freedom to hunt.

"I want to join my mother," she said, squaring her shoulders in determination. "I refuse to cower in this tower, wondering if there are threats waiting in the shadows."

"They're not going to let you do that," Laryn replied.

Pulling a face, Patton agreed. "Orders are to keep you here for now. So, let's wait and see what happens. Our illustrious leaders are likely devising a plan as we speak."

"To do what? Die?" Amelia grunted, sharing a look with Delyth.

Chewing the inside of her cheek again, the mage tasted blood. "No, I'd wager a purse of silver that my mother is going to give the order to leave. She won't want to wait for the Unseelie to come to us, especially if they're here already. By nightfall, the bells will ring across Endara and Ensaycal, and the heralds will be screaming for everyone to evacuate."

Nineteen

Teleri

Part of her remained on the street in Endara. Which part was hard to figure out when her thoughts had become a mess. All Teleri could be certain of was that ruin might descend upon them at any moment, and there was absolutely nothing she could do to prevent it. Eirian had decided the future of their people while they stood in the shadows of an empty building, with soldiers, priests, and common folk watching on. She suspected the part left behind was her willingness to fight for her home, but a voice reminded her that leaving was fighting. It was the people who made the cities, not the buildings. All that mattered was preserving the lives of the humans and elves who lived there.

Anticipation crept down her spine at the knowledge the bells would soon echo over Ensaycal and Endara. Heralds would march from the temples, their hands grasping letters to be read to everyone who would listen. There would be many who would refuse to leave, and Teleri had decided they would not force people to go. They would be honest with their citizens, informing them of the Unseelie in their midst and the truth of the war coming for them. Anyone who remained in their home would be allowed to stay. She hoped that if the enemy knew the two bloodlines had fled, they would leave the hollowed-out shell of a nation alone. It was unlikely, and the tactician side of Teleri knew the Unseelie would swarm the cities to feast upon the defenceless who remained.

Commander Calea had delivered her to the false safety of her home in the middle of Ensaycal. Where the sight of dragons circling her city had once been reassuring, Teleri saw only destruction. The memory of what Briallen had done to her goblin assailant left a bitter taste at the back of her throat. She had never imagined the possibility that she would have to say goodbye to Eirian and her sister on a battlefield. Age was supposed to rob her of another Altira mage. But while the two husk makers would stand between her people and the Unseelie, she would be the one leading them away. It hurt. As the heir to War himself, Teleri wanted to argue that it should be her battling the enemy, but they were immortal, and there was nothing she could do to stop them.

"Mother?"

Shoulders slumping, Teleri turned from the window to smile sadly at her son. "It's time, my love. I've written what I want the heralds to say, and I'd like you to deliver it to the clerks to be copied. When that's done, we can make our way to the central bell tower. As the High General, I will ring the first one."

Yestin hesitated; a flash of the boy he had been flitting across his face. "You don't need to."

"Yes, I do. It is my duty to ring the first bell to warn my people that destruction has come to drag us to the darkest depths of the other side. They may not know it was me, but I will."

"Let me do it."

"No, come with me so you may understand the cost." She wondered if Eirian was preparing to do the same, or if she would let others pull the chain of the massive bell housed within the tallest tower of the temple. "Then we'll return home to prepare our family."

"Is there no other option?" Dipping his gaze, Yestin could not hide the waver in his voice.

She wanted to pull her firstborn into her arms and whisper promises to always protect him. Pressing her lips together, Teleri forced herself to stand tall, her hand going to the cerapter horn hilt of her sword. It was comforting to rub her thumb over the grooves, and to remember the fight the beast had given her. Unlike the Unseelie, the vicious winged horses with their almost unbreakable horns were mortal, and it had been a battle she could win. In the back of her thoughts, a voice suggested she ask Eirian to beg Death to let her wield Eclipse. As War's heir, she could bear the sword capable of killing the First People.

"I need to send Eirian a letter."

He looked surprised, gaze darting to her desk. "Can I write it for you?"

"It won't take long. I'll do it while you run this to the clerks."

The paper in her hand felt like a boulder weighing her down, but Teleri held it out to him. She caught the tremble of Yestin's fingers as he plucked the letter from her grasp. Striding to her desk, the High General refused to watch the emotions wage war in her son's expression as he read what she had written. If the twin cities were destined to fall, she intended for her last message to Ensaycal to convey her full understanding of the situation. Her need for revenge wanted the mad god to learn what they planned. A small part of Teleri hoped it would encourage the twisted god to turn her focus to the distant daoine land of Telmia, where Vartan Malfaer, heir to Life, ruled.

"Are you sure this is wise?" he murmured.

"No, I'm not. But I hope it might distract the Unseelie, redirecting them to someone who will force the gods into action. Why should we endure Thought's hatred?"

"You're talking about dragging the Great Queen into the fight."

"Indeed."

Crossing the space between them, Yestin grabbed her arm, a desperate plea in his dark eyes begging her to reconsider the plan. "This is insanity, Mother. She's as likely to kill you as she is to allow us to march the populations of Ensaycal and Endara to Telmia's doors."

A slow smile tugged at the corners of her lips. "I'd like to see her try. War might side with her for now, but he will not tolerate his wife killing his heir. Let us not forget that he is also the god of peace. We will take their war to them and make them listen!"

"You'll know if I change this."

"Do you doubt me?"

"No. I know better than to doubt you, High General. If this is what you command me to deliver to the clerks for the heralds to announce, then I will do it. But I do it under duress."

She gave his words a sharp nod, and Yestin released his hold on her arm. Saying nothing else, the warrior marched from the office in defeat. A pang of regret stabbed her heart, confirming to Teleri it was unlikely her son would forgive her for trying to force the hand of the gods. Even though it was Eirian's idea, her part was making it public knowledge. There was a small shred of hope screaming from the pit of her emotions that maybe fewer people would choose to remain in the cities if they knew the goal was to march across the lands to Telmia. It was hope that had her reaching for a quill to write her message.

Ask your lord if he would curse me with Eclipse.

Writing the line was agony. No sane person wanted to wield one of the two blades forged by the rage of Death and the fires of Chaos. There was nothing but pity in her heart for the Executioner, whose only fault had been to be the first mortal created by the gods. It was a marvel she had not lost all threads of sanity she possessed. Especially after the events of the Sundering, when the mad god had taken the sword from the Executioner and used it to kill the Ravens and danann who stood by her side. Too many good people had died, and it had caused the rift between the gods to widen irreparably.

Unlike the Executioner, her life had not been bound to the blade. If Death granted her request, Teleri knew she would die by the time her quest was done. Eclipse would claim her blood and her mind, taking a drop for every immortal life it ended. That was the price she was willing to pay to save her people. But first, she needed Eirian to make the request of her god, and for him not to take offence at it. If he did, she hoped Lord Gebael would not strike her down for daring to ask to be allowed to use his sword in battle against the people they had created it to kill. As she rolled the slip of paper, Teleri questioned her wisdom in following through with her idea.

Twirling it between her fingers, she headed for the door. If Yestin returned and she was not in her office, he would make his way to the dovecote to find her. She doubted he would forget she had mentioned sending a message to Eirian. There were multiple dovecotes built onto the terraces of the temple, serving the army officials. Since the destination for her letter was in Endara, she made her way to the nearest one, trusting the keepers would have birds trained to go to Death's temple on hand.

From the fearful stares of the people she passed in the halls, Teleri surmised word of the day's events was spreading. No one dared stop her. There were no warm greetings, only stiff salutes. It bothered her, feeding the sense of unease that had long since taken hold. Fading light filtered in through glass windows framed by the elegant latticework that was so predominant throughout the cities. The shadows it left on the ground were complex swirls that melded into each other, reminding the High General of power sharing. She had done it many times over the years with each Altira mage to pass through her life, and every time it grew more painful.

Halting outside the door to the dovecote, she watched the shadows shift across the marbled floor. Ideas twisted through her thoughts, summoning questions Teleri had no answers for. She pondered them, wondering if Commander Calea or the dragons might have the solutions she needed. It seemed foolish to give voice to the seemingly impossible idea that there might be a way for Eirian and Briallen to share their husk maker abilities with others. The prospect that they could grant the ability to mages linked with them through power sharing felt too much like hope.

Teleri pushed the thoughts aside, determined not to get distracted from the things she knew she could do. There was no point in mulling over what-ifs and maybes. Part of her argued that what she was doing by sending a request to Eirian to ask Death to borrow his sword was a waste of time. It did not matter if it was, but not doing it was letting a possibility slip through her fingers. Even if that possibility had the tiniest sliver of a chance of coming to fruition. As her husband liked to say, nothing ventured, nothing gained. In her tight grasp, the brief letter to Eirian felt like the slightest ray of light on a dark day.

"High General, what can I do for you?" the pigeon keeper spoke without looking away from the bird she was examining. "It's getting late, so I hope you don't have an urgent message to send."

"Just one for the High Priestess."

The woman glanced at the sky, cooing at her pigeons. "There's enough light."

Extending her hand, Teleri offered the rolled-up paper. "Have you heard the news?"

"My life is dedicated to dealing in news. But I suppose you mean the plan to evacuate the cities and run away from the Unseelie army. Yes, I've been informed."

Watching her secure the letter in a tube to attach to the leg of a bird, Teleri did not know what to think about her tone. There was a disinterested edge to it that seemed like the keeper was dismissing the news. But in the fading light, she saw a deep sadness in the pale blue eyes of the elven woman.

"What will you do with all your birds?"

"Bring them with me. They're very intelligent creatures, though many do not see it." She held out a hand, whistling a tune to summon a bird. "This is my fastest flyer."

For a moment, she was struck with the urge to change her mind. All it would take was a word, and the keeper would stop. As though she sensed the High General's hesitation, the woman looked at her, and Teleri opened her mouth to utter the command. In the corner of her vision, she saw the shadows, a reminder of the goblins hiding in her city. Snapping her jaw shut, she nodded her confirmation to go ahead. Whatever the other woman thought about the situation remained unspoken, her eyes narrowing as she murmured senseless words to her pigeon while nimble fingers secured thin leather threads.

"I knew you'd be here, Mother," Yestin said, joining her on the terrace. "The clerks have the announcement and are copying it as fast as they can for the heralds."

"Good. We'll take the long way. People will want to know why the bells are ringing, and if we do it before the heralds can get into position, it might cause problems."

If the conversation bothered the keeper, she displayed no signs of it. As soon as the tube was secure, the pigeon was given a command. Watching the blue-grey bird take off, Teleri felt empty. She did not want to think about what might happen if it never made it to Eirian. Things did not depend upon it doing so, and she intended to discuss it with the High Priestess when they saw each other the next day. But at the back of her mind, she knew there was a chance they might not see dawn. There was nothing they could do to keep the goblins from their chambers, and she might die before she made it to the bell tower. That prospect summoned her magic, making Yestin stiffen in alarm beside her.

"Mother?"

Pursing her lips, Teleri did not reassure him. "I've never felt so small."

"What do you mean?"

A soft sigh came from the keeper. "There's nothing quite like the threat of the Unseelie waiting in the shadows to kill you to make you realise how ineffective you are. How delicate mortality is."

"Indeed," she replied, nodding slowly. "I can't help but recognise my power means nothing."

"You've always been a fair High General, Lady Zarthein. It will be remembered."

"Will it? I'm not so sure. If... when we survive this, I suspect we'll find ourselves a long way from here, and what lives we led will cease to matter. The gods will decide our future."

There was something wistful yet knowing in the faint smile directed her way. Uncomfortable with the conversation, Yestin shuffled, fingers twitching with an obvious need to be active. He was better suited for action, and Teleri knew he was ill at ease when dealing with the administrative side of his job. Bobbing her head to the keeper, she turned and strode back into the building with her son hurrying along behind her. With few people in the hallways, the place felt bereft of the thrumming energy that accompanied them. It was hardly a surprise there were few around. The High General hoped that everyone who could be at home was with their loved ones. Perhaps they would be safe there for the time being, and it would only be her and Eirian's families in danger.

"Would you answer one question?" Yestin's voice was low, betraying his grief.

"I always do if I'm free to."

"Will you lead our people in this, or will you fight alongside the High Priestess?"

Closing her eyes, Teleri tried to gather her thoughts in the correct manner to answer him. "There is nothing I can do to fight the Unseelie, so I will be the one leading our people. But if there was something I could do, then it would be my duty to do it, and I never shy away from doing what is necessary."

His arms came around her in an awkward hug. "I don't want to face this without you, Ma. You're the strongest person I know, and I don't mean your magic. Our people are fortunate to have you."

"Whatever happens, Yestin, I need you to know I love you and your siblings. All of you are so important to me, even if I'm not always the best mother. No parent is perfect, and I pray one day you'll understand the choices I make have always been me trying."

"And that's what matters. There are plenty out there who don't try. You always do."

Teleri chuckled sadly. "Yes, I'm very trying."

"That's not what I meant."

"Perhaps, but it's true. Now, shall we take an evening stroll to the bell tower? Your company would be very much appreciated."

Linking his arm through hers, Yestin smiled grimly. "We're in this together, Ma."

Twenty

Briallen

Briallen covered her ears, trembling at the sound of bells echoing across the city. They had tolled every hour since the announcement went out, and they were wearing her down. With Eirian's home close to the largest bell tower in Endara, it felt like she could not escape. When they finally stopped, her head ached from the tension, and the dreaded voice at the back of her mind reminded the rider they would resume their ringing in an hour. There was no peace in the city, the thrum of fear carrying through the air in a way that set her magic on edge. Her skin crawled as though thousands of ants were covering it, robbing her of any chance of sleeping.

Not that she could have slept if she had wanted to. Memories of what had happened kept repeating through her mind, making Briallen question if there had been other options. Anything that had not involved her tapping into the husk maker power lurking in her veins. Every time she looked at Eirian, she saw the fear that flashed through her eyes. She had not mentioned it, but Briallen knew her sister harboured concerns for her safety that had nothing to do with the oncoming conflict with the Unseelie. There was only one person who could make the stoic High Priestess experience fear because of a power, and that was the god of death.

Massaging the back of her skull, Briallen sat on the balcony of her bedroom, staring at the city. She wanted to shove her belongings in her bag and trudge across Endara to return to the tower where Igraine slept.

The dragons were taking it in turns to watch over the two cities, doing their best to rest when it was not their shift. None of them were sure what the creatures could do about the Unseelie inside the walls already, but at least they could watch for approaching forces. They patrolled alone, leaving their riders behind so they could be of help to Eirian and Teleri. Part of Briallen wished she were as useful as the others, but her sister had barked orders at her to return to the house to eat and sleep. After what she had done, the duine supposed she should have been exhausted, but she felt too full of energy.

Rearranging her legs before she got pins and needles, Briallen contemplated leaving the house to wander the city. On any other visit, she would have headed for a nearby tavern where she knew there were always decent musicians, and the alcohol was never watered down. But with the bells tolling, and the announcement the city was to evacuate, she doubted they would be open. Or maybe they would be so people could have one last night to drink with strangers and commiserate over a tankard of ale. It was impossible to know without going, and Briallen feared the disappointment she would feel if she got there, and it was closed. If she remained on the balcony, she could pretend it was open, and she was missing out on a lively performance where she might pick up a pretty woman to take to bed.

It was difficult to pretend when her skin crept, and her magic twisted against her hold, demanding to be let loose. There was a hunger gnawing at her stomach that was not from lack of food. Even with everything that had happened, and the sound of the bells, Briallen had sat and eaten a decent meal. She possessed magic, and it had been drummed into her to always eat, no matter how she felt, because if she did not provide the power with enough fuel, it would eat away at her body to get what it needed. The more powerful the magic, the more fuel it needed. Drawing energy from an immortal was no small thing, and though it had not left her hungry, she refused to risk the consequences.

Lifting her gaze to the sky, Briallen decided the stars had lost their shine. They were cold and distant, a hopeless glitter on a suffocating blanket of deepest blue. It felt like she could drown in the sky if given a chance. Thoughts clattered around in her mind, each fighting to become the one she focused on. Somewhere among them, the whisper of Igraine's snores confirmed the dragon was not witnessing her spiral of anxiety. As much as she loved being a rider and having the bond, sometimes she desperately needed to be alone. Privacy was a privilege when one shared their mind with a mostly immortal beast who liked to know everything that was going on.

Briallen rolled over onto her knees, intending to sit with her back against the wall. Crawling across the balcony, she halted halfway to watch the shadows thicken, the flickering light of the lanterns hanging from their hooks giving the darkness a depth she should have been frightened of. Familiar boots appeared in front of her, the shadows twisting around them like an eager cat. Tilting her head back, Briallen stared up at Tristan's bemused smirk, and felt the chill brush of his power creeping across her skin. There was something in his green gaze that made her freeze, breath catching in her throat.

"Now this is an interesting development, Bri," he murmured, smirk fading as he leaned down to cup her chin. "I wasn't expecting to find you already on your knees."

Her eyes widened in confusion. "What?"

The shadows curled around her, and Tristan crouched to bring himself closer. "All I've thought about since I saw you in the claws of that Unseelie bitch is getting you alone, so I could finally tell you the truth. I always thought we had time, but this war will not end well."

"What truth, Tris? I don't understand."

"I'm in love with you, Bri. You are the flame that guides me home."

Stunned, Briallen blinked. She could not respond, her voice trapped in a throat that refused to work. All the air in her lungs had been sucked away, and it felt like her heart was trying to beat its way out through her ribs. Where his fingers held her chin, the slight prick of claws pressed into her skin, sending a shiver down her spine. It was impossible to look away from the deep green of his eyes even as Tristan drew her face towards his, their lips meeting in a gentle kiss that swallowed her surprised gasp.

He broke the kiss to whisper, "You're mine, Briallen Altira. You always have been. You just didn't see it. I can't keep going without you knowing how much I love you."

"Tris..."

Dropping to his knees, Tristan shifted to cradle her face, the tips of his claws scratching through her hair. The shadows heeded his call, tugging Briallen forward when she remained frozen in place. When she tumbled down onto her elbows, his hold tightened, keeping her steady so she could lift herself up. Resting her hands on his thighs, she did her best to avoid his stare, making him chuckle. Unable to resist snapping her gaze to his, she swallowed nervously at the intensity directed her way. What Tristan had said fed the confusion in her heart that only stirred when she thought about her feelings for him.

"If I could take you away to somewhere the Unseelie would never find us, I would, Bri. But I know you'd never be happy to run when you can fight to save the ones you love."

"Why?"

Resting his forehead against hers, he sighed. "Because I know the chances of your surviving this war are low, and I refuse to watch you die in battle without speaking my truth."

Tears welled in her eyes at the thought of Tristan being condemned to walk Tir without the people who had filled his life with love and happiness. The reminder of his immortality was a kick in the guts that left her gasping. Flicking a glance at the silhouette of Endara bathed in darkness, and the empty silence between the ringing of the bells, Briallen wondered if Calea and the other Seelie would embrace Tristan once her father was gone. When the Unseelie came for the dragon riders, they would kill everyone they could, swarming through the halls of her home without hesitation. Her imagination presented the idea of Tristan in chains, being dragged back to the Spire to face the wrath of the goblin queen, and the tears broke free, making him jerk back in surprise.

"Why are you crying, Bri?" His thumbs brushed over her cheeks, catching the tears.

"You must run, Tris. They can't take you back. I know the stories about Queen Calista, and what she'll do to you. Ysgarlad will take you somewhere to hide."

Brows furrowed, he opened and closed his mouth, unable to form a response. Digging her fingers into his thighs, Briallen lurched forward to kiss him. She would have missed his mouth if he had not caught her, claws tangling in the mess of her hair. Pulling her head back slightly, Tristan shifted his other hand to her chin, holding it so he could meet her lips without fear of knocking their faces together painfully. Unlike the first one, there was no gentleness in his kiss, only a desperate hunger that made her feel like he would devour her if she did not match it. The shadows slithered over Briallen, stroking her skin as though they were extensions of his fingers. It sparked her desire, and she moaned into the kiss when Tristan's teeth grazed her bottom lip.

"Gods, you smell delicious, Bri." He rubbed his nose against her cheek and made a noise like purring that had her clenching with need. "I meant it when I said you're mine. Until this life rips you from me, I have no intention of letting anyone else have you."

Whimpering when his teeth found her earlobe, Briallen grabbed his shirt, bunching the fabric in her hand. "Please Tris. Promise you'll leave before the fighting begins."

"No, I'm never going to leave while you still breathe. Whatever the Blood Queen does to me will pale compared to the pain of not being by your side for the rest of time."

Carefully releasing her, Tristan pried her fingers from his shirt before standing. Gazing up at him, Briallen did not know what she wanted to say. Part of her was terrified it was a mistake if she let him have what he desired, but a louder voice screamed he was right. They did not have years for her to decide if she loved him as more than a friend, and she did not want to die with that regret in her heart.

"I don't know if I love you like that, Tris, but you're right about this war. Maybe we could have had years to explore our feelings, and maybe in two hundred years I'd have realised I love you. We'll probably never know. Not unless the gods decide to end this without costing us mortals our lives. But I refuse to die without knowing how it feels to be yours."

Twisting into a position that made it easier to stand, Briallen grumbled when the shadows he commanded curled around her arms and legs. They did not actively hinder her attempts, but the feathery touch made her skin twitch. When she finally made it to her feet, she shot Tristan a disgruntled look. His answering smirk was too smug, and it became gloating when the tug of his magic pulled her towards him. Stumbling into his arms, Briallen smacked a hand to his chest, only to yelp when he picked her up, and carried her into the chamber where the light of a single lantern bathed the bed in darkness.

He laid her down, brushing his lips over her forehead. "Don't move."

"Why?"

Shadows entwined her wrists, slipping through her fingers like formless silk to drag her arms above her head. Tristan reached for her leg, lifting it so he could slide her loose-fitting trousers up to expose her ankles. When he trailed kisses along the inside of her leg, Briallen gave thanks she had not bothered to put her boots back on after her bath. Turning his attention to the other leg, he repeated the action, his smug smirk returning at the sight of her squirming. Every touch of his lips sent sparks through her, and she yanked at the shadows holding her arms in place. It felt like Tristan intended to torture her.

"Tris," she whined, attempting to extract her leg from his hold.

Nipping her leg, Tristan held tight, the prick of his claws warning her to behave. "Yes, my flame?"

"Would you stop playing and fuck me?"

"I intend to worship you, to commit every part of your body to memory, and to do so, I must take my time. So be a good girl for me, Briallen, and I promise you'll enjoy it."

Biting her bottom lip, she questioned her ability to do as he asked. Lowering her leg to the bed, Tristan stepped back, a flick of his hand returning the creeping shadows to her body. Their cool brushes against her warm skin made it challenging to pay attention to what he was doing. Hearing muffled thumps, Briallen suspected he had removed his boots and attempted to wrest her focus from where it was happily tangled up in shadowy touches. Watching him slowly unbuckle his belt, she whimpered when a tendril of magic found her nipple. His lips curled in delight at her struggles.

"Relax and let me take care of you."

She wanted to do what he asked, but did not know how. Every other time she had taken a lover, Briallen had been the one in command, and to surrender control, even to the person she trusted most in her life, felt like giving up a piece of herself. Pulling his tunic over his head, Tristan dropped it on the floor beside his trousers before pressing a knee into the bed between her legs. The shadows tightened, keeping her in place while his hands trailed across her.

"You're so beautiful, Bri. Seeing you at my mercy, and desperate for my touch, is something I've dreamed about for so long." His fingers found the buttons of her trousers, releasing them so he could slide the light material down her legs. "I wish you could see yourself the way I do."

Unable to trust herself to speak, Briallen closed her eyes, thoughts chasing after the scratch of his claws. One ran along the arch of her foot, making her whimper and try to yank free. His chuckle was a warm caress preceding the kisses he trailed up her leg. Hands found the hem of her shirt, pushing it up to expose her breasts to his attention. Moving with it, Tristan settled between her thighs, and released his shadows long enough to toss the garment aside. Before Briallen could make use of her freedom, his lips met hers, and she matched his hunger with her own. The shadows returned, wrapping their icy tendrils around her wrists and ankles to splay her out beneath him exactly how he wanted.

Breaking away from her mouth, Tristan dotted kisses down her throat. "I had so many plans, but I ache to be buried in you while you come undone with my name on your lips."

"Please, Tris."

He continued downwards until his sharp teeth found her left nipple, drawing it into his mouth. Briallen moaned as she arched her back, pushing her breasts into his face, and Tristan slipped a hand between her legs to seek her cunt. The slick of her arousal allowed two of his fingers to slide in easily while his thumb circled her clit. Careful to keep his claws in, the goblin stroked the sensitive spot inside her, and Briallen bucked her hips, desperate for more. When he switched to her right breast, he added a third finger, the barest tips of the deadly weapons slipping free.

"Oh, fuck," she cried, grinding into his hand. "Tristan."

Feeling her walls clenching, he sheathed his claws and pulled his fingers out. Letting Briallen's breast pop free of his mouth, Tristan smirked at the desperate surprise on her face when she realised he intended to deny her pleasure. A shadow slithered around her throat while he shuffled into position over her. Wrapping a hand around his cock, he rubbed the head against her entrance, chuckling when she wriggled against it enticingly. Staring at him pleadingly, Briallen held her breath, waiting for him to push into her. She was trapped on the edge of a cliff, entirely dependent on Tristan to deliver her to the other side.

"Breathe, my flame," he murmured, kissing the sensitive spot in front of her ear.

Taking it slowly to give Briallen time to adjust, he released the shadows, letting her move her limbs again. She buried a hand in his hair, the other grabbing his arse as he filled her completely. Moaning at the stretch, her breath hitched when he withdrew, the ridges of his cock rubbing against a spot inside her that had pleasure coiling tightly, waiting to snap. Tristan nipped his way down her neck until he found a spot on her shoulder that clothes usually covered. Driving back into her to the hilt, he bit her hard enough to draw blood, and Briallen felt the coil snap. Pleasure burned through her with each stroke of his cock, making her toes curl. The pressure of his teeth and the lap of his tongue seemed to match his thrusts. Her throat felt hoarse, and she realised she had been screaming his name.

Tearing his mouth from her shoulder, Tristan kissed her hungrily as his climax hit. Swallowing her moans, he stilled, enjoying the feeling of being buried inside the woman he had loved for so long. Her hand was tangled in his hair, and Briallen felt completely relaxed in his embrace. Lifting his face from hers, the goblin gazed at her adoringly, and she managed a tired smile. The energy that had kept her from relaxing earlier was gone, leaving her wondering if she would melt into the bed if he let go. Propping himself up on one arm, Tristan brushed stray strands of hair out of her eyes before kissing her again.

"I love you."

"Tris," she mumbled.

"No, my flame, don't. Let me have hope."

"I was going to say I'd like to do that again."

Grinning, Tristan kissed the tip of her nose. "Good, because you're mine."

Twenty-one

Eirian

"What documents do you want packed?"

Eirian stared at Joshua, mouth stuck in a slightly open position. Her voice abandoned her, leaving her floundering as they threw more questions her way. Eyes darting around her office in disbelief, she wondered if any of the documents held enough importance to be packed up so they could occupy the precious little space they had in the wagons. Thoughts turning to the dozens of libraries in the twin cities, her heart plummeted. So much information would be left behind, and the High Priestess grieved at that fact. If they survived and found themselves forced to make a new home, the things left behind would be irreplaceable. History would be lost, never to be recovered.

Those thoughts turned her mind to the great city of artisans that had already fallen to the Unseelie. It was heartbreaking to know how completely the mad god planned to wipe the existence of mortals from the face of Tir. Worse, because art and knowledge were not exclusive. Losing those things was detrimental to everyone. Shifting her gaze to the open window, Eirian listened to the clang of the bells, and watched a dragon circling Endara. All she could do was hope the Unseelie army would leave the cities intact with most of the people gone. Someone would see the value of what they left behind.

"Eirian?" He placed a hand on her arm in concern. "What's wrong, my High Priestess?"

"I can't wrap my mind around how much we're going to lose. Why should any of the documents in this office go with us when countless books of history are being left behind? These cities are home to thousands of years of knowledge, and we're walking away from them so we can survive."

Grimacing, Joshua nodded. "The librarians are doing their best to select the most important ones. If you want to give the space to them, no one will argue. You're right. There are a lot of documents in the temple and the council records that won't have a purpose once we leave."

"Yes, I think we should. Because maybe we'll get to return, or maybe the survivors will be forced to make a new home, and those books will give them something to start with. Especially anything dedicated to building. We should never forget where we came from, so history books are also important."

"I'll give the orders then."

Rubbing the back of her hand over her mouth, Eirian met his worried stare. "Have you heard from my husband? He's overseeing the various crafting guilds in their preparations, as well as the hurried construction of as many wagons as we have the materials on hand to make."

"No, Eirian, I haven't. I'm sure he's fine."

"You weren't there, Joshua. A goblin threatened my sister, and there's more of them in my city, but I can't do anything about it. I need you to promise me you'll lead our people away from here in my place. The High General has already assured me she will, but I need you to do the same."

He recoiled in horror, and off to the side, a pair of priests gasped. "You're not coming?"

"Of course I am... but if I have to fight the Unseelie to buy everyone else the chance to get away, I won't hesitate. This is my responsibility, old friend. I'm the Altira."

"I can't imagine this life without you in it, Eirian."

Lifting a hand to his cheek, she gave him a sad smile. "I'd rather not imagine it either, but there are worse things to imagine than my death. If fighting until my last breath will save the lives of innocents, then it is a fate I will gladly face. Unfortunately, I fear my sister will be with me."

"Did you have any idea she would be a husk maker?"

"No," she replied, shaking her head in regret. "Maybe if I had, I would've refused to send for her. Briallen is older than me, but she is so young because of her duine blood. She should have the years to grow into her powers, to discover what her animal form is, to find love and start a family."

"The daoine can't escape this war any more than we can."

A priest cleared her throat, drawing Eirian's attention to where she stood with an armful of books. "So, High Priestess, are we packing any of this?"

"No, leave it. None of it is important. The things in this room won't help our people rebuild." Eirian swept her gaze over the shelves laden with ageing tomes, and various artefacts from years long gone. "Let them remain here in case the chance comes to return. There is always hope that the gods will end this war between themselves, and save countless mortals from suffering."

Clasping his hands behind his back, Joshua hated the weight that had seemed to age her overnight. "We should count ourselves lucky if death is our fate. There are worse things waiting for us in the hands of the Unseelie. The Blood Queen won't kill everyone and rob her people of a source of entertainment."

Hearing a priest gulp, Eirian scowled at her assistant, but he did not look guilty. She knew he was right about what the queen of the goblins would have planned. Mortals were the preferred prey for those who had become Unseelie. They would not kill everyone without hesitation; they would capture as many as they could, and select those to be dragged back to the Spire and other cities, where they would be kept captive and forced to breed like livestock. It fed her anger at the gods, and Eirian wished to scream at the ones who created such misery.

"All I can say is if it looks like everything is lost, kill yourselves. Better to stab your own heart than have a goblin lay claim to your flesh." Crossing to the window, Eirian wished to be left alone. "Go help pack essentials. As much food and medical supplies as possible. Things that we will need more than worthless records of a temple soon to be lost to memory."

Joshua made no effort to move while the other priests scurried from the chamber. "Do you want to break down? I'm here if you do, and I understand completely."

"Do you?"

"Yes. I had a moment last night where I just screamed at the walls of my bedchamber."

The thought of her stalwart companion losing his temper brought an amused smile to her lips. "So did I. It's not weakness to break down over situations like this. Better to let it out than let it build."

He crossed the room to stand beside her at the window, staring out at the only place they had ever called home. It was easy to see how badly it hurt to know they would soon walk away and leave it all behind them. The bells would continue to ring until the next day, after which the bulk of the evacuation would begin. Wisdom suggested they should be leaving already, and Eirian did not need to ask the guards on the city gates to know people were doing just that. For most, the day would be spent picking apart their homes and their belongings to take only the barest essentials with them. Neighbours would share what resources they could, though no doubt the greedy amongst them would hoard what they could. Others would bid tearful farewells to those who had decided to remain despite the threat to their lives.

Tracing the line of buildings with her eyes, Eirian tried to commit all of it to memory. She did not know how far she would make it, but she hoped luck would be on her side and she would remain with her people until they reached the distant lands that were their destination. Part of her hope stemmed from sheer hatred for the situation the gods had pushed them into. She wanted to be there when the god of life was forced to intervene to protect her precious heir. It was vindictive, and if things had been different, Eirian would have argued with herself over it being cruel to drag others into the war, but she found she no longer cared. If the gods were determined to ignore their suffering, then she would spread it until they could no longer sit to the side, blind to the pain their creations were enduring.

"This will work," she said quietly, mouth set in a firm line. "I know it will."

Head cocked, Joshua shrugged. "I don't know, Eirian, but I hope you're right. It's better than lying down to take it without a fight. The people will understand. We all know what the Unseelie are."

"It's unfair that we cannot truly fight back. When the gods got bored, they should have made them mortal instead of making new toys. The divide between us cannot be repaired while the playing field is not level. I don't care about the differences in lifespan, just the ability to stab them in the heart and watch them die. Look at the daoine! They don't die of ageing, but they can be killed."

Ice trailed down her spine, and Eirian's breath caught in her throat. She knew what the feeling meant. Biting her lip, she gathered her composure and gave Joshua a sad look. Convincing him to leave quickly would be difficult at the best of times, but she hoped he would believe her need for some alone time.

"Could you let the rest know I don't want them to waste precious space with temple records?"

"Of course," he replied, arching a brow. "Do you need anything else?"

Scratching her cheek, Eirian shook her head. "I need some quiet time to think before privacy becomes a thing of the past. You know what I mean. It'll be hard to snatch a moment once we leave tomorrow."

Bowing slightly, Joshua gave her a pitying look. "I understand. I'll return in an hour to check on you and give you any updates on progress. Enjoy a nice cup of tea, Eirian."

The tendrils of cold wrapped themselves around her limbs, and she watched the priest depart the chamber. Considering the tired ache of her body, the High Priestess lifted her chin higher and decided not to drop to her knees. If Death dared strike her down for not cowering in his presence, then she would embrace her end with the defiance she felt. He emerged from the shadows, icy gaze studying his heir. Eirian looked at him once before pointedly turning her back on the god to stare at the city. Chuckling, Gebael wandered to her desk, running his fingers over the stacks of abandoned paper.

"You're doing the right thing, Eirian."

Thankful her back was to him so he could not see her rapid blinking, the High Priestess took her time to respond. "I'd thank you, my lord, but considering the lack of options available to me..."

Gebael grunted in agreement. "I did my best to convince Shianeni to see reason."

"Don't you dare take credit for my idea."

"Never. My plan was to convince Vartan to come to you. I thought if he got it into his mind to ride to the rescue of his fellow heirs, it would force my wife to act. Your idea has a far better outcome."

She finally turned to gaze at him in amazement. "It does?"

"Yes. I see less death on your path than I do on others. There are so many deaths to come that they have clouded my mind as to the best course of action. All I could do was wait for something to change." Smiling sadly, he rubbed his forehead. "I even thought about taking Eclipse and slaughtering the Unseelie myself, but I saw nothing but destruction for Tir if I walked that path."

"Speaking of Eclipse..." Eirian turned her thoughts to the brief message she had received from Teleri. "I have a request to make on Teleri's behalf. She humbly asks to be allowed to wield the sword in battle should we face the Unseelie. While I can slow them down, she cannot do anything."

It felt like time froze as Gebael stared at her, as unblinking as a statue. His dark brown hair was dishevelled, and it surprised her to spot ink stains hidden beneath the slight curls. They looked as though he had been rubbing his head without regard for the ink on his fingers. Eirian tried to imagine him hunched over a desk working on a report into the wee hours of the morning and had to bite back a laugh.

"No," he said, straightening. "Not Teleri. It would destroy her, and we need her alive."

"I shall let her know."

Returning to her vigil over the city, the feeling of his arms slipping around her waist came as a surprise. Lips brushed over her ear, the press of Gebael's nose against her cheek becoming a chilling presence. He pulled her body against his, but did nothing else. Closing her eyes, the High Priestess wished the touch of her god stirred the excitement she had grown accustomed to over the years. With war looming over her people, she could not find it in herself to feel pleasure in his embrace.

"You won't be facing the Unseelie alone, my darling."

For a moment, hope bloomed in her, but Eirian squashed it down like a dandelion beneath her heel. "Are you planning to walk with your people, guarding our backs against your wife's army?"

"Yes, and I won't be alone. You're right to be angry with us. We have let our people down. Even if Shianeni refuses to do anything about Annawyn, I will not stand idly by. Doing so will condemn Tir back to the barren rock it was when we fell from the stars in desperation for something new."

Wriggling out of his grasp enough to turn to face him, she raised a brow expectantly. "That's why you won't let Teleri use Eclipse. You intend to wield the blade yourself."

"Indeed. Though if I were to let another use it, the only person in this city capable of surviving is your sister. I know what Briallen is; I always have done. You've often feared what I would do to her, but if I hadn't wanted her to exist, she would never have been born."

"Briallen could wield Eclipse?"

Gebael brought his hands to her cheeks. "Don't tell her anything I said. Now kiss me."

Some of her fears melted away like ice in the summer. Tilting her head back, Eirian welcomed his lips against hers. If letting him take his pleasure from her helped to ensure he would remain to fight, she would be the dutiful High Priestess she had always been. His hands gathered the skirts of her robe, bunching them up around her waist so he could lift her to straddle his hips. Wrapping her arms around his neck, Eirian clung to the god, meeting his gaze to find the desire burning in them.

"I am yours, my Lord Death. Always."

Balancing her arse on the windowsill, Gebael brought a hand to her cunt. "Oh, darling, I know."

It surprised Eirian how quickly she became aroused. Part of her knew it was conditioning, that the god had trained her to desire his touch, but the sparks of pleasure from the touch of his fingers on her clit washed those thoughts away. Gasping when he slid two fingers into her, she ground against him, eager for the teasing to be over. He trailed kisses over her neck and throat, nipping lightly so that he did not leave marks on her skin. There was something desperate in the way Gebael moved, suggesting he knew their time was short. Arching into him, Eirian did not plead for more, but the flicker of amusement in his eyes when she met his gaze confirmed he knew what she wanted.

Removing his fingers, Death undid the buttons of his trousers to free his cock. "You're beautiful to me, Eirian. Now tell me what you want."

Tightening her legs on his hips, she groaned. "Please fuck me. I need you inside me."

There was no gentleness in his response, only the shard of ice that was his cock slamming into her. His mouth claimed hers, swallowing the scream of pleasure that had threatened to bring the priests running to investigate. Eirian knew there would be bruises on her arse, and she would feel the ache of his roughness for days. His thrusts were unforgiving, but it was exactly what she needed, and her orgasm crashed into the High Priestess like a wave battering the cliff. She needed Gebael to take his pleasure from her, to banish her fears with his kisses and his chilly touch. Surrendering to it, Eirian tossed her head and bit back her moan when she felt him spilling into her. For a moment, she felt the frozen chains of the Veil wrapping around her, threatening to drag her into the realm of the dead, but they faded when Gebael pressed his face to her neck, his murmured apologies and praises nothing more than a breath on her skin.

"Thank you," Eirian whispered, stroking his hair.

Gebael chuckled, making no attempt to pull out of her warmth. "You're welcome?"

"No, I mean it. I needed that. With everything going on, I needed a reminder that even when the worst is unfolding around you, there can be moments that aren't heartbreak."

"Emotions are such complicated things, darling. I understand."

She gave him a sleepy smile. "And thank you for not letting me attract concerned members of the temple. That would have been embarrassing to explain."

"You are my High Priestess," he murmured, nuzzling her neck. "I'll always protect you."

Twenty-two
Delyth

Standing in a circle with other mages, she linked her magic into the net of wards they were weaving. Above their heads, the massive glass dome of the university glittered with the power already anchored into it. It was a task Delyth relished helping with, and she felt the amazed gazes of her friends as they watched her hands spread, shimmering strands caught in her fingers. A warning whistle bid the mages halt before the rumble of the bells vibrated through the building. They had settled into a rhythm of waiting out the ringing after an attempt to preserve the architecture of the compound had come crashing down on the mages responsible because one had reacted poorly to the sound. With time marching on, unbothered by events, they could ill afford to make mistakes.

Each mage was responsible for helping with the wards before taking a break for a few hours to assist with securing valuable resources. No one knew what the future held, and there was an unspoken hope that they would be free to return to their homes soon enough. Delyth did not dare cast doubt on those dreams when the knowledge she possessed about her mother's plan was not for the general population. But she felt them looking to her as if she held all the answers. They expected leadership from her because she was the daughter of the High Priestess, and an Altira. Sometimes those looks extended to Amelia as though they thought she was as much in the know because she was a Zarthein. It left the warrior uncomfortable, but Delyth was confident she could meet the expectations when push came to shove.

"On my mark!"

Flicking her gaze to the mage in charge, Delyth prepared to throw her section of the ward at the dome. The last ring echoed, the sound dying slowly. They waited several moments to be sure it was done before another shout signalled for the group to release the magic. Inhaling sharply, she launched her power upwards, exhaling as she closed off the threads and watched the net settle into place. There was a collective pause as the mages waited to be sure it had sunk into the glass and stone that faded when no backlash of magic knocked them off their feet. It was too easy to make a mistake when working on wards like they were, and the resident healers had been running around the university tending to those who had suffered the consequences of the tiniest of miscalculations.

Arms slid around her waist, telling her Amelia no longer cared about who saw their relationship. "Have I told you this hour how amazing you are? Because if I haven't, this is your reminder."

"I like it when you tell me," she murmured, leaning back against her lover. "Almost as much as I like it when you put those skilled hands to good use and massage my shoulders."

"There's time for that later."

Jaw clenching, Delyth resisted the urge to remind the other woman that come sunrise the next day, they would depart the only home they had ever known. Beyond the plain surrounding the Bay of Blades, the world was an unfamiliar place. There were a few places they had been, but Eirian had shown her the route they would take, and those lands were unfamiliar. Even if they survived the journey and arrived on the Telmian border as her mother hoped they would, countless would fall on the way.

"Maybe one day, our descendants will return, and they'll find this magnificent building preserved."

Amelia's arms slid away, and she sighed heavily as she came to stand beside the mage. "There's a lot in the cities I hope will survive. Surely the Unseelie won't destroy knowledge."

Bounding over to join them, Laryn slung her arms over their shoulders. "You need to eat after all your excellent work, Del. Lucky for you, Calleth has gone for food."

Her stomach rumbled at the thought, pangs of hunger reminding Delyth of how much magic she had spent. There would be more wards, more outpourings of energy to preserve something of their home. Lifting her gaze to the beautiful glass dome, she admired the shine of magic clinging to each coloured panel. It was a sight she would carry in her heart until the day she died, though she doubted it was something they could easily recreate.

"I'm hungry, so good call," she said, turning her back on the atrium where countless brilliant minds had gathered over the years. "Let's enjoy a meal together while we can."

Patton was waiting for them by one of the arched doorways that led off to one of the many sections of the university. "Come on, he said he'd meet us in the thirteenth courtyard. I can't say what sort of food he'll scrounge up, but hopefully it will be more than bread and butter."

"They'll be using up anything we can't take with us," Amelia was quick to say.

People gave them space, no one eager to delay their preparations for the evacuation. Delyth wanted to walk slowly so she could drink in all the sights that had been her comfort growing up. Every painting they walked by, every mosaic of stone and glass, the countless shelves of books tucked into alcoves for anyone to borrow from. Those shelves were beautifully carved testimonies to the skill of the master carpenters. Magic thrummed through the entire building, much of it the remnants of mages long gone, but who had left their blessings on the institution that had fed their dreams.

"If we survive, and find ourselves unable to come home, I want to set the foundations for a place like this," Delyth said, ignoring the startled looks her friends gave her. "Just because we must flee our home, and leave behind more knowledge than we can imagine, doesn't mean we can't rebuild from what we have. Turning our backs on our history will allow the mad god to triumph."

"You know, that's an inspired plan." Patton lifted one shoulder, smiling wryly.

Screwing up her face, Laryn elbowed him before dancing out of reach of his retaliatory strike. "Fools, both of you. Del might not be saying it to our faces, but I know when the situation is fucked."

Head held high, Amelia kept her hands clasped behind her as she strode along at Delyth's side. "Yes, the situation is fucked. None of us knows whether we'll survive to see tomorrow, let alone the day after. Hope is a fickle thing, but it's well worth clinging to, because without it, there is no point."

They followed a hallway that led them outside onto a sheltered path. It curled around a garden, gum trees dominating four equally spaced points. Delyth knew there was a small shrine at the base of each, with a quaternary knot carved into each as a dedication to the four primary gods. She wondered how many people across both cities were visiting similar shrines to make offerings to their creators in a desperate attempt to change their fate. Her thoughts turned to her mother, and whether Death had returned yet. Eirian had planned on summoning the god, but Delyth had not wanted to ask more questions, not when she knew her mother's faith had been shaken.

Calleth had laid out a picnic in the middle of the garden, and he was sprawled out on his back, arms crossed beneath his head. Food was spread out on the blanket in a display that Delyth had not expected. Sensing a shift in the air, she hesitated, letting the others join the elf on the grass. None of them looked back at her, so she turned slowly, studying the garden and the walkway surrounding it. Somewhere in the distance, a dragon roared, reminding her of their guardians watching from the skies. Her gaze settled on the man sitting on a stone bench overlooking the greenery, and the air of magic around him made her breath catch in surprise. Their eyes met, his sad smile a reflection of the sorrow she felt, and unable to resist the draw, Delyth walked slowly towards him.

There was a book resting on the bench beside him. It caught her attention, the strange swirl of colours suggesting the cover was fabric bound. Her fingers itched to examine it, and Delyth sat with the tome between them. Giving her another sad smile, the man nudged it towards her, and she cringed at the scrape of it moving over the stone. Resisting the urge to snatch it up, the young woman studied it, her mind churning over what the symbols embroidered into the cover meant. A scratching sensation at the back of her neck prompted her to turn her gaze to the man, and she found amusement warring with delight in his eyes. The longer she stared into them, the more she felt like she was falling through space wrapped in a blanket of stars while existence exploded around her.

"You're going to need that, Altira," he murmured, and his voice was silk slipping over her skin. "Carry it with you on your adventures and protect it with everything you have."

"Who are you?"

"Not important. I dare not get too involved, lest I fancy more suffering. Just know that you're not alone, and there is hope. In that book are ideas to change the war, and I know you can weave the threads needed. Your capacity for imagination will lead you to do horrendous things, but they're needed. Without them, humans and elves will be wiped out."

Lips parted in awe, Delyth knew the man staring at her was a god. He was not Death or War, but one of the others who were worshipped by those who needed their blessings for their crafts. Placing a hand on the book, she bowed her head in respect and wondered what he meant by horrendous things. She wanted to ask, to demand an explanation for why he was warning her, except the depth of sorrow in his swirling eyes silenced those questions. When he covered her hand with his, Delyth felt her magic rising to welcome the touch. It sang so sweetly that she had to close her eyes to listen.

"There will always be choices, Delyth Altira. Even when you think your back is against the wall, there are choices. What you do with them is up to you. You have free will."

"Even if it means defying the gods?" Arching a brow, she waited to see a flash of anger.

"Especially if it does. The gods are flawed creatures, fractured and incomplete. Some of them try their best to help. Others cannot help but be jealous of the vibrant freedom their creations have because of the threads of existence woven together so that they might live. In you, that spark is particularly bright."

Delyth wanted to preen in the glory of being complimented by a god. It did not matter to her which one he was; the validation in his compliment thrilled her. As an Altira, she had always thought the only god whose opinion could matter to her was Death, but this nameless man with stars in his eyes filled her with a renewed sense of determination. Hearing laughter from her friends, she glanced their way, watching Patton and Calleth roll around on the grass, wrestling over something.

"They will serve you well on the journey to come."

She wanted to imagine her friends being by her side for the rest of her life, conquering the challenges thrown in their way. "I couldn't ask for better friends. As for Amelia…"

He chuckled, and she shivered at the way it caressed her spine. "The young Zarthein will burn the world for you. As it should be between the children of War and Death. You're stronger together, even across distances that seem impossible to link without the roots of desperation entwining beneath the surface."

"That's oddly specific."

"One day in the near enough future, you'll understand. This war will take you to lands where humans and elves already wage war with each other. I need you to survive, because it is you who will save my bloodline. What you will build together if you win…"

Startled by the wistfulness that overcame him, Delyth hungered to hear more. "What will we build?"

The god half smiled, but did not answer. Power curled around him, exhilarating and suffocating, laden with the promise of creativity. Breathing it in, she could not help where her thoughts turned. Her mother never spoke of how Gebael felt during their encounters, and the tendrils of curiosity wriggled into her mind. If a lessor god felt so good to be around, she suspected Death and the other primary gods would be overwhelming. Watching his eyes flutter shut, Delyth kept quiet, choosing to study what parts of his skin she could see. She wanted to run her hands over the dappled night sky that was draped over the body of someone who looked like they spent their days studying the mysteries of the universe.

"You're beautiful," she murmured, stroking the cover of the book beneath her hand.

Lips quirking, he cracked open his eyes to glance at her. "Thank you. Unfortunately, you're predisposed to find me that way. Such is the nature of the bloodlines."

"Anyone who doesn't find you beautiful is a fool."

"Are you coming to eat, Del?" Laryn waved from her spot on the grass.

Reminded of her hunger, she gave the man an apologetic smile. "She's got a point, but you probably already know. You're welcome to join us."

He smiled, and Delyth felt like she was staring at the sun. "Thank you for the invitation, but I've lingered here long enough. I'd hate for certain others to realise I'm meddling."

"Are you meddling?"

"Oh, little girl," he murmured, leaning towards her with a sly grin. "If I don't meddle, they will destroy this world, and I've invested too much power into the future."

Squirming beneath the weight of his attention, she felt her cheeks burning. "Do you see the future?"

"Not me, but another. We tug on the strings beneath the grand schemes of the others, and they never see what we can do... well, most of them. Your god knows what the truth is."

Understanding struck her like lightning, and Delyth gasped. "I know who you are."

Pressing a finger to his lips, the god tutted. "Tell no one where that book came from or that you met me. I've gone to great lengths to ensure no one will feel my influence."

"But—"

"Hush, Delyth. Don't force me to alter your memories of this."

Shrinking back, she bowed stiffly. "I beg your pardon, my lord."

"And now I feel bad." He cupped her chin gently, lifting it so he could hold her gaze. "I wish you all the luck I can give you. Never let them bind you down in chains of servitude. Too many Altiras have surrendered their brilliance to that wheel. But one day you will find your freedom."

Frozen in place, Delyth could not speak as he rose from the bench. His fingers brushed over her hair, energy flooding her senses, sparking the empty places between the thrum of her magic. Watching him walk away until he was out of sight of her friends, she whined when he vanished. As soon as he was gone, she felt free to move again, and she grabbed the book from where it sat, hugging it to her chest. Relishing the sensations swirling through her, Delyth swore she would not let the god down.

"I promise, Chaos, I am yours. Whatever you need me to do, I will do it."

Twenty-three

Teleri

Teleri nudged her horse into a canter, moving across the rocky ground bordering the road. Wagons stirred the dirt, leaving a choking cloud hanging in the air. The afternoon sun bounced light off the bay, catching the corner of her vision whenever she was foolish enough to glance that way. Soldiers patrolled the road to reassure those who had decided not to wait. People were pouring from their homes, clinging to their meagre belongings and their families as they passed through checkpoints where clerics recorded their names. She had argued against the departure census, but watching the lines of desperate people leaving them behind, Teleri understood the purpose of what Eirian had ordered her people to do.

Families were being torn apart. There were many who held firm in their faith that the heirs of War and Death could lead them to safety. She refused to destroy that faith even if she did not share it. At the bottom of the box where she was shoving stray thoughts, Teleri knew hope was still alive. It had good reason to be, but she knew that if she let it out, she would be in danger of sentiment impeding practicality. The people needed her to be a pillar of stone against the oncoming storm. Eirian had her plans, but the High General would be the shield protecting those she was responsible for. Just like the handful of dragons circling above them was a beacon of safety. A hollow one, but better than nothing.

"Mother," Yestin said in greeting when she brought her horse to a halt next to him. "Is it strange to feel like there are both more and fewer people leaving than I expected?"

Her mouth twisted, the wry smile confirming she felt the same way. "I hope they find safety somewhere. Perhaps this is a better option than everyone heading the same way."

"You think small groups hiding in the hills and forests will have a better chance at surviving?"

"I don't know, my dear boy. All I have is hope."

Yestin stared at a pair of elderly elves staggering along behind a wagon. "I suppose that's all any of us have. Hope and despair. The question is, which one will win out in the end?"

The roar of a dragon swooping low over their heads drew Teleri's attention to the familiar form of Laszlo. Remembering the feel of his scales beneath her, and the warmth of his body, the warrior smiled. She longed to take to the skies on the dragon again, and to experience the joy of seeing her home far beneath her. The prospect of Hadrian pressed to her back was a small pleasure she buried beneath the desire to feel the spray of water as the dragon flew close to the surface of the Bay of Blades.

"They never stop being magnificent."

Snorting nervously, Yestin's horse tossed its head, and he stroked its neck soothingly. Her horse did not flinch, but watching the twitch of its ears, Teleri knew it disliked the dragon. Across her chest, her baldrics sat uncomfortably, their position changed by the way she leaned back so she could continue to watch Laszlo soar. Her sword caught between her arse and the seat of her saddle, the cerapter horn hilt gleaming in the sunlight. Watching the dragon swirl in the air, the High General wondered if his rider was anchored to his back, or if the peropuan was confident in his own wings to keep him safe. She knew the riders were assisting with preparations, acting as a link to what their dragons could see from the sky, but a small part of her wanted to know Hadrian was guarding her.

"Is it wrong of me to hope I might beg a ride?" Yestin drew her attention back to him.

"I'm surprised you've never asked Briallen. I know you've had her over for dinner."

He gave her a sheepish smile. "It felt impertinent."

Unable to resist laughing at his response, Teleri waved at him. "But asking her to join you for dinner was not? My dear boy, you have a confusing sense of things some days."

"I extended the invitation because of the children. She's always been good with them."

Teleri felt deep sorrow at his explanation. It was a reminder of how badly they often treated the half-duine dragon rider. She had always tried her best to be welcoming, but at the end of the day, Briallen was Eirian's older half-sister. Being raised in Bellenden did not help. The differences between them were vast, and she had frequently found the endless enthusiasm displayed by the woman to be somewhat irritating. Reflecting on it, Teleri suspected she had disliked it because Briallen was so different from Eirian, and she longed for the untamed nature of the older sister to be present in the younger.

"You should ask her once we're on the road. Briallen is unlikely to say no," she said, shoulders slumping as Laszlo circled back towards Ensaycal. "Don't miss out on the chance to see the world from the sky, because we don't know how much time we have left. We should enjoy what we can."

"I noticed you've let Amelia remain with Delyth."

"Why would I deny them?"

Grunting, Yestin observed a horse being led past with three small children perched on its back while the adults formed a knot around it. "These things don't matter anymore. I heard the High Priestess commanded that no records from the temple take up space in the wagons that could be used for supplies."

"She can be quite wise." Teleri smiled faintly, remembering her delight at the news. "It's an excellent decision. You can't convince me there are documents in the temple that are more important than food or blankets. By taking a census of people leaving the cities now, she is covering what she needs for population records."

"Are you saying that birth records aren't important?"

"Not right now, they're not. People have their own ways of marking that information. If we're able to return, they'll be waiting. Should we be forced to rebuild elsewhere, then we will start again."

Laszlo was gliding back towards their location, his movement lacking the fancy twists he had put on display before. Cocking her head, Teleri studied the motion of his wings as he banked them before reaching the air above her. They were massive sails framed by powerful limbs and talons that could rend flesh and bone without a problem. She wished the immortality of the Unseelie allowed for their bodies to be torn apart instead of leaving them dependent on husk makers and dragon fire to slow them down.

"Why do you think the dragon is doing that?" Shading his face against the wind caused by massive wings, Yestin peered between his fingers at Laszlo.

Unflinching at the grains of dirt striking her, Teleri watched Hadrian leap from his dragon, his wings catching a current before the mighty beast moved on. The peropuan drifted down, and she saw the broad grin he wore as he got closer. Weapons covered his body, carefully positioned to be comfortable and accessible in flight. She admired the fit of his armour, wishing she could wear the lighter combination of leather and mail the dragon riders used. Someone had once told her that some of the older riders used scales from their bonded as part of their armour. It was another thing she could not help but envy.

"Good afternoon, High General Teleri Zarthein," Hadrian said, landing next to her.

Struck by the desire to run her hands over the leathery surface of his wings, Teleri arched a brow. "Are you the barer of good news, or will I regret setting eyes on your face?"

"I'm sorry to disappoint you."

Yestin hissed, sitting straighter in his saddle. "What happened?"

"Goblins attacked one of your garrisons and set it on fire. Most of the soldiers escaped, but many died either to claws or flames." He dropped his gaze to hide his sorrow. "I'm sorry."

Grinding her teeth, Teleri kept a tight hold on her rage. They had expected the Unseelie in the cities to attack while they could before most of the population was gone. Expectation did not soften the blow of discovering their expectations had been correct. Part of her had clung to the hope that they would do nothing, and the evacuation would go without a hitch. Closing her eyes, the High General offered a silent prayer to Death on behalf of those who had fallen.

"We knew it would happen." She turned her gaze from Hadrian to the lines of people leaving her city, and the soldiers positioned on the other side of the road to oversee them. "All we can do now is to continue on the path we have chosen. At least some of these people may live to see another day."

Stepping closer to her horse, the dragon rider placed a hand on its neck. "You suspected the Unseelie would strike garrisons first. It's a logical conclusion to reach."

"Indeed."

"They might come after you and the High Priestess tonight."

"I wish them luck if they go after Eirian. She won't be sleeping, and if they think they can sneak up on a husk maker, they deserve what will happen. I'll make it hurt."

His mouth twisted in annoyance, and the look he gave her told Teleri she would face a fight if she thought he would abandon her side before dawn. Hearing Yestin muttering, the general turned to her son. Dark eyes so much like her own were filled with anger, threads of it slipping through the cracks in his armour to stir the magic that connected them to the god of war. Sighing heavily, she leaned sideways to stretch out and touch his arm. Nodding in appreciation, the younger man wrestled his magic under control.

"I understand, my sweet boy."

"What about the family, Mother?" Yestin stared at the city. "The children."

"They're gathering in one place with everything they're taking with them. We are doing what we can to protect them against an enemy we can't fight."

Searching the sky, Hadrian said, "We could lure them into a trap. They're not immune to fire."

The two elves stared at him in amazement, and Teleri laughed in disbelief. "Why haven't we thought of that before? That's why dragons are a weapon against them in open areas."

"Possibly because dragon fire is magical, but I'm sure burning a building down on a group of goblins would do more than tickle. It would slow them down."

Her excitement over the idea was short-lived, and Teleri slumped. "Except I don't want to set fire to the cities. It would be nice to preserve what we can in case we can come back."

"Which is a perfectly understandable position to take," he replied, eyeing her thoughtfully. "But I'm talking about something smaller. They'll want to kill as many Altira and Zarthein family members as possible. What if they thought you were ensconced in a particular building?"

"And we set that one on fire? It could work. How would we make them believe it?"

Clicking his teeth together while he thought, Yestin finally said, "By doing it. Just because we go in, doesn't mean we have to stay in. If we pick a building with underground access..."

"We go in, leave by that path, and they'd never know. That's a good idea."

It felt wonderful to have an idea that would allow them to strike at the Unseelie wanting to kill them. An excited buzz crept through her magic, drawing a vicious grin to Teleri's lips that surprised the two men. Patting her horse on the neck, she nodded slowly, running through the list of potential buildings they could use to draw the enemy into a trap. Wherever it was possible, they constructed homes with underground chambers, and many had tunnels connecting them. The main thing she needed to be certain about before proceeding with the plan was protecting other buildings from catching on fire as well.

Gaze sliding in Hadrian's direction, she chuckled in delight. "I think we can do it. It's worth a try. Can you pass the suggestion along to Eirian? If they can try the same in Endara, it would help buy time."

"I'll ask Laszlo to tell Igraine. Do you want to return to the city now?"

There was no chance of confirming her intentions because Yestin had already urged his horse into motion. Shrugging at his mother, the warrior nudged the beast into a trot. Unimpressed with being left behind, Teleri's horse tossed its head, fighting to be allowed to follow. Hadrian flashed a grin at her, his wings spreading in preparation. For a moment, she wanted to command him to remain watching over the people leaving on their own terms, but there was something deeper in his gaze that made her hold her words. Pressing her heels into her horse, the High General chased after her son, mind twisting with possibilities.

A few buildings burning down around the Unseelie might do little more than anger them, but it was a risk she was willing to take. They had so few options available for fighting back that anything that might hurt the immortals filled Teleri with hope. She wanted them to suffer, and she imagined that being trapped in a burning building, unable to escape easily or die, would be an agony that would haunt their attackers. It was common knowledge that it took most immortals years to fully recover from dragon fire and the magic of the husk makers. That was why they were such a threat, and the mad god had done her best to wipe out Death's Ravens, leaving only the Executioner and a few others. Any daoine born with the ability were in danger of the same fate.

Hadrian kept close to her as they followed the road back to Ensaycal. With the long journey ahead of them, neither elf wanted to push their horses if they could avoid it. The soldiers watched them pass by, as did the people making their way in the opposite direction, reminding Teleri that they looked to her for reassurance. Going faster than a trot would suggest something was wrong, and she did not want to cause a panic. Better her people leave in peace. Yestin threw the occasional look over his shoulder to confirm she was still with him, and every time she saw the determination on his face, she offered silent thanks to the dragon rider for pointing out that fire was a weapon they could use against the enemy.

No one made a move to stop them as they entered the city, slowing their mounts so Teleri could take the lead. "I think I know just the place to fool them."

"So do I, but let's check your location first," Yestin replied.

Teleri pointed in the direction she intended to go. "This way. I'm sure you'll agree with me when we get there. It's the perfect location, and it'll help get the children out of the city."

Twenty-four

Briallen

"I hope she knows what she's doing," Igraine grumbled at the back of her mind. *"This feels too dangerous. One wrong move, and they all die of smoke inhalation or the city burns."*

Lips thinning, Briallen balanced on a wall, hand pressed to the warm stone. Soldiers and priests escorted various members of the Altira family along the street below, guiding them to the building near the gate they would leave by on the morrow. Her body ached, protesting the awkwardness of her perch, but she refused to budge. It provided her with a decent view of the road so she could oversee the people approaching, and it was not so high that she would be injured if she needed to jump down to protect her relatives from an Unseelie attack.

Her magic whispered across her skin, reaching for anything close enough to fall victim to the burgeoning power she struggled to restrain. When she took up her position, Briallen had admired the tiny white flowers growing in cracks in the stones, but they had steadily faded into dust as tendrils of her magic sucked the life from them. At one point she had realised that some of the sore spots left behind by Tristan's affections had healed. Part of her wanted to grieve their loss. Thoughts of his hands and mouth on her skin were a distraction she could ill-afford, but every time the shadows shifted, her breath hitched in anticipation of their caress heralding his arrival on her side of the street.

Aware of the danger, the goblin had been behaving himself. Briallen caught sight of him in the shadows of the street, watching her watch the others. They had dedicated their morning to assisting with preparations to leave, and a small part of the half-duine mourned the fate of a city she loved. Endara and Ensaycal were beautiful, and with the destruction of Kinara, their loss would have far-reaching consequences. All they could hope for was the Unseelie possessing a respect for knowledge. To burn down an empty city punished no one but the future generations of people on Tir, including their own.

Spotting Delyth being escorted towards the house, Briallen grinned. The four elves clung close to her, and the firm hold Amelia had on the younger woman spoke of the arguments that had unfolded when soldiers had fetched them. Turning her gaze to the darkening sky, she hoped the idea Teleri and Hadrian had devised would work. If they could trap and burn some of the Unseelie in the cities, it would provide a distraction for the others, allowing them to leave as planned with fewer people chasing after them. They all hoped that care for their brethren would make those unharmed remain to tend to the burned ones. The problem was in ensuring things unfolded as planned.

"I don't want you in there with them."

Briallen sighed, rubbing the side of her neck as she debated responding to the dragon. They had been arguing over it on and off since Igraine had passed along the plan from Laszlo. Her sister had seen the brilliance in it, latching on to anything that would work. Orders had already been spread among the clergy to inform people to keep a flame handy, as well as any flammable liquids that could be thrown on an attacking Unseelie. It was something that everyone could use for self-defence. Except it came with the possibility of burning the city down around them if things went wrong. A dark whisper in her mind suggested that people might not care so much about destroying their home if it meant hurting those who planned to kill them. She understood the sentiment all too well.

Snarling across her mind, Igraine swooped down low above the street, and she turned her face to the wind caused by the passing wings. *"I'm not going to let you die."*

"Careful, Igraine, one might think you'd abandon your duty to the innocents of this land."

"Don't speak to me of duty, fledgling."

Baring her teeth, Briallen did not bother to respond. The dragon could comb through her thoughts anyway, so there was little point in picking a fight. Better to conserve her energy for battling the Unseelie. And for mulling over the way her sister had stared at her sadly. The memory bugged her, like an itchy grass seed caught in her clothing that she could not extract. It felt like Eirian knew something about her that had left the High Priestess unsettled, and Briallen really wanted to know what it was. Even Igraine had commented about it.

Shadows brushed over her legs, and she glanced at where she had last seen Tristan. "I know you're there, Tris. Don't distract me, or I'll tell Delyth you told me you love me."

There was no response from the murky spots where light battled darkness. Dismissing the twisting shadows as nothing more than her imagination, Briallen arched her back, stretching to fight off the stiffness brought about by remaining in one spot too long. A muscle twinged in her back, and her power increased its whispered demands to be let loose. Eyeing a nearby tree, the rider wondered how it would feel the pull the life force from it, turning the energy in on herself. It would heal any injuries she carried, banishing the aches in her limbs, and the early throbbing of a headache at the back of her skull.

"Such thoughts are dangerous, Briallen."

"I know, but I need to train this power. From everything Eirian said, the early stage is the worst. I lack the control to stop it from accidentally killing someone."

"All the more reason you need to stay out of that building tonight. If your tenuous control slips, you could wipe out your kin, including little Delyth. Could you live with that?"

Both of them knew the question needed no answer. Accidentally doing harm to the Altira family was something Briallen would not recover from. Not only that, but if she hoped to avoid drawing Death's attention, she needed to ensure she did not do something as stupid as killing a large portion of his mortal bloodline. A shudder ripped through her at the thought of the god setting his sights on her. Lord General Valerian had always told her to offer her prayers quietly, and to keep her head down lest the powerful being decided he had no interest in allowing a duine member of the Altira line to exist. She knew her father had hoped no dragon would want to bond with her because of the connection.

"Your father can be quite the fool."

She bit back a giggle, eyes tracking another group of soldiers escorting civilians towards the house. *"Just how many Altiras are there? I'm feeling overwhelmed by how many relatives I have that I didn't realise existed. Or are some of these simply important people the Unseelie might go after?"*

"They're setting other traps; this is just for the family."

Recoiling in amazement, Briallen scrambled when her knee slid over the edge of the wall. Huffing at her foolishness, the dragon circled closer, pale sunlight bathing the grey scales and giving them a bluish sheen that her rider found quite pretty. Adjusting her position, she was tempted to straddle the wall to avoid a repeat, especially with how tired she felt. Searching the shadows, the duine waited to see if Tristan would send her a sign of his presence. Nothing stirred on the other side of the street, and though she did not want to be distracted, the lack of movement felt more uncomfortable than it should.

"He's still here, isn't he?" she asked the dragon.

Chuckling, Igraine did not reply straight away. When she had awoken curled up in Tristan's arms, Briallen had suffered an onslaught of delight from the dragon. Her bonded had given them privacy through the night, but her impatience to celebrate a union she had been waiting for had left them unable to enjoy a few moments together as the breaking dawn bathed the bed in soft light. The goblin had informed her that Ysgarlad was equally pleased about the situation, and it left her wondering how any rider could maintain a relationship when they had dragons getting involved.

"They don't unless we approve."

"If I ever find myself owed a favour by a god, I'm going to beg for some changes to how this bond works. Privacy is a nice thing, Igraine. It's not nice to constantly invade our minds."

The dragon huffed in amusement. *"How else are we supposed to keep you lot safe? And yes, our handsome goblin is close. He's patrolling farther down the street to avoid tormenting you."*

Her cheeks burned, and Briallen decided they did not need a flame to set the building on fire when they could just use her. Pushing her embarrassment aside, she swivelled around, sitting down on the wall with her legs hanging over the side. If she needed to jump down, the position would work well enough. Drumming her heels against the stone, the rider nodded to a waving soldier, observing the pair carrying a timber box between them. They were not the first to carry such items into the building, and she knew the contents were flammable, intended to help the fire burn quicker and hotter once it was lit. But there was one thing that kept bothering her about the traps they were setting. Briallen did not know how they intended to know there were Unseelie inside so that the fires could be lit.

"Your sister is coming."

Sitting up straighter, she peered down the street to where Eirian was swarming towards the building. It was the best way she could describe the power clinging to her sister, and a dozen priests buzzing around like flies. Pressing her lips together, she tried not to laugh. Waving when the High Priestess got closer, Briallen prepared to jump down from her perch. Halting a short distance from where she would land, Eirian cocked her head as her older sister launched from above. The impact jarred her ankles and knees, bringing the hungry whispers back to the surface of her mind. Clenching her eyes shut, the rider pushed them down, burying their demands beneath walls of magic she prayed would contain them.

"I wasn't sure you would stay the night with the rest," she said, not bothering to keep her voice low.

Eyes twitching, Eirian kept herself from glancing around. "Well, it's rare that all the family is in one place. This is an opportunity to share a meal before we leave."

"True. Delyth is here, but she didn't look impressed about it."

"My daughter will understand the importance of spending time to-gether."

They stared at each other, and Briallen saw a flicker of guilt pass through Eirian's eyes. She was reminded of her suspicion that her sister knew something about her she was not sharing. Lifting her chin, she spotted Tristan in the shadows farther down the street, a faint smile tugging at her lips.

"Well, we'll be on guard all night. You don't have to worry about the Unseelie coming through the door."

It was a line they had instructed her to use in case they were being watched. While the goblins could strike at any time, using the shadows to move among them without being seen, the mara and strigoi were left waiting for nightfall before they could attack. They hoped the suggestion that the front entrance was the only one being guarded would help encourage an attempt on the lives of the families. Briallen did not know why they were leaving windows and rooftop doors without guards, but she figured it might play into how they planned to know if there were Unseelie in the building.

"Thank you for your diligence, Rider Briallen," Eirian replied, bowing her head slightly.

"*Something is going on,*" Igraine grumbled, swooping over the street. "*I sense a presence in the city.*"

Squinting, she made a show of watching her dragon. "*You don't think it's just Death? Maybe Eirian summoned him. I know she was hesitant to risk angering him.*"

"*Possibly. That would make sense. Zern said earlier that he felt something, but it comes and goes.*"

"*So, like a god?*"

Feeling the dragon's annoyance at her comment, Briallen lowered her gaze to her sister. "I look forward to seeing you later, High Priestess. Enjoy your evening."

It almost seemed like she was going to take a step closer, to say something that would assure the duine that the strangeness was only in her imagination. The slight drop of her shoulders and the twist of her mouth were the only signs that Eirian had changed her mind. Locking on the blue eyes that were so much like her own, Briallen hoped the other woman could see her disappointment. There was no sign she did, but the High Priestess was better trained.

"Have you had any problems with your magic?"

The question came as a surprise, and Briallen stepped back. "I've kept it under control."

"So you haven't killed anything?" Arching a brow, the High Priestess inclined her head at the wall. "Not even the smallest of plants that most would dismiss as insignificant?"

"Well, yes, but that's me keeping it under control."

"I need you to stay out of the building tonight, Briallen. You're a danger to the family."

She nodded so hard her neck pinched. "I know. Better for everyone to keep me out of crowded places. Igraine hasn't stopped lecturing me about the risk."

Eirian's laugh was even more surprising than her initial question. "Dragons are smarter than we are."

"Maybe. I'm withholding judgement."

"*Impertinent girl.*"

"*Hence my decision.*"

Igraine's roar echoed over the city, and Briallen closed one eye, lifting her brows in exasperation. The priests surrounding Eirian stared at her, but their High Priestess smirked. Nodding as she started walking towards the door, she passed close enough to touch her sister's arm. It was a brief moment where their powers curled against each other in familiarity, and their gazes met. Biting her lip, the rider found the flicker of assurance she had sought, a reminder she was not alone in her struggles. They were two husk makers in a city filled with an energy their magic longed to consume. She knew if Eirian had controlled it as a child, then she could do it as an adult who had undergone training already.

"If you can, Briallen, get some rest. Tomorrow will be a long day," Eirian murmured, hand dropping.

"I'll try my best, but someone needs to watch your back."

"That's what the soldiers are for. You should go somewhere safer and let Igraine guard you."

Staring at Eirian's back, Briallen wondered if the comments had been intended as instructions. She suspected her sister wanted her away from the danger they were summoning with their plan. Part of her thought it might be a good idea to get on Igraine's back and stay in the skies until dawn broke over the horizon, bathing them in the light of a new day.

"*That is a good idea.*"

"Aren't I a danger to you?" It was something she had wondered repeatedly since the power had shown itself. *"I'm not getting on your back unless I know I can't drain you of your life."*

"Yes, that would be rather inconvenient. We spoke about it, and the consensus we reached is that you're not powerful enough to kill me. Yet. Give it time and training."

Screwing up her face, Briallen spotted Tristan striding towards her. *"Well, I suppose I didn't harm him last night while I was in less control. Still, I'd rather stay close so I can help if needed."*

Tristan's smile sent shivers down her spine, but it was the brush of shadows that had desire turning her thoughts towards other options. His hands settled on her hips, the prick of claws the barest of sensations through her armour. Leaning in closer, Briallen did not kiss him, even though she wanted to.

"You're going to do what Igraine tells you, Bri. Otherwise I'm going to throw you over my shoulder and get on Ysgarlad so you don't have a choice about it," he said, pressing a kiss to her nose. "And if you're a very good girl for me, I promise you'll enjoy the reward."

"I can't abandon my duty to my family," she argued.

"Your father and sister would be in agreement about this. Without training, you're a risk to the people you want to protect. The best thing you can do is stay away from them."

"Fine."

He wrapped his arms around her, victory summoning a smirk. "I'm glad you're being reasonable, love. Can I still throw you over my shoulder, though? It would be fun."

Twenty-five

Eirian

Shadows were draped over everything, shifting whenever the lantern flames sputtered in the oil. They had not bothered to fill them as much as normal, preferring to conserve as much fuel as possible for the journey. No one knew whether it would be possible to stop at night, or if they would keep moving until they felt safe enough to rest. All resources were valuable when those in need of them did not know when they would secure more. Which left Eirian feeling guilty over their plan to use a lot of oil if the Unseelie took the bait and came after the Altira and Zarthein bloodlines.

Beneath her spread hands, the timber felt cold. A crafter had spent a lot of time sanding it down to an almost perfectly smooth point, treating it with the care of someone who knew it would serve generations. Her family was filtering into the tunnel beneath the building, soldiers escorting the oldest and youngest first. For the trap to work, they needed to stay on the upper level for as long as possible so that their scent could trick the goblins. A candle flickered, melting wax trailing down the smooth pillar to feed the widening pool on the table. Eirian had lit it while she sat in vigil, letting the dancing flame consume her regrets.

Several elderly members of the Altira family had volunteered to remain as bait. They had argued that their time was done, and joining the rest of the evacuating citizens of Endara and Ensaycal was nothing more than a waste of resources. She had wanted to deny them the choice before remembering that countless other families had gone through the same discussion. It was not her right to deny anyone the freedom to decide their fate, no matter how much it hurt those who loved them. Forcing those in their twilight years to trudge across the land hoping to avoid destruction was a cruelty. Eirian refused to be cruel to the people who had already spent their years serving their home.

"Ma," Delyth murmured, placing a hand on her mother's shoulder to squeeze it. "Are you coming?"

Pressing her cheek to the warm hand, Eirian caught sight of the satchel strapped across her daughter's chest that she had refused to let go of. "Not yet. I'll wait until it's time. If they can smell me here, they won't be able to resist. Killing the Altira is one of their goals."

"I'll stay with you."

"No!"

"Please, Ma. Let me support you through this. I know tonight is hard for everyone."

Her heart plunged into an icy river at the desperation in Delyth's voice. The need to be a comforting mother sat at odds with the leader carved from stone. Both sides agreed they needed to protect the young woman, but instinct pleaded to be allowed to pull her into her arms. Sighing heavily, Eirian covered the hand on her shoulder with her own, and said nothing. As long as she did not speak, they could pretend she was going to let Delyth remain with her until they knew the Unseelie had come. All those involved knew there was a chance the enemy would not fall for the trap, but until the sun rose above the city, they refused to lose hope that it would work.

"Why isn't Aunty Briallen here?"

Chewing the inside of her mouth, Eirian decided it was a safe subject. "Too dangerous to have her close to people until she has control over her power. When I came into my abilities as a child, they kept me in an isolated section of the temple grounds with minimal people around me. No doubt the daoine have methods for ensuring a husk maker doesn't do too much harm while learning to wield the magic, but right now, Briallen doesn't have the option available to her."

"You think she's going to accidentally kill people." She hooked her foot onto the leg of a chair, dragging it closer to sit beside her mother. "Could she hurt Igraine?"

"I don't know. Calea said the dragons had been discussing the development."

She thought back to Gebael's visit, and his comment that Briallen could wield his sword in battle when Teleri could not. The deeply suspicious part of Eirian believed the god had something to do with her sister developing husk maker powers. It was his magic, spun into daoine as the only defence anyone had against the immortals. They were called husk makers for a reason. Sucking the life energy from the First People left them as hollowed-out husks made from withered skin and brittle bones until they healed. Something that took a long time, and involved a lot of suffering.

"Do you want to know something I wish?" she asked Delyth.

Arching a brow, the younger woman nodded. "What do you wish for, Ma?"

"I wish the dullaghan could kill immortals."

"That would be handy. What happens when a dullaghan is set after them?"

Frowning, Eirian realised she did not know. "I've never asked."

"Do you think it hurts them?"

"I hope so. Maybe it does something like my power does. Leaves them barely alive, and suffering while they recover. Wouldn't it be nice if Death forged more weapons like Oblivion and Eclipse?"

Delyth's hand dropped to the satchel, stroking the leather while she stared at the single candle in front of her mother. "Perhaps he should. If weapons that could kill them were readily available, it would make things fair for us. Well, fairer. There will never be fairness between us while they're immortal."

"You're right. We cannot be equal with things the way they are. This is why it's so important for brilliant minds like you to escape the destruction headed our way."

"What if they knew what we would do?"

Biting her bottom lip hard enough to feel pain without drawing blood, Eirian clung to the feeling to provide clarity of thought. She knew what the gods were capable of. Death and War could see potential outcomes directly related to their essences. It was entirely possible that the mad god had foreseen their decision to evacuate the cities to make their way across the lands to where Life's bloodline lived. There was no way to know if leaving would only see them walking into a trap much like the one they had planned for the Unseelie who had infiltrated their home. The dragons would do their best to survey the road ahead, but even the mighty, winged beasts had limitations.

Eirian cast her thoughts back to her conversation with Gebael. He had claimed he intended to guard their backs against the Unseelie, turning Eclipse on those whose existence he could not otherwise claim. She hoped he was lurking somewhere beyond the perception of mortals, watching for threats. A small part of her that revelled in his attention believed the god would intervene if he foresaw a threat to her life. With Annawyn making a move against his bloodline, and that of War, the last thing either god would want was for the current heir to be killed, forcing the power to linger in wait until the next was born. It would be too easy to wipe them all out. Gazing at her daughter, Eirian grieved for the vibrant girl she had watched grow. She knew that girl would be lost to the challenges they would face.

"Ma?" Delyth reached for her, but the High Priestess recoiled.

"It's time for you to join the others, my darling girl. I don't want you here when the goblins come."

She looked like she was going to argue, but the satchel shifted against her, and Delyth slumped back on the chair. "Don't be angry with me, but I'm scared, Ma. I know I shouldn't be worried about you facing a few Unseelie, but I can't control how I feel. This whole situation is dangerous, and all it would take is one catching you unprepared for you to be killed."

Sorrow had Eirian stretching over to kiss her cheek. "I could never be angry with you for this. Fear is a perfectly healthy and understandable response to the situation. I'm scared."

"But you're never scared."

"What gives you that idea, Delyth? I'm only human, and none of us is immune to fear."

With wide eyes, the young mage regarded her mother with amazement. Smiling sadly, Eirian turned back to her candle. It felt like she had closed the door on some impossible belief her daughter held about her. There was no point in continuing forward under false assumptions about what strength she possessed. She was the pillar upon which too many people placed their faith, and no pillar is immovable. Sometimes the hardest of stones needed a little extra support, and that included her. Eirian hoped that when they could carve out time to rest, she would be free to let her guard down around Delyth.

"Promise me you will leave the moment they come into the house," Delyth said, rising from the seat to grab her arm in a desperate grip. "I still need my mother. Your death helps no one."

It came as a surprise when her daughter promptly turned and walked away from the table, leaving her there alone. Eirian heard the murmured exchange as Delyth passed the soldiers guarding the chamber. Whatever was said was too quiet for her to make out, but she imagined the young woman was threatening the warriors if they did not ensure she left in time to make it out alive. Chuckling, the High Priestess let her magic unfurl like the petals of a dandelion, delicate threads stretching out to touch against the living things in the building. She found reassurance in knowing she was not alone in her wait, even though she wished she were. Those elderly Altiras had played a part in her younger years, and knowing what death was waiting for them hurt more than Eirian expected.

People often believed she was comfortable with death. She was comfortable with the god of it, but rarely the actuality of dying. It did not matter that, as the High Priestess of Death's temple, Eirian used her powers to deliver willing sacrifices to the Veil. Somewhere in her memories was a count of the lives she had ended, but she tried not to pay too much attention to the number to avoid the bone-aching sorrow it brought. In the eyes of many, the High Priestess was a glorified executioner, and she suspected there was more truth in it than she liked to admit. Part of her delighted at the opportunity to use her husk maker power for what it had been created for. Stopping the Unseelie in their tracks, and making them wish for the death immortality denied them.

A throat was cleared to the side, drawing Eirian's focus from her candle. "Is everything going well?"

"Yes, Your Eminence, it's done. Lady Delyth was the last. The… the um…" His shoulders slumped, and he stared at her apologetically before lifting his gaze to the ceiling.

"I understand. They're in position and ready to do their part."

Tempted to reassure him there was no need to be annoyed with himself for his inability to communicate details regarding the elderly members of her family who planned to sacrifice themselves, Eirian lifted her hand. Before she could touch his arm or communicate what she hoped would be words of comfort, the tendrils of her power she had left lingering through the building twanged in her mind. Nose flaring, she stiffened, waiting for it to happen again so that she could be certain of what she felt.

Alerted by the sudden change in the High Priestess, the soldier dropped a hand to his sword. "Your Eminence? Has something happened? Is it time?"

It was a different flavour of life that slid into her grasp. The goblins did not taste like humans and elves, and they lacked the shimmering brightness of the daoine. Closing her eyes, Eirian spread her magic like a web, letting it pick through the shadows to find the handful of Unseelie coming to kill the Altira family. She had expected more, but another part of her argued that six goblins could do plenty of damage to a building filled with humans. Knowing they were coming, she nodded to the soldier. They needed to retreat into the tunnel below, guarding it in case the goblins found their way down as well. Something Eirian had no plans of allowing to happen. She would turn them into husks first.

"Give the order and then get out of here."

As she rose from her seat, the soldiers jumped into action. They had devised a quick method to alert those remaining behind to set the building on fire, but Eirian had a sinking feeling in her gut that many of them would fall. Leaving her power in place, she surrounded herself with the magic she needed, prepared to suck the life from any immortal who dared get close. As they crept through the shadows, seeking the unguarded entrances, she tracked them in her mind. Her magic begged to be allowed to consume them, and it was tempting. All Eirian needed to do was let go, and they would fall with no fires needing to be lit. But she knew it was possible that she was not aware of all of them.

"Time to go, Your Eminence," a soldier said, returning to her side.

There was something not quite right that scratched at the edge of her awareness. Cocking her head, Eirian inhaled sharply, sensing the tendrils of another with a power similar to hers. It raged like a flooded river, filling the building with a chill that froze her lungs. She knew it was not Gebael, and it certainly was not Briallen. Shoving the soldier away, she forced herself to keep breathing.

"Get out of here!" she hissed, struggling with the magic screaming to be released. "Something is coming, and it's not Unseelie. Now go before I accidentally kill you."

The soldiers needed no other warning. They knew the danger that came with being around a husk maker struggling with control. It was taught to all of them when they joined the army to prepare for the day the current Altira mage died, and a new one was born. She tracked their hasty departure, feeling only relief when they were gone from the building into the tunnel. Opening her mind to the scratching, Eirian staggered at the weight of the whisper that slid into her thoughts.

"Hello little heir. Will you feed me?"

Someone crashed through the door, dragging a struggling goblin behind them. "Did you want to question any of them? Or am I free to do my job here?"

Mouth hanging open, Eirian stared at the tall woman. A long braid of bone-white hair hung over her shoulder, gleaming in the firelight, while a sword was held in her other hand. She wore armour similar to that of the dragon riders, which surprised the High Priestess. There was no need for introductions when the whispering sword in her grasp dripped with shadows and promised to deliver the dark nothingness of its name to anyone who dared get in its way.

"Thank fuck you're here. Granted, this is not how I wanted to meet you, Lady Oblivion."

The Executioner lifted the goblin, pointing at it with the sword. "So, can I kill her?"

"Please do. Let's kill them all."

Twenty-six

Delyth

Time lost all meaning in the dim light of the tunnel beneath the city she would put behind her once the sun rose. At her side, Amelia was a silent presence who could not stop fidgeting with whatever she could get her hands on. Laryn and Calleth sat snuggled together on the floor, backs against the wall while they made the best of the wait to sleep a little. She envied them for the ability to rest, but until her mother joined them, Delyth could not stop pacing back and forth in the tunnel. Soldiers observed her when they tired of staring down the empty tunnel, hoping to see the High Priestess striding towards them. The young mage was thankful it was too dark to see their expressions because she knew they looked at her with sorrow and fear for what had happened to her mother.

Patton was the least bothered by the situation, choosing to spend his time whittling a small piece of wood he had brought with him. She knew what he was doing—using a skill he was developing to keep his mind focused on something unrelated to the danger they were in. All it would take was one goblin tracking their scent into the tunnels for their blood to stain the hard-packed dirt. The broad strap of her satchel sat uncomfortably on her collarbone, the edge of the leather digging into her skin. Adjusting it, Delyth thought about the book tucked safely within. She had wrapped a wool scarf around it for additional protection, and she had not let it out of her sight since receiving it. Part of her longed to tell her mother about it, but with the attempt to trap some Unseelie going on, the young mage had decided it could wait until a calmer time.

Her friends had teased her about how protective she was of the tome. They had believed the strange man she had spoken to was one of the masters of the university, but Delyth's refusal to let them read it amused them a great deal. In her mind, it was a precious gift to be cared for, and studied until every word had been imprinted on the back of her eyes. She wanted the knowledge to bleed through to her dreams, driving her to madness with new ideas that would stretch her magic beyond anything she had previously imagined possible. When the god of chaos gave someone a book of knowledge, Delyth knew it was a gift to be cherished. And with the brief conversation she had with her mother over Death forging more weapons capable of killing the First People, she could not help but wonder if Chaos had foreseen the need to provide her with the schematics for such things.

Gazing at the single lantern dangling on a hook, Delyth wished it were brighter. They were too far apart to provide enough light to read by; otherwise, she could have distracted herself from her fear by sitting on the ground to examine the book. She wanted to know if there were wards written on the pages that could be wielded against the Unseelie so she did not feel useless. So none of them were as defenceless. Anything to shake the awful sinking feeling that had settled into her gut from the moment her mother had told her about what was going on. Delyth was tired of feeling like she was just waiting to die.

"It's the High Priestess!" a soldier called from further down the tunnel.

Spinning, Delyth wanted to run towards her mother, but the soldiers were hurrying ahead of the High Priestess. They pushed past, startling Laryn and Calleth from their sleep. Pressing against the wall to keep out of the way, she heard her friends call for her to join them. Refusing to move, Delyth waited to set eyes on Eirian, fingers clinging to the strap of her satchel. Striding out of the dark between lanterns, the tallest woman she had ever seen accompanied the older Altira. Sucking in a surprised breath, she stared at the pale gleam of a long braid, and wondered if her lungs were going to freeze from the chill accompanying them. There was a heavy blanket of power surrounding the stranger that carried a hint of familiarity, reminding her of when Eirian used her magic to kill.

"What are you doing here, Delyth?" Eirian halted in front of her. "I thought you were going to safety?"

"I couldn't leave without you, Ma."

Cocking her head, the strange woman studied her, and chuckled. "You have a touch of chaos to you, young Altira. The goblins are all dead, and your mother is perfectly safe."

Dropping her gaze to where the strange woman held the hilt of a sword, Delyth realised it was the source of the chill she could feel. Her mind swirled with confusion, a tiny voice suggesting she knew who the other was. It did not seem likely that it was, but shifting her focus back to her mother, the question remained. There was always a chance that Death had done them a favour and sent help.

"Are you the Executioner?" she murmured.

"Indeed, I am."

Patton let out a small whoop of excitement and elbowed Amelia out of his way so he could stand next to Delyth. "You are amazing. Can we see the sword?"

"You don't ask that!" Amelia smacked the back of his head. "Our apologies, Lady Oblivion."

"Better the questions than trying to kill me. That has happened more times than I can count. Now, if I might suggest that we keep moving because those weren't the only goblins in the city." Oblivion made a shooing motion with her hand.

As curious as she was about the infamous woman, Delyth was more concerned about her mother. Releasing her tight grasp on the strap, she stepped closer and awkwardly attempted to hug Eirian. There was a moment of hesitation from the High Priestess before she returned the embrace. With her mother's arms around her, the young mage felt like someone had lifted a weight from her shoulders. Almost as though she had not been certain the older woman was safe until she touched her. The tickle of Eirian's breath through her hair, the familiar way she pressed her cheek to Delyth's head, and pressed her fingers to her spine. It was the same way her mother had done it all her life.

"I'm so glad you're safe," Delyth whispered, tightening her hug. "I was worried."

Kissing the side of her head, Eirian smiled sadly. "I know. Thank you for waiting. I'm annoyed that you did, but I'm so pleased to see you're safe too."

Oblivion cleared her throat, and the sound had the two Altira women pulling apart. She did not move, instead remaining where she was until they were in front of her with the elves. Further along the tunnel, the soldiers waited nervously, their warrior magic influenced by the sword. Eyeing her friends cautiously, Delyth wondered if they were feeling whatever the others were experiencing. Her magic was writhing against her control like a trapped sea serpent, but she did not know what it wanted to do. Part of her wanted to believe the confined space made it worse, but logic countered the argument with facts she could not deny. Clinging to Eirian's side, she nodded when Amelia stared at her.

"So, what happened?" she murmured, curious to find out how her mother had come to be in the company of Death's most feared Executioner.

"The goblins came as we hoped, the soldiers left when I commanded them to, and as I was preparing to play my part, Lady Oblivion arrived. She made quite the entrance," Eirian replied, casting a look over her shoulder at the duine. "She dragged a goblin in with her and killed it."

"Really? What did it look like when it died?"

"A dead goblin."

Scowling, Delyth huffed. "No, I mean, what did the act of dying look like? Was it different?"

"Honestly? It just looked like a quick, but bloody death. I thought it might be different as well."

Disappointment wormed through her, taking Delyth by surprise. She did not know why she had expected a death delivered by a sword capable of killing immortals to differ from any other, but she supposed it had something to do with what was taught about the weapons. In the stories about the Executioner and the sword that shared her name, it was claimed the weapon was a final death. It destroyed the essence of the victim, leaving nothing to cross the Veil to the land of the dead. There would be nothing to be bound to the bones that tied a person in place for eternity. A dreadful fate for most, and a curse endured by all the Altira mages that came before Eirian.

As they walked down the tunnel towards the junction it connected to, Delyth found her thoughts circling the sword behind her. She wanted to know how it worked, and what exactly Death had done to it that enabled its power. The god of chaos had played a part in the forging, just as he had in creating the dullaghan. It left her ever more eager to reach a place where she could finally sit down to examine the book the god had given her. As soon as she could, Delyth planned to pore over every page. But the more she thought about Chaos and his gift, the more she glanced back at Oblivion. There was something bothering her about how the duine had greeted her that filled her with more questions.

Catching her glance, Oblivion flashed a grin in the murky darkness. "I sense your turmoil, young Altira. So full of curiosity, and yet so afraid of where it might lead. We'll have our chance to talk."

"How did you know that?"

"Among other things, I'm a mind mage. It's not my most significant power, but it does what I need it to. Though I'm surprised I can read as much of your thoughts as I can. I expected better walls."

Embarrassment lit her cheeks on fire, and Delyth did not look at her mother or friends. She had believed her mental shields to be excellent. Mind mages serving in the temple had trained her from when she was young, but having someone like Oblivion dismiss her efforts was a blow to her confidence. Eirian touched her arm in what she assumed was an attempt at comfort. One she shrugged off with a scowl, choosing to cling to the strap of her bag. Keeping her gaze locked on the back of Amelia's head, Delyth gathered the tattered threads of pride, weaving them in with her determination. If the walls in her mind were not good enough, she would build them higher and thicker until the Executioner could no longer skim her surface thoughts without putting in any effort.

"So, since we have time to talk," Patton called from his place ahead of them. "What did you do to the goblins? And what about those who planned to remain for the plan?"

Eirian stiffened, and Delyth recognised the way she held herself. There was no need for the High Priestess to say anything, but her daughter was the only one who could read her reactions. She knew her mother had killed their elderly kin. If the Executioner had destroyed the goblins, it meant there had been no need to burn the building down. Out of kindness, Eirian would have offered them a choice. Delyth appreciated what her mother had done, knowing that she had acted to spare them pain. It did not make it any easier. Not that there was any comfort she could offer her mother.

"I killed them all," Oblivion replied coldly, sparing Eirian the need to say anything.

"Why?"

Glancing back at the duine, Delyth envied the calm way she said, "Because that is my job. Don't worry, I asked them first. Not the Unseelie, but the Altiras who had already chosen to die. It wasn't fair to leave them waiting, though several had already fallen to the goblins. The rest were offered the chance to come along with you, remain in the city, or to die quickly and painlessly."

"Thank you." Delyth nodded in respect. "They deserved the freedom to choose."

"Everyone does. There are few people who understand as well as I do what it's like to have no free will. Believe me, it is something I do my best to honour as much as I can."

It struck Delyth as strange that her heart ached for Oblivion. She knew the story of her creation, and she wished she could ask more questions without being impolite. The pale-haired woman behind her was the very first mortal person created by the gods, but she had never gotten a chance to be anything other than the Executioner. Death had laid claim to her before her eyes had opened, and pressed the hilt of the sword into her hand, binding her existence to it. He had made her the first husk maker, creating a type of magic that would become one of the most feared on Tir.

"I wouldn't wish my life on another," Oblivion murmured, and Delyth knew it was intended for her.

"What would happen if they killed you in a fight?" She wanted to turn around and walk backwards so she could watch the duine. "You're one person. Surely numbers?"

Eirian cleared her throat, and Delyth suspected she would have been on the receiving end of a scolding look. "Darling girl, now is not the time to pester Lady Oblivion with questions."

"I don't mind. Your daughter is curious, and she is refreshingly innocent. Many people have asked the same questions, but with ill intentions behind them. Young Delyth merely seeks to satisfy her brilliant mind, and I'm happy to indulge her as much as I can." Flicking a hand at the bag hanging from Delyth's shoulder, Oblivion let a thread of magic brush against it.

"Are you here for my aunt?" The question fell from her lips without thinking, and Delyth frowned.

"Yes. She has come into her husk maker powers, and I'm to help her while we assist your people with their escape. I'm not the only one who'll be helping, either. Your mother already knows, but I intend to summon the hunts."

There was a gasp from Amelia, and the young warrior spun around, forcing Delyth to give her a shove to keep going. "You're bringing the might of the dullaghan here?"

"Don't look so surprised, little Zarthein. The people of Endara and Ensaycal are at a severe disadvantage against the Unseelie, but I have the authority to do something about it. Death's riders will come, and they are angry about what happened to Kinara, so they're looking forward to making the enemy pay. They're not the only ones who are deeply unhappy about the fall of the city of art."

Her imagination offered helpful ideas of what the terrifying headless riders would do to protect her people, and Delyth smiled in delight. "I'm looking forward to watching them exact their vengeance. Kinara was a beautiful place, and I dreamed of seeing it one day. Now I never will."

"We're here!" a soldier shouted from ahead.

Staring at the brighter lights, Delyth decided she was not ready to leave the tunnel. The moment they did, work would sweep her mother away, leaving her with her friends to figure out what to do with themselves. Oblivion would accompany the High Priestess, taking all the answers to questions she had not yet thought of. With the rising of the sun, they would find themselves on the road, leaving their homes behind. For a moment, panic gripped her heart, but a hand on her shoulder filled her with calm. Glancing sideways at the duine, Delyth nodded slowly. She felt the creep of magic like a fog, spreading a false sense of serenity.

"You are stronger than you realise, Delyth," Oblivion whispered, giving her a faint smile.

"I hope so."

She chuckled, half shrugging. "I dare you to prove me right. Too many people have disappointed me over the years. Will you be another one? Don't let time bury your name in the sand, Delyth Altira."

The comment hit her like a wave, and Delyth forced herself to lift her chin and square her shoulders. "I've always fancied having my name in the history books. Challenge accepted."

Twenty-seven

Teleri

The lingering stench of smoke refused to let her forget the screams of the Unseelie trapped inside the burning building. She had remained in the tunnel below, standing watch while it happened. It had felt wrong to leave with the others, and Teleri had commanded the soldiers accompanying her to join the rest. Her vigil had been hers alone to endure, and no one else needed to listen to the agony of immortal goblins being burnt alive. What she had ordered would haunt her nightmares for the rest of her life, however long that was. A part of her questioned the morality of it, but whenever that voice raised its head, a louder one shouted about what they would have done to her family.

Bathed in light, red was painted across the sky as though someone had dipped a brush in blood. The humidity had not changed, but the clouds felt foreboding. Rain would slow the evacuation of the cities, even more so if a storm rolled in off the sea. Staring at the colours, Teleri wished she could enjoy the beauty of it while sitting on her balcony with a cup of tea. It would have been far preferable to being on the back of her horse, watching a wave of soldiers departing Ensaycal ahead of the civilians they hoped to protect. Her family waited on the side, planning to join the convoy with the rest of the city officials. She had reservations about letting them all travel together, but no one would listen.

Her horse tossed its head, impatient to be on the move. Circling above them, the dragons kept watch. All except Idrun and her rider, Val. They had departed the day before to return to Bellenden to inform Lord

General Valerian and the council of dragon riders that Ensaycal and Endara were evacuating. Teleri prayed to War that they would reach the city unharmed, and that when they did, they would find their people safe. A selfish part of her was glad Calea had not sent Hadrian. She found comfort in his company, and the general hoped he found pleasure in hers. The peropuan calmed the tempest of her thoughts, soothing the anxiety that threatened to displace the calm demeanour of the High General.

As though Laszlo sensed her thinking about Hadrian, the dragon circled lower. Inhaling sharply, she caught sight of the rider. His wings were folded close to prevent them from getting caught in the air current created by the fast-moving creature beneath him. Around her, untrained horses shied away from the threat presented by the dragon. Their instincts screamed at them to run, forcing their riders to struggle for control. Aware of the disruption he caused, Laszlo swept back up into the clouds and resumed his circling patrol of the region. One of the other dragons roared in the distance, making Teleri chuckle as she wondered if the pair were being scolded.

No longer caring to remain where she was, the High General nudged her horse into motion. There had been no word of how things had gone in Endara, and she wanted to find out if Eirian was safe. At the bottom of her emotions, Teleri recognised the fear for her human counterpart that threatened to leave her paralysed. If anything had happened to the Altira mage and her family because of her plan, she knew it would destroy her. Nothing the Unseelie could do to her would come close to what the guilt would do. A handful of soldiers trailed after her, unwilling to let their commander go anywhere alone. Their presence did not matter; the only thing that did was reaching the meeting point she had arranged with Eirian.

The dragon tower stood alone against the fading dawn. Wagons, riders, and people on foot made their way out of Endara, aiming to join those leaving Ensaycal. A familiar red dragon stood guard over dozens of riders, and the thread of power connecting Teleri to Eirian drew her attention to a woman standing alone, gazing out over the bay. Bringing her horse to a halt next to the High Priestess, she saw what held the other woman's attention. Ships were setting sail, taking advantage of the tide and the wind to carry them far from the twin cities. They were likely to have as many passengers as possible. She suspected several captains would have taken advantage of the situation, offering places only to those who could pay. Pressing her lips together, Teleri offered a prayer to the god of water that there were no ocean-bound Unseelie waiting in open waters to consume the ships leaving the Bay of Blades.

"We have help," Eirian said, placing a hand on her leg. "The Executioner is here."

It felt like the air had been stolen from her lungs, and Teleri shifted in the saddle to stare at the people gathered nearby. Her eyes were drawn to the two women standing closest to Igraine, and she knew the pale-haired one who towered over Briallen was the one she was looking for. There was something about the way they huddled together that bothered her. Returning her focus to Eirian, she frowned at the slump of her shoulders. Grief cast a shadow over the High Priestess that spoke volumes.

"How?"

"Lord Gebael sent her. He told me he planned to help us, and I assume this is part of that. Lady Oblivion said she'll summon the full hunt to guard us against the Unseelie."

Fear slithered down her spine at the prospect of their people being guarded by the headless hunt. "The dullaghan? I'm not sure how well that will go down with our people."

"As long as the Unseelie don't attack, they'll never know about the dullaghan."

"They'll stay in the Veil?"

Eirian sighed, nodding slowly. "So I was told. I watched her kill goblins, and then I killed my kin, who planned to sacrifice themselves to the fire to lure the Unseelie into the trap. It has been a long night."

Eyes wide, Teleri did not know which of them had endured worse. "I listened to the screams as the ones who came for my family were burned alive. They may still be screaming."

"We should tell her. Maybe she can go back to the trap sites and put any Unseelie out of their misery. As much as I hate them, I can't stand the thought of unnecessary suffering when we can do something about it. They deserve death, and we can give it to them."

"You're right. I'm sure Briallen can help her get to each site quickly."

Arching a brow in amusement, the High Priestess shook her head. Slipping from the saddle, Teleri contemplated hugging her. They were not the most affectionate pair of godly heirs, but knowing Eirian was safe filled her with a need to feel the press of her body. Clenching her jaw, she hesitated before deciding that life was much shorter for all of them than she had long thought it would be. There was no point in leaving things unsaid or undone when, at any moment, the Unseelie could sweep through them. She grabbed Eirian's arm as the other woman turned, and pulled her to her chest, slipping an arm around her waist. Startled, the High Priestess did not struggle free, her lips parting in a silent demand to know what was going through Teleri's mind. Giving her a wry smile, the High General kissed her gently.

"I'm glad you're safe," she murmured, trailing her fingers down Eirian's cheek.

"As am I. You don't have any power to use against the First People, so I think I was more worried about you than you were about me. I'm sorry for what you had to do, but I'm glad you thought of it."

Closing her eyes for a moment, Teleri remembered the screams, and shook her head to banish them. "This is war, dear heart. We will all do things we regret in the name of survival."

"All that matters is that the people survive."

"Tell me I'm wrong to fear that you'll throw yourself into the fight. You're a husk maker, Eirian, and I know you think it's your duty to sacrifice yourself to bring down countless Unseelie."

Resting her forehead on Teleri's, Eirian sighed. "No, you're not wrong. We know it's what I will do if I must. There's no point in holding back when the enemy is immortal."

"Maybe I'm just tired of outliving Death's heirs," Teleri said, the simplicity of her admission surprising her as much as it did Eirian. "I've known for a long time that you wouldn't be my last Altira."

Withdrawing from her grasp, the High Priestess smiled sadly, and shrugged. She entwined her fingers through Teleri's, drawing the general along with her towards Briallen and Oblivion. People watched them in silence, no one daring to interrupt whatever was going on between the two heirs. Beyond the small gathering with its dragon protector, the evacuation of the cities continued. They were not needed to oversee it, and Teleri was thankful for that fact. Settling her gaze on the strange duine woman, she tried not to seek the mighty sword at her hip. There was a buzz of power in the air that made her blood sing, and the High General felt it increase with each step she took towards the Executioner.

"I'm glad to see you're safe, Teleri." Briallen gave her a small wave in greeting. "Igraine said Laszlo had seen you, but Eirian wasn't happy to take her word for it. We were worried."

There was no outward sign of recognition on Oblivion's face, her blank expression leaving Teleri unsettled. Glancing around, she noticed Delyth nearby with Amelia and their three friends crowded close. The sight of them lifted another heavy blanket from her heart, and the High General smiled thankfully. Deep down, she had known they were safe. Eirian would have been a distraught mess if something had happened to her daughter. But there was no confirmation of safety quite like setting eyes on a person.

Squeezing her hand, Eirian nodded to the white-haired duine. "High General Teleri Zarthein, this is Lady Oblivion, Death's Executioner."

Cocking her head, Oblivion stared at Teleri, a flicker of power passing through her blue eyes. "It's good to meet you, High General Teleri Zarthein. Are you as impulsive as the rest of Neriwyn's favourites? I've spent too many years of my life herding reckless warriors."

Teleri did not blink, too stunned to respond. At her side, Eirian bit back a laugh, but the shake of her shoulders failed to hide her reaction. Lowering her head, Igraine blew hot air over the two daoine women, and Oblivion's expression cracked, allowing a smile to escape her mask.

"The dragon tells me I need to apologise for being rude to you, High General. She said she's rather fond of you, and she'll eat me if I do it again. You're most fortunate to be held in high esteem by many."

Her mouth fell open, and Eirian's laughter ceased to be silent. Beside Oblivion, Briallen covered her mouth, doing better than her sister at restraining her amusement. Igraine snapped her jaw, nudging her rider's back in a suggestion to do something.

"Now she's threatening to eat me. Thank you so very much, Lady Oblivion," Briallen grumbled, shooting the older duine an annoyed look. "Igraine said to shut your mouth, Teleri. Before it's filled with flies and dust. She said the stunned fish expression is not a good look."

Rearing back, the dragon growled at her rider, and Oblivion slapped a hand to Briallen's back. "Oh, now you've done it, Altira. It was nice knowing you, even if it wasn't for as long as I hoped."

Shock fading, Teleri pinched the bridge of her nose and wondered if everyone had lost their minds. "Is idiocy something to do with being bound to the god of death, or is it something you manage all on your own? Is it something that afflicts husk makers?"

"There we go." Oblivion extended a hand to Teleri. "You needed a distraction from those terribly unhappy thoughts you've been struggling with. Don't worry, Igraine won't eat us."

"It's an honour to meet you, Executioner. I think. I'm undecided considering all of... this." She waved at the two duine and the dragon before giving Eirian a silencing look.

Holding her hands up, the High Priestess grinned. "I'm nothing more than the audience."

"We left multiple buildings burning with Unseelie caught in them. I don't know if you're interested in putting them out of their misery. Sometimes, mercy is all that separates us from the enemy."

Mirth fading, Oblivion swept her gaze over the line of the distant city. "There's no need for me to do it. My master already has. He's on the hunt while I'm tasked with protecting you."

She staggered, and Eirian was there, a hand on her arm to steady her. It felt like the rug had been yanked out from beneath her, and Teleri suspected she would never find her balance again. Knowing that Death was prowling through the streets of Ensaycal and Endara, hunting the Unseelie who had come to harm the innocent people of the cities, was both a relief and a weight dragging her down. Meeting Eirian's gaze, it was clear the High Priestess already knew what was happening.

"Did you ask him about the sword?" she whispered, hoping her lover was the only one who heard.

Eirian's eyes widened briefly, gaze darting to Briallen in terror before returning to her. "He said no."

"There's more, isn't there?"

"I knew he intended to help us."

The hot breath of a dragon washed over them, and Teleri shifted to stare into Igraine's dark eye. "How can I help you, mighty one?"

"She said Eirian smells of evasion." Briallen shoved her hands into her coat, eyeing her dragon sideways. "And she'll drop me in the bay if I don't mention she doesn't like that you're keeping secrets, sister. I keep telling her they're not important."

Shouts rose in the distance, drawing Teleri's attention away from the small group. As she shifted, she caught Eirian and Oblivion exchanging worried glances, and brushed it off as related to the ruckus. The layer of dust filling the air had settled slightly, except in one spot where it rose thicker than everywhere else. Fear coupled with a need to discover what was going on, had her striding towards her horse. A soldier held the reins, gladly surrendering them to her once she reached her mount. Before she hauled herself into the saddle, she felt the resulting burst of air from a dragon taking off, and glanced up to watch Igraine pass overhead. Horses shied, their nerves about being so close to one of the massive predators warning them of the increased danger of having one fly over them as she had.

"Igraine will check on it for us," Briallen said, joining her at her horse. "My sister remained with Lady Oblivion, but I thought I should stop you from running off until we found out what was happening."

"Eirian is withholding information."

"Well, of course she is. So are you. So am I. Everyone is keeping information to themselves until they know it's needed. I dread to think how much Lady Oblivion knows that we'll never learn."

Rubbing her face, Teleri turned to give the younger woman a look. She watched the slump of her shoulders as she understood what was not being said. Glancing over to where the High Priestess stood with the taller duine, neither of them bothered to continue the argument. They simply waited for Igraine to convey a message through her rider. Studying the shadows under Briallen's eyes, the High General wondered how much sleep the woman had gotten since her power manifested.

"How are you feeling, Briallen?"

Half-shrugging, she grimaced. "That's a complicated question. I haven't slept much, but for multiple reasons. Don't tell Eirian, but things with Tristan have changed."

Teleri chuckled, understanding exactly what she was implying. "Congratulations on finding something good while the world goes to shit around us. I understand the need. Don't tell anyone, but I'm rather enjoying Hadrian's company. These things keep us sane in the darkest of times."

"Really? He's a good man, and I suppose you couldn't go wrong with dallying with him."

"Dallying? Is that an Igraine word?"

"She said a wagon has a broken wheel, and the supplies spilled when it happened. It's holding things up, but they're working quickly to fix it. Soldiers are there, and we shouldn't be concerned." Scratching her neck, Briallen stared at the distant form of her dragon. "She said you should absolutely drag Hadrian by the wing to a secluded spot and take what you want from him."

Arching a brow, Teleri did not know if the dragon's encouragement should surprise her. "Did she now? I love my husband and Eirian. I have no need for more lovers. Let me enjoy Hadrian's company how I want to. There's no point in tainting my imagination with disappointment."

"You should be glad not to have a dragon in your mind."

"I'm sure you're right."

TWENTY-EIGHT
BRIALLEN

It FELT STRANGE TO have someone pressed to her back, arms wrapped around her waist, and the quiet chuckles of delight in her ear. Beneath her, Igraine was the warm, solid presence she always was, but Briallen was hypersensitive to the woman behind her. She could not shake the surprise that had left her frozen when Oblivion announced she would not be flying of her own accord but staying with her. Everything she had heard about the Raven kept rushing through her mind, leaving her fearful of what would come next. The silence from her bonded did not help, but Igraine was keeping out of the conversation, only letting her voice caress her rider's mind when she needed to say something.

"I know this isn't the best time to be coming into your power," Oblivion said, her words snatched at by the whistling wind as they circled lower over the convoy of fleeing people. "But you have nothing to fear. I won't let you accidentally kill anyone."

One of her hands was pressed to a darker grey scale, nails digging into it just so Briallen could feel the bite of pain lancing through it. "I'm not worried because I don't expect to come out of this war alive."

"Well now, we're going to have to do something about that."

"Why?"

The arms around her waist tightened, and for a moment, Briallen thought she heard a dark whisper demanding to be fed. It was not her magic. That had been silent since they had departed the dragon tower. Not even a thread of it felt within reach, and she was thankful for the transient nature of magic when it first began manifesting. Until it settled fully, the ability would come and go in a most unreliable manner. She knew better than to count on it to be available when she needed it the most. For all Eirian's promises to help her learn to control it, Briallen doubted there would be time to even start.

"Because I have a plan, and I need you to survive. This war can be ended. Our Lord Death is doing his best to convince that bitch Life to do the right thing, but she's being herself about it."

Cold claws of fear dragged across her stomach. "Should you talk about her like that?"

"I've said worse to her face."

Gawking, she craned around to stare at Oblivion's cold smirk. "And you lived?"

"Not by her choice. Let me tell you, the pleasure it gave me to press the tip of my sword to Shianeni's heart cannot be surpassed. Nothing will ever feel as good as that... except maybe running Annawyn through. After what she did to my family, it's the least she deserves. The things I'd like to do to her."

"I'm sorry for what happened during the Sundering. I can't imagine how you must have, and still do, feel." Forced to turn forward again, Oblivion surprised Briallen by resting her head on her shoulder.

Magic curled around them, a gentle stroke of ice across skin that felt too hot. She wanted to throw off her riding leathers and the protective gear that kept her from suffering windburn. Igraine banked, her wings going still as she glided across the sky, giving them an unimpeded view of the seemingly endless line of people, wagons, and livestock. Farmers herded cattle and goats along the side of the road, making the ever-present cloud of dust worse. None of those close to Endara and Ensaycal had wanted to remain on their farms, choosing instead to accompany the rest of their people on a journey no one knew the end of. Eirian's plan to lead the Unseelie to the distant daoine land where Life's heir lived was a brilliant one. They just had to survive it first.

"You shouldn't bring up the massacre of her family, my fledgling," Igraine muttered in a corner of her mind, and levelled out, returning to her slow flight as they guarded the people below.

"I don't mind when people mention it, but it depends on why." Oblivion's voice was a warmth across the exposed part of her neck. "Briallen may ask about it considering what she is."

A plume of fire was released from the dragon's mouth, the rumble of her annoyed roar spreading through them. *"She is mine. We are bound. Husk maker or not, she is a dragon rider."*

"My plan for this war includes protecting your kind."

Frowning, Briallen did not look back at the woman clinging to her. She knew the dragons had little expectation of surviving a war between the gods; not with the First People fighting their battles. As powerful as dragons were, they could die just as easily as a human could, but they would do more damage on their way down. Igraine had agreed with her plan to rain destruction on the Unseelie before they died, and to be given hope of survival filled the young duine with dread.

"What is your plan?" Briallen did her best to sound disinterested so that her hope and her dread did not betray the conflict in her heart. "And what do you want from the dragons?"

"After the Sundering, I played my part. I turned my back on my mate, and those who survived. My sister, Malena, plotted and joined forces with King Craven Havard of Diwan. They've made their deals, and had their daughters as they needed to. Our plans stretch far into the future, but they depend on Shianeni doing what is required. We need Annawyn to be imprisoned."

"And what do you want from us?" Igraine snarled, her suspicion swarming across the bond.

Her skin itched from the weight of what her dragon felt. Wishing her mental shields were better, Briallen swore to dedicate more time to building them up if they survived the fight against the Unseelie. A disbelieving huff in her mind told her what Igraine thought of her plan. The faint scratch of the powerful sword did not help the prickly sensation that made her squirm. Neither did Oblivion's arms around her waist, and she swept her gaze over the sky to find the familiar red splotch that was Ysgarlad. Picturing Tristan, Briallen wondered what he would have to say about her companion.

"He is a handsome goblin, and I can understand why you're in love with him," Oblivion murmured, a hint of laughter carried on her voice. "Those green eyes are very distinct. Who was his mother? Or should I ask, who is his grandmother?"

Beneath the fabric covering her face, Briallen felt her cheeks burning. "I'm not in love with Tristan."

"*His bloodline is unimportant!*" Igraine grumbled.

It felt like being trapped between a rock and a hard place with the way Oblivion and Igraine's thoughts circled each other in her mind. Briallen wished she were not the go-between for the mighty duine to intercept everything the dragon had to say. When they had been on the ground, and she had not been touching either of them, it had been easier to deal with. Now that she was pressed between them, their minds were heavy pillars weighing down on her, and Briallen felt the thud of a headache forming.

"Malena is coming to help in this battle. As are a few of the other Ravens. People believe most of us died, but with every new husk maker born among the daoine, a new Raven rises. Unfortunately, our one attempt to help the danann realise the truth was thwarted. Lord Neriwyn saw through our plan and rejected Malena's youngest daughter, sending her back to Diwan."

She had met the queen of Diwan once, and Briallen pictured the black-haired woman with her piercing gaze. The three princesses stood out in her mind because they had been so different from each other. But it was the youngest she had never forgotten. Blessed with an incredible gift for music, the third daughter had performed for the company of dragon riders and their mounts, lulling them to a state of serenity that Briallen wished she could find again. Among the dragons, she was spoken of with awe.

"Princess Silaine is incredible," she said.

"Yes, she is. One day she will transcend us all." Oblivion relaxed her hold on Briallen, leaning back slightly. "They're special girls. Shianeni thinks she knows everything going on, but her ego blinds her. She has no idea the rest of us plot behind her back, preparing for the day when she is gone from our lives. Our Lord Death has a plan, and we're instrumental in bringing peace to Tir."

Igraine slowed, drifting away from her position over the convoy. *"You would dare conspire against the god of life? Are you a fool, Executioner? She would burn us all."*

"I am merely a tool, just as you are, dragon. Lord Gebael has made a sanctuary. We'll fight this battle against the Unseelie, and we'll force Shianeni's hand, but the dragons are doomed. You will fall in the war to come. Except for the few who join me. We will vanish from a battlefield bathed in flame, and from living memory, until the time comes when we can rise again."

The thought of nearly all the dragons dying in an unwinnable battle against an enemy who wanted nothing more than to destroy everyone else broke Briallen's heart. She had known they would die to protect her sister's people, but hearing the Executioner speak of it in an unbothered tone drove the truth home. They would perish no matter what they did.

"No, not all will," Oblivion said, reminding Briallen that she was a presence in her mind. "Your father is one of the leaders who have been assisting. We're old friends. There are hundreds of eggs already safely hidden in the sanctuary we have built. And we have been carefully relocating knowledge. But once we retreat there, the walls will stay in place until it's time. There will be no back and forth."

"*Why?*"

"Because the gods are going into hiding as well, though Shianeni doesn't know it yet. Lady Alyah has seen the path we must walk if we wish to save Tir. They plan to force Life to bind them away with Annawyn, and to lock the First People in the Veil until such a time that it is possible for the gods to be reborn. A plan where they will cover the world with a fog so people do not realise there is anything beyond their borders. It will mean the First People are forgotten. Of course, this will weaken Shianeni, which is exactly what we need to happen if the plan is to work."

Suspicion raged through her, drawing a flicker of her magic to the surface. Briallen did not need Igraine's contribution to know that there were only two reasons Oblivion would share so much information with them. Either they were doomed to die shortly, or she needed them to ensure the plan worked. It felt like the Raven was leading them down a path they had no choice over.

"What part are we to play?" she hissed, glancing back at the woman holding her.

"You're a Raven, bound to a dragon, and you're an Altira. Do you know how powerful that makes you? Even untrained and without your power fully manifested, the pain you will rain down on the Unseelie in battle is nothing to blink at. Lord Gebael plans to let you wield Eclipse in this fight while he negotiates with the others to ensure your sister and the Zarthein heir can lead their people where they need to go. We are bound, Briallen, and on this path, we're stronger together."

Someone had ripped her heart out through her throat, and now she was simply waiting to die. Not even Igraine could speak; the silence in

Briallen's mind was suffocating. Plunging downwards, the dragon swept across the land in a quest to locate a spot she could set down without being observed by the people they were guarding. She knew their sudden departure from the path would draw the attention of the others, but the angry grey beast beneath her would deal with them. Whatever Igraine told her fellow dragons would have to be enough to keep them from giving chase. Especially Ysgarlad. Briallen was not ready to face Tristan when all she could think about was the nightmare Oblivion had delivered to her.

"I want nothing to do with wielding one of those swords!" she said, half hoping the wind would steal her words even though the woman pressed to her back had already read her thoughts.

"Would you rather die?"

"I think I might."

Oblivion laughed, and there was a hint of insanity in the sound. "You're wiser than I expected, Briallen, but you're a fool if you think you have a choice. He won't let you."

There was no need for her to name the person she referred to. Briallen knew it was Death. Spotting a rocky outcrop, Igraine banked towards it, aiming for the side furthest from the convoy. It would afford them some privacy, and shade from the blistering sun. As soon as the dragon touched down, her rider hurried to release herself from the saddle, scrambling down the grey foreleg to reach the ground. Oblivion remained in place, observing the landscape with a relaxed smile. Turning her head to Briallen, Igraine snuffled as she checked the duine over in her usual manner. The protective wave that flooded across the bond reminded the rider that she would not face things alone. She was never alone.

"You look like you're going to be sick."

Scowling at the dragon, Briallen pressed a hand to her stomach. *"Are you surprised? You heard what she said! I don't want this, Igraine. This is not for me."*

Spreading her wings to shade her rider, Igraine shook to dislodge the powerful woman on her back. *"You can get off now, Executioner. We'd like to talk."*

"Then we shall talk," a man said, drawing their attention to where he perched on a boulder. "My darling Oblivion would rather I deal with this because her first choice is to tie you up until it's time."

Igraine lowered herself to the ground, baring her teeth at the man as she did her best to shield her rider. Feeling the icy fingers of power caressing her, Briallen dropped to her knees, head bowed. She did not need to be told who was staring at her with eyes of the purest blue while his hand rested on a sword hilt identical to the one Oblivion carried.

"Forgive our disrespect, Lord Death."

He hopped off the rock, striding towards them without a care for the teeth aimed at him. "You are so different from your sister, Briallen. I'm sorry about this, but my priority is ensuring Tir survives."

A hand touched the top of her head, encouraging her to lift her face to gaze at the god. Gebael arched a brow, gesturing at the coverings that protected her from the harsh environment when flying on the back of a dragon. She felt Igraine's rumbled warning, the threat of a roar that would bring the others of their company to their side. Turning to meet her gaze, Death huffed at the beast, and she snapped her jaw.

"I know we created you lot to have no fear, but even you must admit a little would be reasonable right now, Igraine. Do you want me to kill you?" He waved at her, but Igraine did not recoil from his power. "I won't hurt Briallen! We need her for our plans. But if I have to bond her with a new dragon, I will. So, take that into consideration before you bite off more than you can chew."

With her face uncovered, the duine reached out to the dragon and touched her warm flank. *"Don't do anything foolish, Igraine. Leave that to me. Please. I can't lose you."*

"He won't give you a choice, my fledgling."

"Such is the way of the gods. I'm an Altira, and he is Death. I serve him."

Gebael chuckled, giving her a knowing look. "Don't worry, I don't expect you to serve me like Eirian does. Oblivion would probably try to run me through again. She never tires of looking for an excuse to do so. Now stand up... wait, no, don't. This might hurt, so you're better off staying where you are."

"Don't be a dick, Gebael!" Oblivion called down from her spot on Igraine's back.

"Are you going to stay up there the whole time?"

Briallen could not see what was happening, but the bemused expression on Gebael's face suggested the older duine had responded with a rude gesture. Her heart was knocking at the walls of her chest, reminding her it was still there and someone had not, in fact, ripped it out of her throat no matter how much she felt like they had. Shaking his head, the god unbuckled the scabbard containing Eclipse, and Briallen watched his every movement like he was a snake about to strike. In a way, she supposed he was. She wanted to climb onto Igraine's back and run away before he could press the hilt with its ominous raven's head into her hand.

"This is only temporary, Briallen," he said, holding the blade with one hand on the hilt and the other wrapped around the leather covering it. "But while you wield this sword, you will be immortal."

"What?"

"It's part of the process; otherwise, it would kill you. I have no intention of leaving you bound to it, but for the time being, this is something that must be done."

Power wrapped around her, keeping Briallen from moving. She wanted to fight against the unseen threads, but her gaze was locked on the sword as Death drew it free. Shadows dripped from the blade, calling to the magic coursing through her veins, and the scratch at the back of her mind grew stronger. Lips thinning, Gebael glanced at the terrified dragon before closing the distance between him and the kneeling woman. Drawn by the second sword, Oblivion leapt down from her spot, landing easily despite the height from which she had jumped. Darting over to the other duine, she hovered behind her, ready to offer support once their god was done.

"I really am sorry about this, Briallen. Hold out your hands."

Tears clouded her vision as the tug of his command had her lifting her gloved hands, palms up and waiting for the sword. Gebael placed Eclipse in her grasp, and pain ripped through every part of her. Agony wrapped around her spine, and Briallen wanted to collapse, but the power held her frozen in place.

"*My own pretty Raven. Will you feed me? I'm hungry.*"

Closing her eyes, Briallen let the tears fall as the scratch at the back of her mind became the voice of the sword. "*Yes, Eclipse, I will feed you.*"

Twenty-nine

Eirian

Shading her eyes, Eirian watched the sky. It had been hours since she had last seen the flash of grey that assured her Igraine was near. An odd feeling had settled in her gut soon after her sister's dragon vanished. One she could not shake, no matter what she told herself. At her side, Madoc was a shadow, his silent gaze locked on some distant point. She missed the talkative man she had fallen in love with as a rebellious young woman. Darkness had wrapped itself around him after a day of travelling, a sign the truth of what they were doing had sunk in.

While scrambling to arrange the evacuation of two entire cities, and set traps for their enemy, it had been easy to forget the reality of what was going on. Now they were stuck on the backs of horses, surrounded by a convoy of people without a sense of safety, and filled with nothing but desperation to reach a destination far from their home. It made sense that depression had taken hold of a man who thrived on building. Eirian wanted to encourage him to think and talk about what they might do when they got to where they were going, but she could not. She did not want to be the person who gave him a false sense of hope when they could be set upon by the enemy at any moment.

Their daughter rode with her friends a short distance away. Every time Eirian looked at the young mage, she noticed the protective way Delyth clung to her ever-present satchel. She kept meaning to ask what was so important, but a little voice suggested it did not matter. Most people had something they valued with all their heart. In a small pocket of her coat, she carried a pouch with all the trinkets Gebael had given her. Another held a little notebook she had pilfered from Briallen's things that was filled with sketches of her family and the cities. If her sister had noticed its disappearance, she had not said, and Eirian had no intention of returning it when it held images of things she never wanted to forget.

She caught a flash of red as Ysgarlad circled above them. Even though it was not Igraine, Eirian found some relief in seeing the familiar dragon. If something had happened to her sister, she knew Tristan and his bonded would not still be guarding the convoy. There was no way he would sit idly by while the woman he loved was in danger. But she could not shake the odd feeling, or the whisper in her power that told her it had something to do with what Death had said. The thought of her cheerful sister being able to wield a weapon capable of killing immortals filled her with an inexplicable fear. More so than the thought of Teleri using it. Her elven counterpart was a warrior, and if anyone could handle the responsibility of a weapon like Eclipse, it was War's heir. Not her sweet sister, who smiled so much, and kept sketchbooks filled with reminders to prompt her memory.

"What's bothering you?" Joshua brought his horse closer, and his question stirred Madoc from his daze. "Don't tell me it's nothing. You haven't been able to lie to me for years."

Meeting her husband's gaze, Eirian saw his exhaustion as he regarded her and the priest who had never left her side. "I haven't seen Igraine above us in a while."

Her words had both men searching the sky for the grey dragon. When they failed to spot Igraine, Madoc gave her his best attempt at a reassuring smile, while Joshua shifted anxiously in the saddle. Eirian was thankful for their reaction. It made her feel better about being worried.

"The others don't appear to be behaving any differently."

Grunting, Madoc gave Joshua a look of disagreement. "If they were trying to keep the rest of us calm, then they would do their best to remain in place. Why would they send Igraine and Briallen away?"

"Why wouldn't they? Someone needs to scout ahead, or behind, for the Unseelie."

Siding with her husband, Eirian glanced back at Delyth and her friends. "Because she's my sister. Her absence is the one that myself and Teleri would notice."

As they watched, the red form of Ysgarlad peeled away from her place above the convoy. Tracking her direction, Eirian was the first to spot the shape drifting towards them. The other dragon met it, and they circled each other while the rest approached. If she had not thought something was wrong before, the High Priestess was now convinced there was a problem involving her sister. Fingers of ice trailed down her spine, drawing her attention to a spot off to the side of the road. A man stood alone, watching her, and as she stared back, he vanished. Eirian did not need to see him up close to know it was Gebael. Pressing her lips together, she returned her focus to the dragons.

"See, nothing to worry about," Joshua said.

Studying her, Madoc moved his horse closer. "If you think something is wrong, I believe you, love. You've always had an instinct for these things, and I know not to doubt you."

She wished she could kiss him. The first chance they got, Eirian planned to remind him she still loved him. In all honesty, she knew she loved Madoc more every day, even if they did not always seem to be on the same page. When it mattered, they were a team. While she stared at him, the High Priestess realised she could hear a strange bird call. It was a shrill screech that sounded as though it was getting closer. Jerking around, she stared at the massive hawk plummeting directly towards them. Horses neighed in alarm, fighting the control of their riders. As she watched, the bird suddenly spread its wings, talons extended, and feathers became the gleaming skin of a naked duine.

"High Priestess Eirian Altira?" the woman said, dipping her head in greeting.

Mouth hanging open in amazement at the smooth way the woman had shifted, Madoc did not stop his horse from knocking into Eirian's. "Blood and bone! Do that again."

Cocking her head, the duine arched a brow, regarding him with a bored expression. "I'm Princess Astoria Havard of Diwan, and I bring you greetings from Queen Malena."

Pressing her fingers to her mouth, Eirian wanted to laugh in relief. "Oh, you are most welcome, Your Highness. It is an honour to meet you. Where is Queen Malena?"

"With the Executioners."

It did not slip her notice that Astoria had implied the existence of multiple people capable of killing the First people, and Eirian forced a smile to her face rather than demand to know what she meant. "I'm sure she's happy to see Lady Oblivion again. If you'd like to lead the way, I'll gladly follow."

"Can you fly, High Priestess?"

"No."

Astoria shrugged, waving her hand at the dragons circling in the air. "Well, my mother is with the Executioners on the back of a grey dragon. I understand you know Lady Eclipse."

Her stomach dropped away, leaving her a stunned shell with frozen lungs. At her side, Madoc and Joshua stared in confusion, looking between Eirian and the naked duine standing before them. Any moment someone was going to wake her up, and the High Priestess could brush the entire exchange off as a bad dream. She did not want to discover that Death had bound her older sister to a weapon that would destroy the very sunshine of her nature. Briallen was warmth, and happiness, and hope.

"Ma, what is she saying?" Delyth's voice carried a hint of the horror she felt.

"Lord Gebael has chosen to… curse Briallen with the sword Eclipse," Eirian replied without looking at those closest to her.

"Curse. Interesting choice of word," Astoria said, chuckling. "Very apt."

She wanted to grab the duine and shake her, but people were watching. It was more important than ever that she maintain the composure they expected to see from her. With the evacuation of the cities well underway, Eirian could ill afford to do anything that might upset the process. The danger grew with every passing day, and the only thing keeping people from panicking was the confidence of their leaders. Wherever Teleri was, the High Priestess imagined she would have plenty of things to say about separating the public from the private. Her feelings about what Gebael had done to her sister were a private matter.

"Tell Rider Briallen that I wish to see her."

Magic seemed to run across the duine's skin, a sheen of heat that had nothing to do with the warmth of the day. "They instructed me to remain with you until they join us."

Licking her lips, Eirian contemplated how to respond. Turning her gaze back to the distant dragons circling in the sky, she realised she was in a difficult position. With no authority over the princess, she had no way to compel her to convey the message to Briallen. All she could do was wait for her sister to come to her. She supposed the longer it took, the more time she had to come to terms with what her god had done. There was nothing she could do to change it. Briallen was bound to Eclipse, and any attempt to separate them without Death's assistance would be a disaster for those involved.

"Fine. We'll move the horses to the outer line to make it easier to separate from the convoy when the dragons come. I assume you will fly with us?"

Amused by her brusque tone, Astoria grinned and spread her arms. The shift into her hawk form was as smooth as it had been when she nearly crashed into the ground. Watching her take off without a word, Eirian wanted to scream profanities at the older woman. Hearing Madoc praising the shape shifter's display, she eyed him sideways in frustration. It was easier to press her heels to her horse, guiding it through the lines of people trudging their way to an uncertain future than it was to convince her husband that it had been little more than a spoilt royal showing off.

They followed her, none of them keen to miss out on what was going to happen. Eirian did not need to speak to her daughter to know Delyth was worried about her aunt. The two of them had always been close. People parted to let them through, fearful of being trampled by the horses if a dragon passing over startled them. It was as reasonable a fear as what she felt for Briallen. With rage in her heart, the High Priestess did her best to keep her power under wraps. No one wanted a husk maker to lose control in the middle of a large number of people.

Once free of the suffocating press of desperation, Eirian encouraged her horse to break into a trot. It felt good to move a little quicker, and she was sure her mount was happy to stretch his legs. The others kept up, Delyth and her elven companions spreading out to give themselves more room to move. Searching the sky for the dragons, a sliver of concern curled around her spine when she noticed that most of them had returned to their spots over the convoy. Three of them remained in the same place, and the High Priestess suspected they were Igraine, Ysgarlad, and Zern. As the rider in command, and someone with a long friendship with her father, Calea would question Briallen regarding what had happened.

The hawk hovering over them let out a shrill scream before drifting higher in the air to meet a large black bird flying towards them. They circled each other, and Eirian realised the new arrival had to be Queen Malena. Unlike her daughter, the Raven descended to the ground gradually, her black feathers gleaming in the sun as she set down on the earth. Her transformation was smooth, but lacked the extravagant performance of Astoria. When they were done, the daoine women stood with their gazes locked on the approaching dragons. Only two were headed their way, and the unmistakable red and grey beasts were matched in speed as they came in to land further away from the convoy.

As soon as their riders were safely on the ground, Igraine and Ysgarlad took off again. It was too risky to keep them on the ground where travelling livestock might become frightened by their presence. A fresh wave of dust carried on the breeze created by their massive wings. Coughing, Eirian watched the three people striding towards them. Tristan was gesturing wildly, shadows crawling across the land to swirl at his feet, summoned by the strength of his emotions. Before they reached her group, the High Priestess felt the wall of magic surrounding the two women, and her heart plunged in regret. She met Briallen's gaze when her sister halted beside Astoria, but saw nothing in the blue eyes that mirrored her own. The hilt of the weapon responsible for the change stuck up over her shoulder.

"I'm sorry, Briallen," she said simply, refusing to look at Oblivion. "I didn't know this is what he had planned when he told me you could wield Eclipse."

Giving her a grim smile, Briallen shrugged. "What is done is done, High Priestess. Your people are even more protected now. Queen Malena has news that you need to hear."

"Indeed, I do. I apologise for the manner in which we've met, High Priestess." Bowing her head, Malena offered a warmer smile than the two Executioners. "I'm Queen Malena of Diwan."

"We have little power over the current situation, so we'll make the best of it. It's an honour to meet you, Queen Malena. Now, what news do you have for us?" Eirian did not know if she wanted to hear what the duine needed to share with them.

"They're coming. Astoria scouted their presence to the west, and they'll be upon your people within two days at the most. I have been in contact with Lord General Valerian, and he will be here before then with several hundred dragons and their riders. Unfortunately, other Unseelie armies have struck the dragon cities, including Bellenden. Those coming to help here are in as dire a situation as your people."

Delyth cried out in horror, and Eirian listened to Amelia attempting to soothe her. They had known the Unseelie would attack the dragon cities, but she had hoped they were wrong. Closing her eyes, she let her emotions churn before counting to ten and taking a deep breath, squashing them beneath the heel of the role she had been born to. She was the Altira mage. The Unseelie would regret coming for her family and her people. Meeting Briallen's gaze, Eirian saw a flicker of pain. It fed a sliver of hope that her sister was strong enough to withstand the power of the sword.

"We can win—no, we will win this," Eirian said calmly, lifting her chin as she draped her power over herself like a cloak. "The mad god will regret sending her army after us."

Thirty
Delyth

It was impossible to escape the choke of desperate fear permeating the air. Emotions ran wild, and with every passing hour, more people broke from the convoy, fleeing in any direction except west. Those who held hope for salvation watched the sky, eager to see more dragons. Every time Delyth thought about what Queen Malena had told them, her heart broke for the mighty protectors and their riders. She did not know if her aunt had lost family in Bellenden, and the crackle of power keeping Briallen wrapped in its grasp deterred her from approaching. The woman who looked at her with a frozen gaze was not the aunt she adored, and she wished she could fix it.

All her ideas for discovering how to make weapons to be used against the Unseelie felt wrong. Before Death had bound Briallen to Eclipse, she had not understood the cost. The suffocating weight of their power also helped Delyth understand what it took to create a blade capable of killing an immortal. But even knowing the challenge, her fingers itched to examine the swords. She wanted to pick apart the threads of its weaving of magic, and learn the shape of the wards that allowed it to be a presence that scratched against their minds. No one was immune to the effects. Everyone shifted uneasily when the swords were near, eyeing the two women who wielded them as though they were beasts waiting to attack. Part of Delyth feared Briallen was what they saw her as—dangerous.

Caving to her desire to read the book Chaos had gifted her, the young mage sought the back of a wagon with barely enough room for her to perch. The driver was happy to let her squeeze in, and Delyth loosened the girth of her saddle slightly to give her mount a break while she read. Despite the looming threat of attack, the convoy had not been pushing hard in order to conserve energy. So many people were on foot that it would have been pointless for those with horses to charge off into the distance. Delyth had overheard a plan for mounted soldiers to offer themselves as a decoy to lead the Unseelie away from the bulk of the evacuees. She did not think it would work, but they had few other options.

Her fingers caressed the book. The cover bore no clues of what it contained, and she knew from her previous attempts to read it, the pages were filled. It was a tome that required complete and unwavering attention. Reading it in the back of a wagon while the air was thick with dust was not the ideal place to study a book that deserved devotion. But it was the only choice Delyth had. Her friends kept their distance, watching on with heavy gazes that carried the weight of what they knew was coming. They had seen the change to Briallen, and heard the news of the Unseelie army approaching. Amelia had been the one responsible for informing her Aunt Teleri.

Flattening her hands on the first page, Delyth lowered her head and rested her forehead against the thick paper. "Blessed Chaos, please let there be something I can use now."

There was an odd sense of rightness to praying to Xhaiden that she had never found with the other gods. She knew what the books said about the god of chaos. That he was a lesser god and embodied disruption to the balance. Unlike the average person, Delyth knew things about the other gods, and it made her ponder who exactly was the true threat to the balance. It did not seem like the embodiment of Life cared about her creations. If she had, then she would do everything she could to prevent the mad god from destroying their world. When Death was doing more to protect the living than Life, there were more than a few questions about the gods that needed to be answered.

Hunched over the book to protect it from dirt, Delyth examined the first page. Her eyes followed the swirl of lines around the edge, the twists familiar. They dipped and curled into the text, separating sections like vines in a garden. It felt like it was important to follow the flow, so she trusted her instincts as she read, letting her mind take her where it wanted to go. There were no wards to learn, but she greedily absorbed the lecture on the importance of balance when casting, especially in the event of multiple mages working together on a single task. Every time it brought up teams binding their power together, Delyth lifted her gaze to stare across the lines of people trudging along the road.

Tens of thousands of mages were among them. She knew it was a lot of power, and even more potential. With the right combination of wards, perhaps they could trap the Unseelie, and let fire take care of them. All they needed to do was stop the enemy in their tracks, and allow Oblivion and Briallen time to kill them all. Pressing her lips together as a wave of queasiness struck at the thought of her cheerful aunt dutifully executing thousands of people, Delyth wondered what she was really willing to do. It was a question they would all need to ask themselves. If there was something in the book that they could use, she needed to be sure she had the stomach for the carnage that would follow, because it would be her delivering the plan to her mother and the High General. She would be the one explaining everything while the rest listened and asked themselves if they had the strength to follow through with it.

"What is the deal with that book, Del?" Amelia's voice broke through her concentration.

Swivelling her head to blink at her best friend, the young mage sighed. "It's special, and someone important gave it to me. That's all I can tell you. This book is invaluable."

"Right." Her mouth twisted, and the elf scratched the tip of an ear. "You've been obsessed with it since that master gave it to you. All I want is to understand why."

"Because there might be something I can use to help us win against the Unseelie."

"If there were, why wouldn't the master who gave it to you have said something to the council?"

Closing her eyes, Delyth wondered how she could explain it to Amelia without revealing that the person who had given it to her was a god. Not just any god, but Chaos himself. When she looked at her again, she saw the tired impatience in the dark eyes she adored. It left her questioning whether their relationship would survive the journey to Telmia. Dropping her gaze to the book, the mage could not decide if it was worth worrying about romantic entanglements when the survival of her people was uncertain. There would be no relationship if they died on the barren land they were crossing, and their ashes swept across Tir on a stray breeze, never to be given a proper farewell.

"Please, Amy, just let me have this book. I need to feel like I can help. You're a warrior, and I am an academic. This is all I can do to be useful to you."

"You're not useless, Del," Amelia replied angrily. "I hate it when you suggest you are!"

"But against the Unseelie, I am. Unless I, or someone else like me, finds something we can use against our immortal enemy, then it's best that I keep out of the way, and do what I do best. Read."

Clenching her jaw, the young elf looked for their friends in desperation for someone to support her. The others had stayed back, giving them as much privacy as they could manage. Even the wagon driver had his head bowed, straw hat pulled over his face and a kerchief covering his nose and mouth as protection from the dust. Returning her focus to the book, Delyth carefully turned the page over. A dragon roared above them, the sound serving as a reminder that they were trapped in the agonisingly slow slide of time when they knew something was going to happen, but not when.

"I love you, Delyth Altira. No matter what happens. But I wish you'd let me help you."

"There's nothing to help me with, Amy. Let me read my book, and if I find something useful, you will be the first to know. Please."

Amelia's huff as she peered into the wagon told Delyth how much she hated that there was not enough room for them both. At any other time, she would have been happy to sit next to her lover in silence while they travelled the road. All Delyth really wanted was to feel the warmth of her body against hers, and the tickle of her breath over her skin. They did not know how much time they had to be together. If they fell to the Unseelie, she did not want to die without the taste of Amelia's kiss on her lips. But the suspicious way Amelia stared at the book was a knife twisting in her heart.

Her eyes followed every word scratched onto the page. It was as useful as the first, detailing the different ways in which mages could share power. Some of them were familiar to her from her lessons at the university, but others were new. When the third page laid out the formation for a simple ward that a single mage could do, the instructions for it being woven by a group confused Delyth. Returning to the start of the text, she read it again to work out why anyone would bother doing a team casting of it when one person was enough. As the explanation sunk in, her mind began turning over the possibilities of what they could do with other wards if cast by a team. Turning her gaze to the sky, she looked for the dragons, wondering which one was Igraine.

Thinking about Briallen brought her mind around to the husk maker power her aunt had developed. She could not help wondering what would happen if a team of mages shared their magic with a team of husk makers. Running her tongue over her teeth to keep her agitation under control, Delyth wanted to track down her mother or Oblivion to pose the question. It made sense that under those circumstances, the husk makers would be capable of sucking the life out of more people on a bigger scale. But she did not know how the energy worked, or if they needed an influx of power in order to draw more of the precious life force out of things. Without that knowledge, Delyth did not know if the outline of a plan forming in her mind could work against the Unseelie army.

"I know that look, Del," Amelia said, nudging her horse closer.

She frowned, giving her beloved warrior a torn look. "I have an idea, but no way of knowing if it would work. Not without questioning Lady Oblivion... and then I feel foolish for wanting to bother her with my questions, because if it did work, surely the husk makers would have tried it before."

"Tell me what it is."

"The first few pages of this book go into channelling magic through teams of mages to allow them to cast bigger, more powerful wards. Our cities were probably built using these methods. My thought was, if drawing magic from a team of mages allows husk makers to use their power on a bigger scale?"

Eyes widening, Amelia looked horrified at the idea. "That's a... yeah. I don't know."

"Exactly."

"If they could, then a couple of husk makers might wipe out a city if they had willing mages. I don't know if I want to find out whether it would work. This is the stuff of nightmares."

Waving the comment away, Delyth turned back to her book. "But imagine using it against the Unseelie. They could potentially bring down a legion."

"And kill how many of us in the process?"

"When I see my mother again, I'll mention it to her. Maybe Lady Oblivion will be more receptive if the idea comes from the Altira mage, rather than her young daughter, who doesn't have the same power."

Drumming her fingers on the pommel of her saddle, Amelia thought about where Delyth was going with the idea. "What about things like knock back wards? Imagine a team of shield mages working together on the front line. They could flatten the enemy."

The page she was on held her attention. It was a series of simple wards drawn over the trunks of trees in a line. Small marks denoting distance were set between each drawing. On the next page, the text detailed the possibility of using the underground link of plants to connect the power of wards over a large distance. She found it puzzling to make sense of because it appeared the author was arguing with themselves over whether the idea would work at all. Sweeping her gaze over the landscape, Delyth snorted at the lack of trees, and turned the page again. There was no point in wasting her time on something they could not use.

But her mind kept returning to the possibility of joining husk makers together as a team. She stared at the sky instead of reading the page. Dragons drifted on the currents, their wide circles over the convoy allowing them to watch for problems. They were waiting for Briallen's father and the remaining dragons out of Bellenden. No one was sure how many more would come, and Delyth hoped they would be enough to make a difference. If they could torch the Unseelie, maybe the rest of them could get away while the enemy recovered from the fire. Shaking her head, she forced herself to focus on the page again even though her mind wanted to drift among the clouds.

Once her focus locked onto the words, she found something that made her heart skip a beat. Remembering Teleri's idea to lure the Unseelie into a trap, she realised the ward her eyes refused to move from had a use. It was one she had never seen before, but Delyth had faith she could master it quickly. The ward allowed for the displacement of particles, specifically earth. She imagined how easy it would be for a team of mages to split the ground beneath the feet of the enemy. Once trapped in a chasm, the dragons could bathe them in fire, rendering them unable to do a thing until Oblivion and Briallen killed them. A dark voice at the back of her mind suggested they could close the ground up again, imprisoning the immortals in a tomb they could not escape from. Certainly not in time to prevent her people from reaching their destination and forcing Life to do something about the mad god.

Turning to Amelia, she smiled slowly, and let her glee show. "I have an idea."

Thirty-one

Teleri

"Aunty Teleri!" Amelia's voice had her turning in the saddle to search for the young elf. "Would you get out of my way! No, this is important. Lady Delyth has something for the High General."

Spotting the young woman who looked so much like her mother, Teleri guided her horse towards where they were arguing with a soldier. The moment the officer saw her, he saluted and shrunk back in his saddle. Eyes narrowing at the group led by her niece, the High General signalled for them to approach. She glanced up at the circling dragons, aware that more would arrive at some point. Everyone knew the danger, and enough people had overheard discussions about the downfall of the dragon cities for rumours to spread. Hope was waning with every cluster of people who decided it was not worth remaining with the convoy when they could make a run for it alone.

"Is your mother safe?" she said, levelling her gaze at Delyth.

The mage frowned, mouth twisting before she replied, "Not a clue. I assume so. Wouldn't you know if she weren't? Honestly, I haven't spoken to her since..."

Understanding what she was referring to, Teleri sighed. "I see. What is so important?"

Amelia looked like an eager puppy, squirming in her saddle with an excitement that did not belong on a Zarthein warrior. "Del has a book, and it's full of ideas. She found something we could use."

"A book? Let me see it then."

She watched how Delyth clutched her satchel to her chest, panic flaring in her eyes. It roused her curiosity more than she had expected. Her plan had been to indulge their attempt to feel useful before gently squashing any ideas they had. There was no point in encouraging them to do something stupid. But the protectiveness the young Altira was showing towards something like a bag containing a book was intriguing, and Teleri wanted to see what was worth that reaction.

"Hand it over, Delyth." Extending her hand, she waited.

Shaking her head, the mage refused and gave her a pleading stare. "It was given to me... please believe me when I say that you'd understand if I could tell you. The one who entrusted this book to me is powerful, and I won't risk upsetting him by letting others handle his gift."

Teleri stiffened, her gaze settling firmly on the satchel clutched to Delyth's chest. Letting her magic curl around it, she felt the strange threads of power. They carried a taste like lightning, and a hint of destruction. Lips thinning, the High General regarded the book and the woman holding it with concern. She understood what Delyth had not dared to say. A god had gifted the book to her, but the question was which. Turning to her niece, she studied Amelia thoughtfully. It was obvious she did not know what her lover possessed.

"Tell me about the man who gave the book to Delyth."

Startled by the question, Amelia shrugged. "Tall, darkest skin I've ever seen, handsome. Had a few tattoos sticking out from under his clothes. Powerful. His magic made my skin crawl, and he was only interested in speaking to—blood and bone, Del, did a god give you that book?"

"Xhaiden, Lord of Chaos," Teleri said quietly, cocking her head. "What did you find?"

"There's a ward in here for moving particles, specifically the earth. It's very simple, one that most mages could master in a short amount of time. The book also goes into depth about different methods for power sharing, allowing mages to link and work over a large area."

It did not take long to work out where Delyth was going with her explanation. Covering her mouth, Teleri swept her gaze over the convoy of desperate people. She did not know exactly how many mages were among them, but she was confident they numbered in the tens of thousands. The warrior mages and their shields were under her command, so she had no intention of counting them towards those who could lend their power to Delyth's plan. Everyone else needed to do their part.

"You're thinking that with enough mages using this ward, you could open the ground beneath the Unseelie and trap them in a hole? I like it, and if it can be done..."

"Exactly." Delyth nodded enthusiastically. "Trap them in a hole, and roast them. If we buried them alive, who would blame us?"

Arching her brows at the venom in the mage's voice, Teleri looked at Amelia in surprise. She did not look disturbed by what her lover had suggested, hinting that it was not the first time Delyth had voiced it. While she understood and shared the desire to prevent the Unseelie from doing more harm, she felt a need to remind the young women that they were still people. It was not their fault the gods had created any of them the way they had. That was simply their lot in life, and punishing them in such a dreadful manner instead of killing them was a cruelty that would stain their hearts for eternity.

"They're still people, Delyth. What would your mother say?"

"If it meant Aunty Briallen did not have to use Eclipse as much, she would agree to it."

Clenching her jaw, Teleri felt the reminder like a knife in her gut. She had seen the dragon rider, and the sword that Death had forced on her. In passing, Hadrian had recounted the story Igraine had told the other dragons. The god had not given Briallen a choice before binding her existence to the weapon that now controlled her. Eirian's distress had been plain for her to see, even if others could not. Part of her felt guilt over bringing up the sword, but Teleri reminded herself that Death had probably had his own plan in mind long before she made her request.

"You're right. Have you seen your aunt again?" Glancing at the sky, she could not locate the grey dragon. "Hadrian said she is keeping away from the other riders. Only Tristan dares go near her."

Delyth looked like she might cry for a moment before she squared her shoulders. "No. Will you help me test my theory about these wards? The sooner we figure out if it will work, the sooner we can start teaching as many mages as possible how to do it. That way, when the Unseelie attack, they'll be in for a jaw-dropping surprise. Literally. Their jaws will drop below the ground."

"There was no need to explain your attempt at a joke, girl."

Clearing her throat, Amelia did not hide her amusement. "She tries, Aunty Teleri."

No one would argue about trying Delyth's plan if it came from her. The High General knew it was why they had brought it to her rather than trying to convince a handful of mages to work with the young Altira. Letting her gaze drift over her officers, Teleri considered which of them would not question her orders to assist the High Priestess's daughter. She needed ones who could follow orders without demanding an explanation of where the wards came from. If the god of chaos had visited Delyth, and he had given her a book filled with potential help, then she would be damned to oblivion before she let anyone ruin their chance. Xhaiden was notoriously flighty, and with his bond to Death, it was no surprise he had selected someone from Gebael's bloodline.

"I'll make the arrangements. Have you attempted the ward yet?"

Blinking at her, Delyth paled. "No? When I realised what I had read, I explained it to Amelia first before we came straight to you. I haven't stopped to test it."

"But you've memorised it?"

"Yes, High General."

If the situation had not been so dire, Teleri would have laughed at the scolded droop of Delyth's shoulders. She understood her desire to speak to someone older and more experienced about what she had come up with. Knowing the dangers of trying unfamiliar wards alone without a rational mind, she was even more thankful for it. Eirian could not survive the loss of her daughter to the war. There was no point in praising the young women for not endangering themselves when it had not been their intention, but that did not stop Teleri from thanking the gods for their enthusiasm keeping them sensible.

"Stay here. Take the time to plan how you intend to test it. Don't forget, this is a new ward to you and the others, and with anything new, caution should be taken," she said, nodding to them before she turned her horse towards the cluster of officers watching intently.

As she rejoined them, Teleri felt a change in the air. It was the thrum of power in the breeze that heralded shouts of amazement. There were several dragon roars, some familiar, and others not. Everyone stopped moving, turning their faces to the horizon where a dark line drew closer. Pinching the bridge of her nose, the High General found she was not surprised Lord General Valerian and the remaining people from Bellenden had arrived then. While their presence would help assure the convoy that they were not defenceless, she needed to focus on her priorities. The first being the arrangements for mages to assist Delyth in testing her plan. It was not something she wanted to put aside when it had the potential to save countless lives without relying on the dragons, or the two daoine bound to Death's swords.

"Malek, Senna, Kristyn. I need the three of you to come with me."

Exchanging looks, the officers waved at the swarm of dragons filling the sky. They did not want to miss out on what would happen when their general met with the leader of the riders. When they saw the dark look on Teleri's face, they silenced any protests they planned to make, and nudged their horses into motion. Following her over to where Delyth and Amelia waited with their friends, the three officers did not bother to hide their annoyance. Watching Eirian's daughter straighten in the saddle, her hand resting on the satchel containing Chaos's book, the High General was proud of the determination in her gaze.

"Right, the three of you are going to assist Lady Delyth. She has uncovered a ward that might help us in the battle against the Unseelie, but we need mages willing to test it out with her. You're shield mages, and I think you'll have some suggestions for how we can make this work," Teleri said, waving at Delyth while staring at the officers and silently promising to make them suffer if they refused.

Senna huffed, turning her focus to Delyth. "What does the ward do?"

"It moves earth. Basically, when done correctly, we should be able to open the ground to make a hole." Delyth did not bother to give a detailed explanation, and Teleri watched Senna's stance change.

"Really? Are you sure?"

"That's what my source says. I can show you, but the book is mine, and only for my hands. The High General knows where it came from and understands why I cannot let others have it."

Shifting her focus back to her commander, the shield mage arched a brow. "High General?"

"I'm aware of where the book came from. If anyone tries to take it from Lady Delyth, I'll kill them myself. This is our chance, and I won't let anyone risk ruining it because they can't trust my word, or hers. We're not talking about some novice; this is Delyth Altira, daughter of the Altira mage." She heard the roar of a dragon closer to them and nodded to the group. "Now, I'm relying on you lot to get this sorted. Test the wards carefully. If it works, find some fucking mages to train. The sooner we're sure of it, the better. Stars above only know when the Unseelie might strike."

Saluting her, the three officers and Amelia and her friends did not meet her gaze. Teleri nodded to Delyth and wondered what Eirian would say when she found out what her daughter had done. It felt fitting that she was placing so much faith in the abilities of an Altira when their destruction was coming for them. Touching the hilt of her sword, the High General shifted in the saddle to signal to the rest of her officers to follow her through the lines of the convoy. They needed to be in the open before they could greet Lord General Valerian.

She opened her power to the thread connecting her to Eirian. They would need to greet the riders together, and she wanted to save time by finding the Altira first. It would give her the chance to tell her counterpart what her daughter was doing. Following the distant pull, Teleri led her officers through the throng of people, seeking the open region beyond. It was a barren landscape, all rocky browns and greys with sparse scrub clumped where it could survive. Knowing they had husk makers on their side, she could not resist imagining what it would look like when they sucked the life force from the Unseelie. They would either feed it to the earth or spread it across the army to mend any injuries incurred during the fight. Either way, the land would never be the same.

A massive blue dragon spiralled down to a spot further from the convoy. She watched it move, marvelling at how something so big could be so graceful. Spotting Laszlo and Zern settled into a circular path above the blue, Teleri felt her heart flutter at the prospect of seeing Hadrian again. As she spent more time with the peropuan, she longed for the peace his company brought. The grey form of Igraine plunged down, settling onto the ground near the blue, and their horses skittered sideways, nervous about being close to the dragons. Sweeping her gaze across the land, she followed the tug to Eirian, watching as the High Priestess rode towards them with a group of people surrounding her. There were circling forms in the air—the dark forms of Queen Malena and the other Ravens, as well as the bold hawk that was the Princess Astoria. Teleri had witnessed the marvel that was her shifting, and wondered what it would be like to watch the Battle Hawk fight against the Unseelie.

"I don't know what to say to him," Eirian said the moment they were facing each other. "How do I tell Lord General Valerian that I let Death do what he did to his daughter?"

Grimacing, Teleri shook her head. "There was nothing you could do, Eirian. He knows you cannot command the god of death. Besides, he'd already be aware of it. Come on, let's greet the poor man. He's likely to be in pain after losing his home, and possibly family members as well."

"That's exactly what I'm worried about. Briallen isn't herself with Eclipse in control."

"And there's nothing we can do for her except fight the Unseelie and hope Lord Gebael releases her from the sword as soon as the battle is over. By the way, I'm pleased to inform you that you have a wonderfully brilliant daughter who might have discovered something we can use against the enemy."

Eirian stared at her in bafflement. "She has? I mean, it doesn't surprise me, but also, she has?"

"Someone important gave her a gift. A book. Let's just say, she might bring a little chaos to the fight, and turn the tide in our favour. If it works, and we're able to teach enough mages in time. I'm hopeful, which says a lot. Delyth has help from three of my most trusted officers."

The blue dragon roared, drawing their attention to the handful of beasts waiting for them in a half-circle. People had gathered in front of them, and Teleri was surprised to see several danann there. It was hard to miss the broad wings with their colourful feathers, and she searched for the darker wings of Hadrian in hope. Eirian sighed heavily, resigned to seeing her sister again.

"Well then, let's get this over with," Teleri said, offering an assuring smile.

Thirty-two

Briallen

Igraine's departing wing beats were a drum in her ears, but the empty patch of land was where she needed to be. Fingers fumbling with the fabric covering her face, Briallen tried to silence the whispers in her mind. Unlike her dragon, the accursed sword had no interest in giving her peace. It crooned at her, hungry demands for destruction urging her magic to struggle against her control. She could not stand being near anyone, least of all her father and sister. When Valerian had set his eyes on her, his daughter had seen the sorrow in his gaze, and it had felt as though he was grieving her death along with those of two of her siblings who had fallen in the battle for Bellenden.

She could not grieve. The sword would not allow it. Eclipse latched onto her pain, twisting it into a need for vengeance. All Briallen wanted was silence in her mind, and the freedom to drop to her knees to scream and cry over the unfairness of it all. Her brother and sister might not have always been the most supportive siblings, but they had been family, and they had fallen to the Unseelie. Worse still was the news that mortals marched alongside the First People who answered the mad god's call. Humans, daoine, and elves had betrayed their own to join with those who would destroy them in the end. When the fires of conquest died out, those mortals would find themselves the playthings of their allies.

"We will destroy them all, my Raven."

Screaming in defiance, Briallen undid the buckle of the belt keeping Eclipse attached to her body. It would not free her of the voice echoing through her mind, but it made her feel better to throw the sword as far as she could. The compulsion to fetch it back wrapped iron chains around her limbs. There was no need for the weapon to scold her for her behaviour; it felt nothing but hunger. An insatiable need to consume the spirits of those it killed. All she was to Eclipse was a hand obeying its commands, a puppet on strings constructed by the god it served. Together, they were to be Death's shadow cast between the Unseelie and the light of existence.

"Bri," Tristan said, his hand catching her arm before she picked up the sword. "I'm here."

His shadows curled around her. Under the pale light of the waning moon, his ability was stronger than it was by day. There were countless shadows for Tristan to call upon, and they wrapped her in their cold, silky touch. Kicking Eclipse away, the goblin moved in front of her, his second hand coming to cup her cheek. Briallen clenched her teeth, struggling with the compulsion to turn her husk maker power on him. It was what the weapon was screaming at her to do. To Eclipse, he was not her best friend; he was just another goblin to kill.

"You shouldn't be near me, Tris," she whispered. "I'm not in control."

Resting his head against hers, he sighed, and the shadows brushed over her skin, slithering beneath her clothes. They trailed like fingers over the sensitive spots Tristan knew would make her squirm. A spark of desire broke past the demands to kill him, and Briallen stiffened when Eclipse purred in delight. She did not want the sword to destroy the safety she found in her friend.

"*I see why you don't want to kill him.*" Eclipse wormed into her memories. "*Yes, he is good. We like this. Oblivion says it feels as good as drinking the blood of our enemies.*"

"I'm never going to abandon you, Bri. You're mine, remember. Wherever you go, I will follow. As long as you serve that sword, I will serve it too. Tell it I will drag the Unseelie to your feet so it might feast upon them. We belong together forever and always."

Tears tracked down her cheeks. "You don't understand what it's like, Tris. My thoughts are barely mine. Even Igraine is affected by the sword."

"I know, Ysgarlad told me. She's angry and scared. We love you and Igraine, but all we can do is to be there for you. No matter what, we will be by your side. Death might not have bound us to the sword, but we serve it anyway. Tell me what you need, Bri. If it's someone to kill, I will go right now and find you someone to sink that blade into. All you have to do is say the word."

Her hands slid beneath his coat, feeling the warmth trapped in the layers of clothing all riders wore. His words pleased Eclipse, the sword picking them apart as it decided what it wanted more. It hurt to wrest more control over her actions, but Briallen kissed Tristan, her fingers digging into his waist to pull him to her. She wanted to sway the weapon's desires away from its craving for blood. She knew she should feel guilty for using her friend that way, but suspected some part of him knew.

"Stars, Bri," he murmured, nipping her lip. "Tell me what you want."

"I want you to fuck me, Tris."

Eager curiosity swarmed across the chains binding her to the sword, and Eclipse fell silent. Tristan's mouth found hers again, his hands seeking the clasps of her riding leathers. Her refusal to let go of him turned into a challenge. Briallen feared releasing the tight hold she had on the goblin would lead to the weapon deciding to go back to craving his death instead of the pleasure he could give them.

"*Found you,*" Oblivion whispered across her mind. "*Oh good, you haven't started without me.*"

Snarling, Tristan pulled back, swivelling around to glare at the approaching woman. The Executioner carried something under her arm, and the shadows recoiled from her as she came to stand next to them.

Eyes darting to where Eclipse lay on the ground, Briallen waited for the sword to resume its demands.

"Don't worry, I'm not here to kill you, Rider Tristan."

Eclipse crowed in delight. "*Yes, this is better. Much better. Now we will see.*"

Understanding filled her with confusion that was swiftly drowned out by the desire coming from the sword. "No, please. He's mine. You can't take this from me as well."

Arching a brow, Oblivion brushed a hand over her cheek. "Darling Briallen, if I don't, you'll kill him. Eclipse hasn't got the experience to control its urges. Besides, you're mine now, and what's yours is also mine. He's not my first goblin, and I promise you won't complain about what I can teach him."

His fingers were wrapped around her belt, and Tristan cocked his head, glancing between the two women. "I told you, Bri, whatever you need. This isn't what I expected, but if it means being with you."

"This isn't fair," she whispered, anger and grief lacing her words.

"No, it's not." Pulling her close again, Tristan smiled sadly. "But I refuse to leave you, and I'd rather you didn't kill me. Besides, if she can teach me more ways to please you, it'll be worth it."

Plucking the object from under her arm, Oblivion chuckled as she unrolled it. Shaking the blanket out, she laid it down on the ground. They did not move, clinging to each other as they watched her pull the other sword over her head to chuck it on top of Eclipse. Sweet silence drifted across her thoughts, and Briallen sighed in relief. She doubted the quiet would last for long. Moving to stand behind her, the Executioner slid her hands over her shoulders to her chest, coming to rest over her breasts.

"As long as you are bound to that sword, you're bound to me," Oblivion murmured, nuzzling Briallen's neck. "Some would say the threads binding us make you my wife."

"I am not your wife."

"Don't worry, darling. If things go according to plan, this is only temporary."

Oblivion kissed her neck, trailing her lips along the line of her jaw until she reached Briallen's ear. The nip of her teeth made the younger woman squirm. Meeting Tristan's gaze as he stepped back, she was stunned by the desire burning in the green depths. His shadows crept back, curling around her legs, and from the low chuckle of the woman pressed to her back, around hers as well. They stroked softly, leaving her skin tingling when they moved on to a fresh spot.

"Seems you've got better control over your power than I expected, princeling. I'm going to sit down on the blanket while the two of you strip off all those layers. Riders wear a lot of protection, which is perfectly understandable, but makes it frustrating when you want to seduce them."

The moment her hands left, Briallen felt agony shooting down her spine. It was like someone had cut off a limb, and she knew it was because of the swords. Shoulders slumping, she closed her eyes. Tristan closed the distance between them, his knuckles gently lifting her chin so he could kiss her. For a moment, she could pretend they were alone.

"You can say no, Bri. I won't mind. What I will mind is if you force yourself to do this when you don't want it. They've taken so much control from you; you don't have to give them this." He kissed her again, slower, as though he expected her to decide she was strong enough to refuse. "I will always wait for you, my flame. You are the light that lets my shadows grow."

"I need you," she whispered.

"I am yours."

Keeping her gaze locked on his, Briallen picked up where they had stopped when Oblivion joined them. Her hands shook while they fumbled with the clasps of her riding leathers, and Tristan followed her lead.

Stretched out on her side with her head propped up on her hand, the Executioner watched in silence, but they felt the weight of her attention. The sword was a presence at the back of her mind, and the eagerness it fed down the chain encouraged Briallen to seek the woman bound to its mate as soon as she was done stripping out of her clothes. Beneath her knees, the blanket was scratchy compared to the silken shadows slithering across her skin while she crawled over to Oblivion.

Stroking her cheek, the older woman kissed her softly. "I'll do my best to shield you from them. But there is only so much even I can do to protect us from what they want."

Realising that Oblivion wanted her to focus on Tristan, Briallen turned to beckon him closer. He stood at the edge of the blanket, shadows clinging to his legs as though they were pleading to be let loose on the women. Remaining on her knees, she settled in front of him, and the shadows flocked to her, some creeping past to curl around the Executioner. His cock jutted out, and she reached for it, trailing a finger along the underside before wrapping her hand around it. The moment her mouth drew the head in, Tristan groaned, burying his hands in her hair. It was easy to slip into a place in her mind where sucking and licking his cock was the only thing that mattered, and Briallen welcomed that focus.

"Stars, Bri," he groaned, tugging her hair until she removed her mouth. "Keep doing that and I'll lose it before I've had a chance to please you."

His shadows curled around her like ropes, encouraging Briallen to move backwards onto the blanket. They softened the scratch of the wool, helping her to imagine they were back in her bed in Endara rather than on the ground somewhere while they waited for the Unseelie to attack. Watching Tristan drop to his knees while the shadows tugged her legs apart, she did not flinch when Oblivion's hands ran through her hair. With that touch, a weight lifted from her mind again, and Briallen twisted slightly to stare at the other woman. Following the path of his shadows, the goblin slid his hands along the insides of her legs until he settled between her knees, gaze locked on Oblivion.

"Are you waiting for permission?" Shuffling closer, the Executioner chuckled.

"Yes."

"Do you want his mouth on you, darling?"

Briallen swallowed, nodding when her throat refused to work. Power caressed her mind, drawing her gaze to Oblivion. The other woman wore an amused smile, and the moonlit glow of her skin did nothing to hide the scars and tattoos decorating her body. A longing to familiarise herself with every mark dug into the rider's heart, and she wanted to turn over so she was on her knees as she pleased her mate. When the thought flickered through her mind, Briallen recoiled in shock, but Oblivion's hand shot out to grab her arm. She knew it was Eclipse's thought, not hers, though it only made it hurt worse.

"The more you fight the sword, the more it will cost you, darling."

She wanted to cry, but desire filled her with a need to touch Oblivion. "If I don't fight, it will consume me."

"Trust me, fighting will break you. That is what the swords do. If you surrender and do what it wants, it has no reason to force you to comply. You don't want to become like me."

Tristan's fingers dug into her thighs, his warm breath over her stomach drawing her attention back to where he had settled between her legs. At the edge of her mind, Eclipse purred in delight, eager for the goblin to prove why they should not kill him on the spot. She let Oblivion press against her back, her legs becoming a cage to help the shadows keep her in place. When her fellow rider lowered his mouth to her cunt, Briallen groaned. Hands caressed her breasts, pinching her nipples to roll them between fingertips.

Oblivion's lips were on her ear as Tristan's tongue speared into her. "He looks perfect between your legs, like he was made to serve you. Close your legs around his head, hold him there so he knows his place. Make him beg for the right to breathe the same air as you."

His eyes met hers for a moment before Tristan grazed the sharp tips of his teeth over her clit. The lap of his tongue at her entrance made Briallen hesitate to follow Oblivion's instruction, but he soon had it buried back inside her, his nose pressed into her mound as though he was giving her permission to do it. Shadows urged her legs to close around his head, and grabbing her hand, the older duine encouraged her to bury it in his hair. Tristan slid fingers into her while he had the chance, stroking the tips of his claws against the sensitive spot he knew would make her moan.

"That's right, hold him there."

Arching back against Oblivion, Briallen felt like her nerves were on fire. She rocked her hips into Tristan's mouth, hand pressing his head in firmer. He made no attempt to pull away, his tongue and fingers working together to coax her orgasm to its peak. Lips dotted kisses over her skin, a hand closing around her throat while the Executioner's other hand continued to toy with her breasts. Just as a thread of concern for Tristan wriggled into her mind, teeth latched onto her neck while the hand at her throat tightened. It was enough to send her over the edge, a hoarse scream of pleasure silenced by the hand that had been on her breasts. Shadows tugged her legs apart, freeing the goblin to breathe.

"Well done, princeling." Oblivion released Briallen, cradling the limp woman. "Keep that up, and you might just live to see tomorrow."

Briallen saw the smirk appear on his face as he trailed a claw down Oblivion's leg. The sword lurked at the edge of her thoughts, eager for more, but her body refused to move while it recovered. It was clear Tristan knew she needed time, and his shadows curled around the other woman.

"In that case, Lady Oblivion, allow me to serve you now."

Chuckling, the Executioner stroked Briallen's cheek. "You can start by calling me Liv."

Thirty-three

Eirian

She turned tired eyes to watch the sun creeping over the horizon. Exhaustion was an ever-present companion, and one the High Priestess knew would exact an unforgiving toll. There was a cost to sucking the life from random clumps of grass or the occasional low-lying bush to bolster her waning energy. No one criticised her, but Eirian saw the concern in her husband's gaze. Even Joshua regarded her with the same reproach he had reserved for her younger years when she had been determined to know everything at the cost of adequate rest. The difference between that time and their current situation was that they were equally tired. Everyone was. It was impossible to get enough sleep when the Unseelie army was waiting somewhere beyond sight to attack and destroy them.

In all her years, Eirian had never felt the weight of her role as much as she did while watching the solemn march of her people. Those who remained had placed their trust in her, in Teleri, in the dragons circling overhead. More had fled through the night, unwilling to wait for death when they might survive on their own. She tried not to think about what fate awaited them. Better to pretend they had found safety. No doubt some were attempting to return to the cities they had left behind, hoping with the bulk of the population evacuated, the Unseelie would leave Endara and Ensaycal intact. They had not.

Lord General Valerian had shared that fact with her and the others when he arrived. The dragons had flown over the burning ruins of the two cities, but had not dared land to inspect them. Eirian doubted her heart would ever recover from the loss. Not that it needed to. She had a task to complete. Grieving the fall of her home could come after she had forced the god of life into action against the mad god. If those who knew about the destruction wished to succumb to sorrow, that was their choice. What they had asked was that no one spread the news to the convoy of citizens. There was no need to devastate the population with the tragedy. It could serve no purpose.

Watching the silhouette of a dragon cross the glowing orb of the rising sun, Eirian wondered where her sister was. Thinking about what her god had done to Briallen hurt as much as it did to think about her cities. Gebael had not made his presence known to her, leading the High Priestess to suspect he knew how she felt about his actions. The grief in Valerian's eyes when he looked at his youngest daughter had cut her to the bone. It was a reflection of how she felt. Though neither of them said it, they knew Briallen would never be the same. Eclipse would destroy the cheerful woman she had been. She tried to tell herself it was simply the price of survival, and sacrificing a few to ensure the many lived was barely a price to pay. But Eirian could not convince herself that losing Briallen was worth it. Neither was losing her daughter.

Madoc was gone from her side, his silent presence no longer a comfort. She hoped he was having success with Delyth and the other mages who were working hard to master the ward she had found. It had been beautiful to watch the two of them bonding over the plan, and even Joshua had found reason to smile. They all knew how magnificent Delyth would be when she was older, and the way those who had volunteered to experiment with her ward happily followed her instructions was a sign. No one tried to argue about her youth and inexperience, nor did they look to Eirian for confirmation that they should do as they were told. People simply did it. Even Teleri had watched on in awe as mages fell into line, looking to Delyth as though she was their leader. Part of her supposed it was the truth. As the only one who had presented something they could use in combat, her daughter had stepped up to give the mages a leader.

With the dawning light chasing the shadows from the land, Eirian gave thanks to the gods for allowing them to survive the night. Every day that they lived, they were a day closer to their destination. She knew their task was no small one. Reaching Telmia would take years on foot. If they made it through the Unseelie attack. Her skin crawled with the knowledge that it would come. That night, or the next, but it was coming. They would creep up in the dark, taking advantage of their superiority over the humans and elves to butcher their way through the convoy without hesitation. Some would be kept alive, playthings for the goblins to drag back to the Spire to entertain the Blood Queen. Anyone with Altira or Zarthein blood would be slaughtered on the spot. The mad god wanted her fellows to be without escape from their existence so that she could drag them into destroying Tir.

"Eirian?"

Smiling tiredly, she looked at Joshua and Rince, noticing the healer was carrying a flask in one hand while struggling with the reins of his horse. They were welcome companions, though it felt strange having priests and clerics looking to her for leadership when there was no temple to tend to. People did not need to be reminded that Death was waiting for them. The anticipation of the Unseelie attack served that purpose well enough. She had seen many cast aside their black robes, preferring to don plain clothes like everyone else instead of walking around in a constant reminder of what they had left behind.

Offering her his flask, Rince grimaced. "You look as fucked as I feel."

"Charming." Uncorking the drink, she sniffed it in expectation of smelling a herbal tea. "Is this gin?"

"My expert opinion is to enjoy the small things while you can."

She could not argue with his statement. Taking a swig, Eirian appreciated the burn at the back of her throat. Handing it back, she watched Rince take a mouthful as well while Joshua stared at them in surprise.

"Someone brought a whole wagon, but they're only letting people have a small amount at a time. I've got healer's privilege, since we might need it for cleaning wounds in a hurry."

"Sounds reasonable. I may have slipped a bottle of wine into my belongings before we left Endara. Thought I'd keep it in case I had something to either mourn or celebrate."

Sighing at them, Joshua patted his horse. "I checked on Delyth and her teams. They're working hard to master linking their magic together on short notice. At least a lot of them were doing it recently, so it's fresh on their minds. Are you sure you want to risk your daughter on this task?"

It would have been a lie to say she did, but Eirian knew there was no point trying to stop Delyth from fighting. Anyone who could help, and who wanted to, would do what they could. At least her daughter had something tangible to do. The High Priestess hoped she had been able to dedicate more time to her special book in case there were other wards inscribed on the pages that they could use.

"Do I want Delyth to be in harm's way? Not at all. But there is no safety for any of us. The dragons will fight, and the one rider I could have trusted to get my daughter away... Briallen is a slave to Eclipse, and she will do what the sword commands her to. Which will put her in the middle of the fight as one of the two people capable of killing the Unseelie. Everything else that we do is simply sandbagging a flood. So tell me, Joshua, should I risk Delyth?"

"I understand," he replied, grief giving his eyes a glassy look. "At least she can fight."

"You have a purpose," Rince said, offering the priest his flask.

Accepting it, Joshua scoffed. "And what is that exactly?"

"Those who cannot fight will need people like you to help lead them away from the battle. Until we know where it will happen, we can't make plans, so the responsibility of quick thinking will fall on your shoulders while our gallant High Priestess holds back the enemy."

Eirian nodded slowly. "If I fall, they'll need you to take command."

"If you die, what point is there in going on?" The priest stared at her, a lifetime of unspoken words filling his eyes, and her mouth twisted as she looked away. "If the husk makers and the dragons fall, and Delyth's plan fails, we're all going to die."

"Well, you're a cheerful one." Laughing bitterly, Rince ran a hand through his hair.

"Didn't know being cheerful was a requirement."

Tracking the movement of a familiar red dragon, Eirian wondered how Tristan was coping with Briallen's change. She suspected it was safer for the man to keep his distance from her despite their friendship. It was a pity, because she knew he had finally admitted his feelings to her sister. But as a goblin, he was at risk of being run through by Eclipse, and if Briallen killed him, it was something she would never come back from. Ysgarlad circled low above them, the wind from her wings making the horses shift nervously, and several neighed in fear. Shadows seemed to condense beside Joshua, growing thicker as the red dragon banked.

"I've been looking for you, High Priestess."

Stepping out of the shadows, Tristan pulled the wool away from his lower face. It was strange seeing him wearing the rider's goggles, but Eirian supposed he had probably been patrolling most of the night. When they were visiting the cities, they spent less time high in the sky where temperatures were closer to freezing. He bowed stiffly to Joshua and Rince, green eyes almost black in the low light.

"Is everything going well?" she asked him, wondering if he knew what she really meant.

There was a red mark on his neck that was partially hidden by his uniform. "So far. We've spotted the army on the move. The Lord General believes the attack will come tonight."

"What does the Executioner think?"

"She agrees with the reports from our scouts. It's not like there's much else to say about it. They're there, and they know we know it. All we can do is keep moving."

"Does High General Teleri know?"

Tristan frowned, cocking his head as he eyed his dragon. "Apparently, Hadrian is delivering the message. Lord General Valerian only wants those of us who can mount and dismount without landing to pass information along. The dragons need to remain in the air as much as possible so they're ready."

It made sense, and Eirian wondered if that rule extended to Briallen as well. "Have you seen..."

"I was with her last night. She's coping."

"Is she?"

"High Priestess... Eirian, I cannot say what the sword is doing to her. But I promise you, I am doing everything I can to support her." He flinched, and she saw something nervous in his gaze before he forced a bright smile to his lips. "At least Lady Oblivion likes me. As long as she's around to keep Eclipse under control, Briallen will be fine. She won't do anything she regrets. That's the best we have."

Leaning forward in his saddle, Rince blinked at the goblin. "Do you need some pain relief?"

"That depends on what sort you're offering."

"The good kind." He held out his flask with a grim smile. "Because you're only bruised, not broken."

Eyeing the object warily, Tristan did not move to take it. "What is it?"

"Gin. Like I said, the good kind."

Confused, Joshua stared at the goblin in concern. "You're hurt? Did something happen?"

A faint flush coloured his cheeks, and Tristan accepted the drink. "Just took a tumble from Ysgarlad, nothing serious. I was attempting a flying dismount to ensure I could shadow walk from midair."

She knew it was a lie because the mark on his neck looked suspiciously like someone had tried to choke him. Stomach clenching with anxiety, Eirian hoped her sister had not been the one to leave her fingerprints on his throat. It would not have bothered her if they got rough with each other in the heat of passion, but knowing that Briallen was chained to Eclipse made things dangerous.

"Oh my! Well, I'm glad you didn't break anything. That sounds quite risky. Did you manage it?"

"I'm here, aren't I?" Taking a second swig of the gin, the rider returned the flask to Rince.

Rince snorted, a brow arching as he looked at Eirian. "Perhaps you should limit those dismounts."

Part of her was glad she was not the only one who saw through Tristan's excuse. Though Eirian figured Rince was relying on the information provided by his healing magic. At least he could be trusted to keep what he knew to himself. Rolling his shoulders, the goblin gave them a tired smile before looking up as his dragon made a pass over their heads.

"I'll try my best. At least we'll be busy today making our last-minute preparations. Before sunset, make sure your people are separated. Those willing to fight need to be on the outside of the line. Everyone else needs to keep moving, and they can't look back." Tristan met her gaze, and Eirian nodded in understanding. "That's what I was told to tell you."

Somewhere a hawk screamed, and Eirian wondered if the Diwanian princess was watching them with her sharp gaze. "We'll pass the order along. People have been told to make their choice and commit to it. Delyth has every willing mage working on her plan to trap the Unseelie."

"It's a good plan, and I really hope it works."

Motherly concern flickered through her when she realised he was going to be fighting the people he had been taken from as a young boy. "Are you ready for this, Tristan? I imagine it's hard for you."

"My loyalty is to the dragon riders, not to the people who abused me because I was born a male. Don't worry, High Priestess, I know where my place is. It is beside your sister, and it always has been. I will have her back in this fight, and if anyone dares hurt her, I'll destroy them."

Whistling, Rince held his flask to his chest. "Be still, my beating heart. What I'd give to have someone making those sorts of declarations for me. Best of luck to you, rider. I'll be somewhere in the line, hoping I don't need to patch too many people up. So, please don't pay me a visit."

Bowing, Tristan gathered the shadows to him, and Ysgarlad banked, using her wing to cast a shadow over her body that he could step to. "Good luck. I'll be back with any messages from the Lord General."

Eirian watched him vanish in a shroud of darkness, and part of her envied the ability. She could imagine how useful it was. Though it would be pointless during a battle at night against an enemy made up of people with the same skill. Ysgarlad roared, and she spotted a dark figure moving on the dragon's back, confirming Tristan had made it safely. It still seemed risky to send him when there were multiple danann among the riders. Staring at the patrolling dragons, Eirian was glad Valerian had sent Hadrian to Teleri. She knew her warrior counterpart enjoyed the peropuan's company.

"Well, if today is to be our last day, what does my High Priestess want to do?" Rince asked.

She wanted to curl up in a comfortable bed with Madoc. "I need to rest as much as possible. This battle is going to push my limits, and I'm no spry twenty something year old mage. My power might be great, but my body cannot match it. The joys of ageing."

He hummed in agreement. "Looks like you're in command, Joshua."

Thirty-four
Delyth

"You don't think we're spread too thin?" Delyth stared at her father, nervously chewing her bottom lip as she ran over the possibilities. "If there's a weak spot, the link will fail."

Cupping her face, Madoc did not smile when he knew there was little point trying to assure her everything would be fine. "We've done our best, my dear girl. You have been brilliant, and this is our best chance of defending ourselves. Only you could have united thousands of mages to learn a new ward in a short amount of time when their lives, and those of their loved ones, are in danger."

"Still..."

"You've taken mages of all schools, and you've turned them into a wall to protect the innocent. If nothing else, Delyth Altira, you're allowed to be proud."

Huffing, she rolled her eyes. Her father was right, and she knew it. Glancing at where Amelia stood with their friends, she hoped they would not have to fight. The thought of losing them to the Unseelie filled her with more dread than anything else. If they had to die, they would die together, and nothing else was acceptable. Either they lived as one, or they died as one. Delyth knew better than to tell them that. While Laryn would coo over how sweet it was she put their friendship so high on her list of important things, Amelia was likely to tie her up and throw her over the back of a horse, sending it off with the rest.

"But I'm right to be worried about the ratio of mages?"

"We had a night and a day to prepare for this. If we had longer, then I would say yes, you are right, but the time factor doesn't lend itself to an accurate judgement of skill. All we can do is hope that people recognise the important of shoring up any weak spots in the link as we work and take action."

A master from the university offered her a grim smile, inclining her head at Madoc. "Your father is right, Lady Altira. What you've organised is bigger than anything we've done, and hopefully people will recognise the need for constant adjustment. Each section is responsible for itself."

Above them, the sky was a pale blanket of blue, cloudless and withholding the promise of a spectacular display of colours when the sun set. She was thankful for that. It would feel like an insult if their last day alive was shown out the door by a beautiful sunset. Breathing deeply, Delyth reminded herself that it would not be their last day. Her plan would work. They would trap the Unseelie in a chasm of their making, preventing the rest from crossing. But a small voice kept reminding her they were fighting goblins who could shadow walk. There were still shadows at night, especially with dragons involved. Their fire would provide the light needed to give the enemy an advantage on the battlefield. One that could ruin them.

Patting his pocket, Madoc checked the flask was in place. Healers had done their best to give everyone a small amount of a tonic that would help bolster their energy. Food had been delivered to all the mages, meagre but better than nothing when they would wield their magic in large amounts until they won the battle, or they died. Pockets were stuffed with easy to snack on items, but Delyth wondered how many of them would remember to eat something when they had the chance. Especially the ones whose livelihoods did not rely on using their power. Many of the mages lending their help did not train regularly, and were likely to burn out quicker than the rest. They had argued over where to put them, with many suggesting they should stay back and just lend their power to those working the ward. It made sense when they lacked the skill and precision needed for the task.

Her fingers twitched, sketching out the lines of the ward she had spent the whole day mastering. "What was the signal again?"

"I believe it was dragon fire. Hardly one we'll miss," Patton replied, shifting anxiously beside Calleth. "I hate that we can't see them coming. We're sitting blind."

"A wise commander attacks when they know their opponent is weakest."

He mocked her response, and Laryn elbowed him. The yelp he gave made Delyth smile. Tension was thick among those who were waiting in place while everyone else kept moving. It was impossible for hundreds of thousands of people to travel quickly, but it was the job of the soldiers, the mages, and the dragons to keep the Unseelie from devouring them. Delyth thought it right that such a barren land would be the place where they made their stand. What was going to happen would scar anywhere, but better it be an unpleasant location than one filled with beauty. War was ugly. She did not need to be a seasoned warrior to know that. Death could be gentle, but battle never was.

"I taught her that," Amelia said, moving to stand next to her lover, sliding an arm around Delyth's waist. "Can I get you anything, Del? Have you drunk recently? You need to be hydrated. Eat something."

Madoc smiled, giving them a proud look. "The two of you are a credit to your bloodlines."

"Thank you, Lord Madoc."

"Have you spoken to your parents, Amelia?"

She nodded, and Delyth covered her hand. "My mother is with those who are continuing to move. She's helping to protect the children. Da is with the other archers. Though he isn't sure how much use they'll be in the dark and against the First People."

"They might be immortal, but they're not invulnerable. Take out an eye, and that's not something they're going to grow back. We can't cut off their heads, but we can remove a hand or a foot."

That was what the First People among the dragon riders had told them. It had been repeated up and down the convoy—the only instruction anyone had for the fight. Aim for the eyes, for the hands, for the feet; if a cut was lucky enough, it could incapacitate their enemy for days. They would not die, but they could bleed. Just like they could burn. Delyth had seen the horror in the eyes of Commander Calea and the other First People riders when she mentioned her idea to close the ground back up with the Unseelie trapped in it. Even though it would be a slow and torturous fate for them, the young mage failed to find a part of her that cared. It should have scared her to be capable of such cruelty. Except it did not.

Dusk left pale pinks and oranges mottling the sky. Clouds remained absent, and Delyth wondered if that was a good thing. She could not remember whether cloud cover bothered the dragons. Amelia's hand twisted around so they could lace their fingers together. Leaning into her warmth, the mage wished she could smile. On a different day, she would have been too busy kissing the other woman to notice the creep of darkness. There was a strange chill to the air, reminding her the dullaghan were keeping guard. Everyone had been warned that the headless riders were present, and that they were allies. No one was sure what they could do against immortals, but Delyth doubted they would be there if they were incapable of doing something. It was only logical.

A bird call cut through the fading light, drawing their attention up as the familiar hawk dove towards them. Delyth found her marvellous, the shift between her two forms so seamless that it felt impossible. She had seen other daoine transform, and none of them made it look as easy as Princess Astoria did. The hawk spread her wings before she hit the ground, and Amelia gasped when the naked woman stood in its place.

No matter how many times they saw it, Delyth doubted it would ever lose its impact, and the Battle Hawk knew it.

"They're coming," Astoria said, not looking at them as she stared into the creeping darkness. "Are you ready, Lady Altira? Because if you're not, then I'm afraid it's too late for you to run."

Fear ripped through her, and Delyth wanted to drop to the ground so she could huddle in a ball. It was easy to feel ready for battle when it was still in the future. Her confidence felt like it had been ripped out of her, and the hole left behind filled with every doubt she could experience. Who was she to think she could offer a solution to more experienced mages and officers? Clearly, they were as insane as she was, and the Unseelie were going to feast on their bodies by dawn. Astoria's startling blue eyes narrowed, her head tilted as though she could feel every emotion twisting through her, and Delyth wanted to shrink away from the sympathy she saw there.

"Have faith in yourself, Lady Altira. It's a good plan. He chose you for a reason."

It was the reminder she needed, and Delyth drew herself up. "You're right, he did."

Astoria smiled faintly, turning her gaze to the sky, and Delyth was sure she saw a ripple of fire spread across her skin. "And that one has very specific reasons for his choices."

"How can you be so certain of it?"

"Because he sees things we cannot. The dragons will be careful not to rain fire on the front lines until they've seen your chasm. They'll concentrate on keeping a safe distance from you, but the Unseelie know how to fight dragons, so be prepared. There's always a chance they will turn their bolt throwers on you."

Amelia flinched at the scenario Astoria suggested. "Let's hope they don't."

"Indeed. Have you seen what they can do?"

"Only in pictures."

"Ah." She grimaced, eyeing the four elven warriors with understanding. "If you see combat tonight, I wish you the best of luck in surviving. Fucking stars know it's going to be hard for all of us."

Observing her friends, Delyth was forced to admit it was strange to see them so sombre. None of them had imagined a few months earlier that they would be in the position they were. No one in the convoy could have foreseen the Unseelie coming for their lives. She frowned, a small voice expressing doubts over it, and she stared at the duine princess. It was a lie to say no one could have foreseen what was happening. The gods in all their power were more than capable of knowing what one of their own was up to, and many of them had done nothing. Death and Chaos were doing what they could, but neither of them could stop the mad god without the rest.

A horn blew from some distance away, picking up responses from farther along the lines. Stiffening, Delyth knew what it meant. The lookouts had spotted signs of the approaching army. With the light fading, it was going to be a challenge to tell friend from foe, even once the dragons began bathing them in fire. At least they did not need to fear a wildfire ripping across the land. It was all dirt and rocks, with very little scrub to catch alight. Snorting, Delyth told herself it was the small things that they could count on. Like their magic, and the sharpness of their blades. They could rely on the dragon's fire to burn the Unseelie even if it did not kill them. Eirian and the Ravens could leave the enemy as crippled husks waiting to be put out of their misery by the Executioner and Briallen.

"Good luck," Astoria said, inclining her head. "That's my signal to leave. I hope I see you again on the other side of this. If not, may the Veil bring you peace."

There was nothing else to say as she shifted into her hawk form, taking off into the increasing dark. Her feathers seemed to gleam with their own light, as though flames clung to the tips. Delyth knew little about daoine who shifted into birds typically seen only during the day, but she doubted they were blessed with the ability to see at night. She hoped Astoria would be safe to fly once darkness staked its claim on the land. But even as the thought crossed her mind, distant flares of fire poured from the sky as the dragons attempted to slow the approach of the Unseelie army. Feeling Amelia's hand on her, Delyth leaned into the embrace, fighting the urge to cry. It was too late to lament the unfairness of life, and she knew it was a reminder they all needed. Just like the aspect her power embodied, Lady Shianeni, the great queen of the gods, was as unfair as anything could be.

More fire lit the sky, far enough away that they could not hear the screams. The horns cut through the strange stillness that had gripped the lines when the dragons began their assault. A heavy sigh drew Delyth's attention to her father, and she stepped free of Amelia to grasp his hand. She wished her mother were with them, but the High Priestess was with the other husk makers. Only a handful of them were present to fight, led by Queen Malena. It was odd to think of the Ravens choosing this place to make their last stand against the god who had destroyed so many of them. That they did not have their danann companions fighting with them seemed very peculiar to Delyth until she remembered that many of them had lost their mates during the Sundering. Including Queen Malena. Her mother had taught her about the events that had led to Death turning his back on the gods he belonged with.

"When the second round of horns sounds, it'll be time to make the link," Madoc said, gently reminding her of why they were there. "Are you ready for this, my sweet girl?"

"I wish Ma were here."

His breath hitched, and he squeezed her hand. "So do I."

Taking the time they had to focus her mind on their task, Delyth went over the various twists and loops of the ward they needed to work. The book had gone through different formations for linking power, and they had chosen a straight line because that was what they needed for the plan. In a line, they would be free to push the ward forward into the ground, drawing the earth they were carving back towards them. It would serve two purposes, the first being to open a chasm between them and the Unseelie, and the second to provide some protection from the dragon fire.

"Deep breaths, Del. Remember, feet apart, keep your balance, and sink into the calm."

Eirian might not be with them, but Delyth was happy to be standing shoulder to shoulder with her father. He had mastered the calm needed for massive workings during his apprenticeship. Madoc could stand all day, drawing on his power in measured amounts to layer stone after stone atop each other. Closing her eyes, she pictured the image she had spun as a child. It was a warmly lit room filled with every book she had ever read. Running her hands over the spines, Delyth embraced the serenity she felt when surrounded by knowledge, and wrapped it around her mind as her magic slid into her hands. The horns came again, telling the mages to link. Stretching her power outwards, she imagined she was grasping the hands of the other mages she was joining with.

Wind rushed over them, almost as loud as the buzz of magic in her ears. Delyth watched a plume of fire break the darkness nearby, not daring to count the shapes she saw moving in it. She let the screams melt away, refusing to be disturbed by the sound of unimaginable agony. There was no room to falter as they prepared the weaving of the ward they needed. Magic shimmered in the air, a long blanket of interwoven threads spreading the length of their line. They held it in place, waiting for the right moment to turn it against the ground. Most of them were barefoot, allowing the mages to feel the effects of the ward once it began. Those who were not, possessed a connection with their power that negated the need for unimpeded contact. Her father was one of them, and Delyth suspected most of those still wearing shoes were builders like him, each used to working on massive tasks with no need of extra help.

"Steady," Amelia whispered from behind her, and she found comfort in the woman's presence. "I feel them out there. Their bloodlust tastes much the same as ours."

That ability was why they had warrior mages spread along the line. Most were preparing to fight and die, but they had kept some aside to act as protection for those working the ward, and so they had an additional method of knowing when to begin. It felt like they had taken a collective breath as the shadows grew, long fingers of darkness reaching out to grasp their hearts and inspire fear. The dragons continued to rain fire down on the Unseelie, but Delyth was sure it seemed like there was less than before. She supposed they were not inexhaustible sources of flame. Better to assume they needed to conserve their magic just like any other wielder than to acknowledge that the enemy had probably brought some down.

"Now, Del."

Magic flared brightly along the line of mages as their warrior counterparts told them to act. The threads of the ward grew tight, stretching across a broad section of the land. It was bigger than Delyth had expected it to be, and there was a thrum of power giving it the strangest gleam. No one stopped to consider what it meant when their full concentration was needed to push it down like it was a net capturing fish in the sea. Instead of fish, they scooped earth and rocks, drawing them away from each other. The ward cauterised the ground like a battlefield healer dealing with a wound that needed to be sealed before the injured person lost too much blood. Screams filled the air as the Unseelie plunged down into the chasm waiting for them. They were pushing forward with too much momentum, their eagerness to feast on the humans and elves keeping them from realising the danger they were in.

A hand touched her back, power coursing through her into the ward and spreading through the link to the other mages. She knew Amelia was behind her, but the power was not hers. It felt like the god who had given her the book. Not daring to glance back and risk breaking her concentration, Delyth kept working, drawing the wall of earth further from the other side. They pushed down as far as they could into the ground, carving the chasm deep enough to prevent anyone from climbing out. No matter how many fell, there would be more, each possessed by a desire to destroy her people. The dragons kept back, aiming their fire at the lines further back from where the mages worked. They did not want to provide the enemy with a better view of what was going on.

Breath tickled her ear while more power poured into her to spread across the link, but Delyth did not lose focus as Xhaiden whispered, "Take it all."

Thirty-five

Teleri

Fire filled the sky, the smell of burning flesh filling her nose. She wanted to gag, but there was no relief to be found in doing so. Occasionally, the sound of someone emptying their stomach reached her ears, and Teleri experienced a pang of sympathy. The only way they could escape the acrid scent was to run farther than the wind could carry it. As bad as the smell was, it was the screams that turned her cold despite the warmth of the night. Up and down the line they had formed along the chasm, the Unseelie found themselves unable to escape the trap they were caught in. There was no way to get away from the dragon fire raining down on them.

With the amount of magic filling the area, Teleri could not sense her link to Eirian. Wherever the Altira mage was, she hoped she was as safe as she could be. At least she was not dead. No amount of power in use would prevent her from feeling the backlash of her human counterpart dying. For one of them, she had been far from the twin cities, and it had brought her to her knees in the middle of a battle. Her bloodlust longed to be let loose on the Unseelie attackers, uncaring that she could not leave her post. All it knew was that there was a fight to be had, and it needed to protect Eirian. It was a struggle to keep the power under control when thousands of her fellow warrior mages were waiting.

If everything went according to plan, they would remain waiting until it was over. They could do little against their enemy, and the High General did not want to throw her soldiers to their deaths if she did not need to. As long as they remained behind the lines of mages working their wards, they would be safe. Their job was to protect the valuable magic wielders if the shields faltered, or the Unseelie made it across the chasm. Teleri wondered if the generals in charge of the enemy army would pull back when they realised what was between them and their prey. She did not know how many they were willing to throw into the earth before they gave up and looked for an alternative path.

Watching the dark shapes of the dragons cast against the night sky, Teleri hoped they had not lost too many. She knew the Unseelie had bolt throwers intended for combating the mighty beasts. It was how they had destroyed most of the cities dedicated to them. To some extent, it truly felt like they were witnessing the decline of civilisation. So much knowledge, art, and history had been wiped from the face of their world. Things that could not be replaced. Should mortals survive Annawyn's war, they would fall into decline as they found themselves unable to replicate the achievements of the past. What knowledge they possessed now was what future generations would have to learn from, and only if they could record it before it was lost.

"How long until daybreak?" Yestin whispered. "This night feels like it will last forever."

She wanted to offer him some form of comfort, but her body was frozen in a state of anticipation. "It won't. This night will end, just like all the others. The gods aren't ready to destroy Tir, and so it will continue to turn as it circles our sun. Day will continue to give way to night, and night to day."

"I know that, Mother."

"But I understand what you mean."

Scoffing, the younger elf dragged his boot across the ground, and the sound was a welcome addition to the screams. "I hate this. If only there were more we could do."

"And I hate that you didn't go with the others."

"What, and leave you here to deal with this alone? You ordered Father to protect the small ones, so it's my duty to be by your side. Do try to appreciate my efforts, Mother."

The sarcasm in his words made her laugh, and Teleri reached out to ruffle his hair. "Why did you need to inherit your father's attitude? Considering he's a shield mage, I'm not sure you make up for him."

"Better his attitude than yours."

It felt good to laugh while the world seemed to be falling apart around them. Better to laugh than to let the insanity of their future dig claws of despair into her heart and mind. Her eyes caught what appeared to be a ball of fire darting through the sky towards the ground, and Teleri hoped it was not a dragon. The glowing orb flared, vanishing briefly before it reappeared, heading back to the sky. She thought the movements were too agile for a dragon, reminding her more of a bird striking at a target on the ground before rising to dive again. Recalling the duine princess, the High General wondered if it was her. No one was ever certain of what the daoine were capable of, so she could not dismiss the possibility.

"We're going to survive this, Ma," Yestin said, the surety in his voice making her glance at him.

"But at what cost? The dragons have been so reduced that I can't see how they could ever recover. The Unseelie have destroyed their nesting grounds. How can a handful of survivors save their kind when those who serve the mad god will never let them find peace? As long as the Unseelie exist, we'll never stop being in danger. We need the gods to do something."

"I don't understand why they don't just make them mortal. The daoine are."

Teleri snorted, shaking her head. "Probably because they get entertainment out of this. It's War's arena except the entire world is the fighting pit."

He cleared his throat, shuffling nervously as he looked around. "You don't think it's because they can't? If I were a god, I wouldn't admit if I couldn't do something; otherwise, people would stop believing."

"Our gods have no need for us to believe in them. It makes no difference to them."

A dragon swooped low in front of them, breathing fire on a section of the Unseelie that had stopped on the other side of the chasm. The screams filled their ears, and the smell of burning flesh grew stronger. Someone nearby vomited, their stomach no longer able to tolerate the awful scent. Teleri's stomach churned, protesting against her iron will. She would not vomit. As War's heir, she needed to be a pillar of strength for the warriors surrounding her, and for the straining mages holding the wards in place.

"Then why do we bother to have temples for them? Or to make offerings, and pray?"

"Because our magic and our lives come from them. By acknowledging the importance of their role in our existence, we are demonstrating our ability to rise above them. They might not grant us fairness, but we prove every day that we are better than them simply by living. The gods wouldn't last a week if they had to live the same way as the rest of us. I doubt the First People would do too well either."

Something in her response made him chuckle. "You're probably right."

"Of course I'm right," Teleri muttered, watching another dragon make a fiery swoop over their enemy. "I'm your mother, and it's my job to know these things."

They felt the magic waver and stepped forward in concern. The High General did not know how the mages had held the ward for as long as they had, but she feared they would soon run out of energy. Exhaustion would lay claim to the weaker mages, placing additional strain on the rest until there was not enough to hold the line. Her lips parted, eyes widening as she realised what none of them had voiced. No matter how cruel they thought the idea of burying the Unseelie alive was, they would do it. Not because it was what they wanted, but because their magic would fail.

Hearing her gasp, Yestin touched his mother's arm. "What's wrong?"

"They're going to end up burying them."

"What?"

"When the ward fails, the earth will return to where it was, filling in the chasm with all those people trapped in it. I know Delyth and many others wanted to do that anyway, but the rest said no." Laughing in distress, Teleri rubbed her face. "What fools we are. We cannot claim to be better and then do this."

"It's war, and we're desperate."

"Maybe if they would die from it, but they're going to be trapped until they're dug out."

He sighed, and she realised her son disagreed with her thoughts on the matter. "At least they won't be burning any more, and that's all the mercy they deserve."

"I'm sorry to hear you say that, Yestin," she murmured, lifting her gaze to the stars they could see beyond the circling forms of the dragons, and the smoke. "Because even though they are our enemy, they are still people. We can't know how many of them want to destroy us, or how many are driven to do this by the mad god. Never forget that god is Annawyn, and her power is over our minds and hearts. She can twist our thoughts and our feelings, driving us to do things we didn't think we would. Everything that has happened so far is because she loved her mates so deeply that it broke her when they betrayed her."

The need for something solid to grasp had Teleri reaching for her sword. Its hilt was unblemished by all the hours it had spent in her grasp, no grooves worn into the horn by the frequent rub of her thumb. She had never forgotten her fight with the cerapter: sword and bow against horn, wings, and hooves. They were vicious, bloodthirsty animals, rather unlike their cousins. Occasionally, a few brave people thought to capture cerapter foals, raising them as though they were horses, and carefully meeting their need for raw flesh with livestock, but they were never truly trustworthy mounts. Not like horses. But the High General had always wondered what it would be like to have a cerapter as a companion, a beast that could match her rage in battle.

"Do you wish you were out there?" Yestin's voice held a mixture of wistfulness and fear.

She did. The desire to fight was raging behind the shields holding her magic back. It knew there was blood to shed, and rage to embrace. That the enemy was immortal did not matter to the fury coursing through her thanks to her connection to the god of war. All it wanted was to pit itself against others until it met its match. Part of her wondered if Lord Neriwyn would come and put a stop to the battle if she threw herself into it. He was aware of what happened to her, just as he had been with all previous heirs. Her heartbeat was bound to his existence until she died and the power passed to the first Zarthein born afterwards. The longer the fight went on, the more dragons that fell to the bolts of the Unseelie army, the more Teleri knew she would want to do anything she could to draw the god of war into it just to stop it.

"For so many reasons, yes," she replied, fingers tightening around the hilt of her sword while she swallowed back the bloodlust bubbling through her. "But I know where I'm needed."

"If we lose, do you think they'll kill us quickly?"

"They would want to put an end to the bloodlines as quickly as possible because once they slaughter the Altira and Zarthein children, Death and War will come. Though they're not the gods we need to react. It's that bitch, Life, who holds the power to put an end to this. She can stop the mad god."

Hearing the whoosh of wings, Teleri turned her gaze to the sky in time to see a dragon plunge towards the chasm, fire bellowing from its roaring mouth. A dark figure dove through the air in their direction, wings spreading wide to slow their descent before landing in front of her. In the murky light cast by all the fires, the High General recognised Hadrian staring at her in fear. She was thankful to see him alive, but a bitter voice reminded her he was as immortal as the enemy. Blood trickled down the side of his face, encouraging her to push aside the anger and step forward to place a hand on his arm.

"You're hurt."

Flashing her a tired smile, Hadrian's wings drooped. "It's nothing to worry about. Better me than Laszlo. Things aren't... well, honestly, they're fucked. Lord General Valerian wants you to take your people and run. Now. While we're holding them back. You need to go, Teleri. Please."

Teleri's heart plummeted faster than the dragons that had been shot from the sky. "There was no hope, was there? You're all going to either die or be taken captive to give us what little chance we can get to escape. Even if they don't destroy us, the dragons can't come back from destruction."

"Have a little faith in us," he replied, lifting a hand to cup her cheek. "There's more going on than you can know. You should've worked that out when Death bound Briallen to Eclipse. But all of it will be for nothing if the Unseelie destroy your people. I'm sorry we didn't have more time to get to know each other. In case no one reminds you for a long time, Teleri Zarthein, you are magnificent."

The noise of the battlefield faded into the back of her mind as Teleri held his gaze. Hadrian's hand was hot against her skin, a reminder that he had been in the thick of the fight on the back of a dragon. She wanted to plead with him to retreat with her people, but she knew better. Dragon riders were the noblest of warriors, and short of being ordered for a specific reason by their commander, none of them would flee the battle that was destroying them. Hand trembling, the High General grabbed the clasp of his coat and yanked the peropuan to her so she could press her lips to his. His wings curled forward, shielding them from view as his other hand wrapped around her waist. It was a kiss of regret, filled with a hunger for what might have been if they had been given a different path to walk. Teleri did not care that her son was watching; his father had married her knowing they would have other lovers.

"If you can escape, find me," Teleri murmured against his lips.

Hadrian chuckled, and the hollowness of it told her she would never see him again. "I make no promises, Teleri, I only demand them. Make your people retreat and don't look back."

"You have my word."

"Igraine is going to retrieve Eirian Altira from the fight and bring her to you. Don't let her back into it. She's done her best to help the Ravens, but she needs to leave as well. The Lord General refuses to let his daughter's sister die here, husk maker or not. He promised her." Cocking his head, the rider watched the dragon circling above them. "Laszlo said Igraine wants you to tell Eirian tomorrow that Briallen loves her, and always will, and that she is sorry for the way things must be. She also wants you to tell Delyth to be strong, and to watch her back because deals with the gods always come at a cost."

Closing her eyes, Teleri fought back the tears of grief that wanted to fall. "I promise I'll pass those messages on. Whatever happens, Hadrian, I hope you and Laszlo survive."

Wings flaring outwards, he stepped back, and she sensed the regret in his movement. "We will. Now go, High General. Take your people and run. Run and don't stop. Don't look back, no matter what."

Watching him leap into the air, his powerful wings carrying him upwards to meet his dragon, Teleri pressed her lips together. Each deep breath was a reminder that they could survive. A hand on her shoulder drew her focus to Yestin, the younger elf giving her a determined nod.

"What about the mages and their chasm?"

"It's time to give the order for retreat. I'm sure they have a plan for anchoring the ward even if it won't last forever. Pass it along the line quietly, no horns. We don't want to announce our departure to the enemy. The dragons, the Ravens, and the dullaghan are doing their best to give us time. Let's not waste it, or dishonour their sacrifices." Teleri glanced at the sky, watching more fire raining down on the enemy they could not see clearly. "We live today so we can fight tomorrow."

Thirty-six

Briallen

Blood dripped from the tip of the sword, and it whispered happily. No matter how much it drank, Eclipse never stopped hungering for more. Every life it claimed brought delight across the bond Death had forced on her, but with the delight came peace. As long as she kept moving through the lines of Unseelie soldiers, the sword did not claw at her mind. A part of her identity was free to drift through the murky bloodlust to comment on everything she did. Briallen did not know whether she wanted it to stay or go. It was easier to kill without hesitation when her mind was clouded by Eclipse's desires. With the sword as quiet as it was, it forced the dragon rider to acknowledge that it was her hand driving it through the bodies of those who got in her way.

Too many dragons had fallen. She no longer knew how long they had left before dawn. The only thing that kept her from accidentally killing the wrong person was the guidance of the sword in her hand. It helped that the human and elven forces had been kept out of the fight behind the gaping chasm created by Delyth and her ward. Magic left a strange taste in the air, mixed with burning flesh, and blood. Pride filled Briallen when she caught glimpses through Igraine's eyes of what the mages had done. Except now they were being ordered to run. Her dragon was searching for her sister, intending to snatch Eirian from the battle where she wielded her husk maker power without remorse. Oblivion kept her safe, leaving Briallen free to surrender to Eclipse's hunger. Unlike its twin, the sword in her hand was rarely fed, kept locked away by Death unless he needed it.

"I've got the High Priestess," Igraine's voice was louder than the sword in her mind.

If there was one thing the dragon and the sword agreed on, it was keeping Eirian safe. A part of Briallen kept buried beneath the demands of the weapon was amused by how eager it was to protect her sister. She suspected she should not have found it as funny as she did, considering who her sister was. It made sense that Eclipse wanted to protect Death's heir.

"Take her to the High General." Swallowing, Briallen inhaled deeply, flinching at the awful smell of the battlefield. *"Thank you, Igraine. Make sure they leave."*

There was no answer from her dragon as Eclipse dug eager claws back into her mind, urging her onwards. Aware of what was moving among them, the Unseelie were doing their best to avoid Briallen. Her unsteady grasp over her husk maker powers left her unable to consistently cripple the enemy so she could walk among them as an executioner. She had wanted to be teamed with Eirian because of it, but Oblivion had insisted it was safer for everyone if she fought alone. It was not like the enemy could kill her. As long as she was bound to Eclipse, she was immortal, but not invulnerable. But few dared risk dying in order to get close enough to hurt her, and Briallen was tired of the constant chase.

"Soon we must also retreat, my sweet Raven," Eclipse purred across her thoughts. *"Though I still hunger. Our masters are waiting to release the little fire hawk. We shall watch her burn them brighter than any dragon, and we shall feast on their screams."*

Trudging through the burnt bodies brought down by dragon fire, Briallen did not hesitate to drive the increasingly talkative sword into each suffering person. She hated it, and Eclipse was not as satisfied as it was when she actively fought the enemy. They were being merciful, putting them out of their misery. With only two weapons capable of killing them, far more would be left in agony for years, slowly healing from full-body burns. Deep down, Briallen regretted causing so much harm, but then she remembered what the Unseelie would do to her family, and countless innocents, and it was hard to feel sorry for her part in making them face the consequences of their choices.

A hand grabbed her leg, claws digging through the leather. "Please help me."

Pressing her lips together, Briallen gazed down at the mostly burnt goblin. She could see patches of untouched skin where armour had protected it. Others moaned in agony, no longer capable of screaming. There were so many, and with each passing dragon raining fire down on the lines of Unseelie, the number grew. So did the number of dragons brought down by the insidious bolt throwers designed to cut through the iron scales protecting the mighty beasts. The bolts tore through the delicate skin of their wings, sending them crashing to the ground. Remembering every dragon that had fallen, not just on the battlefield where she stood, but in all the cities the mad god had sent her armies to, Briallen refused to feel sorry for the pleading soldier.

"Help you?" she said, her voice carrying the mocking laughter of the sword in her hand.

Eclipse crowed happily as she drove it into the goblin. Wrenching it free again, Briallen moved on to the next body waiting to be released from life. Her leg stung from the claws that had sliced into her flesh, adding to the many injuries she had suffered. It was easy to push the pain back, letting it feed the rage of the sword. All the advice Oblivion had given her on how to best deal with the weapon had been washed away by the insatiable craving of the blade spun from the fabric of death and chaos with one purpose. Even if Lord Gebael separated her from Eclipse, Briallen knew she could never be the same woman she had been before he chained her to a bloodthirsty sword with no morals.

Her attention was drawn to the sky as she felt the brush of wind moving across the battlefield. Those dragons still living were making their way to the other side of the chasm to guard the departure of the people of Endara and Ensaycal. It was all part of the plan Oblivion, her father, and the gods had devised without telling Eirian and Teleri. The only reason she knew about it was that, as the wielder of Eclipse, they had to tell her. Briallen wondered how the rest of the surviving dragon riders would react when it came to light that they were going to fake their destruction at the hands of the Unseelie. Fire would consume the region, fuelled by the combined efforts of the Ravens turning the land to ash, and while it did, the plan was for them to vanish before the smoke cleared.

"Our mates are calling for us," Eclipse murmured, and she felt regret twisting through her mind. *"We must go to them. There will be more blood to drink on the way."*

"Why are you still hungry?"

"Because he will take me away from you, my pretty Raven. I will be alone again to starve until he lets me out. And you will miss me as much as I miss you."

The prospect of missing the sword bothered her. She knew what her fate was. Oblivion planned to lock the surviving dragons, their riders, and the Ravens behind a wall of magic intended to keep the world out and them in. People would avoid the region she had picked, remote and windswept, but capable of sustaining their population, especially with husk makers living there. They would remain until it was suitable for them to be freed. What that meant, Briallen did not know, and the other woman had not bothered to tell her more. Being trapped for an unknown length of time with Oblivion filled her with dread. All she could do was hope that once Death took Eclipse back, she would cease to be a focus of the Executioner's attention, freeing her to find happiness with Tristan.

"We like that goblin. He is ours."

"Yes, Tristan is ours. I hope he's safe," she replied, squinting into the strange darkness.

Sighing, Briallen realised she had been moving through the Unseelie without paying attention. Fresh blood dripped from her armour and the sword, and her magic crackled at her fingertips, eager for use. There were moving figures ahead, the swirl of shadows around them a sign of who they were. Embracing the numbness of the sword, the dragon rider stretched her power outwards, sinking it into the group of goblins heading in the same direction as she was. Without training, it was a struggle to draw from so many at once, but the flood of energy filling her was greeted with delight from the weapon. Eclipse helped her more than Briallen would admit. It knew a great deal about the intricacies of the power, and so much more. Something that did not cease to amaze her considering it was a sword. When she let it take over, it was easy to drift through the wealth of knowledge Eclipse possessed, and allow it to keep her from grasping what she was being driven to do.

They moved among the shuddering husks to deliver blissful mercy. She knew the burns were terrible to heal from, but what a husk maker did was something worse. There was no escape from the power; it sucked the life out of a person. It was the reason Death had created it. Flush with the stolen energy, Briallen felt her injuries healing. The pain in her leg from the dig of claws faded, and the exhausted ache in her bones was washed away. Immortality did not prevent her from feeling the cost of battle. Her arms hurt from constantly wielding the sword; her skin was tender from the sweat soaking the layer of linen between her and her armour; and inside her boots, her feet protested every step. When it was over, Briallen hoped she could sleep for a week. A gnawing pit in her stomach reminded her that there was a cost to using her magic that could only be delayed by the energy of others.

With no more fire illuminating the sky, the dragons retreated into the darkness above the chasm. The closer she got to where Oblivion was waiting, the more obvious the thrum of magic was. If she had not had Eclipse, Briallen would have feared the mages had been left behind while the rest of the fleeing citizens of the twin cities escaped. Thankfully, it was the power of the god of chaos keeping the chasm in place, preventing the Unseelie from giving chase. It wrapped around her, reaching for the threads of itself that were bound to the sword, giving it life where no weapon had a right to such an existence. And Eclipse reached back, leaving the woman caught in a whirlwind of screaming chaos in her mind. The only thing that allowed her to cling to sanity was the pull of the one other person enduring the same thing.

Oblivion's hand settled on her cheek, and Briallen found it easier to breathe. The two swords were blissfully silent, happy to bask in the touch of their wielders. At the back of her mind, Igraine pushed through the chaos, pressing comfort into her rider. It hurt to admit the sword had changed their bond, and she hoped that once Lord Gebael took his weapon back, they could find their way back to something like they used to have. No dragon deserved to have the whispers of a bloodthirsty entity whispering in their mind. Taking a step closer, Briallen let Oblivion slide her hand from her cheek to the back of her neck, fingers digging into the base of her skull as blood-splattered lips met. Lost in the swirl of magic, and the taste of the other woman, she forgot the battlefield.

"There you are, my darling wife," Oblivion murmured against her mouth when the kiss ended. "Did you have fun? I wish the light were better so I could see how soaked in blood you are."

She hated it when the older woman called her wife, but there was no point arguing. "I wouldn't call it fun. At the start there was some fighting to be had, but once the Unseelie realised what I am..."

"You became the Executioner instead of the soldier. That is what we are, Briallen."

"How was my sister?"

Chuckling, Oblivion kept her hand on Briallen and turned them to move toward the chasm. "Angry. Her power as a husk maker is not quite the same as ours. I suppose it's because she's the Altira."

The comment had her frowning. "What do you mean by that?"

"We're powerful, but the Altira is connected to our master in ways we are not. I'm not able to draw the life from as many at once as Eirian. Watching her fight was beautiful."

Thankful her sister was no longer on the battlefield, Briallen found a smile to wear. It felt wrong to do so, but she needed to feel something positive for a moment. The closer they got to the chasm, the worse the swirl of Chaos's power became. But there was more. An icy thrum warned her that Death waited ahead, and Oblivion's grip on her neck tightened in warning. Listening to the excited chatter of the sword in her hand, Briallen was thankful she was not the only one experiencing it. The woman at her side was enduring her own talkative weapon, though she was better able to block it out. Further back, brave Unseelie moved through the crippled remnants of their fellows, seeking to find out why the dragons had withdrawn, and the husk makers had taken flight. Briallen almost laughed at herself for considering them brave when she knew they were the ones ordered forward while the commanders held the rest in wait.

Her gaze was drawn to a pale form in the darkness. Flames caressed the skin of the Diwanian princess, her brown hair tumbling over her shoulders and back. When Briallen met her amused gaze, she thought she was drowning in blue fire. Astoria cocked her head, shifting her focus to the man standing next to Death, and the rider huddled closer to her fellow. She was uncertain of what the gods had done to the hawk shifter, but memories of watching the older woman plunge in and out of the fight as a flaming bird lingered in her mind. Oblivion's hand left her neck, slipping around her waist to hold her close, and Briallen wondered if she was as uncomfortable with the situation as she was.

"Is it time?" Oblivion demanded, her tone bored.

"You could at least pretend to show me some respect," Gebael muttered, glancing at them. "We're all gods here, apart from the two of you. Don't make me regret giving you a friend."

Eyes widening at his comment, Briallen stared at the flaming princess. "You mean the three of us?"

Digging her fingers into her hip, Oblivion whispered, "Hush, darling. Astoria is in between. Until she dies, she's mostly not a god, but Lord Xhaiden has bound the power of fire to her. The god of water finally has a wife to call his own. I wish Charnel luck."

If it had not been for the arm holding her up, Briallen suspected she might have collapsed. The god of chaos had made a new god. She had not realised it was possible, and the questions swirling around her mind demanded answers. Purring in amusement, Eclipse offered them, drawing her thoughts into its grasp, while slipping its control over her body into place. Sensing the shift in her, Oblivion frowned, studying the clench of her jaw in the light provided by the burning woman.

Approaching, Death gave the appearance of someone unbothered by the destruction surrounding them. "Malena and the other Ravens have joined the dragons. It's time for the two of you to do the same. Dawn is approaching, and you need to leave while it's dark."

"I thought you wanted us to help my niece?" Huffing, Oblivion shifted her feet, throwing a concerned look at the princess. "It would be nice if you kept me informed of changes to the plan."

"I am informing you, Oblivion. Right now."

"Earlier would have been nicer. Then I could have used my magic instead of conserving strength for a fight you've now denied me. That's not very nice of you, Master."

Gebael pinched the bridge of his nose, sighing heavily. "Thank the stars you have manners, Briallen. Perhaps you can teach Oblivion how to be polite."

"No thank you," Briallen replied, and the cheeriness of her voice surprised her.

His eyes narrowed in annoyance, shifting from her to the Executioner. "Don't corrupt her."

Gasping in horror, Oblivion made a point of kissing Briallen's cheek. "I would never! My wife is the sunshine and sweetness to my darkness, and I rather like that."

"Need I remind you that this is only temporary, Oblivion?"

"Is it though? How certain are you that you can unravel what you've done without killing her? I won't complain if I have to keep her and her pet goblin prince. Having the Blood Queen's grandson under me is a pleasure."

Dismissing the glaring god and mocking duine, Briallen turned her gaze to the sky. She felt Igraine's approach, and Eclipse loosened its hold on her enough to let her enjoy the anticipation of taking to the air. It had become clear the sword loved flying on the back of a dragon just as much as she did. Wind swept over them as the grey beast landed a short distance away, her hot breath tickling over their skin.

"We can argue about this later, Oblivion. Right now, you and Briallen are going to get on the dragon and leave. The others are waiting. Don't force me to order you." Gebael flicked a hand at the swords, and Briallen listened to Eclipse bemoaning its sudden cleanliness. "Briallen, it's time to go."

The whisper of his power tugged at her thoughts, and the young half-duine bowed stiffly before extracting herself from Oblivion's grasp. Giving the princess another look as she sheathed Eclipse, Briallen understood what they had meant when they told her that fire would consume the region. Chaos had created a god of fire, and though Astoria had not died and been reborn into her full power, she could wield enough of it to do the damage they needed her to do. Perhaps it would even kill her in the process, but Briallen doubted it would. She suspected that only the gods present were aware that Xhaiden could do what he had done. It was dangerous knowledge to possess.

Igraine lowered herself to her belly, making it easier for Briallen to climb up. Listening to the distant argument between Gebael and Oblivion, she settled into the saddle. The bump of her saddle packs reminded her she needed to mask her face before they took off, and she fumbled in the dark to find the wool coverings that she had shoved into the bag for herself and her fellow. She knew the other woman could fly on her own, but Oblivion had admitted to wanting to stay close to her. Impatient to go, Igraine snapped her massive jaw at the arguing pair to remind the Executioner that it was time. Eclipse laughed at the back of her mind, and Briallen heard the other woman's mutterings as she climbed up.

"He's a fucking prick."

Doing her best to relax as Oblivion's arms wrapped around her, the rider replied, "He's Death."

"Well, we've done what we can for this war. It's up to your sister to get her people where they need to go so she can put an end to this. Now it's time for us to vanish from the world."

Spreading her wings, Igraine launched into the sky, and Briallen held tight to the pommel of the saddle with one hand while the other pressed the wool mask into Oblivion's hand. "This better be the right thing to do, wife. Because I promise you will regret it if it turns out to be a mistake."

Chuckling, Oblivion nuzzled the side of her head. "I'm starting to really hope Gebael can't separate you from Eclipse because I think I want to keep you."

"The feeling is not mutual."

Thirty-seven

Eirian

Exhaustion ate at her, but the muscular arm around her waist kept Eirian from tumbling off the back of the horse. Teleri was a comforting but silent presence pressed against her back, the peacefulness of her magic soothing the ache of her own. She had poured so much power into the Unseelie, and as much energy as she pulled back into herself, the High Priestess felt the cost. Her skin prickled almost as badly as if she had performed a cleansing. The power of a husk maker was deceptive. Other mages thought the draw of energy allowed the wielder to escape the usual costs of using magic, and to some extent, it did. But soon enough, the shakes would set in, and the scratch of her power beneath Eirian's skin would drive her to distraction at the very least. At worst, she would endure the itch, tearing at herself until she drew blood to ease the discomfort.

"You're fidgeting, dear heart," Teleri murmured, adjusting the position of her arm. "Care to tell me what's bothering you? I've never known you to be so quiet as you have been since we started riding."

"I have an awful feeling we won't be seeing any of them again."

"Eirian..."

Darkness offered no relief from the flashes of memory churning around her mind. "You know I'm right. We've left the last of the dragon riders behind to keep the Unseelie from giving chase."

"Everyone knew the risks involved. There's no guarantee that we're going to survive this either. They're doing what they're supposed to do. The strong protect the weak."

"And my sister?"

"Is the second strongest of them right now. Remember the benefits of what your god has done to her."

There was no need to be reminded of the cost to Briallen when Death bound her to his sword. She had seen the darkness lurking in her sister's gaze, and watched the change it had brought upon her. Eirian doubted she would ever forgive herself for what had been done. Part of her knew it was irrational because Gebael must have had the plan in mind well before she asked him to let Teleri wield Eclipse. But despite being the younger of the two of them, she felt a responsibility to her sister. One she had neglected.

Lips parting, Eirian debated how to respond. "And when she's left standing on a battlefield of the dead and dying, with the corpses of the dragons and their riders surrounding her? What then?"

"This is the cost of war, Eirian Altira. We all know it. If you think Briallen wasn't fully aware of what the battle would take from her, then you're doing her a disservice. She's young for a duine, but she's not a child. I'm not sure anyone born of a god's bloodline is ever truly a child. Besides, Igraine bonded with her years before it was acceptable, and you've got to trust that a dragon knows things."

"I don't know if I wish I were as detached as you."

Teleri's arm tightened around her waist for a moment before going slack. "I'm not detached. I feel everything, just like you. But I know none of it helps. Right now, our focus has to be on surviving. Everything else will slow us down. Do you want to die, Eirian?"

"Of course not!"

"Then you fucking bottle it all up, and think about nothing but surviving. Your daughter and husband are riding over there, just as exhausted as you are. Just as frightened of what the future holds. We've lost people, and we'll lose more. What we can't do is give in to our emotions; we can't let them break us because that's exactly what the mad god wants. She wants to tear us apart as she destroys us."

Eirian did not want to close her eyes out of fear of what would play out in her mind. Everything the High General said was the truth. For all their efforts to escape the Unseelie, the real enemy was within them already. Annawyn was the god of their minds, her power insidious as it slithered through their thoughts like a taipan in the grass. There was no defence against her, only the hope they would make it to their destination with enough of them left to enact the plan they had devised. A frightened voice that sounded too much like Briallen whispered at the back of her mind, suggesting their plan might not be theirs at all.

It was entirely possible the mad god wanted them to flee to Telmia, where Life's heir waited. If they dragged King Vartan into a war against those who had sided with Annawyn, and forced Shianeni to react, the consequences would leave no part of Tir untouched. They were playthings, and there was nothing to stop the gods from wiping the world clean to start again. Eirian feared the voice would grow louder with every passing day they remained alive. In some ways, their escape had been too easy, and the voice hinted it had been done on purpose. The god of thought wanted them to flee Endara and Ensaycal. She wanted them to force the other gods to do something instead of ignoring her.

"What if this is her plan?" she whispered, and Teleri stiffened behind her. "To gather heirs in one place and force the other gods to act. It was always about her jealousy, and if they save us, it will only prove her right. You can't deny that our escape has been... convenient."

"Never repeat that thought to anyone else, Eirian."

"I would never."

The weight of Teleri's head against hers was a comfort. No matter what happened, Eirian knew she could count on the other woman to hold her up. Gazing at the stars, she wondered what they would find if they reached their destination. She had studied the maps, doing her best to memorise every detail of the land they were crossing. King Vartan was not the only heir waiting for them where they were heading. Annawyn's bloodline ruled over a region near Telmia, and she remembered the one time she had met someone from the Kaetiel family. They were distinctive with their golden curls and blue eyes that resembled a perfect summer sky. Almost as though they were the light to the Zarthein dark. Knowing the draw she felt for Teleri, Eirian realised they would be forced to confront the same pull to the other two.

"Do you think it will be strange when we meet Vartan?"

Teleri snorted, pressing a gentle kiss to the side of Eirian's head. "Of course. It's probably been a long time since he had anything to do with the other bloodlines, let alone an heir."

"What about the Kaetiels? They're over that way as well."

"True. The real question is whether they're on our side or hers. After all, she is their god, and I imagine she would keep a tight hold on them to prevent them being used against her."

Blinking slowly, Eirian considered what she had said before replying, "What if she doesn't care about them? If she wants to kill our bloodlines to prevent the other gods from passing over to their heirs, then surely she'd want to kill her own as well."

"Unless..."

"She wants everyone in the same place so she can take us captive."

Sighing heavily, Teleri rested her head on Eirian's shoulder. "I'm too tired, Eirian."

"So am I, but I can't make my mind shut up." She shifted slightly, the prickle of her skin robbing her of any chance of sleep. "And the cost of my magic is only making it worse. I've never used it so heavily."

"What can I do to help you manage it?"

If they had been somewhere safe, Eirian would have asked for a sedative to help her sleep through the worst of it. That was what they did for anyone experiencing the itch from overuse of magic or performing a cleanse. Except they were stuck on the back of a horse, far from their home, on the run from an immortal army determined to destroy them, and in short supply of sedatives. Closing her eyes, Eirian listened to the steady beat of hooves all around, and wondered how many mages wrapped safely in the arms of a soldier were experiencing the itch. None of those who had lent their power to the earth-moving ward was riding alone to prevent them from passing out and falling from the back of a horse. Being doubled up meant they could not travel as fast, but better to go slow and stay alive.

"I don't think there's anything we can do."

Snorting, Teleri teasingly brushed her lips against Eirian's ear. "I'd offer to distract you, dear heart, but it seems highly inappropriate right now. Though I imagine it's what my niece is offering your daughter."

Her eyes slid towards where she knew Delyth rode with Amelia. "With everything she has done, I rather hope Delyth is so exhausted she's sound asleep. She needs the rest."

"I'm proud of her."

"So am I—so proud it hurts. I want to cry in awe at what my daughter managed."

"You need to tell her that when you get the chance."

Eirian planned to. She wanted it to be the first thing she said to Delyth in the light of day, when they took a moment to stop and eat. There could be no long breaks for anyone until they knew they were safe. Though the illusion of safety was something they would all question. If they had the chance to make camp for a night, the High Priestess suspected she would close her eyes and sleep the whole time.

"Sometimes I feel like I failed her as a mother."

"We all feel that way. At least you've been present in her life. How much of Yestin's early years did I miss because of my duty as War's heir? While he learnt to walk, I killed people. You got to hear Delyth's first word, watch her steps, read her bedtime stories, but I didn't get that with my first son."

"Madoc and I wanted more children, but when it never happened, it became easier to pretend we were happy with just Delyth."

Feeling Teleri's finger stroking the thin gap in her armour where she had loosened the lacing to ride easier, Eirian looked forward to shedding the layers of leather and mail. She rarely wore it outside of training, but knowing she would need to fight the Unseelie, she had brought it with her from Endara to wear into battle. In their rush to get away from the battlefield, there had been no time to strip out of it. At least if the itch got bad, Eirian knew it would prevent her from scratching her skin badly enough to hurt herself. It was a small mercy in a sea of torment.

"I never asked," Teleri said, and Eirian heard a hint of guilt in her voice. "I always thought you were simply dedicated to your role, and Delyth was part of that dedication. You had her because it was expected of you to contribute to the continuation of the Altira line."

"Why would you ask? I wouldn't have been the first Altira mage to do so."

"I've always admired your relationship with Madoc. You chose him despite all the people telling you not to. No one considered him an appropriate man for the High Priestess of Endara, and you didn't care what they said because you loved him. And then you let him be the man he is without forcing him to change. Many others would have demanded he bow to the ritual of the temple, but not you."

Letting her thoughts drift to her husband, Eirian wished he was the one with an arm wrapped around her waist while keeping her safe on the back of a horse. But his efforts in helping Delyth and the other mages had left him in the same position she was. A small smile tugged at the corners of her mouth when she imagined Madoc slumped over the neck of a horse, snoring loudly, while a soldier did their best to keep him from falling off. Her husband had always been able to sleep anywhere, and she had found him doing so in odd places over the years.

"He's a good man, Teleri, but so is your husband. If we're able to rebuild, I want to change the way we worship the gods."

Teleri made a sound of disbelief that Eirian found amusing. "Who are you, and what have you done with the High Priestess of Death? Change the way we worship the gods?"

She hummed in confirmation. "Indeed. If there is one thing I'm learning from everything we're going through, it's that the gods don't deserve our worship. They might have created us, but they did so for their own amusement. Does the cow worship the farmer who plans to butcher it to feed their family?"

"We've never approached worshipping Lord Neriwyn the same way you do with Lord Gebael, but if I'm honest, Death is perhaps the only one who deserves it. Your rituals honour those who have passed more than they do any god. Death is honest with us mortals. He doesn't make promises, nor does he demand our obedience. All he asks is that we live, and honour the gift of existence by being our best."

There was no lie in what Teleri said, and that was why Eirian was confident she would not face repercussions from Gebael for changing things if she got the chance. She suspected he would be the first to say his fellow gods did not deserve worship. People needed to stop praying for intervention from divine creatures who neither heard them, or cared to hear them. If they survived the war foisted on them by the neglect of their jealous gods, Eirian knew they would have to learn to live for themselves. Instead of thanking the gods, they could thank each other and those who had come before them.

"You'll help me change things, won't you, Teleri?" she murmured, settling her gaze on the distant horizon. "I can always count on you to redirect me when I take a step in the wrong direction."

Watching the sky grow lighter, the High General sighed. "Why don't we focus on surviving first?"

They fell silent, neither willing to take their eyes from the slow rise of the sun. Light broke over the horizon, chasing the shadows across the land. Eirian felt a desire to look back, to search the distance for any sign of the dragons, but she could not bring herself to. She knew if she looked back, there would be nothing there. No dragons or their riders, not even the Unseelie army giving chase. There would be nothing but shadows and a land that would not forget. It was scarred permanently by what they had done, and even once the wind had swept away the ashes, it would bear the mark of war. Looking back would only bring heartbreak.

Eirian kept her face turned to the sun, and let the shadows fall behind her, while Teleri's arm tightened around her waist. Beneath them, the horse plodded on, following the path set by the haggard convoy of humans and elves who had fled Endara and Ensaycal with only the hope of survival in their hearts.

EPILOGUE

SILAS

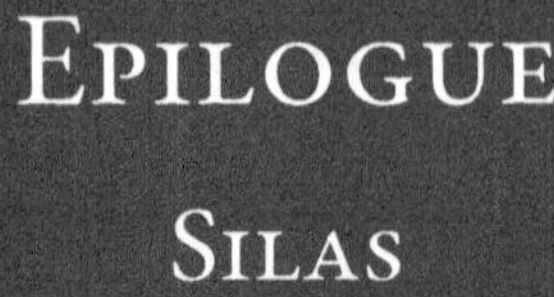

THE BOW WAS WARM in his hands, but it was not the weapon bothering him. Glancing at the small boy on the ground beside him, he wished their parents had not insisted they go to the range together. At eight years of age, his younger brother had developed his magic, but not the skill needed to keep it quiet. Instead of being free to focus on shooting a target, Silas was left with the constant scratch of an undisciplined mind mage battering his mental shield with enthusiastic hail.

"Are you going to keep shooting, Silas?" His brother grinned broadly, distracting Silas with the gap in his teeth. "I wish they would let me learn to shoot a bow. Why won't Ma and Pa let me?"

Silas ground his teeth, sweeping his gaze over the training soldiers. The promise of war was an ever-present shadow in their lives. Unlike his younger sibling, he was well aware of the whispers of an uprising. People knew the god behind the Unseelie was bound to his family, and their kingdom was only a small one surrounded by hungering nations that saw the Kaetiel bloodline as a means to an end. Many of his relatives had been removed from Holroyd, and quietly slipped over the border to Telmia where the daoine swore to keep them safe.

He wished he could go with them when they took his brother, and the last few closer family members remaining in the city. But King Vartan was heir to the god of life, and he was the heir to the mad god. The very person the other nations wanted to capture. As long as he remained distant from the rest of the Kaetiel family, they would be safe from being murdered in their beds. Or so he hoped. Reminded that his brother knew nothing about the dangers of the world they lived in, Silas sighed and ruffled the golden curls that gleamed in the sunlight.

"Maybe when you join the family in Telmia, you'll be able to learn," Silas said, plucking an arrow from the quiver his brother held.

"Do you think so? I can't wait to see a duine shape change."

Squinting at his target, Silas imagined it was the god who tormented his dreams before drawing his bow. "You'll be staying with King Vartan. They say his husband transforms into a horse."

Hitting the middle of the board with a satisfying thud, the arrow joined the others he had shot. For a moment, he felt a flicker of power escaping the walls he had buried his magic beneath. It had gotten challenging to restrain it, and Silas had no intention of letting Annawyn use him to drive his people to madness. As long as he held onto hope that the other heirs would make it to his land alive, he knew he was making the right decision. Death himself had visited to assure him they were coming as quickly as hundreds of thousands of people on foot could.

It was information he kept to himself. No one else knew, not even his aunt, the queen. They did not need to know until after the people of Endara and Ensaycal had crossed the Red Desert into the human lands that bordered their own. When the Valkera family, the heirs to Chaos who ruled over the mighty oasis city in the middle of the Red Desert, sent messenger birds to prepare, he would share what he knew. Silas understood what the plan was to force an end to the destruction tearing Tir apart, and he knew what role he needed to play. He would stand with Eirian Altira, Teleri Zarthein, and Vartan Malfaer against the might of the gods, and they would demand things be changed.

Lining up another target, Silas kept his mind on the plan. He was willing to die to bring down the god responsible for his existence. Whatever it took to save Tir from its creators. Until then, he needed to focus his efforts on remaining sane.

ACKNOWLEDGEMENTS

Returning to writing an epic fantasy was an interesting trip. Especially this particular story. The events in The Fall Duology shaped Tir and exploring them gave me opportunities to delve deeper into certain characters who would otherwise have remained nothing more than historical figures mentioned in passing. While Briallen and the dragons don't make a reappearance in the second book, if you have read To Charm a Hawk, you'll know how their story went. Don't worry, they'll be back.

To Beau, my wonderfully patient husband. Thank you for always being there for me. Without your support, none of this would be possible. You are my rock, my heart, and my safe place. I love you so much. And to my children, keep being the delightfully crazy demons you are.

To Freya, I still miss you. Every damn day.

This one is for you, Anita. Over the years, your support and friendship have been invaluable. Thank you for everything, I am eternally grateful.

As for you, Natasha Madden, thank you. For being my sounding board and my beta. Most of all, for being my friend. Let's keep reaching for those stars.

Callai, keep being tough. Keep fighting. Keep being amazing. I'm lucky to call you my friend. You have been through so much and I will never stop admiring how you refuse to let it defeat you.

You know what I'm going to say to you, Chloe. You should be writing. I'm still waiting. Don't make me send you glitter bombs. You know I will and I won't regret a thing. I'll even support Jess doing the same.

To the rest of my team, thanks for all your support. I appreciate you a lot. You do so much for me. Thank you.

To Mel, thanks for everything. Especially the cute animal videos. And Jess, thanks for keeping Chloe on her toes. She needs it. To the rest of the PageHeart group, thanks for being such a supportive community. You're all awesome. Never forget that.

My love and gratitude to my family. None of this would be possible without you. I hope I continue to make you all proud.

Finally, to my readers. Thank you. For every page you choose to turn. For every comment. All of your support and encouragement. You are the wind in the sails of all authors. Keep doing what you're doing, and we'll keep writing books for you to devour.

About the Author

Joyce Gee is based in Mandurah, Western Australia. Growing up among the rainforests of Far North Queensland, she loved to vanish into the other worlds hidden within the trees. When she isn't writing, she enjoys drinking tea with a book to read, pottering in the garden, camping with her husband and their two children, or escaping with her camera to capture the beautiful landscape of Western Australia.